To Kelvin

GW00865378

Many

for your support
and I hope you
enjoy my first
novel.

Michael
3
v,
11

# SCORPION'S TALE

*Bromley Coughlan*

authorHOUSE®

*AuthorHouse™ UK Ltd.*
*500 Avebury Boulevard*
*Central Milton Keynes, MK9 2BE*
*www.authorhouse.co.uk*
*Phone: 08001974150*

*First published by AuthorHouse 2/18/2011*

*ISBN: 978-1-4490-5597-4*

# Acknowledgements

This book is the product of six false starts, thirty years in conception, fifty years of experience and nearly five years in its execution. Written initially in long hand in a series of note books, it has been lovingly typed and edited by my wife. This is therefore a truly collaborative effort, and the fact that it is being published under a *nom de plume* that is a mixture of our maternal grandparents' surnames is in itself reflective of the result.

The length of time it has taken to write this Christmas 'stocking filler' is due in part to long gaps between inspiration, and that it was mostly penned during long-haul flights or around swimming pools on holidays to the following: Mojacar - Spain (thrice), Heraklion – Crete, Colombo – Sri Lanka, Dubai (thrice), California, Cannes, Harrisburg – Pennsylvania, Warsaw, Meribel (twice), Louisiana, Abu Dhabi and finally Canada. There should be a thank you to our sons, who have endured the disruption caused by this book, which filled large parts of holidays and weekends.

It has been a long journey, but now complete, the books that have been sitting on our beside tables can now be read. *B.C.*

# Friday Morning
# The Lamb

*Drunk, Disgraced, Desolate!* I - Marcus Edge - stared into the empty bottom of my pint glass. It was only half past eleven, on a grey and miserable November Friday morning, I had necked two pints of beer in less than half-an-hour. Sitting on a stool in The Lamb, a traditional public house in Leadenhall Market near the centre of the City of London a beacon for the insurance and banking communities, I mused that even the 'spit and sawdust' nature of The Lamb was changing with a new restaurant on the upper floors. How many other words beginning with the letter D could I think of to describe my self-pity before I succumbed to another drink?

In less than only eighteen months I had plummeted from high-flying Lloyd's of London insurance broker to a down-at-heel self-styled unqualified loss investigator. *Divorced* another D word that would soon apply when my estranged wife started to formalise our separation.

At thirty five I was the toast of the Lloyd's insurance market but nearly twelve months had now passed since my fall from grace. The Captain of Lloyd's Rugby Club; an active member of Lloyd's under 35's; youngest, and most successful, divisional managing director in one of the world's largest insurance brokers. Sought by every recruitment consultant, I was top of their 'hit' list, because to persuade Marc Edge to join another broker would not only make a major contribution to their annual budget - but also establish their credentials as a major force in the insurance recruitment consultancy marketplace.

*Desperate!* Another D word. The obvious trappings of the successful yuppie were long gone. Loss of the Porsche plus the modern duplex in East London's fashionable Docklands were both bearable - but losing Mércédès was the worst of all. Mércédès was my wife of only six months before my disgrace and daughter of Lord Masterson, Chairman and owner of a rival niche insurance broker. In their private moments, Mércédès would call me her *Dependable, Daring, Desirable* Marc - that seemed a lifetime ago.

On the verge of tears I was shaken out of my reverie by a familiar voice, "A bit early for that; isn't it old chap?"

I looked up to see the gleaming white teeth of Knapp-Pahl Sethia shining back at me from one of the broadest smiles in the London insurance market. K-P was so called because his initials were much easier to say than his name, plus he was more than slightly nuts. He could hardly be described as a typical member of the Lloyd's insurance community. Highly educated at Harrow, he was expelled at fifteen after being discovered in flagrante with one of the younger female members of staff. He joined Her Majesty's Royal Navy. After an embarrassing incident involving a submarine and a foreign ship, he resigned his commission, and like most of its inhabitants he fell into the world of insurance broking. It wasn't that the Royal Naval experience helped him in his new career of a marine hull placing broker, nor his command of - at least - half a dozen languages, but the fact that at six foot three inches tall - in his stockinged feet - and weighing over twenty five stone, K-P seemed to have no trouble to persuade underwriters that they should underwrite the risks he broked. K-P waddled around the City of London, his girth and thickness of thighs making an immediate impression, when visiting an underwriter at his box in the Lloyd's Building. His size and joviality also belied a fiercely loyal and competitive rugby player - giving him the ball five metres from the opponents' try-line was tantamount to a certain score. Only his inability to reach the break-down point in open play, and the fact that he had run out of second row partners, had meant that he had retired from the game of 'egg-chasing'.

"Never too early" I replied, "And yourself? Business slow today?"

K-P feigned a hurt expression, giving me a soulful look. Responding to the jibe he puffed out his enormous chest and announced, "I'm here on official *Lammers* business".

I smiled for the first time in a long time, "Oh yes – what's that then?"

"I am booking the new restaurant upstairs for the annual Christmas dinner to be held in early February. When everyone's non-alcoholic resolve is at its nadir." K-P cackled.

I and K-P were two of the founding members of The *Lammers*, a society formed by like-minded practitioners drawn from various careers and disciplines of the London insurance market, each veritable connoisseurs of gastronomy and wine - in quantity if not quality. Paying a monthly subscription, the society held a number of important events throughout the year which often involved dining, drinking, golf days and visits to the races. The only pre-requisite was to be a frequent visitor to The Lamb hostelry, and for being slightly bonkers.

My dark mood returned to my face, "I'm not sure I can make the next event."

"Why's that?" K-P had a mischievous glint in his eye.

"I haven't paid my subs since the summer" I was feeling even more uncomfortable as K-P tried to keep a straight face.

"It's been taken care of." K-P replied.

"How?"

"I've paid your *Lammers* subs for this and next year. Want another pint?" K-P crossed the bar in two large waddling strides.

I was deciding whether to be happy or angry at my friend's generosity. I decided on the former as my new pint of beer was set down in front of me.

"You welcomed and helped me when I came to the City with your friendship and no preconceived ideas because of the colour of my skin. It's the least I can do." K-P continued "If it wasn't for three children all under the age of six you would be welcome to stay with Jane and me."

K-P had met and fallen in love with Jane, as tall as him but a red-headed, fiery, skinny secondary school maths teacher. They still lived in K-P's two bed-roomed flat in Mile End, with children seemingly popping out every year.

"When are you going to buy a proper house K-P?" I asked.

"What, with the Olympics less than three years away? Plus, I can be home in twenty minutes from my office.

Enough time for a quick lunch and other refreshments" K-P left unsaid the obvious as he took a long draught from his pint with most of it disappearing down his gullet. "We are hoping that the noise of the children will drive the neighbour's barmy, then we will buy their flat for a knock-down price, because of the noise of the inconsiderate neighbours."

K-P finished his beer before I had even started my fresh drink and stood-up "I'll see you lunchtime; perhaps? Need to catch an underwriter before he wakes up."

# Dawn Saturday Morning
# Bishopsgate Police Station

I tried opening my eyes, but the eye-lids wouldn't move, I felt sure some bastard had sewn my eyelids together. My head was raging with pain. Lips swollen, I could have sworn they were the size of bananas, and the taste of warm sickly blood inside my mouth coincided with a massive wave of nausea. I started vomiting uncontrollably, the bile exiting my body from both mouth and nose.

"You dirty bastard!" yelled a voice from nearby.

The voice echoed around the room, and the echoes suggested there was plenty of concrete and steel in the room. I was still retching violently and I discerned rather than heard the noise of firm footsteps on an uncarpeted floor. There was a distinctive metal-on-metal sound followed by a middle aged and authoritative voice shouting "Quick fetch the doctor!" I don't need a doctor I want an optician because I can't open my bloody eyes. The waves of pain and nausea were replaced by oblivion – I passed out again.

The smell of vomit receded slightly and I felt warm soapy water on my face. The left eye flickered in response to the attention - light but no images appeared.

"Keep your eyes shut please", I was instructed by a kindly but firm voice with an accent similar to K-P's "I need to clean your face to assess the injuries".

What injuries I thought to myself? Then the nauseous feeling returned but the stomach was empty. At that moment the dull pain which had been running between my right shoulder and right hip increased with each of my racing heart beats, and then reached a crescendo with me screaming like a banshee.

The voice was quietly instructing me to "Keep still I want to find out how many ribs they broke".

Injuries! Broken ribs! Shit I feel bloody awful and I can't remember anything. What time is it? Memories were very vague of the previous evening. Where has my Yacht-master watch gone? What will Mércédès say? She bought my beautifully expensive watch as an engagement present; I had sworn to myself that no matter how low I sank I would never sell or pawn my Yacht-master.

"Where am I?" I mumbled.

"Bishopsgate Police Station", was the doctor's reply "and before you ask - I'm the duty police surgeon" the voice conjured an image of a man of Asian extraction in his early thirties. The doctor wiped my forehead, eyebrows, eyes and cheeks with some antiseptic lotion. "When did you last have a tetanus injection?" he enquired.

I didn't answer his question immediately. After a few moments I replied "Quite a long time ago, a lifetime ago - a very different life!"

A functional interview room soon replaced the concrete cell. I was sitting uncomfortably across the table from two police officers. The discomfort was due to a number of reasons - the pain in my side was still searing and the painkillers administered by the doctor were accompanied with the advice that a further two doses would probably be required before the effects would be felt properly and then perhaps the pain might lessen. With only one eye open, coupled with the embarrassment of the smell of my own stench, was the fact that I simply could not remember what had happened – this in particular seemed to annoy the younger of the two people sitting opposite me.

"You were found face down in Middlesex Street at eleven thirty last night" stated the older and shorter of the two police officers in his estuary English accent.

"You then tried assaulting one of our officers" chipped in the younger impatient female police-officer. She's in a hurry to get nowhere I thought.

"We brought you here to arrest you, when you passed out. When you regained consciousness, we summoned the doctor to establish the extent of your injuries. Three broken ribs, facial cuts and lots of bruises" continued the shorter policeman.

"From the smell of you I guess it's pointless to ask whether you remember anything."

It was phrased as a question but the policewoman wanted to wrap this up quickly and continue to climb up the greasy pole that was her career. I shrugged my shoulders - words were too painful. I remembered only dark shadows from last night, it brightened when I thought of K-P, and brighter still when the image of Mercedes lying in our bed came into my head - then the dark clouds returned as I remembered that that was part of the previous life.

The police station's phone was offered to me for '***ONE CALL. NOT INTERNATIONAL AND NOT MORE***

***THAN THREE MINUTES*** was displayed on a notice above the handset. The police had returned my mobile to me, even though I had no credit; I carried the phone anyway because it contained my contacts of that distant previous life. K-P was not answering, my brother had disowned me - through shame - and my parents were visiting my sister in Australia. Mércédès was now shacked up with my archrival and nemesis. I certainly was not going to give them the satisfaction of seeing me in this state.

"Hello, Sir Hugh Masterson speaking" said the voice from the other end of the phone. Sir Hugh Masterson was a self-made shipping magnate, extremely wealthy (tens if not hundreds of millions), a member of the Committee of Lloyd's, my former boss and for a short time my father-in-law when Mércédès and I married. Even though he was a member of the Committee of Lloyd's when they gave me a life-ban, he kept in touch and inferred that he advocated that such a punishment was too draconian, but that he had been outvoted.

I explained where I was, and I did not know how I'd got there, adding that I was a complete mess without money, keys and a change of clothes. The voice, which still retained a trace of a Rhodesian accent, simply - and without questioning - said that Samuel (his chauffeur) would be there in about an hour and he hung-up.

# Saturday Morning
# Journey to The Hall

The older shorter policeman, 'Sergeant Brian Smithson' was the name on his security badge, said I was very lucky not to be charged with assaulting a policeman - thanks very bloody much I thought aloud inadvertently *sotto voce*. The policewoman tried to change his mind so she could add me to her monthly quota. Sitting around the station was wasting time; she wants to be out and about, catching as many people as possible transgressing the law. Successive UK governments had nearly destroyed one of the icons of our society, 'The British Bobby' on the beat. I was about to share my thoughts with this latest product of the system when the moment was broken by another policeman entering the room with news that my lift had arrived and that the doctor said it was OK for me to travel; however, any worsening of the headaches and I should go to hospital immediately.

"And the next time you embark on a twelve hour drinking spree try and eat something!" was the parting shot of Sergeant Smithson finally showing his paternal and pastoral instinct that was missing from his younger colleague.

It was a sunny bitter cold morning when I walked out on to Bishopsgate. Parked in front of the police station was a claret red Range Rover with blacked-out windows. Upon seeing my bedraggled figure the passenger door windows electric motor whirred into action and I found myself staring at Samuel's broad face. His teeth were not as white and true as K-P's but against his ebony black skin the effect was startling.

"Good morning Mr Marc", I was unsure if he was smiling in friendship or laughing at the bedraggled man in front of him, "Sir Hugh thought the coat on the back seat might be welcoming". The last word pronounced full of East African intonation. More like Sir Hugh wanted to protect the leather seats of his beloved car. With all of his fortune he could afford a fleet of Bentleys, but no, that would be too ostentatious and conspicuous. 'You can take the man out of Africa you cannot take Africa out of the man' Sir Hugh would often say.

Very quickly we were gliding smoothly through London's East End passing by the Royal London Hospital at Whitechapel as Samuel informed me there was fresh coffee in the compartment in the right-hand door and croissants filled with ham and cheese in the compartment below the computer/television screen in front of me. The Range Rover had been whisked away as soon as it had rolled-off the production line, to a specialist firm in Kent which customised cars for their 'special' customers. Even when I pushed Samuel in the privileged son-in-law times, he would not divulge the details or extent of the customisation, other than it cost as much again as the original price of the top of the range model. I was amused that Sir Hugh had now even required Samuel to wear gloves when driving, as I looked at the new soft leather gauntlets. The leather steering wheel and the gloves even matched!

I drank the freshly made coffee from the fully integrated Nespresso machine, and then feasted hungrily upon the croissants filled with a Bayonne crut jambon and delicious slices of Emmenthal cheese. Whereupon I considered the dichotomy that was Sir Hugh Masterson's predicament with his former son-in-law; we were birds of a feather, both self-made men in a society that is still trying to rid itself of nepotism and the old boy network.

Sir Hugh Masterson had been born in what was originally British Nyasaland that merged with Southern Rhodesia to form Rhodesia. Sir Hugh Masterson's grandfather, entitled but penniless had emigrated from Scotland between the world wars, and joined the grab for land in Africa. Avoiding the 'white-trash' in Kenya his grandfather became a significant if not rich landowner at the start of World War Two in East Africa. Sir Hugh's grandfather survived the war but his only son, Sir Hugh's father, was attracted by the lure of Spitfires dog fighting over the patchwork fields of Kent. He left his bride at home with his father, Sir Hugh's grandfather, knowing that she was pregnant and made it as far as Cape Town where he was lost at sea en route to England.

Sir Hugh's mother a fresh-faced English rose died broken-hearted in the act of childbirth. His baronetted grandfather - Sir Hugh Masterson - and his grandmother, raised Sir Hugh. But it was his grandfather he idolised, who in turn doted upon his son's progeny and his future legacy.

'A chip off the old block' people would say when the two Hughs were seen together, and doubly so even though they were two generations apart. 'Big Hugh' and 'Little Hugh' not only looked alike, but they had the same mannerisms and walk. When they spoke it was even more eerie - the same Rhodesian inflection and Scottish lilt if only an octave apart.

It was not as though 'Big Hugh' had any reproach about how he brought up his own son. It was the fact that he might run out of time, given his age, to teach 'Little Hugh' all he knew. Their bond was so strong that 'Big Hugh' had to barely raise his voice in all 'Little Hugh's' childhood, and to the day he died 'Big Hugh' never laid a hand in anger upon 'Little Hugh'.

Not that the Mastersons could be considered soft; hard and fair was probably the consensus. Samuel's great-grandfather was at 'Big Hugh's' side from the beginning and his family have been entwined with the Mastersons ever since.

'Big Hugh' died in the 1960s during Ian Smith's unilateral declaration of independence (UDI) 'stand-off' with the then British Prime Minister Harold Wilson. Apartheid was going to tear Rhodesia apart in 'Little Hugh's' - now Sir Hugh – opinion. The Mastersons had lived with apartheid if not openly embracing it. Sir Hugh himself was besotted by the only daughter of a rich Goanese merchantman. He knew that such a union would be deemed unacceptable in the introverted community of white Rhodesia. Slowly, skilfully and very profitably he sold most of the Mastersons assets in Africa, and when Sir Hugh, his Goanese wife and his grandmother arrived in February 1971, he was very liquid in the world of post decimalisation United Kingdom.

Sir Hugh's now father-in-law had persuaded him that the future was not to be found investing in the traditional industries of the United Kingdom, especially with the battle between the government and the powerful unions looming large. Furthermore, his father-in-law saw the rise of manufacturing in the third world, particularly South-East Asia once the conflict in Vietnam and surrounding countries finished. They invested in a new container ship and started the company Masterson shipping. Home initially was London, first Notting Hill Gate where his beautiful Goanese wife gave birth to Mércédès his daughter. In the space of only three years they had moved five times, in what was the crazy world of house inflation in the early 1970s. Sir Hugh Masterson was no snob, and quickly assessed which was the next upcoming area in London and cranking-up the size and value of his home at each transaction. Then miraculously, when the property crash came at the time of the secondary banking collapse, he was in rented accommodation 'between properties'. It was then he heard of The Hall in an area north of London south of Cambridge, still very rural, where people rode to hounds and the government was planning the third London airport at Stansted. He found the ideal seat for his 'ancestral' home near a village called Rickling Green between the A10 and A11 – there was no M11 back then! The Hall was in the hands of a stockbroker on the verge of bankruptcy and desperate for cash, which Sir Hugh had aplenty.

His luck was not confined to Sir Hugh's personal affairs. In the same period his company had grown exponentially by acquisition, usually when the counter party was in need of funds quickly, to complete a transaction or to survive. Lord Weinstock coined the phrase 'Cash is King', and Sir Hugh Masterson was a devotee of the creed. Along with shipping companies, he acquired a transport company, and a freight forwarding company attached to which was a small Lloyd's Insurance Broker. He also obtained a minor share in the Port of Felixstowe. The British financial press coined the phrase 'The Scorpion' when describing Sir Hugh, because he came out of Africa, and immobilised all in his path.

Business was good but it came at a price. His wife, the gorgeous Goanese beauty, never settled in England particularly with the continuous moving of houses. Whilst Sir Hugh was building his empire one day she returned to Goa to see her mother and simply decided to stay there.

# Late Saturday Morning
# The Hall

I must have dozed off because the next thing I remembered was being shaken awake by the Range Rover passing over a cattle grid that signalled imminent arrival at The Hall, which awoke the searing pain in my head and ribs. The next dose of painkillers was now due!

The house was not the prettiest of buildings. It was constructed for a Swedish Count in the early days of the 20th century, and the prevailing gaudiness of a large Edwardian House was much in evidence. The Count hightailed back to neutral Sweden at the outbreak of World War II, especially because he was married to a Jewish beauty. In his haste he left behind certain heavy dark wood items of furniture and a 1908 Rolls-Royce Silver Shadow, where the chauffeur had to drive open to the elements whilst the occupants travelled in enclosed opulent luxury behind him. The car remained in the barn and was now unserviceable as the engine had been requisitioned - or stolen - in the dark days of 1941. Later in World War II, after the arrival of *overpaid oversexed and over-here* Americans, The Hall played host to the US Air Force Officers, as The Hall was in striking distance of a number of US air-strips in that part of East Anglia.

As the car drew up to the front door, the Scorpion opened it. Dressed in an open-neck shirt and jeans, he greeted his estranged son-in-law with,

"My god you look bloody awful. It is Saturday and there is no-one in the house so I suggest we go out to lunch and then you can tell me all".

I had not looked at myself in the mirror since the police-station. One eye was firmly shut with mammoth pounding in my head and on the side of my torso. I felt sure that the bruising would be entering the red-to-magenta phase, before the pain subsided, and the dark shade of blue replaced by a purple phase.

Sir Hugh was looking at me with the quizzical half-mocking hawk-like expression he often wore. A tallish man, he had more than a passing resemblance to the late-lamented actor Sir Ian Richardson. The effect was heightened as they both spoke with the same Scottish lilt, although traces of Sir Hugh's Rhodesian accent was still obvious, usually too late for people to notice by which time the entrance to an exclusive restaurant had been secured.

Not that Sir Hugh was particularly interested in expensive high-class restaurants, unless it was part of a wining and dining ritual that secured a deal in his favour.

"Come on" he said as he strode towards an out-building.

The downstairs of the old stable block provided garage space for Sir Hugh's cars and upstairs the original botheys had been converted into a very nice self-contained flat for his grandmother, but since her passing they were now Samuel's quarters.

Sir Hugh climbed into his Land Rover Defender - his favourite car because it reminded him of his days in Africa. The fourth car in the garage, after the *hors de combat* Rolls-Royce; Range Rover and Land Rover Defender, was an old Peugeot 505 shooting-brake with three banks of seats. Before the plethora of four-wheel drive cars, the Peugeot workhorse was held in the highest esteem in East Africa, for its comfort and resilience on difficult roads.

"Where are we going?" I mumbled through swollen lips, to try and slow the whirlwind that was Sir Hugh Masterson.

"The Cricketers" he shouted above the noise of the engine and the rattles associated with the short wheelbase aluminium workhorse Land Rover, as we sped down the drive.

A frantic fifteen-minute drive through the lanes of West Essex brought us to the village of Clavering.

# Saturday Lunchtime
# The Cricketers

It was into a picturesque English setting that we drove and headed for the Cricketer's Arms pub-restaurant. Today the village was empty other than a couple of hardy walkers taking advantage of the bright but weak November sun.

The Cricketer's itself was busy, if not heaving, as was the case during most of the summer every Thursday to Sunday. A gastro pub-restaurant with a well established reputation, until the son of the owner shot to fame as a funky TV chef. Word had spread on the grapevine, and now 'foodies' from far and wide sought out the Cricketer's.

"Hello, Sir Hugh", the barman greeted us as we entered the hostelry.

"Hello George" Sir Hugh replied. "Can I have a table for two in the restaurant please?"

"Certainly." We were led through the bar with the question "Can I get you a drink while you contemplate today's fare?" The barman said in a mock ostentatious tone.

"A diet coke for me please, and a pint of the guest bitter, for my son-in-law." Sir Hugh answered before I could think whether drinking whilst taking painkillers was a good idea.

George looked at me askew as Sir Hugh added "Poor lad's been in the wars."

Given the events of the past eighteen months that was probably the biggest understatement in the world; but I was still feeling the glow of being referred to as his son-in-law in the present tense, until I reasoned that Sir Hugh probably did not want the hassle of explaining why I was no longer his son-in-law. That might show potential weakness in public that The Scorpion would abhor.

The drinks arrived and I ordered homemade tomato and pepper soup and pasta in arrabiata sauce, both of which I felt I could manage with my swollen lips. Sir Hugh chose dressed Cromer Crab, followed by fillet steak and a salad.

"So what happened?" enquired Sir Hugh. I managed a noisy slurp of soup with a shrug of the shoulders which was a major mistake as it was a catalyst to transform the dull ache in my side into a searing throbbing pain.

I grimaced and mumbled, "I don't remember much at all. I had gone to the City for an appointment with Eric Jones at half past ten, he's Claims Manager at Neptune Re [1]. He telephoned me Thursday to say that he potentially had a very interesting situation he required investigating. He felt it would suit my 'particular' skills and background - he was being his enigmatic self."

"That sounds like Eric" said Sir Hugh "he has been on a number of Masterson's claims. He is a maverick and a bloody pain in the arse!" Sir Hugh had become quite het-up

---

1.  Re – Stands for Reinsurance

but quickly regained his composure and asked nonchalantly "What was the issue he required investigating?"

The starters were quickly cleared away to be replaced by the main course, "I don't know" I replied picking up a fork and spoon.

I wasn't looking at Sir Hugh, I was more concerned as to whether it was better to try and feed the pasta via the side of my mouth, where the lips were less swollen, or try a full frontal assault. I chose the latter and the noise of pasta slurping caused a number of heads to turn with faces frowning; I mimed an apology pointing to my lips.

"Perhaps smaller pieces might be easier?" Sir Hugh jested, his eyes dancing with laughter.

I didn't have the appetite for a session of verbal jousting with my father-in-law, so I carried on recounting what I could remember of the previous day's events.

"Eric didn't show at the meeting until gone eleven o'clock. He was red, flustered and obviously very cross. I have crossed swords with Eric for many years and whilst he is prone to blow his top, from time-to-time, I have not done anything to cause offence recently. Eric quickly apologised, embarrassed, he explained, that the red tape was driving him mad, and that he wanted me to do some work for Neptune Re, but the Compliance Officer had 'gotten wind' of my potential appointment. Accordingly, the Compliance Officer was insisting that before I could work for them I needed to increase my Professional Indemnity insurance limit to two million pounds and I had to agree an onerous contract." I managed another spoonful of pasta, the occupants of the nearby table muttering and raising their eyebrows, tut-tut-ting.

"'Someone is against my appointing you' Eric had said 'but I will not have my independence or integrity questioned – so don't let me down Marc' and we agreed that I would do the necessary as soon as possible with Neptune Re increasing their fee to accommodate any increased costs I incurred."

"Oh!" said Sir Hugh as he finished his steak.

I was regretting ordering the pasta, I swear it was growing on the plate, and cooling quickly into a congealed lump of unappetising carbohydrate. I twirled more on my fork when he told me that they have recently been the subject of a routine visit from Lloyd's, so perhaps that is why they are being so prim-and-proper.

"Are you allowed to tell me that Sir Hugh?" I let humour creep into my voice but saw that Sir Hugh was not amused.

Neptune Re was a specialist marine reinsurance company based in Bermuda with a Syndicate (or 'box') in Lloyd's that was formed shortly after the disasters that befell the World Trade Centre and elsewhere on 9/11, when there was a dearth of capacity in the worldwide insurance Market.

Sir Hugh had a number of conflicts of interest to manage. Firstly, Neptune Re was the leading reinsurance company that provided reinsurance protection to an established 'P&I' (Protection and Indemnity) [2] Club who insured Masterson

---

2 'P&I' Club stands for Protection and Indemnity and were formed as Mutual Insurance Companies by the owners of shipping. Whilst an established mutual and owned by the policyholders the P&I Club often sought and obtained restructure protection to take out the 'peaks-and-troughs' by a Treaty (whole account or part of an account) or facultatively (individually)

Shipping's own vessels. Secondly, he was Chairman of Judge, Palmer and Gown, a Lloyd's insurance broker. JPG were my former employers, and where I first met Sir Hugh, and JPG placed large amounts of business with Neptune Re, and placed Neptune Re's own treaty retrocession reinsurances. Thirdly, he was currently on the Committee of Lloyd's and heading a sub-committee looking at outsourcing by insurers and brokers.

"I'll ignore that laddie on the basis that you're unwell." Was the crisp response from Sir Hugh.

With my pasta half eaten and my napkin covered with red blotches, I pushed the plate away and continued with my tale.

"I couldn't increase my Professional Indemnity limit before the weekend, so I agreed that I would return Tuesday morning with my revised Cover Note, so we could dot the 'i's' and cross the 't's'. Only then could he advise me further as to the nature of the investigation but he said that I should be prepared to travel and it might not make me many friends."

"I tried calling Jimmy Black at JPG, my broker who arranges my insurance cover. I was told he was off-sick and would be back on Monday." My lips were stinging from the talking and spicy pasta sauce, I reflected that it was an appalling choice for lunch given my particular predicament. I continued after a long draught of the guest bitter, "I left a message for him to call me as soon as possible on Monday, at which point the available credit on my mobile was exhausted."

I drew breath and took a further two long welcome draws from my beer, less noisily this time as I was starting to master drinking the cool liquid, and wondered whether I could survive on beer for a week as the pasta had beaten me.

The main course was cleared away and we both declined pudding or cheese. An eerie silence befell us, the dining room was nearly empty, the table next to us rushing away to have 'tea and scones' in Cambridge.

I continued my tale of woe, "I had been walking past The Lamb on my way home and had just spent precious money on a tube fare for what was a false start. I was in the doldrums and a couple of friends were indulging in a 'hair of the dog' following a large 'thirsty Thursday' evening. They bought me a couple of pints and then K-P bought me one more."

Sir Hugh's face brightened at the mention of K-P's name. K-P had been an usher at my wedding. My parents insisted my brother should be my best-man whereas my choice would have been K-P. We held the reception in a marquee on the lawn of The Hall. After Mércédès and I had left for our honeymoon, Sir Hugh and K-P discussed the merits of India and East Africa over a bottle of vintage champagne cognac, until the weak rays of dawn crept over the horizon.

"It becomes a bit blurred after lunch especially with no food. I do remember bumping into that toffee-nosed smarmy bastard Tony Eastwood!"

"Careful sonny," intoned Sir Hugh "he may be - as you put it - a 'smarmy bastard' but he is now my daughter's partner. When your divorce is finalised he may become my next son-in-law!"

I was startled if not surprised by the news. I had worked my way up from the grass-roots at JPG, joining after a short dalliance with accountancy; I had spent twelve very happy years with JPG. Given Sir Hugh's other business commitments he was not often in JPG's offices, leaving the day-to-day running to the Managing Director John Eastwood. John Eastwood is one of the nicest and most respected men in the London insurance market. Under his tutelage, I started to make a name for myself as a Marine Hull placing broker.

I had been in the market for seven years when one day, whilst my section leader was off ill with appendicitis, I took a call from Masterson Shipping. I was advised that Sir Hugh Masterson had concluded a deal buying a fleet of ten container ships from the liquidators of a French company. JPG had twelve hours to put the cover in place before the market closed for the New Year. The liquidators own policies would expire at midnight on 31st December. It was Friday the thirtieth of December and those underwriters who had not taken a break between Christmas and New Year were looking forward to the long weekend, and the prospect of a prosperous new year. I cajoled, hounded and bullied the underwriters into providing cover immediately at less than the current premium rates, as it would be 'looked upon favourably' by Masterson Shipping at their renewal in April.

To achieve the full agreement of underwriters meant tracking down a number of them in various wine bars in the City. I accosted the last remaining underwriter at King's

Cross Station before he left for Scotland (he threatened to report me to Lloyd's but never did so). Sir Hugh knew my name and thereafter I worked on the Masterson Shipping account, amongst others. After two years I took over the section, and was promoted to the position of Associate Director and then the Account Executive when my boss was in turn promoted to Executive Director.

Every year Sir Hugh Masterson held a barbeque for all the senior staff of his various businesses. I made the 'cut' the year I became an Associate Director of JPG. At thirty-one, the world was my oyster and during the barbecue John Eastwood introduced me to a gorgeous brunette the same age as myself.

"Mércédès, this is Marc Edge, one of our 'superstars' with the future of JPG in their hands." John's introduction was gracious and hugely flattering, but all I could think of was the future with this gorgeous beauty in front of me.

I must have been staring goggle-eyed at Mércédès, because I didn't show any sign of life when she held out her hand with an accompanying
"How do you do Mr Edge?" John Eastwood nudged me hard in the ribs as Mércédès repeated the greeting.
They both smiled broadly when my eyes jolted back to reality.

John then informed me that Mércédès was Sir Hugh Masterson's daughter, and that she'd recently returned from New York, where she had been working very successfully for a fashion magazine. I was still captivated by Mércédès' smile and nearly did not hear John saying that his son Tony and Mércédès had been childhood sweethearts and he knew that

Tony was hoping they could continue their relationship now Mércédès had returned from New York.

"We'll have to see about that John." Mércédès said politely, not wishing to offend one of her father's closest friends and colleagues.

Making her apologies that she was the hostess, Mércédès left John and me, but during the rest of the evening my eyes followed her everywhere. Each time she turned to me, she caught me looking at her, and she would smile with her eyes seeming to sparkle.

I was captivated by Mércédès, and was racking my brains as to how I could arrange for us to meet again, when a cloud drifted into my mind. That cloud was Tony Eastwood.

Son of John Eastwood, Tony Eastwood could not have been more different from his father. I first came across him at JPG when he would spend part of his holidays whilst he was at university doing 'work experience'. Tony's idea of 'work experience' was very different to the other members of JPG staff who were known as a lean and mean machine. Rolling in at half past nine in the morning, he would usually swagger about the office until half past ten, then go out into the insurance market with the brokers and have coffee and bacon rolls. After half past eleven he would see one or two underwriters with something high profile but not too difficult, then he would disappear to lunch on expenses, until three o'clock. The afternoon was not too strenuous either, a return to broking until half past four - when it was teatime with other brokers and underwriters. Back in the office about five o'clock, for half an hour, when it was a return to the wine bars for an 'early doors'. This was followed by dinner – he hardly ever put his hand in his pocket, and if he did so he would bitch and moan about being an impecunious student.

Good looking with long foppish hair, his cocksure manner with the female staff was only matched by his arrogance and pomposity at other times, bragging that he would be running JPG shortly after graduating from university.

His father had a blind spot for Tony, and Tony played John Eastwood well. Most Fridays Tony would have a day of total abstinence arriving at the office at eight o'clock, working through lunch and finishing at six o'clock when most other people had gone home for the weekend. He did this for three reasons: firstly, the accumulation of alcohol over the week meant he wanted to be quiet, nursing a hangover from 'thirsty' Thursday; secondly, his father usually did a tour of the firm Friday lunchtime and there he would be, diligently working at his desk when most other souls will be enjoying a well-earned drink after an often hard week's work; thirdly, at the end of the day he would be able to cadge a lift home with his father, to the family home near Colchester.

The young people in the firm were dreading Tony's graduation when he intended to join JPG full-time in a privileged position. Some of the more vociferous were even talking about leaving JPG to work elsewhere. Tony graduated, and took that summer off to travel as a reward from his parents for his hard work. October loomed and then at last some common sense prevailed. It was rumoured Sir Hugh had heard about Tony's antics and persuaded John Eastwood that if Tony was going to be taken seriously at JPG he needed experience at another firm. So through his father's contacts he joined the Graduate Trainee Scheme at Inter-Continental Insurance Brokers Inc. As the name implies, Inter-Continental is a Global broker, US-owned and diametrically opposite to JPG as a small niche broker. Despite their fundamental differences of size and culture (JPG a family firm with staff pulling in the same direction whereas Inter-Continental was a firm built on process, economies of scale and a 'hot-bed' of back-stabbing and politics) in the marine insurance arena the two firms were considered to be the leading brokers in the London insurance market.

Tony Eastwood suited Inter-Continental's culture perfectly, and progressed well, climbing the hierarchy in the US owned firm. Our relative seniority in our respective firms and the insurance market was well known so that we naturally became rivals, each having equal success at new business acquisition as well as retaining existing accounts. We also were both active members of Lloyd's under thirty-five's, but other than that our worlds rarely collided until fate took a hand.

A chain of events, which subsequently unfurled, started not long afterwards. Tony became a member of as many clubs and societies as possible, where he could weave his particular form of charm. Most doors were flung open to him, being the son of John Eastwood. The *Lammers* had been formed by K-P, me and a few other members of the Lloyd's Rugby Club. Tony had badgered one of the members who worked at 'Inter-Continental' to propose him for membership. As set down in the rules of the *Lammers*, any prospective member should be invited along to an event to be vetted. It was a race evening where Tony's ostentatious nature pissed every one off, including his proposer, who ignored him completely from the third race. Tony felt it was

K-P and I who blocked his entry to *Lammers*, when in truth no one voted for him at all!

Worse was still to come during the evening of the Lloyd's under thirty five's ball in the autumn of the same year. Mércédès came as Tony's guest and, as I understood later, he had been trying to woo her ever since her return from New York. Mércédès was polite and friendly but keeping her distance from Tony. During the evening Tony became more and more inebriated. Towards the end of the evening, Tony thought he was the alter ego of John Travolta's character in 'Saturday Night Fever', except he wasn't and was crashing into other dancers all over the dance floor. When the disc-jockey switched the mood to the Bee Gees' 'How Deep Is Your Love?' he drew an already embarrassed Mércédès towards him. She resisted. He grabbed her by the waist. I'd been working late and had a big rugby match at the weekend so I was pacing myself during the evening. I walked onto the dance floor and trying to salvage any awkwardness, I said to Tony,

"Excuse me but I don't think you can keep the most beautiful woman in the room all to yourself all evening. May I have this dance?"

Mércédès smiled and started to reply "That would be..."

When Tony cut across her with "Get lost Edge, you upstart!"

I smiled wolfishly putting my arm around his shoulders in an outwardly comradely manner, bringing my thumb and forefinger to either side of the back of his neck, and squeezed hard.

I whispered in his ear "Let the lady go please?"

He tried moving, but I increased the pressure, and he yelped like the pup he was.

Mércédès was released and in one swift movement I swept her onto the dance floor, with no one but the three of us, knowing what exactly had happened. K-P watching from a distance, with his wife Jane, had a good idea though.

From that night onwards Mércédès and I saw each other nearly every day, and fell madly in love with each other, hungrily devouring each other at every possible opportunity that good manners would allow. I was brought home to meet Sir Hugh and Mércédès' very elderly great grandmother. It was the New Year, three years after I had made a name for myself, sorting out the insurance for when Masterson shipping bought the ten container ships from the liquidators of the French company.

It was obvious Sir Hugh knew who I was, and seemed genuinely pleased at the bond that was burgeoning between me and his daughter, but I was certain that his geniality and *bon homie* shown at his home would not translate to the business environment and the offices of JPG.

Our relationship developed quickly with Mércédès moving into my one bed-roomed flat in London's Butler's Wharf. In the May, following the New Year when I met her great grandmother at The Hall, I supported Mércédès at her great grandmother's funeral.

My own parents instantly fell in love with Mércédès when we visited them in their north Norfolk home. My mother and Mércédès talked for hours, I think Mércédès missed her mother and great grandmother more than she would admit to me, or even herself.

Mércédès job in London was demanding, with long hours which matched my own. Weekends were a relief and whilst Mércédès enjoyed watching rugby now and again, she preferred to return to The Hall, where she could exercise her two horses. Saturday evening I would either travel to The Hall, wearing my bruises as trophies, or we would meet back at the flat and 'slob' in front of the television with a take-away curry.

After one year of being together, I proposed to Mércédès, and she gleefully accepted my engagement ring. Sir Hugh was very happy too, as we had spent many hours together at the weekends, easy in each other's company.

I had identified that my position at JPG might become difficult after our marriage, particularly when Sir Hugh had persuaded John Eastwood that Tony should follow his career - at least initially - elsewhere. I was constantly being approached by head-hunters, and had always turned them down, but six months after I proposed to Mércédès, I received a call from Christopher Richardson of Executive Recruitment and Research who offered to buy me lunch. He outlined a very attractive and lucrative proposal from Inter-Continental to head-up their Marine Hull Division. The package effectively doubled my – then – salary, and the 'golden hello' would go a long way to covering the deposit on a duplex apartment in London's Docklands, which Mércédès and I had set our hearts on. The apartment was based in a complex having its own gym, swimming pool, shop, bar and restaurant on site. Initially Sir Hugh was not pleased when I told him in a private moment that I was 'under-offer' from Inter-Continental. I explained to him the reasons why, and afterwards Mércédès said that secretly he was pleased that I wanted to prove myself elsewhere.

My rivalry with Tony Eastwood was heightened by this move. Tony was in the running to head the Marine Hull

Division, and when he was told of my arrival he blew his top, saying he would never work for me. Inter-Continental had not foreseen this eventuality, and Tony had powerful friends in the organisation, so they moved him to the smaller Marine Cargo Division where he was temporarily appeased with the courtesy title of Divisional Managing Director.

"Are you OK?" Sir Hugh asked me, and I was back at The Cricketers with the hurt of my swollen lips, aching ribs and the loss of Mércédès to Tony Eastwood.

"Can we finish this later please Sir Hugh. Suddenly I am feeling tired, very, very tired" I replied.

# Dawn Sunday Morning
## The Hall

I awoke sweating, in pain and confused! In my semi-conscious state I was vaguely aware of my surroundings and of the events of the past forty eight hours. I was suddenly brought to full consciousness by the pain running down my back from my right shoulder to my right hip. I reached out in the darkness and found the painkillers together with a tepid glass of water. The act of swallowing the pills put paid to the notion of any further sleep.

I turned towards the only source of light in the room, an old alarm clock, whose luminous hands seemed to be shining as bright as an electrical clock. I knew the sensation was only relative, but it revived a mixture of both good and bad memories of my first stay at The Hall.

The metronomic ticking of the alarm clock was very soporific and I lay my head back on the soft goose down filled pillows. *My eyes were just closing when I heard the door handle move and slowly the door opened. Framed by the doorway was the unmistakeable silhouette of Mércédès. The vision was made even more sensual by the glow of the lights from the landing revealing the soft yet toned curves of Mércédès lithe supple body through her negligee as though it was an irrelevance.*

*"What are you doing here?" I whispered.*

*"Shh!" she put her finger to her lips as she gently stepped out of her apparel and mounted the bed and me. Sitting astride my groin she rode me long and slowly as though she was gently exercising her equine mounts. Keeping me teetering on the edge of an orgasm, and then dismounting me so that I might take her in my arms, and pull her close to me.*

*"Careful not to wake anyone my darling", she breathed in my ear. The bed groaned sweetly as we made love quietly, each feeling the other pulse and flex with desire.*

*After making love we fell asleep in each other's arms. Then Mércédès was screaming at me,*

*"You bastard! You are a fucking cheating bastard!! You lied to me, you lied to my father, and you lied to your work colleagues and your friends. I hope you rot in hell!! Tony Eastwood may be a chinless wonder, but at least he's honest - and I trusted you!!" She picked up the alarm clock and hurled it at me. Only by a supreme effort was I able to both dodge the clock and stop it smashing into the dressing-table mirror.*

I was lying on the floor when I heard myself crying,

"I am innocent Mércédès! I am innocent!!"

"What's going on?" the lights went on and Sir Hugh was standing in the doorway in a pair of striped flannel pyjamas.

"I-I-I w-was telling Mércédès" I sobbed "that I was innocent."

"On the telephone?" he enquired.

"No, she was here" my voice was still croaky.

"You've just had a dream. Mércédès phoned me after we returned from lunch, and I told her that you were staying with me for the weekend. She felt it better if she and Tony stayed in London. Apparently Tony remarked that he saw you on Friday and you were determined to have a bender! It's still early so I suggest you have another couple of hours' rest and then a hot bath. I'll have Samuel bring up some breakfast at nine o'clock, and then we'll fill your lungs with some November North Sea air."

Sir Hugh shut the door, and I considered the ridiculous vista that had confronted the baronet at five o'clock on a Sunday morning. I was still lying on the wooden floor clutching the alarm clock crying. Now is that any way for a city professional to be acting? I smiled at the pragmatism of Sir Hugh, wondering where someone can still buy flannel pyjamas that fastened by drawstring? I was wearing an England rugby T-shirt and boxer shorts and mused the generation gap. I laughed; a croaking sound came from my throat, the crying not fully buried.

I was definitely awake now, as if I feared the thought of further dreams. I kept playing over the events of Friday in my mind. Up to the early evening everything was very vivid, but after then until the early hours of Saturday morning in Bishopsgate police station everything was still a fog. Dark shapes and shadows came and went. I closed my eyes as if trying to focus my concentration; I felt sure I'd stayed close to Liverpool Street Station after leaving The Lamb. The bars of Spitalfields were vaguely in the background, a typical watering hole for the JPG personnel, and there was something else vaguely familiar. Yet the more I tried to pinpoint it, the further it would slip away from my mind's eye.

I decided to try and forget about Friday, and found myself thinking about the last three years. I moved from

JPG to Inter-Continental in the autumn of 2007, and took-up the post of Divisional Managing Director of the Marine Hull department, and Tony Eastwood having the similar title in the smaller Marine Cargo department. We were both directors of Inter-Continental's Marine Company, and after only six months I was invited to join Inter-Continental's Executive Committee, but Tony was not!

Tony Eastwood had been successful whilst at Inter-Continental, forming strong alliances both inside and outside the company. Some of these friends were powerful, in both the market as well as Inter-Continental, but his style of management differed greatly from my own. Tony's approach was to form a clique of people, whom he had recently promoted, and it was mockingly described as 'Tony's kitchen cabinet'. It was all very well if you're in the club, but it created petty jealousies with an environment of 'back-biting'.

I changed nothing for the first three months, but after the New Year holiday I spoke to a number of my senior colleagues and unveiled a plan for the year ahead, and beyond. The insurance market had hardened terrifically after the 9/11 disasters, but in truth the market had been too soft for too long, and was long overdue for a re-alignment.

Before I 'rolled-out' my plan to the department, I had a series of private interviews with individuals of the 'kitchen-cabinet', which he had left behind in the Marine Hull department. I explained that the 'kitchen-cabinet' would be disbanded, in favour of a more open and inclusive forum. If this did not suit the individuals concerned, then I would have no problem if they wished to join Tony in the Marine Cargo department. I was refreshingly surprised that only two of the ten interviewed chose that course of action. My motives for the changes were not totally restricted to levelling the playing field, but I also suspected certain members of the 'kitchen-cabinet' to be still loyal to Tony, and were subtly trying to undermine my own efforts.

The changes were "like a breath of fresh-air" according to Max Huntley, Chairman of Inter-Continental's Marine Company. Max was also one of the Inter-Continental Group's three Deputy Managing Directors. Max was a product of Harvard Business School, and despite his button-down Brooks Bros shirts, he had assimilated well since moving from New York via Bermuda to London. He had given Tony Eastwood his head and he was pleased with the results, although Tony's English public school antics were barely tolerated but not embraced.

Following my arrival, not only was the Marine Hull department a happier place, but it was much more profitable. In the first six months of the year we retained every major account, and we were on the right side of two of our client's own mergers, plus we won three major accounts (two from JPG which did not please Tony's father, John Eastwood).

The year continued in much the same vein, and my elevation to Inter-Continental's Executive Committee meant time at home with Mércédès which seemed like stolen moments, as each of us was rushing between work appointments. We were both spending lots of time on planes, trains and automobiles. Time spent with *Lammers* and the Rugby Club was also at a premium, and the lack of training resulted in me being dropped from the First XV. I was not overly concerned, especially as Max Huntley had given me a special and secret task to perform. To undertake this task would require me spending large tracts of my time at my desk, outside office hours, including weekends.

Two years previously, the New York State Attorney General decided that the international insurance broking community was corrupt and defrauding its' clients. Mr Elliott Spitzer accused the leading broking houses that they were earning undisclosed commissions from insurers, furthermore at each renewal he alleged that no competitive alternatives were really being sought. This lack of competition and enhanced commission payments was a cosy arrangement but one which Mr Spitzer wished to break. The result was catastrophic for the insurance broking community as these contingent commissions were hidden from clients, who either paid a fee for broking services, or the broker took part of the premium at the normal rate of brokerage. The problem was that firstly there was collusion between the insurers and the brokers, and secondly in certain areas the brokers' earnings (by aggregating the normal rate brokerage and these contingent commissions) could be in excess of thirty percent of the premium. My assignment was to establish the extent of the contingent commissions earned throughout Inter-Continental, and to suggest various best practices to soften the blow, left by loss of this income. The practice of paying volume discounts in the insurance industry was not a new phenomenon, in the days of yore it was termed 'postage'; it was a legitimate payment to the London broker, as he brought the business to the insurers 'by-hand' rather than through the postal system. Furthermore, the trust and development of a relationship between clients and the same insurers, by renewing year-after-year, can be invaluable. This was particularly relevant in the event of a difficult claim, which might, or might not be specifically covered by the policy wording. Mr Spitzer swept aside all the brokers arguments and protestations, with a subsequent massive loss of earnings, profit and trust in the insurance broking community.

The consequences were swift and the cuts were deep. Very few areas of large brokers were unaffected. Previously profitable areas were made loss-making overnight, and the large bonuses awarded by the executives to themselves, had stopped. The eventual job losses followed quickly, as well as other draconian changes, such as expense accounts being cut to the bone. And the area that suffered the most was entertainment between brokers and insurers!

I had been chosen by Max Huntley to undertake the assignment, because I was new to Inter-Continental, and not tainted by previous arrangements. JPG by comparison had never earned contingent commissions, and as a niche broker JPG promoted a tri-partite relationship between their clients, underwriters and themselves with no hidden payments! By the end of that year the assignment was nearly completed, and I heard on the grapevine that a number of Inter-Continental's middle management had felt that I had acted like an over-zealous policeman. I was being snubbed and shunned by my peers. Max Huntley told me not to worry, as they would accept the position, once the changes I had suggested were implemented and started to take effect. Uncomfortable but undeterred, I continued about my business and at the end of 2008, Mércédès and I were married with our honeymoon on a remote Caribbean Island.

When I returned from holiday, early the following year, Max Huntley announced that he had another assignment for me. He would like me to look at the frequency of claims certain Marine owners were suffering. Max sat on a cross-market committee with one or two of its members muttering that something was 'not quite right'. But I never got to begin the assignment.

One of the clients I had won from JPG was a Dutch large privately owned company. My contact at the client, who was responsible for their Marine insurance, I had known for some years and we became friends. They were then bought by a much larger Dutch publicly listed company. The various executives and managers in the small company were rewarded very richly, with the result that my friend bought a house in the Caribbean. My wedding had been a lavish affair, with Sir Hugh spoiling his daughter, but I had kept arrangements of the honeymoon to myself. It was my Dutch friend's wedding gift to loan me his house in the Caribbean for two weeks, and he chartered a private plane to fly us there from a nearby island, from where scheduled transatlantic flights operated.

In February of 2009 I was called into Max Huntley's office one Monday morning. Max had a face like thunder; he said nothing, and simply passed to me an e-mail from the Chairman of my Dutch client, addressed to the Chairman of Inter-Continental. The email advised that with immediate effect their account was to be transferred back to JPG, and Inter-Continental would forgo any brokerage and fees for the current policy period, until the outcome of certain internal and external investigations had been completed. All communication was to be conducted through the Chairman of Inter-Continental and the Chairman of the Dutch company. On no account should any other employee, or associate of Inter-Continental, make any attempt to contact anyone else from the client.

The email continued that their investigations would probably result in police charges being brought against former officers of their Group of Companies, and that Inter-Continental should expect that certain of their employees may also be interviewed by police, in the course of the investigations. The email finished by saying that the Dutch company hoped that Inter-Continental would comply with this request promptly by providing every assistance and access to any relevant papers.

I looked up from the email bewildered and surprised. I'd spoken to my friend Paul van de Kohl only the previous week and he was his usual happy-go-lucky self, just returning from a short skiing break with his latest girlfriend.

Max addressed me with a firm tone "I expect you to adhere to the instructions in the email Marc." He continued, "I want all the placing slips and the client correspondence files on my desk by 'close-of-play' tonight. How much brokerage was expected to be earned this year?"

"Give or take, half a million Euros." I replied.

"Has it been booked in our system yet?" Max queried.

"Not all of it, just the initial deposit of three hundred thousand Euros," I explained "I presume you want me to reverse it?"

"Yes," Max nodded "it's going to make a big hole in our first quarter's figures."

I desperately wanted to speak to Paul van der Kohl, to find out what the heck was going on! Max's lack of friendliness made it obvious that I was under some kind of suspicion, but what wrong-doing I had no idea. Paul and I had been friends for five years, and before Mércédès and I were together, Paul and I would see a lot of each other. He was ten years older than me and divorced. We would holiday together, both having the same sense of humour. I also introduced him to rugby. He played once, in a friendly, and he swore that he would never again go on a pitch with such well-spoken animals. Once he heard the phrase 'that football is a gentleman's game played by hooligans whereas rugby was the hooligan's game played by gentlemen' he would use it at every possible opportunity. Paul loved the social side of rugby, particularly the fact that well-to-do English debutants were attracted to the game. He would come over from Holland whenever he could. Paul was happy to be a spectator joining our home and overseas tours, as an unofficial beer manager.

Trying to phone Paul on anything other than his mobile was always impossible. I reasoned that if he was under suspicion then there was a good chance that his calls and messages were being monitored. E-mail was obviously out of the question. I spent the rest of the day ensuring that all the client's files were in good order, with all recent e-mails filed in the right chronological order. Someone was supervising me from Inter-Continental's Legal and Compliance department, a sanguine Scotsman called George White, whom we nicknamed 'whiter-than'. Max had telephoned saying he – George White – was for my own and Inter-Continental's protection. The placing slips [3] were retrieved from the placing brokers slip cases, and certified copies were taken for Inter-Continental's records. My own e-mail account was locked-down so that all current and historic emails that were directly, or indirectly, relevant to the client were isolated and copied into a separate e-mail account. Whilst this was happening on the placing side of Inter-

---

3    A placing slip is a summary of the insurance contract prepared by the insurance broker and is signed by the underwriter prior to issuance of the policy document

Continental, the claims and accounts departments were undertaking a similar exercise. At lunchtime I was able to slip away to buy a sandwich; I made sure I'd left my mobile phone on my desk in full view.

I was a creature of habit, and usually went to the same sandwich shop for my lunch. The shop boasted that they sold the most expensive sandwiches in the City of London, and far from this putting-off customers there was always a queue of about fifteen minutes from noon to two thirty every weekday. I knew that I wouldn't be missed for at least thirty minutes, and being a Monday I was able to buy my sandwich in less than the normal time. Before returning to my desk I stopped at one of the conference rooms, and tried to phone Mércédès, who was in New York on a business trip for a few days. She was just about to start her breakfast meeting, with an important potential advertiser, so it was a hurried conversation. I played down the situation, saying that I had some problems at work, and would call her later that night before she went to dinner.

I could tell that Mércédès was distracted elsewhere and said, "Ok, fine. Love you!"

I then phoned the private line of one of my former colleagues, and former girlfriend, in JPG's Marine department.

"Carla Nottage." Came the voice from the end of the phone.

"Hello." I replied softly.

There was a slight pause and then Carla spoke in a very businesslike voice, "I'm sorry but Mr Eastwood is out of the office for three days, in Holland with our Senior Broker, and Claims Manager."

"Thanks." I said and then hung up.

Carla had been very loyal to me when I worked at JPG and our fling was long finished when Mércédès came on the scene. Carla was John Eastwood's personal secretary, but this was not a full-time role, and she enjoyed working with the Marine department at JPG. Carla had given me all I needed to know. No-one at JPG was allowed to talk to me about the client, and that John Eastwood himself was supervising the transfer of the business back to JPG. Whilst we were friends, he felt that if I'd not breached the 'non-compete' clause in my JPG employment contract when I moved the client for Inter-Continental, then I had 'sailed very close to the wind'.

The afternoon dragged by interminably. By five o'clock, the placing slips, placing files, claims files and all accounting documents were all on Max Huntley's desk. Max was out at a meeting with the Chairman. He left a message with George White that I should go home and report back at half-past eight the following morning. Once again I was reminded that I was not to talk to anyone about the client other than Inter-Continental's Chairman or Max himself; furthermore, this was to include my wife and definitely NOT Paul van der Kohl.

I returned home to an empty flat, racking my brains as to what had caused the problem. I poured myself a large glass of red wine, and as I was drinking it slowly I remembered the last time Paul had visited London, he thought he'd lost his mobile phone. This was a disaster for Paul, as his phone was permanently attached to his ear, and I jokingly suggested that one day he would have to have it surgically removed. Paul bought a cheap pay-as-you-go phone at Schipol Airport. Over the weekend his younger sister phoned me to say she had found the phone in her car, as it must have fallen under the seat when she took him to the airport. Gerda was always mothering him, especially after his divorce, and they were a close family. Paul left the new phone at our flat saying he could do with a spare in London.

I found the phone and dialled Gerda's number. She picked up on the first ring.

"Paul?" she asked.

"No, it's Marc in London." I continued without hesitation "Gerda is Paul alright?"

"I do not know Marc?" She replied in a stilted voice near to crying.

"He called Friday to say that his office had been searched whilst he was away skiing. He sounded upset."

"Do you know where I might be able to contact him?" I enquired.

"N-n-no. Yes, yes he's here. He's just walked in." Her voice sounded relieved and excited.

I heard a brief gabbling in Dutch, and then Paul came on the phone "Marc, I will call you back in one hour on the phone you are using. I must speak quickly to my sister."

He hung up before I could say anything, even though I was bursting with questions.

It was an hour and a half before he called back, and no number showed up on the mobile phone when it rang. The voice at the end of the line was steady but tense.

"Hello Marc. What's happening in London?" It was his usual phrase whenever he started a conversation with me.

I explained quickly about the email from his Chairman to the Chairman of Inter-Continental.

"Former Chairman," he interrupted "I was sacked on Friday."

"What's going on?" My voice was quiet but sounded strained, "What's this about a police investigation?"

"I fucked-up royally Marc, and inadvertently I have dragged you into my fucking mess."

Paul loved using the word 'fuck' at every opportunity, proud that one of the most common and evocative words in the English language was Germanic in its derivation. Although I had (on more than one occasion) told him its popularity was due to "FUCKIN" written on the stocks, if a couple in the middle ages were caught committing adultery, they would be punished 'For Unlawful Carnal Knowledge In the Nude'.

Paul continued "Listen, I do not have long because shortly the police will have enough evidence to arrest me, especially when a bank in the Dutch Antilles is forced to provide them with certain information. The bank is now open for business, and they will have to give the details to the police later today. I need to disappear for a while or I will be spending a long time in gaol.

Paul was always quite flash and very generous with his money. I, and latterly Mércédès, had benefited considerably from his generosity and a dark thought was entering my mind that perhaps it was not his money in the first place!

"Marc, I will tell you all very quickly. My divorce cost me a lot of money, and I was intent on enjoying myself, once I was free from Frieda." There were no children, and Paul had a succession of buxom blonde girlfriends, each never lasting more than a few months.

"Do you remember that I always requested that you invoice the gross premium, and that the return of commission was invoiced to a subsidiary?" Paul's voice became quieter the more he spoke, like he was confessing his sins.

"Yes," I said "half of the twenty-five percent brokerage allowed by underwriters."

"Hmm," Paul carried on "well I diverted the return of commission to an offshore account for the last five years."

"How much was that in total?" I asked.

"Over two million Euros." His voice was in a whisper.


I groaned audibly because this would probably mean that I might be named as an accomplice in a fraud, and that the Financial Services Authority guidelines, in respect of client accounting had been breached.

"I am afraid there is more," Paul continued "I used the money to purchase shares in the old company, and made three times that amount when we were bought."

"So?" I queried.

"Well - I used the money when I visited you in England, and when you and Mércédès visited the Caribbean, I claimed all the costs back as company expenses."

"So you were laundering the money." I said and thinking that was not too bad – just a slap over the wrists.

"But the problem for you is that I needed two signatures for the Dutch Antilles bank account. The other named account holder is you Marc!" Paul stopped talking as the enormity of the situation sunk in.

"H-how?" I was stuttering.

"I forged your signature and got a copy of your passport when I arranged the visa for the Rugby Tour to South Africa a few years ago. I am sorry Marc, I thought it was foolproof; but accounting regulations have tightened up over time, and the auditors of publicly listed companies are much smarter. It was picked up during a routine audit of the overseas divisions' premium allocation."

"What happens now?" I was fearful to ask.

"Tell them you had nothing to do with it, and I'll do the same in a letter I am writing before I disappear." Some humour had crept back into Paul's voice. "To add insult to injury the company is going to bring an action against directors of the old company, alleging that we mis-stated the affairs of the company. My former colleagues have made it clear that they in turn may well sue me, for any losses they suffer, to defend themselves."

"What will you do? Where will you go?" I said, as I was thinking how to break this to Mércédès, whilst she was fond of Paul, she said he was always too full of himself.

"I don't know yet. I'll probably go to Rotterdam and see if I can steal myself away on a ship to somewhere faraway. I know enough people at the docks to be able to at least buy some thinking time."

"I don't suppose returning the money and saying sorry is going to help?" I asked hopefully.

"No, because a lot of it has already gone; I was able to transfer a tidy sum out of the Dutch Antilles Bank Account, before it was frozen on Friday. Keep this phone safe and I'll call when I can." And with that Paul rang off.

I sat for a while, reassuring myself that I should be alright when Paul wrote his letter, although I knew that there would be a lot of oil to pour on troubled waters. I tried phoning Mércédès, but only got her voicemail, and I dozed off in the armchair.

I was woken at four o'clock, by the flat phone ringing furiously. I picked it up and it was Mércédès shouting at me,

"What's happening Marc?"

"Why?" I replied.

"Daddy phoned, he told me that you were being reported to Lloyd's and the FSA, and what did I know about the police investigation into the affairs of Paul van der Kohl."

I was shocked that Sir Hugh already knew what was going on. Then I reasoned that as Chairman of JPG he must know what was going on.

"I have just spoken to Paul…." I started.

"You have done what?" She was yelling now. "I've been told that you must not talk about the subject, and definitely not to Paul!"

I blushed, realising that perhaps I should have waited until Paul cleared me of any wrongdoing, before admitting to talking to him.

"It's OK Mércédès, I have done nothing wrong or anything untoward."

"I always said he was a smart-ass." She talked briefly about her trip, and that she had another breakfast meeting in the morning. She said she needed to go to bed, and we could catch-up tomorrow evening. I could tell she hadn't been convinced by my pleadings of innocence.

I could not sleep after my telephone call with Mércédès. I ran a hot bath and soaked for a couple of hours feeling a lot better and felt sure the problem would blow over in a few days. The Market would focus and gossip on something else within a day and my news would be tomorrow's chip papers. I was at Max's desk for half-past eight as requested and he also seemed more relaxed than the previous day.

"Why don't you get out of the Market for a few days?" He suggested.

"I've just come back from holiday. Am I being suspended?" I asked, feeling myself tense up.

"No, not at all," Max replied a little too quickly "it's just the Chairman wants to make sure everything is ship-shape. He doesn't want tongues wagging unnecessarily. Why don't you visit some clients and prospects overseas?"

I pondered the idea for a moment or two. "Ok, I will see if I can get a flight to the US today. Mércédès, my wife is there on business and I feel uncomfortable talking on the phone about the situation. She already knows from her father - Sir Hugh - that I may be implicated in something. What can I tell her?"

It was Max's turn to ruminate before answering, and for the first time in two days he smiled. "Well, if the Scorpion knows then I guess it's spreading round the market like wild-fire. I will clear it with the Chairman, but I suggest you explain all to her in person, rather than on the telephone."

"I'll call the travel office to make a flight booking." I was thinking out loud.

Max interjected my thought processes "Speed is of the essence, and the bureaucracy in getting transatlantic flights is painful, I should know! Book it yourself, and I will make sure you are reimbursed when you return."

I was back in my flat by half-past nine. I picked up my passport, threw some clothes into a holdall. Just as I was leaving I remembered Paul's old phone. I glanced at the screen, and saw that there was a missed call from Gerda, hopefully telling me that Paul was able to hitch a ride on a ship. There was a voice message; I had no idea how to retrieve a message from the Dutch mobile-phone company. I tried '901', '121', '111' and '100' - all of which resulted in Dutch gabbling from a recorded message - no wonder the Dutch people speak good English; their language is unintelligible to most!

I took a taxi to Paddington, and I was on the Heathrow Express by eleven o'clock. In the taxi I considered calling Mércédès, but decided against it because she had been up late, and had an early breakfast meeting. I would surprise her that evening, and take her to our favourite Italian Restaurant, *Il Forno* for dinner. I did, however, try to call Gerda but got no reply. At what I thought was the appropriate point, I left a message asking that she call me back.

I arrived at Heathrow and went to Terminal 3 handling the Virgin flights. At the ticket sales counter I asked for availability of flights to New York that day (Tuesday) to be told they have nothing to New York, or Newark New Jersey, whatsoever. I cursed myself for not checking before I left the flat. The tickets sales staff suggested another route via Barbados, with a connecting flight to Miami, followed by an internal flight to New York. If all went to plan I would be in New York by midnight but no dinner in *Il Forno*! It would be cheaper to purchase tickets onwards from Barbados, when I arrived there, and I was also assured that there were plenty of seats available.

I bought my ticket on my own private credit card, to earn my air miles. Passing through to the departure lounge I decided to go straight to a restaurant to have a full English breakfast; I was starving because all I had eaten since Sunday evening was a sandwich.

Just as I finished my breakfast Paul's mobile phone rang.

"Hello Gerda, is Paul on a ship?"

I could tell it was Gerda, but I could not understand what she was saying. It was a mixture of Dutch and English and she was crying down the phone line.

"Whoa, hold-on Gerda I can't understand a word you're saying." I shouted down the phone.

There was a big sniff from across the North Sea, and she started again in a very shaky voice, "Paul is in hospital in a coma."

"What!" I was nearly shouting.

"It was a freak accident at the docks at Euro-port. He slipped on an icy rail and banged his head on the concrete. He's unconscious, and the doctors may have to operate, if there are signs of a blood clot. At the moment he's stable." Gerda was starting to regain her composure.

"Should I come over to Rotterdam?" I asked.

"No, that might not be such a good idea, for either of you at the moment."

"Do you know if there was a letter on him when he fell?" I was being insensitive. But I was worried because Paul, the only person who could clear me, was lying in a hospital bed in Holland.

"No, why do you ask Marc? Anyway the police have confiscated all his possessions."

"Gerda, I am on my way to the US on business, and to meet Mércédès. I'll call you back in about ten minutes, if that's ok?" I said checking my Rolex Yachtmaster.

"Ok, I'll keep my phone with me. Bye." And with that Gerda hung up.

I was just thinking that things could not get any worse when I heard my name being called over the tannoy "Would Mr Marcus Edge please report to the information desk where an urgent message awaits him?" Came the pleasant voice of a female announcer.

I walked over to the desk and said, "Hello, I am Mr Edge."

At that point two men in shabby suits sandwiched me, the taller and leaner of the two opened his wallet, and flashed me his police warrant card.

In barely a whisper he said, "Would you mind accompanying us to answer a few questions? Please do not make a fuss; it will give the tourist industry a bad name." The other policeman picked up my holdall, which was the beginning of twelve hours of questioning.

I knew at once the outlook was bleak for me and without the letter from Paul I was sunk. During the following hours things went from bad to worse, when they found Paul's old phone and a single ticket to the Caribbean, rather than New York which was the plan agreed by Max. Mércédès, when questioned, had no idea I was travelling to New York, which the police thought was very strange for people married so recently! Furthermore, Mércédès had told Sir Hugh that I had spoken with Paul, and as Chairman of JPG, he had reported this back to Paul's former employers.

I was released at two o'clock in the morning, but I had to surrender my passport. When I tried calling Mércédès, her phone was switched off and so I left a message at the hotel for her to call me. I arrived home at four o'clock and Mércédès was sitting waiting for me - her bags still unpacked. She was furious and accused me of lying to her.

"Daddy is sending Samuel to pick me up. I am going to spend a few days at The Hall, to think things over."

In fact she didn't return to the flat until many weeks later, when she collected her clothes, and left her keys on the coffee table. Mércédès was never to step foot in the flat again.

At six o'clock, Gerda rang on the flat phone to say that the doctors would be operating on Paul to remove a blood clot. At seven o'clock I had a call from Max Huntley to say that I was suspended forthwith; and my salary plus benefits were payable for six months, or until the outcome of the police investigation. I immediately spoke to a well known tough civil lawyer, to advise me on my position. His retainer was the equivalent of three months salary, but I thought it was a worthwhile investment. In fact it turned out to be a complete waste of time, because whilst Paul's operation went well, he didn't and still has not regained consciousness.

The police did not press any charges against me; they couldn't whilst Paul was in this state. As soon as my passport was returned to me I went to Holland, to help Gerda keep vigil beside Paul's bed. After two months Paul was allowed to be moved to a nursing home, now off life-support, but he still had not regained consciousness. The doctors felt that his brain was preventing him from waking up and facing the music. During the time Paul was in hospital, I stayed with Gerda and we became close, very close. Mércédès distrusted Gerda almost as much as Paul, but for very different reasons. Gerda was exactly the same height as Paul (over six feet tall), with a great figure, which was always bronzed. A good tennis player and skier, sport was a shared interest for the three of us. She lost her girlish awkwardness and became a very attractive young lady. Gerda had a series of suitors, but she shared Paul's *joie de vivre* and none of them lasted for very long, which meant that Mércédès was always wary of Gerda being a rival for my affections.

Inter-Continental's pastoral tendencies only stretched so far, and the FSA wanted to make an example of high-flying executives breaking or flouting their regulations.

The Inter-Continental Contract of Employment was very prescriptive and according to their compliance department I had breached rules by: returning commissions – without the Chairman's agreement - to an entity different from the one paying the premium; as well as accepting gifts of a substantial value (e.g. a holiday in the Caribbean) without declaring such to Inter-Continental. My solicitor postured as much as he could, but from early on he advised that the position was hopeless. He felt the best course of action was to negotiate six months severance pay, and twelve months benefits - mainly healthcare and life insurance - or until I had found full-time employment elsewhere. Given his fee, and that Mércédès was no longer sharing in the costs of the flat, I needed all the money I could lay my hands on. I accepted Inter-Continental's offer that my solicitor negotiated, as I felt I could get another less paid position, relatively easily. The day after I accepted Inter-Continental's offer I received two letters. One from the FSA, saying they considered me to no longer be a *fit and proper person*, and the second letter was from Lloyd's of London advising me that I should attend a disciplinary hearing in 30 days.

These letters were very bad news indeed, because if found guilty it would be very difficult to obtain a senior position in either an insurance company or an insurance intermediary. My younger brother worked for an insurance company as an underwriter and had always been a bit priggish, but now he looked at me as though I should crawl back under a stone. He was so embarrassed to share the same name as me. Mércédès was gone, and we had signed a pre-nuptial agreement so there was no money from that direction. I put the flat on the market. After the mortgage and the legal fees were paid, I had barely enough to buy a bed-sit above a shop in Hackney. My parents stood by me, but they were more interested in seeing their grandchildren in Australia and spent six months of their time 'down-under'. My rugby and *Lammers* friends remained intact and while they all liked Paul none of them was surprised, and some felt I had a 'blind-spot' for him.

That was all many months ago, and since then Mércédès had filed for divorce. I was scraping by, as an unqualified claims investigator, which needed no qualifications nor FSA or Lloyd's approval. What I did need was a client, and they were scarce, which is why the offer of an assignment last Friday had been crucial.

# Sunday Lunchtime
# A14

The weak November sun was creeping into my bedroom. It was the first bedroom I had ever slept in when I first visited The Hall, situated at the end of the landing near the back-stairs. Sir Hugh and his grandmother's rooms were the two nearest the top of the main staircase, with Mércédès' room opposite Sir Hugh's. The main guest bedroom was beside his grandmother's and Mércédès' bedrooms. There were two bathrooms, one next to Sir Hugh's bedroom and the other opposite the bedroom in which I was staying.

The bathrooms were old-fashioned with large enamel baths from when the Swedish Count lived at The Hall. After the death of his grandmother, Sir Hugh knocked through his bedroom into the room which was his grandmother's, and installed a modern en-suite wet area, with an ultra-modern shower. The shower included a large plate sized shower head, and a number of jets at strategic points in the cubicle, which also boasted a seat. Mércédès and I could only dream about having a shower there together. In addition to the shower, the room was also Sir Hugh's dressing room, and private office. The decor and artefacts were a homage to his grandfather and their African homeland Rhodesia (now Zimbabwe). Only once had I been able to visit Sir Hugh's inner sanctum, escorted by Sir Hugh himself, otherwise the room was locked, even to Mércédès with only Samuel and Sir Hugh as key-holders.

It was a cold morning and I soaked in the bath until I heard a knock at the door. Samuel announced that breakfast was in the bedroom, and Sir Hugh hoped I could join him on a drive to Felixstowe. Sir Hugh would be leaving in forty minutes; it sounded like an invitation, but I knew it could not be declined.

Samuel had found some of my clothes I had left at The Hall, and not collected since that fateful day when Mércédès returned from New York, and left me. A new razor and toothbrush, still in their packaging, were also placed strategically in the bathroom. I completed my ablutions, ate breakfast and dressed in my old clothes, which now hung loose on me. I knew I'd lost weight; the lack of business luncheons and alcohol had seen to that. My side was still aching with a dull constant throb, until I put on my shirt, when the searing shooting pain returned. I had to sit down for a moment or two, for fear of fainting.

Sir Hugh was waiting for me in the main study, off the entrance hall, and he greeted me with a smile.

"Ha-ha! There you are, and on time. Thank-you. Samuel's picking up a business associate of mine, who arrives at Heathrow this afternoon, so I thought we could take the Peugeot. Are you well enough to drive?"

With the pain whilst dressing my initial reaction was to decline, but yesterday's charge to The Cricketers, and the fact that since selling the Porsche I had not driven for a while, I agreed to drive.

Sir Hugh continued, "I thought I could drop you off at Stansted Airport on the way back; there are always good connections to London from there on Sunday. Do you have your things with you?"

I pointed to the plastic bag of a well-known supermarket in my hand "Thank you Sir Hugh but…"

Sir Hugh interrupted me, before I became too embarrassed, and said "Don't worry I'll buy your ticket. Come on let's go or we'll miss the best part of the day."

The Peugeot was already outside the front of The Hall. Sir Hugh was dressed casually but carried his briefcase with him. It rarely left his side.

"You don't mind if I read a few papers as you drive?"

Again it was phrased as a question, but no answer was expected so I didn't give one other than a smile. I started to think that the trip to Felixstowe was not solely for the benefit of my health, but I was being utilized as an unpaid chauffeur, so that Sir Hugh could work whilst Samuel collected Sir Hugh's next houseguest. I couldn't complain so I focussed on the drive.

We had been travelling mostly in silence for almost half-an-hour, on the A14 heading for Felixstowe, when Sir Hugh looked up from his papers.

He must have been reading my mind, "Marc, this is very good of you to give up your Sunday, to drive me to Felixstowe."

Not at all Sir Hugh, I thought to myself; I was going to do bugger-all anyway after receiving a severe pasting on Friday, and spending the night in jail. I had no money or keys, and you took me in as your son-in-law, which I suppose technically I was if not practically. Nothing needed to be said, so I kept my mouth shut and was quiet.

"So what are you going to do next?" Asked Sir Hugh.

"Well I thought I'd give K-P a call - he'll be back by the time I reach London - and he has a spare key for my bed-sit."

It was Sir Hugh's turn to smile; it was a condescending look reserved for parents when dealing with a recalcitrant child. Before Sir Hugh spoke again, I quickly carried on "Oh, you mean the bigger picture!"

Sir Hugh nodded and he smiled again, a lot more sincere this time. "Yes."

"Well I'll be back to Neptune Re tomorrow, after I have spoken to my broker about increasing my Professional Indemnity insurance. I hope they will advance me a retainer, I need the cash, and the bill for the increased cost of insurance will not be due for forty-five days." I finished speaking just as we passed the junction for Bury St. Edmunds.

"So do you know what they want you to do?" asked Sir Hugh.

"No" I replied "other than it was an assignment that would suit my particular skills - whatever they may be."

"What about their normal claims investigators?" Enquired Sir Hugh.

"Apparently they might be conflicted." I replied.

Sir Hugh returned to his papers, and I started to enjoy the drive, on what had turned out be a bright November day. The roads were not crowded, with the traffic moving steadily. The Peugeot was a joy to drive, and its age meant that the engine and gearbox were properly bedded down, so when I needed the power in the mid-range the car would pick up speed quickly and easily. On the outskirts of Ipswich

Sir Hugh glanced at his watch, before putting away his papers in his briefcase.

"Marc, I thought as you had a late breakfast that you could probably manage without food until mid-afternoon, when we can grab a burger and chips at Stansted Airport?"

"That sounds good to me." I said.

"Ok, then perhaps we need a drink, and so does the car. At the next petrol station pull-in please?" Sir Hugh instructed.

It was fifteen minutes before I saw the signs for the Services, a petrol station together with a Little Chef. As I indicated and slowed down, Sir Hugh asked that I drop him at the Little Chef, and could I fill the tank with fifty pounds worth. A crisp fifty pound note was lying next to the gear lever.

"No problem." I said, but inwardly I groaned knowing that there would be raised eyebrows in the kiosk, when I presented them with a new high denomination note. It took more than a few minutes, after I pulled up at the petrol pump, to work-out how to open the petrol cap.

My actions must have seemed very suspicious, and whilst my lips were less swollen, the bruising was still evident on my face. The fuel cost a few pence less than fifty pounds. When I presented a crisp note the young girl rang her till bell, summoning the supervisor. A man only a few years older than the girl came to her side. She whispered animatedly in his ear, and when she looked at me she blushed brightly.

"Do you have any other method of payment sir?" The supervisor asked.

"No." I said.

The supervisor held the note up to the light, checked it against something behind the desk. "Sorry for asking, but we have experienced a number of frauds with fake fifty pound notes. Is that your car?" The supervisor was remaining polite, but there was a muttering in the queue behind me.

"No," and the supervisor was startled by the candidness of my reply "the owner of the car and the bank note is in the Little Chef. I'm merely his driver for the day. We can go over and ask him if you want? But I would not recommend it!"

The supervisor held the fifty-pound note under another light, and said "No, that won't be necessary."

A task that should have taken five minutes, had taken nearly fifteen, and I was expecting Sir Hugh not to be best pleased. He liked things and people to be on time. As I looked through the glass door of the Little Chef I could see Sir Hugh talking on his mobile phone. When he saw me he finished his call.

"I am sorry; I haven't ordered a drink yet!" Sir Hugh apologised "That was Samuel," he continued "apparently he mis-read the arrival time of my associates' flight. He will not be home until later this evening, so it is just as well we will be eating late this afternoon."

Whilst we were waiting for coffee I asked Sir Hugh if I could borrow his mobile phone to call K-P.

"Certainly, what is his number?" Sir Hugh's mobile was as private as his papers, so he keyed the number, before handing me the phone. There was no reply from K-P's phone, so I asked him to call me on my mobile as soon as he was able to do so.

Sir Hugh fixed me with his blue eyes "Laddie, I think the ban served out to you by the FSA and Lloyd's, was over-the-top. I advocated your position, but as your father-in-law I was conflicted."

I smiled embarrassingly; I seemed to be doing a lot of that over the weekend.

He continued ever businesslike, "We are, however, where we are. But you can't continue carrying on living from hand to mouth. You can't return to JPG, but I have a number of business interests outside the insurance industry, and you are still young enough to start again. The situation with Mércédès is delicate, and she is impulsive like her mother." Sir Hugh blushed involuntarily "Also her relationship with Tony Eastwood needs some space to develop – or die!"

It was my turn to blush now.

Seeing that I was about to speak, Sir Hugh put his hand up to silence me, and put forward his proposition. "The person arriving today at Heathrow is Mércédès' grandfather, and also my business partner. He wants to extend our operations in China and the Far East; as a result we need to recruit a Regional Manager in Singapore. The person must be trustworthy, and despite this tomfoolery with Paul van der Kohl, I think a son-in-law will satisfy those credentials."

I blushed again, this time with pride, rather than ire.

Sir Hugh continued, "The position would include a flat rent-free, and if we construct the employment contract the right way, we might be able to minimise the amount of tax you would have to pay. The starting salary would be one hundred thousand pounds."

I was completely flummoxed, because all my financial worries would be over in one fell swoop. I stammered, "I-I-I don't kno-o-ow what to say?"

"Say nothing for now," Sir Hugh smiled benignly "think about it, and let me have your answer before Thursday. Mércédès' grandfather returns to Goa then, and I would like to have the position sorted by then; and by the way, I won't say anything to Mércédès until after you have made your decision. Come on let's go. I have an appointment in half an hour."

We returned to the A14, and Sir Hugh briskly directed me to the Port of Felixstowe. I knew that Sir Hugh had invested in the Port of Felixstowe, and curiously I asked whom he was meeting.

"Oh, one of my ship's captains, he sails tomorrow. I like keeping in touch with as many of my managers as I can, to keep a finger on the pulse. You will find that out for yourself, if you accept my offer?"

I dropped him at the gates of the Port. He suggested that I have the car and take time to think over his offer. He then asked that I return at three o'clock to pick him up. He gave me another fifty-pound note, saying that it should be enough to cover the train fare back to London, plus some spending money for the next day or two.

"Marc, would you mind just checking the spare wheel for me please? Samuel is taking the car in for its MoT [4] this week. He was going to make sure all is ok, but now he will be back late it will be dark, so he won't be able to check it."

"Not a problem Sir Hugh." I replied.

---

4    Ministry of Transport Test

# Sunday Afternoon
# Felixstowe

I drove into Felixstowe itself and parked close to the promenade. Dutifully I discharged Sir Hugh's task by thoroughly checking the spare wheel, taking it out of the boot and ensuring the jack was also working. I then walked along the promenade for an hour or so. The warmth from the November sun was losing its battle against the gentle but cool breeze of the North Sea. Felixstowe held many good childhood memories for me. My uncle was the financial controller of a hotel in the centre of Felixstowe, and in the summer holidays - after my eighteenth birthday - I stayed with him. The visit was not all benevolence, the hotel was on its last legs, and I was cheap labour. Initially I worked in kitchens as an assistant, learning how to wash pans 'properly' with scalding water, and how to bone and roll a turkey – so as to get the most servings possible when roasting. I also spent as much time as I could, waiting at table, which I enjoyed the most, especially Saturday nights when there was a new intake of young girls to woo with the bright lights of Felixstowe (or not). A brassy waitress from Birmingham also took me in hand, who took it upon herself to fill any gaps in my education of the female sex, until my uncle sent her packing back to the Midlands.

I was smiling at the memories, but I was brought back to the real world by shivering against a North Sea breeze. My old fleece was no match against the elements as the sun weakened. My fellow promenaders were better prepared. They all seemed to be leaning into each other, taking their last sun of the year, before winter closed in. I went into a café and ordered a pot of tea.

Sir Hugh's motives behind his offer were not very complicated. I was potentially an embarrassment to him, whilst I was still around the London insurance market. As his son-in-law plus his support at the Lloyd's of London hearing would all be seen as a potential weakness that someone could use against him in the future. The Scorpion could never be seen to be weak!

With me out of the country, the position between me, Mércédès and Tony Eastwood would also be less complicated. Despite my hackles rising every time I heard his name, he played no part in my problems, just a vulture playing on the carcass that was my marriage and career. After my fall from grace at Inter-Continental he was brought in as temporary Divisional Managing Director of both the Marine Hull and Marine Cargo departments, and dismantled most of my changes, re-establishing cronies in his 'kitchen-cabinet'.

I looked out from the café as the sky darkened; it seemed to reflect my mood, but there was salvation and hope awaiting me in Singapore. I decided to accept Sir Hugh's offer. Who knows, in a few years' time I might even be accepted back into the London insurance market? Things were on the up - I even had a free pot of tea - as the café didn't have enough change for the fifty-pound note.

I was walking back to the car when K-P phoned. I gave him a full explanation of everything that had happened since Friday night, adding that I couldn't remember a thing, and I had lost my keys. Once he knew I was in the land of the living, K-P was phlegmatic about the sequence of events. He asked where I was now. I told him, and he was more than a little bit surprised, when he learnt that Sir Hugh had come to my rescue on Saturday. And even more surprised when I told him what else was in the offing.

"What does he want?" K-P asked in mock seriousness.

"I will tell you later my friend," and before he could reply I asked "will the kids be settled by seven o'clock?"

"Yes, I hope so," said K-P "why?"

"Well, could you call me then please, because if I'm not back in London I should not be very far away? Perhaps you could pick me up from Liverpool Street Station and drop me off at my flat, bringing my spare key with you?"

I could hear that K-P had covered the phone with his hand, presumably so Jane his wife couldn't hear him agreeing to meet me on a Sunday evening. "No problem." K-P lied badly.

"Sorry, I will make it up to Jane, and my godchild." I was godfather to K-P's and Jane's eldest child, and Mércédès godmother to the youngest. I caught myself thinking how I would be able to fulfil my commitment whilst I was in Singapore, and without seeing Mércédès at family functions.

Those thoughts were banished when KP answered "Ok I will call you about seven o'clock."

Sir Hugh was at the same place where I dropped him three hours earlier. I was there spot-on-time, which obviously pleased him; he shivered as he got into the car. "Turn the heating up please, and let's get on the move, I need some food inside me to ward off the cold.

We were soon back on the A14, and the traffic had become even sparser than when we drove to Felixstowe earlier, although the number of lorries signalled that a ferry had recently arrived from the continent. Sir Hugh could not read his paper in the gathering dusk, so he talked about Africa, and even with central heating he had never been able to cope with the cold dampness that was Britain in the autumn and winter. His reminiscences were fairly predictable, and at the Bury St Edmunds Junction, he asked whether I'd given his proposition any further thoughts.

"Of course I have," I replied "but you said no answer was required until Thursday."

Sir Hugh merely smiled.

"What timescales are you looking at?" I asked.

I sensed rather than saw Sir Hugh looking at me, as though his prey had taken the bait, and he started to close in for the kill. "I would like you to start as soon as possible, it will about a month - to six weeks - to arrange a work visa, Singapore can be quite particular in that respect. The initial contract would be for three years, subject to six months' notice on either side, with a large bonus should the full three years be completed."

Despite the fact I was driving, I turned to him and said "Three years is a long contract!"

It was as though Sir Hugh had been expecting the question "Not for senior managers in overseas postings. The investment in the infrastructure, and other aspects makes three years a minimum term. We pay only a proportion of your salary to you locally, the balance is paid to an offshore bank of your choice, and a generous bonus is paid at the end of the three years. The bonus depends on the profitability of your sector of responsibility, which can also be taken as stock options in Masterson Shipping."

Sir Hugh's white teeth shone in the beams of the oncoming vehicle's headlights. I could see the reflection in the windscreen to indicate he was smiling again. He was enjoying himself. I felt bad that I had assumed his motives were only to make his life easier; perhaps he felt partially to blame for my predicament, as he had given me too much too quickly - including Mércédès. But then again, we had always enjoyed a good relationship, even before I became his son-in-law.

His coup-de-grace came as we approached the Junction for the M11.

"Why don't you go out to Singapore next week, to get a feel for the place?"

Sir Hugh had his keep-net slowly encircling me, and I was close to being snared. The momentum was broken by the M11, always busy on Sunday afternoons with families returning from weekends in East Anglia. There had been an accident and traffic was crawling. Sir Hugh directed me off the motorway at the first opportunity, and we drove towards Stansted Airport on the back roads, via Saffron Walden and Elsenham.

Stansted Airport was buzzing, the days of the old Nissan huts and turbo-prop planes were long gone. Wide bodied jets now operated daily from one of the longest runways in the United Kingdom, and fierce local opposition to further runways was now looking pointless. We had decided on eating at a hotel near the airport, rather than the airport itself. I was unsure whether it was a reflection that I was 'nearly on the team', or that Sir Hugh was unlikely to have the full meal awaiting his return to The Hall; nevertheless the Beef Tomato and Mozzarella starter, followed by Filet Steak and French Fries was absolutely delicious. The painkillers were definitely on top of my injuries, and my appetite had been catapulted by the fresh North Sea air, and was back with a vengeance! I even managed cheese and biscuits, and other than a small glass for Sir Hugh (who would be driving from the hotel) I demolished a bottle of Chianti Reserva. Sir Hugh looked on confidently, when I told him I had decided to accept his offer. I said that I could visit Singapore in a couple of weeks, by which time my parents would be contactable in Sydney, when I would be able to give them the good news.

"I will call you tomorrow to start the paperwork," said Sir Hugh "come on lets get you on a train before the wine takes affect and you fall asleep!"

## Sunday Evening
## Return to London

It was six o'clock when Sir Hugh dropped me at Stansted Airport. A Stansted Express train was due to depart ten minutes after Sir Hugh headed back to The Hall. I thanked him profusely for his generosity and was sound asleep before the train had reached Bishop's Stortford. My mobile rudely awakened me, it was K-P, and we agreed to meet on Bishopsgate in ten minutes. I had been asleep for over half an hour and my mouth was dry; but my stomach was full, and I had money in my wallet. Plus a well-paid job offer in my pocket. My head was still spinning with the turn around of events, in just over forty eight hours!

K-P met me in his own Peugeot shooting brake. His decision to drive this car was not because of any nostalgic reason, but a pragmatic and logical decision, when having to accommodate the baby and booster seats needed for his young family.

"I have been driving one of these today," I chirped-up "and it was a lot tidier than this one!"

"I hope Sir Hugh took over before you started topping up the alcohol levels from Friday." K-P retaliated.

"Was I really that bad on Friday?" I enquired.

"I had to steer you away from Tony Eastwood. You were fighting drunk." K-P was talking whilst negotiating the road to Shoreditch.

"Oh! Thank goodness for that, if you had not done so perhaps Sir Hugh's offer might not have been so forthcoming." I felt very stupid.

"I tried to take you home when I left at nine o'clock, I was already in deep shit with Jane and could not stay out any later, but you were determined to carry on." K-P paused and then said "I blame myself for getting you into the state you were in."

"So do I!" And we both laughed.

As we drove to my flat, I revealed to K-P the details of the offer, from Sir Hugh.

"That's fantastic Marc." K-P was genuinely pleased for me.

"You can organise a trip to the Hong Kong Sevens for the *Lammers*."

"You sod, if you think that lets you off the hook for next year's tour arrangements you're much mistaken." We laughed again.

He pulled up near my flat with "Ok, let me make sure you get home safely tonight."

I was feeling very tired and did not have the energy to argue with my friend. The traffic outside my Hackney flat was busy even on a Sunday night. But it was nothing like the crescendo of noise it builds to in the morning and evening rush hours, particularly Friday and Saturday when the evening and nights were punctuated by police and ambulance sirens, wailing incessantly.

Hackney had the misfortune of being one of the poorest boroughs in the United Kingdom which is probably why I was able to buy a bed-sit there outright. With no regular income, the chance of a mortgage at a sensible rate of interest was not a viable option, and I could walk to the City and the West End. I would not have been able to afford the cost of commuting if I lived outside of London. The downside, in addition to the traffic noise, was that I lived above a shop that was closed less time than I was asleep. What convenience the shop location presented was offset by the noise and rubbish it generated.

"What will you do with the flat?" K-P asked as if he was reading my mind.

"Rent it probably," I replied "I should be able to do that quite easily. The rent would be the minimum charged by letting agents, but the return on capital a much better investment than a flash apartment in the Docklands."

The downstairs entrance had a Yale-type lock, but the flat door itself had a seven-lever deadlock, as well as another Yale-type lock. K-P had passed me the spare set of keys, and I was trying to turn the key to open the deadlock.

"It is stiff, it won't move." I tried the key once more.

"Here let me have a go you weakling." The keys seemed minute in K-P's massive fists. He tried turning the key, and then he wiggled it again, turning to me he said "It would help if you locked it first you idiot!"

"But I always lock it." I said as the door swung open.

"Oh shit," was K-P's response to the devastation that confronted us "I'll phone the police."

I was too stunned to speak, and felt the blood rushing from my face, whilst the throbbing was returning to my side

"The sooner I leave this place the better." I said to myself.

# Dawn Monday
# Hackney

The traffic outside my 'bijou and well-appointed one-bedroom flat' (as lavishly described by the estate agent who sold it to me) was already stationery at seven o'clock, signalling that the Monday morning rush-hour was well underway. And dawn was yet to peak its head over the horizon.

The shop beneath my flat was already open and doing a roaring trade with the early morning commuters, which would continue right through the day - every day including bank holidays - until half past eleven at night, other than Sundays when Shariz (the owner) closed the shop at half past seven. I was fascinated at the industry and dedication to trading by Shariz. A quiet man with keen eyes and a large amount of nervous energy, he was never still whether it was serving customers, stacking shelves or general wheeling and dealing. The shop was a 'corner shop' come grocery store, and inside the shop Shariz had all manner of items for sale from ironmongery to lap-top computers. Shariz's brother was often in the shop when he wasn't running his general maintenance, lap-top repairs and decorating business from the storeroom at the back of the shop. Always courteous, I would be greeted with 'Hello Mr Marc' every time they saw me. The convenience of the shop and helpfulness of the proprietors was initially wonderful, but was now too overwhelming, and I yearned to be able to lie in bed without the constant punctuation of the shop door opening and closing.

As I lay in bed I thought to myself, 'This will all be behind me when I accept Sir Hugh's offer to work in Singapore'. I was still feeling stiff from where I had received the Friday night beating, but the pain had dulled sufficiently for me to consider some exercise. Sir Hugh's offer was on my mind and I wanted to think things through, and I did this best when I was jogging or swimming. I didn't feel like going to the swimming pool as it was a frosty morning but a run appealed with the cold sharpening my brain cells. The first part of my run was always difficult with an irregular breathing pattern, avoiding pedestrians, cars and the dreaded push-bikes. Push-bikers in London are supremely arrogant. They believe that because they are doing their green 'bit', they can totally disregard the Highway Code, and anyone else on: the roads, footpaths, pavements, and particularly the canal tow paths!

I was still thinking about how to teach cyclists a lesson by pushing one of them into Regents Canal, when I found myself in the haven of Victoria Park. My running and breathing now had a steady rhythm and the weak sun-light was glistening on any ice covered water. Winter was on its way, and the thought of Christmas in the UK with no money was not a pleasant image. The glittering prize of a well paid job in Singapore brought a smile to my face, as I completed the first of three laps of the park. I was mentally ticking off 'things to do'. I would phone Sir Hugh as soon as I returned to my flat, so that the paperwork (visas and work permits) could commence. He had said that the process would take four to six weeks, and in my mind I hoped that I could be on a flight before Christmas Day. My parents were not due to return from Australia until February. Perhaps they might stay-over en route in Singapore, for a couple of days, to celebrate my positive turn of events? My passport was in order for another five years, and my bank manager would be extremely happy to hear of my news. I would rent my flat, and I felt sure there would be plenty of takers, because of the relatively cheap tariff I was prepared to accept. I felt sure that Shariz would be able to find a corner of his storeroom for any bits-and-pieces I wanted to leave in London for a few years.

Despite trying to focus on what was needed to be done to facilitate a quick move to Singapore, my thoughts kept returning to the break-in of my flat over the weekend. K-P had helped me clear up the mess, and I phoned the police who were less than helpful; they issued me with a Crime Number, and asked me to call back once I had identified what had been stolen. The more I thought about the break-in the more I thought something was wrong. I couldn't put a finger on what was troubling me, but it was as though something was out of focus. The more I tried to concentrate on what was wrong, the fuzzier my mind became.

I was so deep in thought I was not aware of the bicycle on my shoulder, until its rider shocked me into reality.

"Get out of the bloody way!"

I turned to see a very peculiar combination. K-P astride a heavy mountain bike! He was wearing his usual broad smile, enjoying the moment, as he knew my abhorrence towards cyclists.

The girth of K-P's thighs meant that they would not point forward when he peddled his bicycle, so he pedalled his bicycle with his heels rather than the balls of his feet. This plus his stout body resulted in him sitting very upright and appearing as though at any time he would topple backwards. Although he did not look the part, K-P had become very adept at manoeuvring himself on the machine, around the London traffic and its pedestrians.

Jane had bought him the bicycle, when he gave up playing rugby, in an effort to ensure K-P kept fit. One disobeyed Jane at one's peril. K-P had embraced the bicycle, as it was a good excuse to get out of their cramped flat, if they had a bad night with one of their young children. So it was not unusual for K-P to suddenly pop out of nowhere when I was out running.

"Morning," I replied "couldn't you sleep?"

"No, sleep is not a problem when the nights are cold. Anyway it was after midnight before I went to bed last night, thanks to you!"

"Huh!" I grunted as I picked up my pace again. We continued for a couple of minutes in silence, around Victoria Park, and were now being joined by other joggers and canine lovers walking their dogs.

As I passed the entrance to the park for my third lap, K-P began to speak.

"You know that whoever broke into your flat was either a professional, able to gemmy both the dead lock and the Yale, or they had a set of keys. The spare set you entrusted to me is normally buried in my sock drawer, thus away from little hands in my household, and that's where I found them yesterday afternoon after we spoke when you were in Felixstowe. Whilst you were starting to tidy the flat I examined the two locks. There did not seem to be any new scratches, therefore the burglars were either very professional, or they had your keys. This raises the question as to why would a professional risk breaking in to your flat when, quite frankly, there is nothing worth stealing." A broad smile was fixed across his face.

He asked "Did you have a tag with your address attached to your keys you lost on Friday?"

I turned again towards him sharply, and even though he was holding up his hand to stop me speaking, I answered "Do you think I am an idiot?"

"Therefore if it was not a professional, whoever gave you a pasting on Friday night and took your keys either knew you or they knew where you lived. If I am right, the assumption that you were the victim of a random beating by local East End thugs, should probably be discounted."

I said nothing and carried on running. It was as though someone had just adjusted the fine focussing on a camera lens, and suddenly the things about the break-in that were troubling me disappeared, and I could see clearly.

"K-P, you're much better at this investigative stuff than me. Why don't we set up in business together?"

"Because I have a wife and family to feed!" Before I could fire a retort, he continued "I must be going now, as we have overseas clients in town this week. I can probably make coffee late tomorrow afternoon, if you are in or around Lloyd's. Ciao!"

As K-P's bulky frame disappeared out of the park gates, I thought how much I would miss him when I was in Singapore. But I had to start rebuilding my life, and I would not get a better offer than Sir Hugh's. I finished the third lap of the park, and then headed back towards my flat, with K-Ps pearls of wisdom ringing in my ears.

I kept trying to retrace my footsteps of Friday, but I could only see vague memories after six o'clock, and everything just seemed to be dark shadows. I was back at my flat before I could focus on the next item on my 'things to do' list. Shariz was just dealing with a customer, but there was no-one else waiting.

When he had finished serving he greeted me with "Hello, Mr Marc, how are you doing?"

"Some good, some bad Shariz, and how are you doing?" I replied.

Shariz looked down at the floor shaking his head "Business is always difficult Mr Marc."

I smiled inwardly, thinking to myself that he was doing very well, especially with the hours he spent in the shop, and with an unpaid extended family to draw upon to run the various businesses.

"Shariz, I will be moving out of my flat soon." I announced.

Shariz looked crest-fallen "Oh no Mr Marc, I hope it is not because of my little business. I thought we were good neighbours and friends."

"No, no, Shariz, I have been offered a three-year contract in Singapore, and I intend to rent my flat whilst I am away. In fact, I wondered if I might store some of my furniture and possessions in your store-room."

"Of course Mr Marc, that would be an absolute pleasure." Shariz was obviously relieved that he was not the reason for my departure; although truthfully I would be pleased to move on.

I smiled, and without breaking a beat, Shariz always the business man said "My rates will be very reasonable. I will be able to offer two tariffs, one with, and one without insurance."

I smiled again and merely nodded "Shariz, were you in the shop all weekend?"

"Yes, on Saturday but Sunday was my cousin's birthday, so we closed the shop. Very bad for business. Why do you ask? Did you need something?"

I looked around to make sure no-one was in ear shot and - other than an elderly gentleman - the shop was empty. "Not exactly, my flat was broken into between Saturday morning and Sunday evening."

Shariz looked shocked "Oh dear Mr Marc, what was stolen? As I said the shop was closed on Sunday."

"Nothing or it appears nothing!" I replied "Did you see anything unusual on Saturday?"

Shariz thought about my question for a moment, and then shook his head with the palms of his hands facing upwards "No, Mr Marc, sorry!"

Another person now required serving, and there were two others just entering the shop, so I said goodbye and made my way upstairs to my flat.

The run had loosened me up, but after talking to Shariz I was starting to stiffen and my side was aching again, so I popped another of the painkillers and climbed into the shower. Despite replacing the shower-head when I moved into the flat, the water pressure was low, and so the shower was pathetic. I thought of Sir Hugh's fantastic shower room at The Hall, and vowed that when I was in Singapore any accommodation had to have a decent shower, especially with the high humidity. After ten minutes I felt the effects of the warm water, mixed with the pain killers. I felt ready to go into the City, to meet with Neptune Re, and tell them that unfortunately I could not accept their assignment. I thought about just phoning Eric Jones, but felt I should tell him in person.

The suit I wore on Friday was ripped, torn and smelt of vomit. Time for a clear-out, and the suit was the first item in the black disposal bag, when I heard my mobile phone ringing and answered the 'withheld number'.

"Hello, Marc Edge."

"Good morning Mr Edge," an American female voice greeted me "this is Ms. Syrani, Sir Hugh Masterson's private secretary. Sir Hugh wondered if you would be able to meet him at half past four today, in his private office in St. James's, to discuss the finer points of the offer in Singapore."

Ms. Syrani's clipped New York accent left little doubt that it would be unwise to decline the appointment. I remembered Ms. Syrani from my wedding, recalling that she had befriended Sir Hugh's grandmother and wife, when they first came to England from Zimbabwe. When Sir Hugh's wife returned to Goa, Ms. Syrani would accompany Sir Hugh to events, which required a partner. Ms. Syrani was nearly six feet tall, with classical good looks, and her greying hair complimented her bearing as a woman of authority. I had asked Mércédès whether Ms. Syrani and Sir Hugh were an item? Mércédès said she was unsure, but she did know that Samuel and Ms. Syrani fell-out in the early days, and did not see 'eye-to-eye' with each other which meant she rarely visited The Hall and almost never stayed overnight.

"Yes, yes, that would be fine Ms. Syrani." I accepted Sir Hugh's invitation.

"Good, do you know where Sir Hugh's private office is located in St. James's?" Ms. Syrani asked, her voice more relaxed, and the New York twang more pronounced.

"Vaguely; I know the building." I proffered, trying to be helpful.

"When you arrive, make yourself known to the concierge. He will direct you from there, please do not be late!"

"Good, things were definitely on the move." I said to myself.

I felt excited that I had been invited to Sir Hugh's private office. He also had offices at Masterson Shipping, as well as JPG. I had visited both of them; the latter on numerous occasions, but Sir Hugh's London pied-a-terre and private office was another matter. Mércédès had pointed it out, when we were in the West End one evening, saying that she had only been there on a few occasions herself.

As I put the mobile into my pocket, I noticed that it was displaying ten missed calls and the voicemail was working overtime. I had run out of credit on my 'pay-as-you-go' tariff. Then I remembered I had change from the fifty pound note, after paying for my ticket from Stansted Airport. I quickly ironed a fresh shirt, sought out another suit, and went downstairs to the shop to buy a ten pound top-up card for my phone.

As I paid Shariz for the phone card, he said "I am unsure if it is connected to your break-in, but very early Saturday morning I had four or five phone calls, but when I answered there was no-one at the other end of the line."

"Thanks Shariz, I will mention it to the police." Leaving Shariz to deal with his next customer.

# Monday Morning
# Bus journey to the City

I rarely received any phone calls and to have had eleven, including Ms. Syrani, before nine thirty on a Monday morning was unheard of in the last few months. I was, therefore intrigued why, I had become so popular. I quickly entered the code, from the phone card, and then dialled my voicemail number. As I walked towards the bus-stop, I remembered that I had lost my overcoat on Friday, and that I should try and find it.

"You have eight new messages." My digitalised voice mail announced to me.

"Hello, Mr Edge, this is Sir Hugh's private secretary. I will call again shortly after nine o'clock, to arrange an appointment for later today."

I deleted message one.

"Marc, this is Gerda, sorry if I have woken you up. I have a few days holiday, and I thought that I might come to England next weekend, to do some Christmas shopping. Is that good for you? I visited Paul yesterday, but there is no change. Talk to you later – big kisses."

"Oh shit." I murmured to myself at the bus-stop. Gerda and I had promised not to fall in love with each other, and neither of us had uttered the *L* word, but the truth was that we were very compatible and very easy in each other's company. The thought of not seeing Gerda, every six weeks or so, filled me with dread. More that once, when I was sitting alone in my flat; I had thought that Gerda would be a wonderful mother, as well as a very accomplished and sensitive lover. Our shared sporting interests made us more compatible. I had previously put these idle thoughts down to loneliness, but I was starting to realise that the feelings I had for Gerda, were far more deeply rooted. Gerda had a good job in Holland, this plus Paul's condition meant she was unlikely to move to Singapore, but we could probably meet three or four times a year. Perhaps the three years would be a good test on the permanence of our relationship. I saved the message so that it reminded me to call Gerda later tonight, to tell of my news, as well as saying yes to the next weekend. If Gerda saw things the same way as I did, it might be a really super weekend.

"Hello Marc, this is Jimmy Black at JPG. You left me a message on Friday. I am in the office until eleven, and then I will be off to Lloyd's, so if possible can you call me before then. Many thanks."

I saved Jimmy's message, and decided to call him after I had spoken to Eric Jones, at Neptune Re.

In fact the next message was Eric, asking me to come to his office at eleven o'clock. I noted the time in the calendar facility on the phone; I also added the appointment with Sir Hugh, at four thirty.

The bus arrived and I clambered aboard. I surveyed my fellow passengers, who were definitely a different crowd from the commuters, most of which were required at work by nine o'clock on a Monday morning. There was a mixture of students, mothers-with-babies or pre-school children, and elderly passengers. They seemed to all know each other, and I wondered if they came on the bus mainly to have a chat. I was able to find a seat at the back of the bus, where a student had his earphones firmly in place, which was just as well because a tirade of abuse followed when I listened to message two.

"Marc you are such a wanker. I came to work today to be confronted by my work colleagues, all giggling because you were off-your-face on Friday making a spectacle of yourself outside The Lamb, trying to pick a fight with Tony Eastwood. If that wasn't enough, you actually get yourself into a fight, arrested and end up spending the night in gaol! And to cap it all off you didn't even warn me, your own brother, so I could prepare myself before I came to work. You are so bloody selfish, and the sooner you realise you have no place anymore in the London market the better! So why don't you just sod off!"

"Hmmmm, Joshua's not in a good mood today" I said to no-one in particular, as I deleted his message.

Joshua was four years younger than me. I introduced him into the world of insurance when he worked for JPG one summer. He did not like the cut and thrust of the broking world, and whether it was the fact that I was successful at JPG or that he was attracted to the technical aspects of the underwriting role, but he - in his own priggish way - declared that he was a 'better farmer that hunter' and joined a Lloyd's syndicate as an underwriting assistant. He was steadily climbing the corporate ladder, very careful to develop and maintain his profile in the market. Thus my disgrace and ban from Lloyd's tarnished his profile, for which he never would forgive me.

The sixth message was from Carla Nottage of JPG.

"Hello, Marc, it's Carla, you probably don't remember but you were with us on Friday night, boy were you flying! Anyway, when you disappeared, you left your coat behind and I picked it up and took it home with me. I have brought it in with me today, so if you're around, give me a call. Bye."

That was good news because the coat was a dark blue 'British Warm' crombie, with a velvet collar, made fashionable in the early seventies by Michael Caine in the film 'Get Carter'. It was part of a uniform worn by young thugs called 'suede-heads' in the nineteen-seventies, but crombies were very much the winter attire of choice for workers in the City of London, particularly Lloyd's insurance brokers who would be in and out of air-conditioned buildings all day long.

The next message was not so pleasant; it was my long suffering Bank Manager who was reminding me of our appointment for the following day to discuss the state of my account and my overdraft facility. I had forgotten about the meeting, so I entered it in the calendar with far less foreboding than when he suggested the appointment to me, a couple of weeks ago.

The last message was the most unexpected and probably the most unwanted.

"Marc, its Mércédès, please do not call me back, just listen. Daddy has told me about the offer he has made to you; I think he's mad, gone off his rocker and I have told him so, but for some very strange reason he likes you. Tony told me about the fiasco on Friday night, with you making a complete arse of yourself, and then you end up in a fight. Marc, I am going to Goa to visit my Mum for a month. When I get back, do yourself a favour and be in Singapore."

It was the first time I had heard Mércédès voice for some months, for a change she was not shouting, and it sounded reasoned. However the underlying message was clear that she had moved on – and so should I.

The bus was now on Bishopsgate and I had forty-five minutes before my meeting with Eric Jones at Neptune Re. I alighted from the bus and found myself outside Bishopsgate Police Station. It was only forty-eight hours since I was last here, and in that short time my life had changed, unbelievably for the better. I had the offer of a well paid job and an apartment that would befit a regional manager of Masterson Shipping, potentially all my financial worries were over. Also, in a strange way the phone call from Mércédès gave me closure, and I felt as though a weight had been lifted off my shoulders. The pasting of Friday night, and break-in of my flat, was just the flotsam and jetsam upon the sea of life.

Thinking of the break-in made me realise that I was standing outside Bishopsgate Police Station, I don't know why, but I just felt the urge to go inside.

"Good morning Mr Edge." The voice came from someone standing behind me. The word 'mister' was heavily emphasised. I turned and saw the older policeman from Saturday morning standing with a cup of tea and a biscuit in his hands.

He continued "How can I help you?"

I could feel myself starting to blush like an errant schoolboy, but I ploughed on.

"First, I would like to apologise for my behaviour on Friday night, and for any offence I may have given to you and any of your colleagues, and I wondered if I might have a quick chat with you if you have the time!"

I could see his expression change from lack of interest to one of idle curiosity.

"I am on my tea break for fifteen minutes, so I can spare a few moments. Let's sit in this interview room."

He used his piece of shortbread to point towards a room across the corridor. The room was much more appealing than the environs the last time he and I were talking.

"I'm sorry but I can't remember your name, Sergeant?" His three stripes were very evident on his epaulets.

"Sergeant Smithson," he replied "and if you think that a few well spoken words this morning will mean that Friday night is forgotten about, you are very much mistaken. I have seen it all too often, well-bred and well-mannered gentleman working in the City, you have too much to drink and the veil is lifted. You behave like guttersnipes, and what's worse you do it with an arrogant swagger, believing you are above the law."

Before I could reply he continued "And Mr Edge you are no stranger to controversy. Are you?"

Sergeant Smithson was smiling, but his voice was very serious.

"Paul van de Kohl is still in a coma, and you're still under suspicion by the Dutch police, of being an accomplice to a major fraud."

He was positively beaming now. In this age of technological advances I should not have been surprised that the British police would not be aware of my recent difficulties.

As if he was reading my mind he volunteered "Saturday morning can be a bit slow in the City. So I checked what we knew about Mr Marcus Edge. Quite interesting, particularly the article written in the Daily Telegraph, 'Edge on the edge' was a very illuminating account of your fall from grace and ban from Lloyd's of London."

It was my turn to smile.

"I'm pleased that my past antics gave you so much amusement."

The smile was about to fall from his face so I quickly raised my hand

"Only joking!" I added.

"Why are you here Mr Edge?"

The policeman was probably thinking he could spend his tea-break more profitably than bantering with me.

"I want to tell you about the events of the past weekend, after I left here on Saturday morning, and ask you a question - please?"

Before he could interrupt I pressed on "My soon to be former father-in-law......"

"Sir Hugh Masterson?" He wished to show me how informed he was of my predicaments.

"Yes-yes," I continued hesitantly "he invited me to stay for the weekend, and has been incredibly generous. He has offered me a good job in Singapore; however, whilst I was out of London my flat was burgled."

The policeman asked "Burgled you say."

I nodded.

"How did they gain entry?"

"That's the question, or should I say dilemma. Were any keys found on me when I was brought in by your colleagues on Friday? Because when I checked the door, and the locks of the flat, there were no scratch marks. I think they used keys – my keys!"

"What type of locks do you have?"

"A seven lever deadlock plus a 'yale-type'; what is also strange is that nothing seems to have been taken! I notified the local police last night at Bethnal Green, but their only response has been to issue me with a Crime Number."

"I'm not surprised," said the policeman "unfortunately there are many more pressing issues for my colleagues at the Bethnal Green nick."

I was thinking to myself that a position within the City of London police force would be far more pleasant, than a similar position in the Metropolitan Police, which covered the rest of London.

He continued "I suppose you have jumped to the conclusion that whoever gave you the beating on Friday night, stole your keys, and then risked breaking into your flat for fun to take nothing."

It sounded quite a ridiculous scenario when Sergeant Smithson voiced my thoughts.

"To be fair there's not much to take." I muttered

The pragmatic policeman in him came to the fore again; "You said you were an investigator, yes? So ask yourself the following questions: Who knew you would be out on Friday and where you would be going? Who knew you would be away for the weekend? Who knows where you live? I'm hoping you were not silly enough to leave your address on the keys! Do you know if you had your keys with you when you were attacked? It was much more likely you offended someone - given the state you were in - and they decided to have some sport whilst teaching you a lesson."

He shrugged his shoulders to indicate the chat was over, and stood up motioning me towards the door.

"If I were you I would forget about it and accept Sir Hugh Masterson's job offer. Goodbye Mr Edge."

'Goodbye' was emphasized in the parting sentence inferring that he did not want to see me again.

# Monday mid-Morning
# Neptune Re

I arrived at Neptune Re's offices fifteen minutes before my appointment. When I asked for Eric Jones I was told he was in a meeting until eleven o'clock, which is what I expected anyway. I went to the toilet. Whilst I was washing my hands I had a close-up look at my reflection. The bruises were still evident on my face, but much more worryingly, I found a number of grey hairs. I thought I should really accept Sir Hugh's great offer.

"Grow up and stop pratting around like an adolescent teenager." I said to myself.

As I re-entered Neptune Re's reception Eric Jones hoved into view.

"Ah, there you are Marc, follow me please. Did you have a good weekend? It looks like you were playing rugby again."

The smile in his eyes gave away the fact that he knew more than he was letting on.

Nevertheless I responded with, "Very good, thank you Eric." I replied.

He would soon learn that my weekend would mean that I would not be able to accept his assignment.

Eric led me to Neptune Re's 'in-house' café, where, en vogue with a lot of other city offices, Neptune Re had a café that was run by one of the well known coffee franchises. They were very proud of this new facility. The coffee was terrific, plus it was subsidised for their employees, but of course the firm benefited from their increased productivity, because the ubiquitous trips to the coffee shop outside the building had been reduced.

Having collected our coffees we found a couple of comfortable chairs away from the main throng of Neptune Re's employees taking their elevenses.

"Eric, since Friday my situation has changed significantly." I started.

"How so?" Eric enquired with a questioning smile.

"Well," I hesitated for a moment, deciding whether to give him the edited highlights or the full story. I chose the latter "on Friday I ended up having a bit too much to drink, and was in a fracas ending up in Bishopsgate police station."

"Yes I know." He said.

I flinched and immediately started to feel myself flush-up "Then what was that reference to rugby all about?"

He was smiling "I thought I'd give you the opportunity to dodge the issue if you felt you needed to; but you didn't, for which I'm pleased. I ought to warn you that an e-mail has been 'doing the rounds' this morning, I think it originated at Inter-Continental."

"That shit Tony Eastwood spreading muck I bet." I thought aloud.

Eric continued, the smile not as broad as a few moments earlier, "One of my colleagues brought it to me this morning, trying to dissuade me from appointing you to investigate this matter for us. I have told him to mind his own business, and that you have few friends at Inter-Continental, so e-mails from them regarding Marc Edge are unlikely to be without bias. Apparently Max Huntley is still angry with you following the loss of one of the world's largest marine accounts, which has affected their results for last year, as well as the budget for this year. But more than that, he's lost the confidence of his Chairman, as he has been accused of serious mis-judgement when he hired you."

This was news to me, but not altogether surprising; the mood within Inter-Continental when things start to go wrong, is appalling. They're like a pack of hyenas preying on the latest soft target. This 'dog-eat-dog' attitude cascades from the top, as it is the way their Chairman behaves, which I experienced at first-hand when I was invited to my first senior management meeting. The Chairman rounded on the finance director - someone who had been working with him for twenty years - and he was smiling as he rammed the knife (metaphorically) between his friend's shoulder blades. I remember that I actually felt a chill over my body, as I witnessed it happening, and the goose-bumps remained afterwards. Max Huntley was a chameleon, and would react very badly to the Chairman destroying the image he had spent a lot of time and money crafting.

I took a swig of my coffee, and told Eric about my subsequent good fortune "You may be aware that Sir Hugh Masterson is - for the time being at least - my father-in-law."

Eric nodded.

"Well he kindly gave me refuge on Saturday, as I had lost my keys and had no access to my flat until Sunday evening. Sir Hugh was in a difficult position when Lloyd's of London disciplined me, and has let me know that he thought the ban was harsh."

Eric raised his eyebrows but said nothing, so I continued "Anyway over the weekend he has offered me a very lucrative position in Singapore for three years in his shipping company - not insurance related - and he wants me to start as soon as the paperwork is sorted out. So Eric," I paused and took a deep breath "thank-you for considering me, but I think my days of claims investigating are over, and I have to decline your assignment. What's more, the cost of more insurance would leave me with very little money in my pocket."

He looked sad for a moment and said nothing. I felt embarrassed so I filled the void.

"I am sorry if I have wasted your time."

Still he said nothing. He sat very quietly ruminating, his chin resting on his fingers of both hands, which were extended like a steeple, the pads of the fingers on the opposite hands touching each other. After what seemed like an eternity he finally uttered a sound but no words.

"Hmmm."

A few more moments passed and he looked up.

"Do you have any idea how long it will take to put the papers in order?"

"I am not sure; but I would like to be in Singapore before Christmas."

Then I volunteered that I would be meeting with Sir Hugh that very afternoon to discuss the finer points of the contract.

"Hmmm." He said again and at that point he looked up and fixed me with his steady gaze. "Well we don't have too much time do we?"

"For what? I'm sorry but I don't ......"

Before I could finish my sentence Eric interrupted "I'm paying for your coffee, so please pay me the courtesy of listening to me. Unless you have somewhere else you have to be at this very moment?" An edge had crept into his voice, but then again he wasn't recognised as being one of the best claims managers in the London Insurance market for nothing. I merely shrugged my shoulders and shook my head.

"Do you remember that Perestroika claim?" Eric asked me.

The correct name of the Perestroika claim was *Nima S.A.R.L. –v- Deves Insurance Public Co Ltd*, but commonly referred to as the Perestroika claim as that was the name of the vessel. The claim was brought initially by *Nima* who bought a cargo of rice to be shipped by the Perestroika from Thailand to Dakar, and the defendant was an English insurance company incorporated in Thailand. The claim and subsequent appeal was won on quite boring technical legal reasons by the insurance company; however the underlying facts were interesting. The rice was never delivered, and it was alleged that the Perestroika was in fact a 'phantom vessel', because the shipping company never intended to deliver the cargo at Dakar, but that the vessel had proceeded to Dubai where the cargo had been discharged and the vessel's name had been changed *en route*.

"Yes," I replied "why?"

"Last week a cargo ship bound for Harare via Beira, Mozambique, from Gdansk in Poland was reported missing, and despite a search being initiated in the Indian Ocean, no wreckage has been found."

"Was there any bad weather in the area when the ship last reported its position?"

"Yes, but nothing the ship shouldn't have been able to cope with, even though the vessel – *Sea Cargo III* - was registered in Liberia to an Indian company Patel Sea Cargo & Co. The vessel was thirty years old and not fitted with the latest gizmos; but what's strange is that there was no distress signal, the ship just disappeared."

It was my turn to say "Hmmm," followed by "what was the vessel carrying, and why are you not letting the insurance company investigate the loss? You are a reinsurance company."

Eric checked his notes "Specialist marine parts. Yes, the insurance company is investigating with a very respectable firm of marine loss adjusters."

"So what did you have in mind for me?" I asked sceptically.

Eric paused for a moment then fixed me with a stare "This is not the first time this has happened. On two previous occasions smaller cargos, so not raising much attention, have disappeared along with their vessels. Again the cargos were bound for Southern Africa."

"Was it the same shippers, same origin and same destination?" I enquired.

"No, totally different, and the insurance company was not the same either."

"Over what period did these disappearances occur?" My mind was racing now.

"Twelve months." Eric smiled. He had hooked me and my own curiosity was doing the rest. "As a reinsurer we're able to see trends and join the dots when others can't."

Eric finished then offered me more coffee which I accepted.

"How could I have helped when the insurance companies have all the resources that a large loss adjuster can offer?" I was curious how Eric saw me.

"You would come from left-field, you're cheap and no-one would take you seriously," I was starting to flush up again, and before I said anything he continued "but you would be able to operate in the shadows. Most people think you are sitting at home, so you shouldn't be missed, and you wouldn't be asked what you are working on. What's more I have seen you schmooze and work a room. You are able to get information out of people."

"That's all very flattering - I think – but I cannot afford to pass up Sir Hugh Masterson's offer" I said in an apologetic tone.

Eric sat quietly for what seemed a long minute, whilst I drank my coffee.

Eventually he looked up at me and our eyes met "Marc, I totally understand your position and hope that it goes well for you."

I felt relief as though Eric was releasing his hold over me.

"However, I can give you five hundred pounds for a couple of days snooping around for me. No contract. No increased insurance will be required; this would be an unofficial task with just a verbal report back to me." He added "No one else is to know! I am sure you can do with some cash for new clothes? You said you are unlikely to be in Singapore before Christmas. Please can you spare me just a couple of days?"

Eric had presented his case like the expert negotiator he is. I was feeling guilty that I was about to decline. I was in a dilemma and reasoned that perhaps I could spare the time, whilst still keeping any snooping very low key.

I heard myself acquiescing to Eric's request "Ok, a couple of days shouldn't be a problem, but where on earth should I start, I can't be flying out to the Indian Ocean."

"Oh no," Eric smiled "you can start much closer to home, very close in fact!"

"What do you mean?" I was puzzled by his remarks.

"The Captain of *Sea Cargo III* is – or was – John Hennessey and used to work for a shipping company based here in United Kingdom. His twin brother – Mark Hennessey - still does." He was really enjoying himself now.

"Well which shipping company is it then?" I asked, bored of Eric's games.

"Masterson Shipping, of course." He announced.

# Monday Lunchtime
# Liverpool Street Station

I left Neptune Re's offices with two hundred and fifty pounds cash in my pocket, and a promise that the other two hundred and fifty pounds would be paid, after I gave Eric his verbal report. He gave me his personal mobile telephone number, and said that - within reason - I could call him out of work hours if the need arose.

I couldn't see that it would do any harm having a nose around, and whilst Masterson Shipping was the starting point, they were not implicated so I didn't feel any conflict of interest. Anyway, I wasn't on their pay-roll yet.

I phoned Jimmy Black, to be told he was in the Lloyd's market. I left a message asking that he phone me, after he returned at lunchtime from seeing insurers. I then asked to be transferred to Carla Nottage.

"Hello, this is Carla." Came the voice from the other end of the phone.

"Hi, this is Marc." I replied "I got your message and wonder if we can meet, to pick up my coat?"

"Sure," said Carla "I'm on lunch break in half-an-hour. Do you fancy a quick drink?"

"Oh no!" I groaned "I'm still recovering from Friday."

Carla giggled.

"It's not funny," I said in mock seriousness "and I've not long taken a painkiller prescribed by a police doctor."

"Yes I heard about your fracas, and that you ended up in Bishopsgate nick. Frankly I'm not surprised you ended up in jail. You were being obnoxious to just about everyone."

"To you as well?" I asked.

"No, not to me."

I was relieved.

She continued, "Ok what about the coffee bar on Liverpool Street Station, just after half past twelve?"

"It's a date."

"No it isn't." Was the sharp reply from the other end of the phone.

After Carla and I finished our dalliance, she hooked up with a guy she met at the gym, which was local near to her home. A very fit person, he came to one of the Rugby Club's training sessions. I thought he was a bit boring, and in love with his own body. He would never have lasted, or enjoyed, a full rugby match.

Before making my way to the rendezvous with Carla I called by my bank, on Leadenhall Street, and spoke to the cashier confirming my appointment with the manager for the following day. I also paid in one hundred and fifty pounds to my current account as a sign of goodwill, which hopefully would be the shape of things to come.

I reached Liverpool Street Station just before half-past twelve, and made my way to the coffee bar. I marvelled at how the station had been transformed, becoming a hive of commercial activity; with big modern screens providing train information, as well as the latest financial and national news clips. The planners and developers had certainly got it right, and the development was continuing with designer shops adjacent to the station.

The late autumn sun of the previous day was no longer in evidence, and, whilst not raining, the clouds were gathering and the breeze increasing in strength. My Crombie overcoat would be very welcome, when it arrived. I walked into the coffee bar, and couldn't see Carla. I decided to grab a table, before it became too busy. I was just clearing away the debris from the previous diners when Carla walked in.

"Hi" I greeted her as she walked up to the table, dressed in a warm fleece jacket and black trousers, my coat draped over her arm.

I stood up to give her a peck on both cheeks.

"Gosh you really did get a good 'slap' on Friday." She giggled as she observed my bruises at close quarters.

I stood back and just gave a very bad impression of a vulnerable Stan Laurel. Carla sat down and handed me my coat. I checked the pockets for the 'lost' keys, but just found my leather gloves, which triggered a faint memory.

"Thanks Carla." I thanked her, and added "I am going to have something to eat. Would you like to join me?"

"Have you got any money? You were pleading poverty on Friday."

"Yes, thanks to your boss." I smiled.

Carla looked at me quizzically.

I answered her questioning glance with "I'll tell you over a sandwich."

We each chose a sandwich, and decided to share a third. The sandwiches plus a coffee each, was making a dent in my newly acquired funds, but a cheap price to recover my coat.

"Ok tell me what has happened?" Carla said between mouthfuls of her brie and rocket sandwich.

I gave a full account of what had happened after I woke up on Saturday morning up to Sunday night, including the offer from Sir Hugh, but I kept the Neptune Re task for Eric Jones to myself.

"Did you know that your antics are all round the market? An e-mail has been doing the 'rounds' since first thing this morning." Carla told me before taking a sip of coffee.

"Yes." I replied.

"Did you see how many attacked you? Why did you call Sir Hugh? When are you going to Singapore?" Carla's questions were being fired at me with no let up.

"Stop, stop please?" I managed to abate the inquisition.

"No, I didn't see anyone. Anyway, why do you think that there was more than one person involved?"

"Well you can look after yourself Marc; with all those muscles?"

I was unsure if she was mocking me, but she was smiling at me coyly, and she had had first-hand experience. She winked and I laughed. I thought privately that her fitness trainer boyfriend probably had to go to work for a rest!

"Did you see anything when I left the bar on Friday night?" I enquired.

"I-I'm not sure," she was hesitant and my interest was heightened "no one from the bar. I felt sure there was someone hanging around outside, but I can't be sure because they kept themselves in the shadows."

"Did you see their face?"

Carla just shook her head.

I continued to answer her remaining questions.

"I don't know why I phoned Sir Hugh. I hope to be in Singapore before Christmas."

I was saved from further interrogation by my mobile phone. I looked at the screen, it was Jimmy Black. I excused myself and took the call. I explained to Jimmy that no additional insurance was now required, and in fact I would probably be cancelling my current insurance. I asked whether there might be some premium returned. He said he thought the answer was likely to be yes, but that he would check with the underwriters first.

Carla was drinking her coffee as I finished my call with Jimmy Black. She told me that my name was usually mud in JPG starting with John Eastwood, but when he saw the email this morning he said 'poor lad'.

"Don't you think that's strange?" Carla carried on "Especially as you were trying to pick a fight with his son, Tony!"

"Yes that is strange." I muttered more to myself than to Carla.

# Monday Late Afternoon
# St. James's

Despite the worsening weather, it wasn't raining but it only seemed to be a matter of time, and now reunited with my overcoat and gloves I decided to walk to St James's. I had plenty of time from when Carla returned to work, until my late afternoon appointment with Sir Hugh, and his business partner Mércédès grandfather.

I walked along the Thames path from the City of London alongside the Embankment, then I turned into Parliament Square, and across into Green Park. The solitude of walking when one has time on one's hands is a pleasure, which I have long enjoyed since my long coastal walks with my father in North Norfolk. We would sometimes walk in silence, just appreciating each other's company, whereas walking with Gerda we could chat for hours. Catching up on all the little things we missed by not seeing each other each day. Recently conversations had included plans for holidays and weekend breaks, and I was beginning to tell when she did not agree with me, her pace would quicken and be accompanied with the phrase 'Catch-up because I can't hear you'.

The walk had given me time to form the questions I would ask Sir Hugh about the nature and the role of the job in Singapore. I also decided to ask him if he could give me the details of his Captain whose brother was the master of the vessel which mysteriously disappeared in the Indian Ocean the previous week.

It had taken me just under a couple of hours to walk to Jermyn Street, and I was still an hour early. I decided to visit various shirt and suit makers in Jermyn Street, to gather ideas for lightweight suits and shirts. After visiting two men's outfitters I quickly surmised that it would only be ideas that I would be gathering, and that I would have to buy my suits and shirts in the Far East, where - hopefully - they would be a fraction of the price of the Jermyn Street shops.

It was a quarter past four when I announced myself to the concierge of the building, as requested by Ms. Syrani, which served as Sir Hugh's private office in a very smart Victorian building.

"Sir Hugh Masterson's office is in the garden flat - at the back of the building." The concierge informed me.

"I'm a few minutes early and I wondered if you could direct me to the facilities?" I requested politely, too politely as I was greeted with a totally incomprehensive look of the person behind the reception desk.

"Where are the toilets please?" I tried a different tack.

"Ha," uttered the concierge "they are behind me."

He pointed to the wall where the outline of a door was barely visible, and as I walked towards the wall the door opened, presumably from a switch behind the desk.

"Please push the button on the other side of the door when you have finished." The concierge added as I entered the secret door.

A lot had gone on since the last time I had been to the toilet, and it was very hot in the confined space despite it being November, so I opened the vent in the frosted glass windows. I had been sitting only for a moment or two, when I heard a raised voice, which I instantly knew to be that of Sir Hugh. The Scorpion didn't blow his top too often, but when he did it was usually without any warning and like a volcano, spitting and hissing in all directions. I had witnessed it on one previous occasion when Tony Eastwood had tried to seduce one of the female members of staff, and Sir Hugh took him aside and told him that he was a disgrace to JPG, and his father.

The Scottish lilt was unmistakable, and more pronounced as the crescendo increased. But even though I listened very carefully I couldn't hear a word of the tirade, nor to whom it was directed. The second question was soon answered, because as I returned from the toilet, I saw Samuel leaving the building. He didn't see me, and whilst I would never be able to tell if his ebony face was flushed in anger, it was evident from his receding figure that he had been sweating, and I overheard him mutter to himself, "Bloody Eastwood." And wondered what Tony had done now.

I felt a small smile cross my lips, and once again was pleased that my fortunes were changing, for the better.

I was sitting in one of the French style chairs in the building's reception, when Ms. Syrani emerged from another secret door similar to that leading to the toilet.

"Marc, it's good to see you again. Sir Hugh will be pleased you're on time. Would you be so kind as to follow me?" Said the lady with classical good looks, and in my opinion even more attractive than the last time we met at my wedding. I wondered whether Ms. Syrani had paid a trip to the plastic surgeon.

I was about to say that I had been there for a few minutes, but something made me hold back, and I wondered if Ms. Syrani had taken pleasure in Samuel's carpeting.

We walked through the door within the wall and almost immediately another door confronted us. It reminded me of visits to the headmaster's study at school. When the second door was shut, the outside noise was completely eradicated. We descended a half-flight of stairs.

The eeriness created by the closing of the double door in the confined deep pile carpeted corridor soon ended as we descended another half flight of stairs to the garden flat at the rear of the building. Immediately we reached the bottom of the stairs I understood why I could hear the raised, but muffled, voices whilst I was in the toilet. The rear of the building was bathed in the week grey November sunlight, because there were French windows in the centre of the room with bay windows either side. The French windows were open and outside was an elderly grey haired Asian gentleman smoking a cigarette whilst talking into a mobile phone. I recognised him immediately as Mércédès grandfather, Phillipe de Silva, he was an urbane man and his good looks displayed traits of the Portuguese ancestry running through his veins.

Sir Hugh was also on the telephone, at his desk, which was situated in one of the bay windows. Ms. Syrani ushered me to one of the armchairs in the other bay window.

"Would you like a cup of Earl Grey tea, Marc?"

"Yes please." I replied.

Within seconds a bone-china cup and saucer appeared on the small table in front of the three armchairs, with a choice of lemon, whole or skimmed milk. I helped myself to a slice of lemon and popped last of the course of painkillers prescribed by the doctor on Saturday morning, into my mouth wondering how Sir Hugh accommodated meetings of more than three people; perhaps that was never contemplated or required.

Phillipe de Silva returned from the garden, through the french windows, reeking of the strong French tobacco which he adored, and came straight towards me with a broad smile.

"No-no do not get up Marcus. How happy I am to see you again?" He seemed genuinely pleased and shook me heartily by the hand. "I am sorry for your recent misfortunes and that you're no longer with my granddaughter; but let me assure you that you will always be part of our extended family, and it is fitting that you will be joining our family business - I hope?"

The last words left me in no doubt that I would be accepting Sir Hugh's offer, which was slightly disconcerting, but the warmth of his greeting gave me the feeling that he was relieved to find someone Masterson Shipping could trust for their Singapore Office.

As Phillipe was just sitting down, Sir Hugh joined us and I stood up to shake his hand.

"Please sit down my boy, it is good of you to give up your time at such short notice." There was a playful glint in Sir Hugh's eyes, as if to say 'Did you have anything better to do?'

I kept my thoughts to myself "Not at all Sir Hugh." I then sat down between Sir Hugh and Phillipe.

"Since yesterday I've been giving some thought to your 'pay-and-rations' whilst you are in Singapore," he started and I began to fear the worst "and I believe I mentioned the figure of one hundred thousand pounds a year as a salary. Plus a fifty per cent bonus if you complete the three-year assignment, achieving the fairly conservative profit margins determined in consultation with you. In addition you will have the use of a flat for the duration of your appointment in Singapore."

"That is how I recalled our conversation yesterday, and it is very generous Sir Hugh; however, you mentioned that as much as possible would be paid offshore into a tax-free account."

"Yes, and that is the aspect that has been focusing my attention, for a couple of reasons." He replied with a smile on his face. "The tax authorities throughout the world are tightening up on such practices, and if you're unable to show that you paid the tax and country where you earned it, then you could be taxed by the United Kingdom Inspector of Taxes, if you wish to repatriate your earnings back to the United Kingdom. We do not want to make you a tax exile. Also, I am aware that what little equity you accumulated was all but lost when you split up from Mércédès."

I was unsure where this conversation was going, and I nodded agreement to Sir Hugh's last comment.

He continued "The credit crunch and subsequent recession has not hit property prices in the Far East to the same extent. In fact they are still climbing in Singapore. One of the main reasons is because Singapore is fast replacing Hong Kong as the financial centre, being more attractive because it is beyond China's political sphere of influence and the increasing pollution spawned by China's rapid industrial expansion. Singapore will also be of increasing importance within Masterson Shipping, as the Board of Directors have decided that focus of growth for the group will be Africa and the Far East. You may be wondering how this might change your basis of remuneration."

Again I nodded my head and his smile broadened as he outlined his proposition.

"I calculate that, if supplemented by genuine business expenses for client entertaining, a salary of thirty thousand pounds should provide you with a reasonable standard of living. Therefore, if you're prepared to accept that as your salary, Phillipe and I are prepared to treat the remainder of your salary plus the bonuses - for the three year period - as payment for the apartment in which you will be living. At today's values the property is worth five hundred thousand pounds, and in three years time could be worth in excess of seven hundred and fifty thousand pounds, all yours tax-free."

It was all I could do to prevent my jaw-dropping.

"I hope that means we can quickly sign the necessary papers and send you for an acclimatisation visit within a couple of weeks. Also you won't have to carry on with any further investigations. If you need an advance of five thousand pounds we can arrange that upon your signing of the contract of employment." Sir Hugh was smiling benignly.

"Thank you very much Sir Hugh, I don't know what to say."

Which was the truth, and certainly it was not the time to ask about the brother of one of his ship's captains.

# Monday Evening
# Hackney

Sir Hugh and Phillipe had an important dinner with dignitaries from Africa that evening, and Ms. Syrani ushered me quickly from the garden flat in St. James's, but not before we had agreed that I would return the following day at nine o'clock with my passport. It was explained to me that by the time I returned Sir Hugh's lawyers would have prepared a contract of employment. When I signed the contract that would enable me to have access to the advance, of five thousand pounds, at which point the paperwork for work permits and visas could commence. A signed contract of employment for three years, together with an advance of five thousand pounds would be a very good peace offering for my forthcoming interview with my bank the following day, to which I was now looking forward to with relish, rather than the usual foreboding.

I caught a bus on Piccadilly towards Liverpool Street, where I could change buses, and return to my flat in Hackney. The wind had been increasing with rain in the air. I was very grateful to be reunited with my crombie overcoat. The rain meant the traffic had slowed and the evening rush-hour had commenced earlier than usual. I was not concerned because the time on the bus allowed me to evaluate my current situation, as well as plan the telephone conversation I would be having that evening with Gerda.

When I was working at JPG or Inter-Continental, I would often find that I could best measure the effectiveness of any holiday, the longer it took me to get back 'up-to-speed' after returning to work, the more rested I had been on holiday. I felt as though I was emerging from many months of hibernation, and slowly – very slowly – the cogs were starting to turn, and I was picking up the pace. The main side-effect of this increased mental activity was the constant feeling of hunger. Tonight I would treat myself to an Indian take-a-way meal, washed down with a bottle of gewurtstraminer, after I had spoken to Gerda.

As soon as I returned to my flat I would start to look for my passport. I had failed to spot it the previous evening after the break-in and my continued search had been interrupted that morning by the telephone call from Ms. Syrani. I waved at Shariz as I went past his shop; he was busy with the evening trade of schoolchildren returning home, it was a time when he needed to have his wits about him to try and ensure there was no pilfering. I opened the door and everything seemed to be as I had left it in the morning.

"Good, no one has returned." I said to myself.

I pondered whether it was worth spending the money to change the locks. I convinced myself that I would need to change the locks as I was going to be renting-out the flat whilst I was in Singapore. I would feel a responsibility if the flat was broken into again by the person with my keys. It was half-past five and Gerda would not phone for at least another hour. I put the kettle on and went downstairs to see Shariz.

There was no one in the shop and he greeted me with "Hello Mr Marc, have you had a better day than yesterday?"

"Very good Shariz, thank you: Is it possible that your brother-in-law could change my locks for me please?" I asked.

"Yes Mr Marc it will cost just a few pounds." He looked almost embarrassed to tell me it would cost anything. No wonder he was such a successful businessman.

"Don't worry, I have money Shariz, and cash too!"

His face instantly brightened "It will be fixed tomorrow Mr Marc, and I'll keep the keys with me in the shop, so you can collect them up to ten o'clock in the evening."

Another two customers had entered the shop and his eyes were darting to see where they were. I bid him good night, and he immediately asked his new customers if he could help them.

I returned to the flat, saw that the kettle had boiled - I went to the tea caddy and opened it to find my passport amongst the teabags. I was surprised, but then again not, because I would often hide my passport in the tea caddy. However, I felt sure that I had looked in the tea caddy the previous evening. I stopped to think carefully and re-trace my steps. I thought I'd used my passport recently and could have sworn it was with other documents. I made myself my pot of Earl Grey tea and looked around the flat. I found the other documents quite quickly, so perhaps I had left my passport in the tea caddy after all.

I busied myself by sorting out my clothes into a pile of what I would be taking to Singapore, another pile for storing (mainly ski outfits) and a final pile for those to be thrown out, which I called 'the Oxfam pile'. I wanted to keep myself from thinking about the impending telephone call with Gerda. Leaving her in Europe was the only blot on the landscape of my new good fortune.

It was almost exactly at half past six when my mobile rang and it was Gerda.

"Chuss." Her soft voice came from the end of the phone, and I could feel my resolve starting to melt.

"Chuss." I said in reply.

"How are you my darling Marc? I have missed so much not talking to you since last Wednesday."

This was going to be harder than I thought, so I decided to plunge in at the deep end. "I have missed talking to you, and I'm really pleased that you will be coming to England this weekend; because I have some very good news on the job front. Also, I want to talk to you about our future as I see you and I being together - as a couple."

"Oh Marc do you really think so? I've hoped for the same thing for such a long time, but from your voice I sense all may not be straight-forward, no?"

I could imagine Gerda at the other end of the phone and wished I was sitting next to her.

I first met Gerda when she had just left university. She was about four inches taller than me. I had read that the Dutch are - on average - the world's tallest nation, I would banter with Paul that this was probably due to the amount of dairy products they consumed. Fair haired with a golden tan she seemed clumsy, with a permanent blush whenever I talked to her. In the early days of our acquaintance the only time she could relax was when we played sport, either together, or with Paul and occasionally with Mércédès.

Her tall athletic frame, plus a good eye-to-ball co-ordination meant that every game was hard fought. Her tennis game was much classier than my own, meaning I had to work very hard to stop her walking all over me. Unlike most women her breasts were not a hindrance to her sporting activities. There was a stirring in my loins, picturing her small glistening breasts pressing against my chest and feeling her long hard nipples, set within large aureole, trying to pierce my skin as we would roll on top of each other during our glorious and languorous love making. Being with Gerda felt right, the love-making to be savoured over a long period, rather than the frenetic sprint with Mércédès which felt more like a hundred metre dash. I actually smiled thinking about poor Tony Eastwood and wondered if he had the stamina to last the course; then I remembered that Mércédès was going to visit her mother in Goa, which should give him some respite for a few weeks.

"Gerda there is no easy way of breaking the news. Sir Hugh Masterson has offered me a position as manager of the Masterson Shipping Office in Singapore, for three years on lucrative terms." I blurted out in one breath.

"What are 'lucrative terms'?" enquired Gerda, and whilst Paul and Gerda spoke very good English, it was their second language.

I explained about the proposition that had been outlined to me that afternoon by Sir Hugh Masterson and Phillipe de Silva.

"My goodness that is a wonderful offer. Not in insurance either. Why?" Gerda sounded rightly curious.

"To be honest I don't know, and no one is more surprised than me, but Sir Hugh felt sorry for my predicament."

"How so?" Asked Gerda.

I then recounted events from Friday lunchtime up to Monday evening.

When I had finished, there was a muffled sound from the other end of the phone.

I broke the silence with a question "Gerda I would like you to come with me?"

There was a sniffle and Gerda quietly responded "I would love to come with you Marc, but I won't leave Paul while he is in his current state. Perhaps if he shows signs of improving we can re-consider? I am truly sorry, I really am."

"My darling I totally understand, but I don't think that I can let this offer from Sir Hugh pass by. I feel I must give it a good try. And at the moment we are only together every six weeks or so, which is about eight or nine times a year. If I accept Sir Hugh's offer I would be able to fly to you at least four times each year, and it could be for at least a week at a time. We could ensure we would fit in with your work commitments, and for more than just a fleeting weekend - quality rather than quantity."

Gerda giggled from the other end of the phone, as she knew exactly what I was referring to.

"More importantly we will have capital behind us, which will help us to set up for the rest of our lives." I hoped I was not sounding too pompous.

"I know Marc that what you say sounds plausible, but it is a lot to take in over the telephone. I will think about it, and we talk about it again at the weekend. I am sure it will be ok, also I have some news for you."

"Yes." I replied.

"You know the doctors had been trying some new therapy on Paul?" Gerda reminded me.

"Ah-ha." I tried not to sound too vague.

Gerda's persistence had resulted in the doctors trying a number of different therapies and techniques. Sometimes it was difficult keeping up with the latest therapy. If Gerda heard hesitation in my voice she did not remark upon it, and she explained to me that Paul's brain activity had increased over the last few days. This was not the first time this had happened. On previous occasions these had proved to be false dawns. Gerda was forever hopeful that Paul would snap out of his coma with no ill-effects. I was less optimistic, but I knew that Paul was a very competitive man, and he had verve for life. Also, despite the fact he dropped me into the biggest pool of shit in my life, I was desperate for him to recover; not only for my own sake, but more so for Gerda's sanity.

After we had finished talking about Paul's condition, which ended with me sounding as positive as Gerda, I asked when she would be arriving at Stansted Airport.

"I won't be travelling by plane." I could sense that she was being playful. "I will be bringing the car so I can return with Christmas gifts and food. Will you be coming to Holland for Christmas?"

I took a deep breath before replying "No I don't think so, Sir Hugh would like me in place in Singapore by Christmas, so I can 'hit the floor running' before the New Year."

"Oh that soon?" I could tell that Gerda was upset, which was hardly surprising, given all that had been thrown at her in less than half-an-hour on the phone as well as putting all her plans into disarray.

"What about we have a Christmas together in Singapore?" I suggested.

"That is possible, I suppose, perhaps I can think it through."

Trying to keep the momentum going on a positive note I asked "So when will I see my beautiful Dutch girl?"

Gerda giggled again "I am taking the afternoon ferry from the Hook of Holland, if they don't cancel it. The weather is supposed to be miserable for the next two days, but it should be better by Friday."

The Dutch were almost as obsessed as the dwellers of the British Isles about the weather - perhaps because both countries had such similar and variable climates.

"I should be with you by late Friday afternoon."

"I can't wait my darling and we have so much to discuss and plan for the future." I said with as much feeling as I could convey over the telephone.

"I know Marc, but as I said earlier it's just so much to take in over the phone, but I've been hoping that you felt the same way as me. So it is good we can now talk openly about such matters my love." She added "I will be OK by the weekend."

I knew that she would be thinking about every aspect over the next few days; making lists and notes of the smallest details.

"I have to go now. So I can start preparing for the weekend." This was Gerda's code for her to do the work that she brought home from the office.

"Ok my darling, and I too will be busy over the next few days, so please send me plenty of text messages to keep in touch. See you Friday and I love you!!" I said before blowing kisses down the phone lines.

Gerda blew kisses back "See you soon my lover – chuss."

I sat quietly for a few minutes recalling the conversation with Gerda, and realised that our relationship had taken a massive leap forward, also how easily the change of the basis of our relationship had been. There was no drama or suspense, which had happened during a similar conversation with Mércédès, when I asked her to move into my flat. A smile flickered across my face, as I thought how quickly the phoenix was rising from the ashes of despair. I was actually looking forward to my appointment with my bank the following day.

I was feeling very hungry by the time I visited my local Indian restaurant, returning with a take-a-way meal, plus a bottle of wine bought from Shariz.

All was good with the world and I was fast asleep before ten thirty.

# Tuesday Morning
# St. Katharine's Dock

I was awake by seven o'clock and in Victoria Park fifteen minutes later for a run; back in my flat showered, suited and booted by eight o'clock. There had been no sign of K-P whilst I was in Victoria Park, and I knew it would be difficult to catch up with him during work hours and evenings, because he was hosting overseas visitors this week. I wanted to talk about the passport episode, explain the details of Sir Hugh's latest offer, which included equity in the Singapore flat. I always respected and appreciated K-P's opinion on many and varied things. He possessed high intelligence; this together with his naval training meant he was able to evaluate and approach problems in a very pragmatic and logical way. Also, I wanted to find out if he, Jane and their children were available for lunch with Gerda and me on Sunday. I decided that I would try and call K-P early the following morning at home.

Just as I was leaving my flat for St Katherine's Dock and the rendezvous with Sir Hugh Masterson, my mobile rang.

"Hello, Marc Edge speaking." My voice was crisp and clear, but it was instantly put to shame by the clarity of Ms. Syrani's voice at the other end of the line.

"Good morning Mr Edge, Sir Hugh wondered if you could come to the Masterson Shipping offices this morning at nine o'clock. Sir Hugh would like to introduce you to one of the other regional managers who currently is in London.

The Masterson Shipping head office overlooked St. Katharine's Dock. Whilst it was the centre of the group's shipping activities only thirty, mainly administrative, staff were employed in the London offices. The offices were well within walking distance from my flat, in the time available, even though rain clouds were looming. I confirmed that I would be there in good time. I waved at Shariz as I left the building, and started walking briskly with my old JPG golf umbrella under my arm, as I headed towards Victoria Park for the second time that morning.

I exited Victoria Park on Grove Road and decided to walk alongside Regents Canal towards Limehouse Basin. From Limehouse Basin I took the Thames Path, past the old wharves that had been morphed into swanky apartments, right along to St Katherine's Dock. Whenever I have the opportunity, I use the canal towpaths, and I was amazed that more Londoners didn't walk them more regularly. Only a stone's throw away from heavy traffic, the canals offered a respite of peace and tranquillity, only to be broken by my pet hate - cyclists - silent assassins. Even though the towpaths were clearly signposted to warn cyclists that pedestrians had right-of-way, and that cyclists should ring their bell when approaching, too few did so. They could pass at speeds approaching twenty miles per hour. It was very frightening when someone passed you from behind at such speeds and with no warning. On more than one occasion my umbrella had clattered the spokes of a cyclist's rear wheel, and when the riders face turned in astonishment, teetering on the edge of the canal I would say 'Sorry, I didn't hear you'.

Mércédès would complain any time this happened, whereas Gerda suggested that they should be arrested, and have their bicycles confiscated. I smiled at the thought of seeing Gerda at the weekend.

The weather was on the change, with the clear blue skies of the previous weekend being well and truly replaced by the blustery squally grey rain clouds, now covering London. It had been a remarkably warm start for November, but in only a few weeks I would be sweltering in the Singapore humidity, which was another reason to smile.

Despite the gathering rain clouds I had stopped to watch an industrial barge negotiate the locks at Limehouse Basin; it was pleasing to know that the waterways of London were playing an important part in the construction of the two thousand and twelve Olympics, with many tons of building materials and top-soil being transported via the waterways. From a very young age I had always been fascinated by the mechanics of the canal locks, knowing that these highways of yesteryear were at the heart of the important and intricate development of London as the commercial centre of the world. The canals were the link to the outside world for the industrial Midlands, and further north, the birthplace of the Industrial Revolution through a grid of canals and rivers.

With the barge safely through the lock I continued on my way up the Thames Path, towards central London, aware of an air ambulance helicopter above me heading towards the helipad at the Royal London Hospital. I was suddenly conscious of a sense of foreboding. I told myself to stop being stupid, it was only for three years, and an apartment fully paid for at the end of the period. I quickened my step and clipped along the cobbled streets and paths, reaching St

Katherine's Dock just before nine o'clock. Just as I entered the Masterson Shipping building it started to rain.

The Masterson Shipping offices were among a number of tenants in a large nineteen seventies office block, having the grand title of 'International House'. I took the lift to the top floor, having first announced myself to the seemingly disinterested security guard on the ground floor. I walked into the reception area of Masterson Shipping, and before I had the opportunity to speak, the pretty receptionist lifted her head and held her hand up, to indicate she was speaking into her headset.

Finishing her conversation she smiled and said "Good morning Mr Edge, Sir Hugh will be arriving in a few short minutes. Please take a seat and help yourself to a coffee or other drink."

I politely thanked her but declined the drink and browsed the magazines; most of them had ships on the covers which should not have surprised me. The reception door opened and I looked up to see a swarthy man, of about my own age, walk into the foyer and address the receptionist.

"My darling Sonia, you are looking very beautiful this morning, and I cannot resist asking you to accompany me to dinner tonight."

The receptionist was fighting not to melt into his eyes, and succumb to his Omar Sharif intoned voice.

She blushed and replied "Mr Aziz I'm very flattered, but I must decline, unless you also issue an invite to my husband."

Mr Aziz laughed and I caught sight of his gleaming white teeth, but was distracted by the glitter of the large quantity of gold that adorned his fingers and wrists. Before he turned away from the receptionist's desk, I could see that Sonia had straightened her back pushing out her chest, thus revealing much more of her deep cleavage and the edge of her bra.

Aziz swung round to address me "I presume you must be the baronet's former son-in-law? Being a scot he can't ignore his crofter's instincts to help the wandering 'black sheep'."

I was stunned on many fronts. How did he know who I was? How did he know so much about me? How did he have the affrontery to address me in such a way? But before I could recover and be angry, he walked over to me and impossibly his smile broadened, offering me his hand.

"Have I put Mr Edge on edge?"

His infectious laugh got the better of me and I relaxed and chuckled taking his hand with "Mr Aziz, you must be Masterson Shipping's regional manager from Dubai."

It was Aziz's turn to look quizzical.

"Touché, but I actually live in Abu Dhabi. Let's go for a smoke?"

"Sorry I don't." I replied.

"Never mind, join me anyway on the balcony before his Lordship commands our attendance."

He led me across the reception towards the toilets and the fire escape. I could hear Sonia tutting as we passed her desk. We passed through a kitchen area and exited at a door marked 'Fire Exit', onto a balcony overlooking St Katherine's Pool, during a brief respite from rain. Aziz lit up his pungent un-tipped French cigarette with an enormous gold lighter.

He smiled, "Whilst Phillipe de Silva is alive this balcony will always be a haven for us smokers. Sorry I have not properly introduced myself. I am Omar Aziz."

We shook hands with me confirming that I was indeed Marcus Edge; however, until the divorce was finalised I was still technically Sir Hugh's son-in-law. Aziz, which he told me is how he liked to be addressed, was instantly likeable. His *joie de vivre* was suited to his playboy looks, and I could guess that he would only have to look at any woman with those dark brown eyes, for her then to fall into his arms and shortly afterwards his bed.

"So should I accept Sir Hugh's offer?" I asked Aziz.

"Why not?" He replied "You're young, free and single are you not?"

"Not exactly." I replied.

He continued, "Even so it is a well-paid position, and you're having a crap time work-wise here at the moment, no? I would think that it is a 'no-brainer'."

Again he stunned me, firstly by how much he knew about me and secondly his liberal use of colloquial English phrases. He broke into his infectious laugh as he drew heavily on his cigarette, but all I could do was to smile in response. I was about to ask him how he knew so much about my position, when I was thwarted by the ring of his mobile. It was a brief call with Aziz only uttering 'OK' to the other caller before hanging up.

"Sir Hugh is on his way up in the lift." Aziz quickly stubbed out his cigarette before escorting me back to the reception.

"Thanks Sonia." He blew a kiss at the receptionist and again she blushed.

We had just sat down, when Sir Hugh and Phillipe de Silva entered the foyer.

"Good Morning Sonia, hello Aziz and welcome Marc." Sir Hugh strode up to me and shook me warmly by the hand "Thank you for changing your plans and joining me here in St Katharine's Dock this morning." He paused for an instant "I think, however, you will find it to your benefit. Please come through and Aziz would you be so kind as to join us?"

Sir Hugh led us into a sumptuous boardroom with a large plasma screen at one end, on which was displayed a map of the world with a number of different coloured dots placed on most of the land masses - as well as some in the blue of the seas and oceans. Sir Hugh smiled when he saw I had brought my JPG umbrella. Sonia had followed us into the boardroom and passed a large brown envelope to Sir Hugh, after which Sonia asked me whether I would like any tea or coffee.

"Coffee with some sparkling mineral water, please?"

Sir Hugh was examining the contents of the envelope that obviously pleased him because he grunted his approval and walked over to me.

"Marc, the lawyers have been busy overnight and prepared a Contract of Employment, also here is a cheque for five thousand pounds. Time is of the essence because Phillipe and Aziz are flying off to Dubai this evening, and we would like the opportunity of sharing our plans with you today. Unfortunately, we are unable to share any information with you until you have signed the terms of this Contract of Employment. I am sorry to put you under pressure, but perhaps we could leave you for twenty minutes so you can read the Contract of Employment. When we return I am sure we will be able to answer any questions you may have, hopefully to your complete satisfaction."

With that Sir Hugh turned on his heel and walked out of the boardroom, with Phillipe de Silva and Aziz following in his wake. I tried reading the Contract of Employment but my head was swirling, and I felt giddy and slightly dizzy. I kept looking at the cheque for five thousand pounds lying beside the Contract of Employment. I stood up and walked around the room to try and calm myself and then I heard the laughter of Aziz, who I concluded must be on the balcony having a cigarette with Phillipe de Silva, and his words of a few minutes earlier 'why not?' was still resounding in my ears. Returning to the table determined to read the document properly, I went straight to the remuneration section and saw that it reflected Sir Hugh's proposal of the previous day, and signed both copies of the Contract of Employment just above the signature of Sir Hugh. I checked my watch for the date, and noticed that whilst Sir Hugh had dated his signature with today's date, at the bottom of the last page a document reference had been deleted and it bore Sunday's date. 'Shit' I thought to myself he had known all along I would accept his offer. Then I reasoned that perhaps he just wanted to prepare in advance following our early dinner on Sunday. I put the cheque in my jacket pocket.

The moment I signed the document my head started to clear, and the beginning of a headache that had been developing in the area of my recent injuries just disappeared. I had taken the 'king's shilling' and was a Masterson Shipping employee bound for Singapore. I spent the rest of the twenty minutes trying to decipher what the different coloured dots meant on the world map. I also began to think about the future of Gerda and myself.

My new employers returned to the boardroom and Sir Hugh beamed when he saw the cheque was no longer on the table. For a second time that morning he shook me warmly by the hand.

"Welcome on board laddie!" The Scottish brogue was very noticeable, and I saw warmth in his eyes that I had not seen since my wedding day.

"Ok Marc, I am sure your natural curiosity would mean that you're dying to know what the different coloured dots represent on the screen?"

"Well, I assume the white dots in the seas and oceans are your shipping fleet. As some have moved since I have been in the room, I guess their position is being tracked by satellite in 'real-time'."

"Excellent but that was far too easy." Chipped in Aziz.

I continued "The green dots - I presume - are Masterson Shipping smaller offices throughout the world, and the yellow dots are the larger regional offices, given the location of the dots in London, New York, Rio de Janeiro, Dubai, Mumbai, Cape Town, Singapore and Sydney."

It was Phillipe de Silva's turn to laugh and with it "You said he was quick on the uptake Hugh."

Sir Hugh picked up the remote control and pushed a button, at which point about twenty new red dots appeared; which were clustered around the East Coast of Africa, India and throughout the Far East.

"This Marc is our expansion plan. We wish to broaden the base of Masterson Shipping so that our African and Asian activities will - in five years time - be at least half of the Group's turnover. The opportunity for further expansion in Europe, North and South America is too difficult, and we foresee the Chinese and Indian economies growing unabated in the next twenty years. Our Singapore Office will be a key in that development, and we will require that you work closely with Aziz. Aziz will be your colleague, but I wish for him to also be your mentor, and tutor. Would this be a problem?"

"No not at all." I answered genuinely.

Sir Hugh passed to me another brown envelope "This contains a key fob on which there is certain information that will be of use to you before you visit Singapore, as well as a return ticket to Singapore for a week on Friday. I apologise for being so presumptuous, but I wanted to show you how keen we are for you to start as soon as possible. The length of the trip has been planned for one week, and you will also find details of ten apartments that we think you might be interested in viewing whilst you are in Singapore. We have reserved a room at Raffles Hotel for a week, plus temporary membership at a well known sports club, which has a great gymnasium as well as being a popular meeting place for a number of young expatriates working in Singapore."

A credit card sized piece of plastic then followed.

"This is a security pass for this building and we will have a desk and computer made available to you in a couple of days. You may wish to bring yourself up to speed with the current trading position and the three year business plan for Masterson's Far East operations. Aziz and Phillipe, as I mentioned earlier, are leaving tonight for a business trip and will not be returning before you visit Singapore, so Aziz has today suggested that he catch-up with you in Singapore."

I nodded and smiled towards Aziz and his eyes were inscrutable, but I felt sure the time spent in Singapore with Aziz would probably be quite alcoholic, and a flurry of nightclubs and expensive restaurants.

As if he could read my mind Sir Hugh continued "If you come back to this office, in a couple of day's time, please speak with Ms. Syrani and she will finalise your travel arrangements to Singapore. By time we should also be able to give you a gold corporate credit card that is issued to all regional managers. There is no credit limit but they have to explain to me personally what expenses have been incurred, and as long as they are reasonable, appropriate" he cast a sideways glance at Aziz "and not excessive! I will be tied up on a number of personal and business matters until Tuesday next week, so if you have any queries before then please contact Ms. Syrani."

He smiled and offered me his hand to shake, which indicated that my interview was over, and I dutifully complied saying how excited and grateful I was to be given this opportunity and relished the challenge. I said goodbye to Phillipe de Silva and thanked him as well. I said *au revoir* to Aziz and that I looked forward to seeing him in Singapore in ten days time. I was sure his left eye gave me the faintest of winks, which easily could be mistaken as a little tick.

# Tuesday Mid Morning
# Leadenhall Street

It was ten thirty and I was walking back towards Tower Hill Station, battling to hold my JPG golf umbrella in the gusting wind, and trying to phone K-P at the same time. I was still in a daze with the speed of events, wishing to seek his counsel to keep my feet on the ground, but his phone automatically switched to voicemail. I left him a message to call me, but knew he would probably be unable to respond until the following day.

I walked past the ubiquitous tourists en route to London's most popular tourist destination, the Tower of London, and then continued up the slight incline away from the River Thames into the financial district of the City of London. The excesses of the late nineteen nineties and the beginning of the new millennia had come to an abrupt end in the autumn of two thousand and eight, with certain banks and insurance companies staring into the abyss of insolvency. Governments from both sides of the political spectrum quickly mobilised to 'guarantee' or take state ownership in a number of these companies to try and avoid a recurrence of the Great Depression eighty years earlier. Despite the populist view that 'fat cats' of Wall Street and the City of London were to blame for the excess in lending and development of convoluted financial products that only a few understood, it was a raw fact that the world economies needed these individuals otherwise the world economy would stagnate. The government's response was more regulations, which appeased the voters, but in reality the regulators would always be behind the innovative and imaginative minds of the financial wizards that will always be attracted to the world of financial wheeler dealing. The invisible earnings of these individuals was of paramount importance to both the USA and UK to keep Wall Street and the City of London as the premier financial centres in the world, thus attracting and keeping the finest individuals.

I mused that the increased regulatory powers of the UK's Financial Services Authority probably resulted in my own harsh treatment. Walking past Lloyd's of London – my old hunting ground – with five thousand pounds in my pocket as a golden 'hello' to my new job in Singapore, I wondered whether everything had in fact turned out for the better, as perhaps my marriage to Mércédès was never destined to be a long-term relationship. My high spirits suddenly dipped for an instant as I thought of Gerda, and the fact that we would be apart for long periods of time whilst I was stationed in Singapore. I turned the corner and saw my bank, and my mood changed for the better, as I could not wait to be able to give my beleaguered relationship manager some good news.

Stuart Myhill was a good solid employee of my bank whose origins were north of the border, as was Stuart's. The government now owned the lion's share of the equity as the price for saving the bank from collapse, which was caused by the recklessness of the former management when acquiring another bank with billions of toxic debt. Stuart would not be considered, or even sought, for promotion within the bank. He was approaching his retirement age of sixty with eager anticipation. Stuart had shared in a private moment that his wife and he would be moving to Spain as soon as he retired. His only daughter had finished university and was training to be a doctor; he had sold his three bedroomed semi-detached mortgage free house at the top of the market in two thousand and seven and was living in rented accommodation so he could take advantage of the falling property prices in Spain. He was hoping to swoop on a five bed-roomed villa with its own swimming pool, near Marbella, within a few months.

I was a bit of a thorn in Stuart's side. During my years of climbing the greasy pole of insurance broking, he had extended to me credit in the form of overdrafts, mortgages and credit bonds, earning him good 'brownie' points – if not commission – along the way. We had become, if not friends, good business acquaintances, and would exchange Christmas cards and celebrate each others birthdays. My sudden demise was a shock and disappointment to Stuart. Whilst he never said anything, he was possibly the subject of ridicule in the bank, particularly when he was interviewed by the police about funds in the Dutch Antilles. He stuck with me, trying to assist me as far as he could during the last twelve months, even though I suspected his every move was being closely monitored by his senior management.

It was ten to eleven when I walked into the bank, announcing to a spotty youth on the front desk who I was, and that I had an interview with Stuart Myhill at eleven o'clock. The youth said that Mr Myhill was in a brief meeting which was due to finish in five minutes. He asked whether I would like to take a seat until the meeting had finished.

I sat in one of the arm chairs and was leafing through the latest edition of 'Stuff' to see what were the latest gadgets in vogue, including the new electronic devices being fêted as the 'must have' gadget for Christmas. I looked at the latest mobile telephone and thought that if I purchased it, I could throw out my IPod, digital camera and current mobile phone. It would be easy to take to Singapore. In the past I had wasted money on similar items when they were the 'must have' items; I reasoned that the latest mobile phone would itself be out of date within a few months, and I would resist until my current phone was *hors-de-combat*. Anyway my eye had been caught by a flamboyantly coloured Vespa retro-scooter that had stood the test of time and would be very practical in both London and Singapore.

Whilst browsing the details of the scooter, I became aware of raised voices in one of the interview rooms behind me; the door was closed so the voices were muffled but I distinctly thought I had heard my name. I was straining to listen with the magazine in my hands, which I was pretending to read, purely for show.

Just before eleven o'clock the door opened and Stuart came out of the interview room, his face flushed and eyes on fire.

"Oh!" He said embarrassed when he saw me sitting so close to the interview room, which confirmed my suspicions, that I had indeed been the subject of the raised voices of a few moments earlier.

He regained his composure quickly and greeted me. "Good morning, Marc. Thank you for coming in today. My Area Manager is on one of his routine visits, and would like to sit in on today's meeting. It is normal bank procedure and I hope you don't mind?"

Stuart was a hopeless liar and perhaps that was a redeeming feature and a reason why promotion had passed him by.

"Not at all Stuart." I replied po-faced, resisting the urge to smile.

Stuart showed me into the interview room and a ginger haired man who I assumed to be in his mid-thirties, stood up to shake my hand. The hand-shake was not as firm as I would have liked and the clamminess of his hand indicated that he was not looking forward to this meeting, and it was going to be far from routine.

Stuart offered me tea or coffee and I accepted the latter; I was enjoying myself as both Stuart and his Area Manager poured themselves each a glass of water. Stuart could sense that something was amiss and that I was far too relaxed for the situation. When the Area Manager reached into his briefcase for his papers I smiled at Stuart, and tried to imitate Aziz's faintest of winks earlier that morning, but was far to clumsy which bewildered Stuart even more.

Stuart was about to commence the interview when I decided to ease his obvious discomfort.

"Stuart, I am very pleased that this meeting with you and your Area Manager has been scheduled for today, because I have some good news for you."

Stuart looked quizzical and the nameless Area Manager remained aloof.

"Yesterday I was given a new commission by Neptune Re."

Stuart was tensing up again and starting to sweat as he probably thought I was going to try and appease them with a few days of consultancy work.

"This will provide me with some pocket money until I take up my new position as regional manager in Singapore for Masterson Shipping."

I reached into my inside pocket, and brought out one of the two brown envelopes which Sir Hugh had given to me earlier.

"Here is a cheque for five thousand pounds that will go a long way to clearing some of my overdraft limit. I also have a duplicate of my signed Contract of Employment with Masterson Shipping. I am visiting Singapore in ten days time, with a view to moving there before Christmas, thus being in situ for the beginning of next year. I have decided to rent my flat during my time overseas and I expect the rental income will clear the balance of my overdraft in less than twelve months."

Stuart was smiling broadly and relaxing into his chair, as he read the Contract of Employment, to confirm the veracity of my statements.

Stuart passed the contract to his Area Manager and said "Marc, I am so pleased for you, and the fact this offer has come from your former father-in-law must make it so very special."

"Yes, I was in a bit of a scrape at the weekend and he has been tremendously helpful since then."

Before his Area Manager had finished reading the contract, Stuart asked whether I needed to extend my overdraft in light of these new circumstances. I smiled broadly, as indeed did Stuart, as we both could see the Area Manager was becoming more frustrated by the minute. Being ginger he was obviously going to be very prone to blushing and this morning was not going the way he had planned, perhaps it was his wish to get rid of two problems at once. A bad account (i.e. me), and an employee who was out of touch and should be asked to retire early, which was not in Stuart's meticulously detailed plans. At the mention of extending my overdraft facility the Area Manager's whole head became bright red, clearly visible through his closely cropped hair, and I was expecting steam to start to appear cartoon-like from his ears.

I decided to play nicely "Thank you Stuart, but I think the current facilities should be sufficient given the fact that Masterson Shipping will be issuing me with a corporate credit card later this week."

This was the final straw for the Area Manager, who made his excuses, thanking me for my time before beating a hasty retreat.

As soon as he left the room, Stuart and I burst into laughter.

Stuart then looked me straight in the eyes and said "Thank you Marc."

I was back on Leadenhall Street by half past eleven with my bank interview over, and I was thinking what to do for the rest of the day. I walked up to Liverpool Street Station to find out the time of the trains to Felixstowe, so that I could start looking into the Neptune Re matter. The weather was rainy and blustery, and if I was going to try and do some sleuthing I would need to change out of my suit and overcoat, into something more suited to the weather and the task. I made a note of the train times for the following morning and walked back to Leadenhall Market and the Lamb.

Whilst *en route* I called my brother. I thought I should make my peace with him, and let him know of my change of fortune, plus he could let my parents know the lie of the land when he spoke to them next. His mobile rang and switched to his voicemail. I had prefixed his number with '141' so he would not know who was calling him. I rang the Lloyd's of London switchboard and asked to be put through to Cuthbert's syndicate. When I was connected I asked to be put through to Joshua Edge.

"Hello!" Joshua replied hastily.

"Hi, it's Marc."

"Yes, what do you want?" The curtness of his tone was all too familiar over the last twelve months.

"Are you free at lunch-time today?" I asked.

"Why? I hope you're not looking to scrounge from me again?" His tone hardened even further.

"No, I have money – and good news".

I remained calm and upbeat. Joshua was obviously curious and agreed that he could spare thirty minutes at a quarter past one, but he would not be seen anywhere with me near Lloyd's of London, so we decided to meet at a coffee shop on Liverpool Street Station.

I had an hour and three-quarters before I met with Joshua, so I called Carla at JPG and asked whether she fancied an early lunch, and I said that I would be paying.

"What, two days running?" She asked, and then she reminded me that she was now 'spoken for' and I had left it too late, if I fancied her.

"Ok, hands up; I wondered if you could do me a favour please?" I asked.

"Hmmm." Was her non-committal reply.

"No nothing untoward. I just wondered if I could borrow the last two weeks editions of Lloyd's List?" I added that it would help me in respect of a new job I had just landed.

Carla said OK, and we agreed to meet at noon in the same coffee shop as the previous day, on Liverpool Street Station.

# Tuesday Lunchtime
# Liverpool Street Station

I went directly to the coffee shop and ordered myself a large cappuccino. When settled with my drink I re-read my Contract of Employment. I felt quite humbled by the trust that Sir Hugh had placed in me to be able to fulfil the role as his Regional Manager in what was planned to be his next big investment. The back copies of Lloyd's Lists would help me come up to speed with the latest news in the shipping industry. Whilst I was at JPG I put into place a system where the back copies would be kept for at least three months, and if ever I had a free lunchtime (which was not that often) I would buy my favourite sandwich and hide myself away in a conference room to catch up on the news. As insurance brokers it was always helpful to be aware of the latest news when speaking with ship owners and other clients. Now I was going to be the client I reasoned that I should be equally well informed.

Just before Carla arrived I put a call into Bishopsgate Police Station and asked to speak with Sergeant Smithson. The police officer told me that Sergeant Smithson was unavailable until two o'clock, and would I like to leave a message. I said that I would call him back later.

Carla arrived on time.

"Gosh Marc, you look great. I would never have recognised you from the person pissed as a newt on Friday or even the person in the same suit yesterday. What drugs are you taking? Can I have some please? I might dump my boyfriend for you!"

We both laughed and hugged each other, and Carla hung on just an instant too long for platonic friends. I could feel her breasts pushing against me and she had obviously just put on some perfume. I kissed her on the cheek and sat down knowing that the attraction between us was not completely dead – whatever Carla might say.

"The only drug is money and a job!" I announced proudly.

"What another investigative case for Edge & Associates? By the way, are there any other associates beyond the bank?"

Her jibe at any other time might have hurt, but not now.

"You are correct that I have a new investigation, but additionally I now have a proper full time job. In fact we will be distant colleagues".

Carla looked at me with a very puzzled face "Lloyd's of London and the Financial Services Authority would never allow you back into the insurance market this quickly. Marc, what the bloody hell are you talking about?"

The people at the next table turned to look at us upon hearing Carla swear. Carla had always had a ripe turn of phrase, which could embarrass John Eastwood and other members of JPG's senior management team, but her work ethic and dedication made her worth her weight in gold. Her fish-wifely moments were soon forgiven and often ignored within JPG.

I continued with my news, "You are now looking at, with effect from this morning, Masterson Shipping's new Regional Manager for Singapore."

"Holy shit, Marc – you *are* on drugs!"

The couple on the table next to us 'tutted' out loud.

"Ssssh Carla, or I will be arrested again, and twice in a week will be too much!"

Our neighbours were obviously uncomfortable sitting next to a gangster, and fled the café leaving their half-eaten sandwiches behind.

Carla giggled "I hate people listening into private conversations Marc, and sorry if I made you feel uncomfortable."

I was not sure whether Carla was just referring to her ripe language or our earlier embrace.

I waved the incident away, saying it was nothing, but that seemed to sadden Carla.


"Right then, what do you want to eat and drink?" I asked Carla and she perked up at the change of subject.

"Well Mr Edge, as you are now reeling it in again, I will have a smoked salmon with cream cheese sandwich, a slice of carrot cake, with a large cappuccino, please?"


I went to the counter and bought Carla's lunch, as well as my own, choosing both the same sandwich and drink.

"No cake Marc?" She asked when I returned.

"I thought I might have some of yours." I replied.

We ate and talked continuously for the next forty-five minutes, Carla fascinated by the generosity of Sir Hugh. I held back telling her how much I would be earning, and the details of the flat.

"Well as I said yesterday, John Eastwood did not recoil at the sound of your name on Monday, so perhaps Sir Hugh has been talking to him?" Carla observed as she finished her coffee.

I diplomatically asked about the back issues of Lloyd's List, adding that as I was an employee of a group company, she should not feel guilty about lending them to me.

"I don't give a damn. Since you left JPG no-one really reads them after a week so they go into the archives. Before I came to lunch I put in a request to archiving and they should be ready by three o'clock." She looked at her watch. "I need to be going now Marc. Come by JPG after three when you can collect them from reception."

She gave me a peck on both cheeks, a squeeze and then returned to work.

I suspected that Carla's comment about not giving a damn was not true. One of the reasons why she had come to lunch was to find out why I wanted the back copies of Lloyd's List, before agreeing to hand them over.

It was one o'clock. I checked my mobile phone for messages. There were none, but I expected that the jungle drums would soon be beating when Carla returned to JPG and the insurance market heard of my appointment with Masterson Shipping.

It was just after quarter past one when my brother walked into the coffee shop. He looked around twice before acknowledging me, and then he made his way towards my table. I knew that he had seen me the first time he looked around, the second was to see who else was in the coffee shop that would witness his liaison with the bad-boy of the market, which might be used to embarrass Joshua in the future.

Joshua hated embarrassment; he liked everything to be nice and neat, with no fuss. As he made his way towards me I was struck by the likenesses and the differences between us. Firstly he was at least two inches shorter than me; in itself that was nothing remarkable as I stood only three inches under six feet tall, but his frame was similar to my own if not more pronounced. This made him look heavy. His abhorrence to anything sporty (I loved sport and would take any opportunity through my life to run, swim, throw, hit, catch both people and objects) meant that he now carried a paunch. He had the same – almost black – hair as me, and whilst mine was greying he was losing his and he combed it backwards to reveal his prominent forehead. He dressed as a city gent in a dark blue pin stripe suit and outside of the City of London he would look faintly ridiculous. Both of us were quick to temper, but he was much more introverted with his glass always half-empty; whereas I was much more gregarious and – usually – my glass was always half-full.

"Well you look sober." Was his opening salvo.

"Good afternoon to you Joshua." I offered my hand in welcome.

"Huh!" He grunted in reply, and barely shook my hand.

"Would you like a cup of coffee, and I presume you have eaten already?"

"I haven't had a chance yet! We are in the middle of finalising business plans for next year, so can I have a filter coffee, and a panini of some sort….please?" The last word was added as an afterthought.

When I returned with his food and drink, plus another espresso and glass of water for myself, he was muttering to himself as he checked his mobile phone for messages.

"How are Joan and the children?" I enquired politely.

"Fine." He responded, embarrassed that I was prying into his private life. "Come on, spill the beans, Marc. I can see you're dying to tell me of your latest good fortune." He almost spat the words out of his mouth.

I gave him a fairly full account of what had transpired over the last five days. As I spoke to him, rather than being pleased I could see his brow started to become knitted, a frown started to spread across his face. I ignored him as best I could.

"The potential down-side is that I will not be able to see Gerda for long periods of time."

He had finished his panini and he could contain himself no more. "If you are innocent," he emphasised the word 'innocent' as if to draw attention to its unlikelihood "then why the heck do you persist keeping in contact with that shit Van der Khol's sister?"

"Firstly, Gerda has nothing to do with Paul's mistakes, and secondly Paul is still my friend."

I was still talking in a normally modulated voice, but I could hear that my words were becoming more clipped.

"Anyway when he comes out of his coma, I am sure he will have an explanation as to what happened, and he will clear me."

Joshua had never liked Paul especially as the *Lammers* had welcomed Paul but not Joshua. I had tried to get him involved in the *Lammers* when Joshua first came into the insurance market but my friends were less forgiving than me. 'Joshing Joshua' was good sport and they had poked fun at him un-mercilessly. He did not have the strength or type of character to poke fun back at them, blaming me for trying to make him uncomfortable and ridiculous. He had taken it badly when I pointed out that he needed no help from me to make him look ridiculous.

Joshua must have been reading my mind, because he was getting redder in the face by the minute.

He started to rant "Marc, you are so bloody lucky. All your life you just breeze around by being an over grown schoolboy, and most people fall for your prankish rugger-bugger attitude. When the hell are you going to grow up? It's not fair that you fall on your bloody feet every time. Sir Hugh might feel sorry for you, because of Mércédès, but he had no right to rescue you from your plight. You deserve to suffer!"

His eyes were starting to well up with tears as the emotion and vitriol continued to pour out of his mouth.

"What makes it worse is our own parents always jump to your defence. It's always been the same 'Marc this, Marc that'. 'Hasn't he done well'? 'Isn't he unlucky to have fallen among thieves'? "No, it isn't unlucky! You deserve it because of your poor choice of friends!"

Tears were actually rolling down his face, with thirty years of frustration pouring out of him in thirty seconds.

"Joshua, yes I might be able to choose my friends, but I can't choose my family, yet you are all I have!"

This was too much for Joshua, and he stood up.

"Please go to Singapore as soon as possible, so I can get on with my life without being constantly haunted by you, and your actions!"

He managed a half-smile as he turned on his heel, and walked out of the coffee shop with his handkerchief covering his face; barely missing a young mother and her child, who were just coming into the coffee shop.

I was stunned and sat for a few moments trying to collect my thoughts. I had always been suspicious that Joshua had been jealous of me, but not to the extent that he had just revealed, and at that moment my thoughts were broken by a text coming through on my phone.

It was from Joshua *'Sorry Marc. It's my problem, not yours. Good Luck'*.

Before I had a chance to reply it was followed by another text from Joshua *'By the way, Tony Eastwood came to the box today and asked for your mobile number. I gave it to him'*.

My brother had never mastered text shorthand.

I replied *'Thx love 2 U all'*.

# Tuesday afternoon
# City of London

It was just before two o'clock and I was now awash with coffee, but I wasn't ready to give up my seat in the corner of the coffee shop. I went to the barista and ordered a large mug of chai latte. I asked to borrow a pen from the barista. When I returned to my table I pulled out one of the envelopes that Sir Hugh had given me earlier that day, and started to make a list on the back of the envelope:

> *Things to do!!*
> *Police – Lock? Passport?*
> *JPG – pick up Lloyd's List*
> *Felixstowe – tomorrow?*
> *K-P – weekend*
> *Gerda – book restaurant*
> *Sort clothes – buy light suit*
> *Masterson – visa/work permit. Call Ms. S*
> *Estate Agent – organise flat rental*
> *Parents/Sister – write letter*
> *Eastwood – what does he want?*

My pen lingered over the last item. I guessed that he had been briefed by Mércédès, or Sir Hugh, about the position in Singapore so I doubted that he was going to tell me not to take the job. I was curious. Also why did he not just ask Mércédès for my mobile number, and then I recalled that Mércédès was going to return to Goa to spend some time with her mother. I assumed that would mean she was unlikely to return for at least four weeks, which might include Christmas. Perhaps he was going to gloat that he would be spending his first Christmas with Mércédès. I smiled; 'I couldn't give a damn' I thought to myself – and I meant it.

I decided to get on with my 'things to do' and vacated my table at the coffee shop, much to the visible relief of the baristas, they probably thought I had taken-up permanent residence; also they cannot have failed to have noticed the fruitiness of Carla's language, nor Joshua's highly charged emotions.

I walked towards Bishopsgate Policy Station, stopping *en route* to check the train times from London to Felixstowe via Ipswich the following day. When I walked into the police station, Sergeant Smithson was behind the front desk.

He looked up and welcomed me with "Good afternoon Mr Edge, I almost didn't recognise you without the blood and bruises."

I managed a half-smile in reply.

He continued "How can I help you - again?"

"I was wondering how many similar incidents to my own you have experienced in the last couple of months."

"We can have anything from six to twelve incidents on any Thursday or Friday night."

I persisted with my questioning. "What about that particular area around Spitalfields? You said you thought it might be a gang of youths?"

"Yes that is correct. I said that because not far away, across Great Eastern Road, there are housing estates where there have been a number of problems." He paused for a moment "But to be frank the incidents have been between rival gangs, rather than picking on anyone from the City."

"Was that the only reason you thought it might have been a gang?" I could see I was about to lose his attention shortly, so I added "Please!"

Sergeant Smithson pushed away the papers he had been pretending to read and answered my question.

"Well it was the extent and nature of your injuries that led us to believe it had been more than one person involved. Also, usually, when there is a fracas involving a 'city gent' it is normally a one-on-one situation. Why do you ask Mr Edge?"

His use of the phrase 'city gent' was obviously being used mockingly.

I reiterated that I thought the break-in at my flat was a sham, and the tell-tale signs that the door had been forced were in my opinion artificial, also I suspected that a key had been used.

Sergeant Smithson made no comment.

I continued that after I searched my flat, on Sunday night after discovering the break-in, the only thing that had been definitely missing was my passport, but after our conversation the previous day when I looked again yesterday evening it was in its normal place – in the tea caddy.

Sergeant Smithson laughed ironically "The tea caddy, gosh, how surprising! I bet your mother used to put the housekeeping money in the tea caddy when you were a boy?"

I nodded.

He continued "You had an emotional weekend and I suggest you missed your passport on Sunday. As to someone singling you out, how would they know you would get as drunk as a skunk on Friday?" He had enough of my story and decided to conclude the discussion, "Anyway the break-in is the responsibility of the Metropolitan Police, not the City of London police. Good day to you Mr Edge".

I left the police station in a clearer state of mind than when I had entered it, because I felt sure that it had not been a random beating and that I had been singled out. But why me? Had I really offended someone so much on the Friday that they followed me and lay in wait? I doubted it. Almost next door to the police station is a library, and I went inside and asked to be directed to the reference section.

# Tuesday Afternoon
# Bishopsgate Library

I looked for the maps of the British Isles and in particular East Anglia. There was a large scale map of Felixstowe showing the town centre – which I knew quite well – and the port area. I had dropped Sir Hugh outside Gate 2 on Sunday, and reasoned that his ship's captain had been not far away. Gate 2 was the entrance to the Trinity Terminal, and I surmised that one of the Masterson Shipping vessels moored there would probably be the best starting point. I used my mobile phone to take a photo of the map of the Port of Felixstowe in case I needed it on my walk from Felixstowe Station the next day.

It was just after half past two as I left Bishopsgate Library, and I tried K-P again expecting his voice mail, but unexpectedly he answered "Hi, Marc, you OK".

"Very good" I paused "almost too good. Are you free for a coffee?"

"Sorry, Marc, I am totally tied up with my overseas clients. I only have ten minutes now because they are doing a quiet bit of shopping. They should be gone by lunchtime Thursday. Perhaps we could meet for lunch then?"

"Perfect," I replied "I will call you Thursday about one o'clock to arrange a rendezvous. Also are you and Jane free at the weekend?"

"I think Sunday is pretty clear. Why?" He asked.

"Gerda is over and she would love to see all of you – especially the kids – also I think I may need some moral support as she seemed a bit non-plussed about the opportunity in Singapore."

He responded just as I hoped he would and the friend he is "Don't worry about Gerda. Jane and I will work on her. Sorry, have to go now – see you on 'thirsty' Thursday."

I laughed and made a mental note to have a large breakfast on Thursday, and also that Felixstowe would definitely be Wednesday.

It was still blustery and raining lightly when I started the walk to the offices of JPG. I arrived just before quarter to three.

"Hello, Mr Edge." I recognised the broad cockney accent of Joe who was the concierge on the ground floor reception of JPG.

Rather than go with a dolly bird receptionist, John Eastwood had retained Joe shortly after he left the City of London Police. Joe had been widowed at a young age, and his only progeny was a daughter now living in the Middle East, with a husband involved in the construction industry. Joe lived in a flat on the JPG premises, which was a Victorian building owned by Sir Hugh. Joe played a full part in a number of JPG's activities which belied his position on reception. In his sixties he was still a force to be reckoned with, both physically and intellectually, keeping his ear very close to the ground.

"Miss Carla said you would be popping in to pick up a package."

"Yes, Joe." It was good to see him, and I told him so.

"Thank you, Mr Edge." He motioned for me to take a seat. "The package isn't quite ready, so please take a seat as you must be tired after your exertions over the weekend involving my former colleagues of the constabulary."

He then gave me a big wink and a smile as I sat down.

The insurance market usually closed for lunch from one o'clock until a quarter to three, so there were a number of brokers passing through reception. It was pretty even between the number who totally ignored me and those who came up to say hello. Just before three o'clock, John Eastwood walked into reception and saw me sitting there. He hesitated for a second and I thought he was going to come across to me, but he had second thoughts and carried on but did nod his head in my direction. I responded with a smile. Perhaps the ice was melting as Carla had suggested.

At that moment a messenger arrived at reception and passed to Joe a package of newspapers which I correctly assumed were for me.

"Mr Edge, your package is ready." He called across to me. "Let me find an executive case for you."

He pulled out a Lloyd's of London carrier bag. He was enjoying himself, as ever poking fun at the JPG youngsters.

"Thanks Joe." I replied genuinely.

"Look after yourself Mr Edge" he said as though I might be in difficulties.

# Tuesday Late Afternoon Hackney

Despite the feel of rain in the air, I decided to walk back to my flat, especially as I wanted to visit a couple of Estate Agents on Bethnal Green Road, as well as picking up something to eat for supper.

I briefly met with three Estate Agents; each had a similar view that my flat would be easy to rent, because the effects of the recession meant that fewer people were prepared to buy properties, so there was an increased demand. Also the Olympics were sufficiently on the horizon to be a positive factor, as I would be letting the flat during the games period. The rental income would start from between three hundred to four hundred pounds per week and could be index linked over the period. With a quick bit of maths, I calculated that gross rental income for the three years of my appointment should generate at least another forty thousand pounds.

Feeling even more chipper than before, I went into a supermarket on Bethnal Green Road buying fresh pasta with a spicy sauce, garlic bread; plus a reasonably priced bottle of red wine for my supper.

I was passing Shariz on my way up to my flat when he called out to me.

"Mr Marc, my brother has changed the locks to your flat and here are the keys – two sets."

"Thanks Shariz, can you keep one set until the weekend when I will give them to my friend K-P. How much do I owe your brother?"

"The cost of the new locks was sixty pounds but my brother can re-use the old lock."

I looked puzzled.

"There was no damage to the old lock; my brother thinks that it was not forced or picked. So he will give you a ten pound discount."

I gave him fifty pounds which cleared me out of cash. I thanked Shariz for his and his brother's help sorting out the locks so quickly.

As I let myself into the flat, I racked my brains to think who would want to break in unless it was someone who thought I had more that I did! That would rule out anyone in the City as they knew I was broke. A number of my friends had paid over the odds for second hand furniture and DVD players, and other gadgets, when I moved out of the duplex in Docklands.

I busied myself by continuing to sort out my clothes into the three existing piles. Unsurprisingly the Singapore pile was the smallest! Most of my short sleeved shirts and t-shirts had seen better days and the latter were only good to me for the gym or the beach, I was even unsure if the tee shirts were even up to the beach. The 'oxfam' and storage piles were by far the largest. I put the give away in two black plastic bags and the storage pile in an old suitcase. I decided to deal with the 'oxfam' pile straight away.

I was about to take them outside when Shariz caught my eye.

"Mr Marc, can I help you?"

Whilst always helpful, this was an example where his helpfulness verged on being intrusive. I explained what the bags were and what I was proposing to do with them.

Shariz said "Don't bother with them yourself. If you leave them in the workshop at the back I will deal with them."

Shariz was a proud man and would not openly take any charity for himself or his family, but I felt sure that his offer was not for purely altruistic reasons, and that his extensive family might have the pick of the contents of both bags.

I put the bags in the shed behind the shop, and just before returning to my flat I asked Shariz whether I could store my clothes with him that I would not be taking with me to Singapore.

"Of course, Mr Marc."

I sat down to eat my supper just at the time an important football match was being broadcast. Whilst rugby was my first love this particular game was important for both sides and had been highly publicized. It turned out to be an intriguing and absorbing affair. By the time it had finished at ten, I realised I had finished all the pasta, garlic bread and the bottle of red wine, the latter was supposed to have lasted a second night.

The news was not very interesting with two reports looking back at events over the last twelve months - the recession and the power sharing agreement between the main two political parties in Zimbabwe. Neither story was particularly optimistic, so I listened with half an ear, whilst

I washed up my supper utensils and crockery. After the weather, which was much more pertinent to me in view of my trip to Felixstowe the following day, I decided to go to bed. I checked my phone and saw I had a text from K-P saying he, Jane and the family would love to see us Saturday evening or Sunday lunchtime.

# Wednesday Morning
# Hackney

The punches were raining down on me as I was on the floor. I tried to curl up into the foetal position, only to be punched or kicked in the middle of my back. I attempted to kick my assailant, but only managed to crack my shin on something hard. This was not a fight that I had any chance of winning. I decided to lie doggo. The punching and kicking stopped immediately, and then I felt hands searching my pockets. They found my keys and took them from my jacket pocket. I lashed out but missed my attacker who hit me very hard on the back then again across my face. I passed out.

I woke up from my very vivid dream on the floor of my bedroom, my shin hurting from where I had kicked out and caught either my bed post or wardrobe. I clambered back into bed, checking my watch for the time. It was half past six and I lay very still on the bed trying to recall as much of my dream in consciousness as it occurred in my unconsciousness. I felt sure that my discussions with Sergeant Smithson and Shariz had jogged my memory during my deep sleep - aided by a bottle of red wine. I felt sure that it was only one person who attacked me and they were very strong. They definitely took my keys. I had not lost them en route in my drunken stupor on Friday.

Whilst I was sure about what had happened to me, the memories of a vivid dream are hardly going to be of interest to the police, or anyone else with the exception of K-P. I would tell him about it the following day.

I had decided to catch a train to Felixstowe after ten o'clock to take advantage of the 'cheap day return' fares offered by the train operating company. So I climbed back into bed trying to go back to sleep, but the weather had worsened and the wind and rain beat heavily against the windows of my flat, giving me no chance of further slumber. As I rested I thought how global warming and climate change in the United Kingdom had started to alter the seasons, with October winds coming in November and snow hardly ever expected until the New Year. The prediction of a café society in London did seem quite fanciful as I listened to the drumming of the rain.

No chance of a run in Victoria Park, I elected to go for a swim at the Burdett Road Baths, which involved catching a bus. On the bus I sent a text to Gerda saying that K-P's family were free either Saturday evening or Sunday lunchtime; although my preference would be Sunday as we wouldn't be out of bed all day Saturday! I finished the text by saying I loved her and was longing to see her. Her reply came almost immediately. 'Lovely idea but shopping is important for Saturday, so yes Sunday but not too early! Love u 2! X'.

The pool was busy that morning and the usual time I devote to thinking whilst swimming was given up to concentrating on avoiding other swimmers. It was half-past eight before I was back on the bus, now crammed with school children heading towards Mile End and beyond. I was back in my flat just after nine o'clock when one of the Estate Agents - whom I visited the previous afternoon - called my mobile and asked if they could come and view the flat to measure up today. I said that as long as they were finished by ten o'clock, that would be fine. This meant I would be on the eleven o'clock train to Ipswich.

I used the time to skim through the back issues of Lloyd's List that Carla had loaned me. The recession had affected shipping. Already I had gathered from the various discussions with Sir Hugh that he saw air freight reducing in the long term; this plus a resurgence of shorter voyages by ships was one of the reasons for Masterson Shipping's expansion in the Far East to create a hub there. Sir Hugh also felt that eventually Africa, once they resolved a lot of their political issues, would be an area for development that Masterson Shipping would also handle from Singapore.

The Estate Agents arrived within fifteen minutes of phoning. I suspect their urgency was driven by a wish to be the sole agent for the letting. I quickly showed them around the flat, and then retrieved my ski-jacket and a wick-away vest from the storage suitcase. Whilst the estate agents were doing their stuff, I took the suitcase with my storage clothes down to the shed, taping a label on the front on which I wrote 'MARC'S STORAGE STUFF'.

On the way back up to the flat I saw that the postman had delivered a postcard from my parents in Australia. The front was showing the Australian Rugby team which they knew would wind me up. The reverse side carried the following message, 'G'day! Having a wonderful time with Patricia, Garth and the kids in their school hols. Goin' 'walkabout' til Dec so out of reach. Don't panic. Love Mum & Dad x'.

So if everything went to plan I would have visited Singapore and be on my way back to London by the time they re-surfaced. At least that was another thing crossed off my 'Things To Do list'.

True to their word, the Estate Agents were finished by ten o'clock and, as expected, they wanted to be the sole agents because they felt sure they had the ideal tenant 'in the wings'. I said yes to their request writing a post-dated cheque for the gas and electric certificates for the following Monday, as well as signing an agreement with them to be sole agents.

The rain was lashing down at quarter past ten when I left my flat, heading towards the bus stop. I looked more like a polar explorer with my insulated 'bobble hat', ski jacket, gloves and walking trousers, which would dry out quickly, and walking shoes. An umbrella would be of no use whatsoever. A bus arrived quickly and, despite the weather, scooted along the route and I was on the eleven o'clock train bound for Ipswich with five minutes to spare.

# Wednesday Afternoon
# Felixstowe

It was after half past twelve when the train rolled into Felixstowe Station, after I had to change at Ipswich. I spent most of the journey time leafing through a selection of Lloyd's Lists, which I had brought with me, trying to glean anything more about the situation, which Eric Jones had asked me to investigate. I was also trying to bring myself up to speed generally with the latest news in the shipping industry. What was clear was that Masterson Shipping's size of the market had not diminished since the start of the recession, in fact it had probably increased with the acquisition of two small operations, one based in Brazil and the other in Dubai. I had only been interrupted once during my journey; it was whilst I was waiting for a connection at Ipswich. My lawyer, Chris Worcester, was catching up on his voice messages from Friday. I told him that the reason for my enquiry had now passed, however I did tell him about my wonderful change of fortune.

"I hope you didn't sign a contract until I have had the chance to vet it?" He asked.

"Well, you see it was very awkward, and there was a 'hello' cheque just sitting there, plus the situation with regards to the flat in Singapore. It was just too good to ignore." I was stuttering down the phone.

"Enough Marc, enough!" He saved me from more embarrassment. "I am sure it will be OK. Sir Hugh is a tough businessman, but from what you have told me, he seems to have thrown you a lifeline. I doubt he has screwed you over, well not too much anyway."

"I will send you a copy of the contract tomorrow, that's when I am hoping to go to start at Masterson Shipping's office, and I will scan and e-mail it to you."

"Fine," said Chris "what about a work permit, and a visa?"

"Sir Hugh's private secretary at Masterson Shipping is looking into that for me. I hope to be going to Singapore for a reconnaissance next week."

"Marc, if you want I will cast my eye over the work permit and visa applications."

"Thanks Chris!" Our conversation finished just before the connecting train from Ipswich to Felixstowe departed.

My conversation with Chris had made me oblivious to the weather, and when I arrived at Felixstowe I was confronted with rain driving hard in the strong winds. I found the bus stop which served the Port and checked that there were hourly departures via services 75 and 76 to Walton Avenue near the Port. The bus would take fifteen minutes, or so; normally I would have walked, but even dressed in my ski jacket and walking trousers, the weather had put paid to that idea. I retreated to the station, buying myself a hot chocolate and a ham sandwich whilst waiting for the bus to arrive.

I looked around at the station, which was familiar from my late teens, when I used to come and visit my uncle to work at his hotel. Yet the station had a very different feel to that sleepy seaside town that I remembered. The Port of Felixstowe, proudly bathing in its own self-publicity as Britain's Premier Port, had seen to that.

The bus schedule was true to form, and there were about a dozen other prospective passengers who suddenly appeared as the vehicle approached the station pick-up point. These were mainly male passengers and a great number having their origins in south-east Asia – I presumed most came from the Philippines. By the looks on their faces they were probably looking forward to being on the high seas and away from the British autumn weather.

After a quarter of an hour the bus arrived at Walton Avenue which was the closest bus stop to the Port Gates. Walton Avenue was also the start of the A14, a major road link that stretched from Felixstowe across England to the M6 south of Rugby. Not only was it a major boon for the development of Felixstowe, but it was one of very few major routes in England that did not start or end in London, running east to west, rather than North to South.

From the Walton Avenue bus-stop travel was by foot and the weather had not eased. As I approached the Gate of the dock, I could see that security checks were being made of all pedestrians as well as vehicles. I had foreseen this eventuality and had brought my business cards showing *M. Edge & Associates - Claims Investigators* together with an old Lloyd's of London photo ID from when I was with JPG, that they omitted to collect when I left to join Inter-Continental. More than once in the last eighteen months the combination of my business cards and a Lloyd's of London pass had unlocked a number of doors closed to the general public. The security officers were in deep conversation with a group of Filipino looking gentlemen. I positioned my business card in a seemingly nonchalant fashion over the Lloyd's of London pass, but in fact it was carefully positioned so as to cover the JPG name. The security guards hardly gave me a second glance as I took off my bobble hat so they could check my picture on the Lloyd's of London pass.

I walked purposefully towards the police headquarters; Tomline House lay behind the police headquarters, which would be the starting point for my investigations. It was nearly a quarter to two when I walked into the reception of Tomline House. I breezed up to the desk and smiled broadly at the young girl seated there. Her high cheek boned face responded quickly to my smile. I tried to charm some information from her.

"Hello, I guess you haven't had many visitors today with the weather like this?" I said.

"No, you're only the second visitor since I started at nine o'clock." She volunteered freely in her soft East Anglian accent.

When she spoke to me she pushed back her shoulders which had the effect of showing off her large breasts, which were accentuated by her woollen polo-neck sweater. I had to concentrate very hard to keep my eyes on a spot between her eyes. I suddenly felt a longing and desire to see, feel and touch Gerda. Friday could not come quick enough for me.

I pulled out my Lloyd's pass and flashed it in front of the receptionist's eyes explaining that I was a claims investigator retained by a large marine insurance company. The fact that Neptune Re was a reinsurance company might only serve to confuse the issue. I said that I was being asked to conduct a spot audit with the Masters of certain Masterson Shipping vessels before they sailed. As I told my pack of lies, I was surprised how plausible they sounded to me.

I continued "I understand that two vessels are due to sail later today and one on Saturday."

She told me that the departures for today had been postponed until at least eight o'clock in the evening, because of the bad weather, and the situation would be reviewed by the Harbour Master at seven o'clock.

"Unless the wind stops this afternoon I doubt anything will leave port today," she added "which is good for your audit, because the Master and the crew are likely to be bored kicking their heels this afternoon."

"Can you tell me where the three Masterson Ships are docked please?" I asked.

"One is here in the Languard Terminal and two are over in the Trinity Terminal." She replied.

"Thank you very much, you have been very helpful."

I gave her one of my winning smiles, and she responded by smiling back at me, her shoulders pushed back further and I couldn't help but notice that her nipples were hardening beneath her woollen sweater. As a throw-away line I asked if she had the names of the masters of the three vessels. She said not, but that if I went to the Masterson Shipping offices in Centenary House they could help me.

"Of course! How silly of me not to think of that?" I tried to cover my tracks as best I could.

The offices of Masterson Shipping were very close to Gate 2, which is where I had dropped Sir Hugh Masterson on Sunday in the sunshine; nothing like the wet and wild conditions of today. I had no idea how I was going to be able to speak to the Captains of any of the vessels without arousing their suspicions, certain I was not going to be able to blag my way on board any of the vessels. The wind had increased in strength since I had arrived in Felixstowe, but the rain had stopped; either the eye of the storm was approaching or the clouds had deposited their contents across the UK before reaching East Anglia. It was therefore unsurprising that East Anglia had the lowest rainfall for the whole of the UK.

The second vessel I came to was a Masterson Shipping container ship. A junior officer was overseeing the loading of what looked to be the crew's provisions. I walked up to him and spun my story.

"Hello!" I was nearly shouting so that my words were not being carried away on the wind. "I am looking for the father of a friend of mine, who is the Captain of a Masterson Shipping vessel that I understand is currently in port."

The young officer said "Is your friend from Russia?"

I replied "No."

"Then he is not the Captain of this ship," he continued "there are two other ships over at the Trinity Terminal."

I thanked him, although I already had this information. It would be a longish trek across to the Trinity Terminal, especially as I would be walking head long into the strong wind blowing from the west. I pulled down my bobble hat and started my hike.

It took me thirty-five minutes to walk over to the Trinity Terminal, passing the Dooley Ro-Ro Terminal *en route*, by which time it was fast approaching quarter past three. All the berths were full, probably because of the suspension of the arrivals and departures. I started making my way westward along the line of vessels moored in the safety of the port, away from the high waves visible outside the Orwell Estuary. As I looked out towards the North Sea I thought of Gerda, hoping that the weather would improve before Friday, thus not affecting her ferry crossing from the

Hook of Holland to Harwich. If the Masterson Shipping vessels had not been departing until the weekend, I could have delayed my visit to Felixstowe until Friday, and met Gerda as she came off the ferry. I decided to text Gerda, 'Near Harwich and thinking of you. Can't wait for Friday? Love Marc x'

The two Masterson Shipping vessels were the last two on the dock. The first one I reached was completely shut up. I reasoned that it was the one due to sail on Saturday. There were signs of activity around the last vessel, where a crew member was acting as a security guard to stop unwanted guests coming on board. He was of oriental appearance, and I thought my Lloyd's of London pass might prove to be the key to eliciting the information I was seeking. I flashed my pass and asked whether the Captain was on board. He did not seem to understand so I tried in my broken Spanish -presuming he was from the Philippines. This seemed to produce at least some response.

"He not here." The sailor was trying to be helpful and pointed at the number '2' on his watch, and added "Gone."

I thanked him and turned away to return the way I came when he tapped me on the shoulder and added "Not far."

I made my way back along the dockside, the wind now behind me, but the rain had returned and my trousers were becoming very wet. As I approached the end of the dock I thought about going into Centenary House and asking at the Masterson Shipping offices if they knew where Captain Hennessey was. I was worried that someone might take a closer look at my credentials, and then make a call to the Masterson Shipping Offices in St Katherine's Dock to check the veracity of my story. I decided against doing so, because I might be the shortest serving employee of Masterson Shipping, at one day!

With the weather worsening, I decided that I had done enough to justify the money I had accepted from Eric Jones, and that my visit to the Port of Felixstowe had been a fool's errand. I felt hungry and thirsty as I walked back past the Dooley Ro-Ro Terminal. On my journey from Tomline House, towards the Trinity Terminal, I noticed signs for the Seafarer's Centre. I hoped I might be able to get a hot drink and perhaps a meal there.

The Seafarer's Centre was buzzing with so many ships in port, most of whom were waiting to see if the weather improved in the next few hours sufficiently, for the Harbour Master to allow shipping to resume. Hot drinks were available, and I was soon in possession of a hot steaming mug of tea together with a thick piece of fruit cake, which I hoped would keep me going until I returned to London.

Seafarer's Centres are spread across the world, and I recalled that there was usually a chaplain on duty. Looking around the canteen area I couldn't see a chaplain at that moment. My tea was too hot to drink, so I wandered towards the reception, asking a middle-aged woman if the chaplain was available.

"My husband is just with someone at the moment. If you do not mind waiting he should be free in about fifteen minutes."

"Thank you. By the way do you know Captain Hennessey?" I asked.

"Why yes? That's who my husband is currently speaking to," the chaplain's wife enlightened me.

Returning to the canteen, I made sure I was seated in the eye-line of the office door behind the reception. It was nearly half an hour before the door swung open and out walked a middle-aged portly man, followed by an older taller man with a weather-beaten tanned complexion, the owner of which I presumed to be Captain Hennessey. He shook hands with the chaplain, checked his watch and walked into the canteen, towards the counter where hot drinks were being served.

I waited until he had bought his drink and was seated before I went over to his table. He was blowing his nose and his eyes were slightly red which made me wonder whether he had been crying. He saw me out of the corner of his eye, looked straight at me, with the keenest blue eyes I had ever seen. The effect was enhanced by the tanned skin which was accompanied by a white beard and moustache.

"Do you mind if I join you please?" I asked.

"Why is that Mr Edge?"

I was stopped in my tracks.

"It is Mr Edge, isn't it?"

It was all I could do to stop my jaw dropping.

He carried on unabashed "Mr Marcus Edge, new regional manager of Masterson Shipping's Singapore Office. Please sit down."

My instincts told me to run-away, but I knew that would have been the wrong thing to do. I tried to brazen out the situation.

"Yes, you are absolutely right. I struggled to re-capture my composure. "Sorry you completely surprised me, how do you know my name?"

Captain Hennessey smiled, and his tone resembled that of a benevolent uncle.

173

"I have been working for Sir Hugh Masterson for a long time. During that time I have been a frequent visitor to his office in London and at The Hall. During the time either talking to, or waiting for, Sir Hugh I would often be staring at the photograph of his daughter's wedding and the man who had made Mércédès so happy!" He was enjoying himself "On Sunday I met with Sir Hugh, and he said you had driven him from The Hall."

I knew that I could be in trouble if I said too much, so I kept quiet, merely smiling and nodding, whilst desperately trying to think of a reason why I was in the Port of Felixstowe on a windswept Wednesday afternoon in November.

Luckily Captain Hennessey was the gregarious sort and continued "And late yesterday, all the senior managers received an email advising us of your appointment. So why are you here?"

"Everything has happened so quickly over the last two days," I started "and next week I am due to be flying out to Singapore. I have worked in marine insurance for a number of years, but never for a shipping company before." I carried on with my cock-and-bull story, becoming more confident with each word. "I picked up a number of back issues of Lloyd's List." I motioned towards my – now soggy – document case that I had been carrying around with me "and came to Felixstowe to try and get a feel for what it's like to be in and around a major port."

Captain Hennessey was looking sceptical and I was sure he was about to dismiss me as a liar.

I quickly added "But coming from an insurance background I believe risk management could be improved to reduce insurance claims, and I had the idea that we – Masterson Shipping – should consider the crew completing a pre-voyage questionnaire to determine whether there are any patterns that could be discovered that could help the

Master of a vessel whilst on that, or future, voyages." The lies were tumbling out of my mouth thick and fast. "In fact I told the receptionist at Tomline House that Masterson Shipping had already implemented these additions to their – or should I say our - Risk Management Strategy. I think she was quite impressed."

Captain Hennessey laughed "I am sure she was, and what have you learned today Mr Edge?"

"Not a lot because of the weather," I admitted honestly "everyone seems to be here."

Captain Hennessey surveyed the canteen, probably in a manner to when he was on the bridge of his ship "Yes, it is very popular today. We can't go too far afield in case the weather changes, and sitting on board whilst the ships are tied-up alongside the dock is not pleasant in these high winds."

I wanted to change the subject but at the same time I did not want to arouse any suspicions. So I asked "What's it like to have Sir Hugh as a boss? I was protected from him when I worked at JPG."

"He is a hard man to please, but when you do so he will reward you well."

This seemed to bear out my knowledge and experience of Sir Hugh.

"But do not get on the wrong side of him" Captain Hennessey was continuing to talk but his eyes seemed to be in the middle-distance "or consequences can be dire."

A moment of silence descended upon us. He caught himself and looked back at me with those keen blue eyes. "You've been given a second chance, Marc. Don't screw it up, and make sure the reason you came to Felixstowe was the one you told me!" His staring eyes seemed to be boring into my soul as he delivered his warning.

He excused himself to go to the toilet and returned a short time later.

He looked at his watch "Gosh it's nearly five o'clock, I must be getting back to my ship to see the latest news from the Harbour Master. And you Mr Edge will no doubt be returning to London?" It was more a command than a question.

"Yes, there is a train to Ipswich leaving in about thirty minutes from the station, so I'd best be making my way there sharpish." I shook hands with Captain Hennessey and added "Thank you for your time and advice."

His hand squeezed a little harder "Good luck and be careful."

The wind had dropped to a strong breeze, but the rain had returned, and it was dark. I walked with my head down for two reasons, firstly to protect my face from the rain, and secondly because I was ashamed with myself as the day had proved to be a complete waste of time. If I had a tail, it would have been firmly tucked under my bottom, as I scurried out of the port.

I was back on Walton Avenue at the bus stop across the road from where I had alighted a few hours earlier. There was no-one else waiting for the bus and, to avoid missing the train to Ipswich, I thought I would have to trek into Felixstowe. Just at that moment a small red mini pulled up and the passenger window opened. I bent down to see who had stopped; it was the young receptionist from Tomline house. "Hello, we met earlier. Do you remember me?" She asked.

"Yes of course I do. How can I help you?" I offered politely.

She laughed "It is me who can help you. There won't be a bus for ages and you will get soaked. Hop in."

"Thank you." I said as I got in the car.

"Where are you going?" She enquired.

"The station if it's not too far out of the way please. I would like to catch the train to Ipswich so I can get a connection to London." I explained.

"You'll be lucky," I turned to face her as she was pulling away from the kerb "the wind has brought down the overhead line near Ipswich Station, and nothing is going in or out for a number of hours yet. I live in Ipswich and can drop you at the bus station, to see if there is a coach back to London."

"Thank you, that is very kind of you. My name is Marc." And careful not to brush against her ample breasts, I offered my hand which she briefly shook, whilst not taking her eyes off the road in front of her.

"Mine is Stacey and, before you ask, I am not in the habit of picking up strange men at bus-stops."

"So I'm a strange man am I?" I replied and we both laughed.

We chattered constantly on the journey to Ipswich, which was stop-go in the rush-hour traffic, made worse by the weather conditions. The radio was turned low, but, every ten to fifteen minutes, our chatting was interrupted by the local radio traffic alerts, which confirmed the position at Ipswich Station that no trains were likely to be running until the following morning.

Stacey had only been working at the Port of Felixstowe since May, when she had finished her HND in Hotel Management. She said she wished to work abroad in the hotel business, but that the right job hadn't come along yet.

Although she didn't say anything directly, I discerned that she had just come out of a long relationship.

"And you are a claims investigator?" She asked "I bet that's interesting with lots of travel."

"Unfortunately most of the work is desk-based and the pay is sporadic." I answered a little too honestly. "But all that is about to change and I am about to take up a permanent post in Singapore before Christmas."

I often was bemused about how much people will reveal to strangers.

"Will your wife or girlfriend enjoy Singapore?" I felt it was not an innocent question.

"I'm getting divorced and my girlfriend lives in Holland, looking after her brother who is very poorly, so she will only be able to visit from time-to-time."

"That's a shame. I would love to work in Singapore," Stacey replied as she briefly turned to smile at me.

It was after six o'clock by the time Stacey dropped me at Ipswich bus-station.

"Good luck in finding a coach to London." Just before she drove away she asked for my card and scribbled a mobile number on the reverse. "If you get stuck, give me a call. I'm only washing my hair tonight."

I smiled and shook her hand saying "Thanks very much."

Ipswich Station was an absolute zoo, with hundreds of people swelling around looking for transport to London, as well as in the other direction towards Norwich. The situation had been made worse by an accident on the southbound carriageway of the A12 between Ipswich and Colchester, which was affecting coaches to London. I was thinking whether I should accept Stacey's offer. I checked my mobile, which had been on mute since I arrived in Felixstowe, and saw that there were two missed calls from a number I did not recognise plus two text messages.

The first message was a reply from Gerda saying 'Me too. X'. I buried my card with Stacey's number into one of the deep pockets of my ski-jacket. The other was a message from my voicemail, informing me that I had two messages. Both were from the same person - Tony Eastwood. The first one asked that I call him back 'at the earliest opportunity' and was timed at five o'clock. The second one was only ten minutes ago with Tony saying it was important that we talk as soon as possible.

I called his number and it answered on the second ring.

"Hello, Marc?" He sounded almost civil.

"Hello, Tony, how can I help you?" I asked.

"Where are you?"

"In Ipswich bus station but going nowhere fast. Why do you ask?"

"I am going to the States on business early tomorrow morning and I have some important information I must give to you before I leave."

"You can tell me now, can't you?" I was becoming impatient and felt my heckles rising.

"It is just not what I can say to you. I have something to give to you;" he sounded genuine "it is very much to your advantage and is important."

"OK, it looks like the only way I can get back to London tonight is to take a coach to Stansted Airport and then catch a train to Liverpool Street Station from there."

"That's perfect because I am currently at The Hall, picking up some clothes I need for my trip." Before I could say anything he answered the question that was forming in my mind "Mércédès left for Goa this morning."

So that was who Sir Hugh was meeting after me yesterday; no wonder he shooed me quickly out of his office.

Tony continued "Let me know what train you will be on from Stansted Airport; make sure it's one that stops at Bishops Stortford, and I will be on the platform at Bishops Stortford. We can travel back into London together.

"OK."

I was curious what he could have that was important and to my advantage. Everything he had done in his life had been to disadvantage me. Perhaps with Mércédès won, he was being less of an up-start. He could have her; I now knew I loved Gerda.

"I don't think it will be much before nine o'clock," I warned him.

"Not a problem. Sir Hugh is staying in London tonight and I am sure Samuel can make some supper before running me to the station."

I am sure Samuel would not love to do that. Tony still expected people to run about at his beck and call.

# Wednesday Evening
# Bishops Stortford

It was half-past six by the time I boarded a bus for Stansted Airport, and I needed to be steadfast to retain my rightful place in the queue, as most of the London bound travellers had woken up to the fact that a bus cross country was the best route home. Like locusts they headed towards the coaches for Stansted Airport and Cambridge.

The accident on the A12 was causing mayhem to even get out of Ipswich, so the A14 was proving to be the most popular route. A journey that typically would take an hour and a half, took longer than two and a half hours, and it was already past nine o'clock when the bus driver announced our arrival at Stansted Airport. I had nestled into the corner on the back seat of the bus with a heater directly under me. I had fallen asleep even before we left Ipswich. The rest was very welcome, and whilst I couldn't remember what I had been dreaming about, I felt sure it involved Gerda and her impending visit to London at the weekend.

As I woke, I felt my mobile phone vibrating; it was the same number as previously, so I guessed it was Tony Eastwood. I waited for it to stop vibrating, and then I sent a text saying we had only just arrived at Stansted Airport, and that I would call as soon as I knew the time of the train to Bishops Stortford and London.

I made my way to the station underneath the Stansted Airport Terminal. I always enjoyed flying from Stansted and did so as frequently as possible. Built originally for American Bombers in World War Two, it has one of the longest runways in the UK. When the 747 carrying the Space Shuttle visited the UK, Stansted Airport was one of the few airports that could be used. The Nissan huts and turbo-propped aircraft had been replaced by an award winning designed terminal building housing a number of budget airlines. The passenger traffic at Stansted Airport had grown enormously; now vying to be larger than Gatwick. There had been some successful local opposition to arrest Stansted Airport's expansion with one or two further runways being laid; although most people were unaware that the foundations for the second runway were already laid. Also there are a series of tunnels under parts of the airfield so should there be a hijacking of a plane in the United Kingdom, they might be sent to Stansted Airport, where they may sit in an apparently desolate remote corner of the airfield, the hijackers blissfully unaware that their operation is being literally undermined by special forces operating right beneath their plane.

The Stansted Airport rail link direct into the City of London had made it a firm favourite with European business travellers; even for long haul flights, when sometimes I had used Stansted Airport, preferring to transit at Schipol in Holland rather than travel to Heathrow.

The next train would be leaving in twenty minutes, and I tried ringing Tony Eastwood, but his voicemail cut in straight away. I left him a message giving the train time and added that I would be in the second carriage. As soon as I had settled into my seat my mobile started vibrating again; I reached for it and saw it was K-P.

"Hi there." I said *sotto voce* into the phone.

"Marc," it was K-P "where are you? Do you fancy a quick drink?"

"I would love to," I replied "but I am on my way back from a wild goose chase in East Anglia. The trains are disrupted and I don't think I'll be back until about eleven. Plus I will have a travel companion?"

"Hmmm" was the guarded response from K-P, "what would Gerda say, Marc?"

I laughed "No a male companion; Mr Tony Eastwood no less."

"What!" K-P sputtered down the phone "Watch yourself Marc."

"He says he has something that will be to my advantage." I explained. "Mércédès has gone to Goa to see her mother, and Tony's off to the USA on a business trip, and he says that he needs to speak to me before he goes."

"Well just you be very careful Marc. Perhaps we can catch up tomorrow?"

"Ok my friend."

As soon as I had hung up, my phone vibrated to say that I had a message. Whilst I had been speaking to K-P, Tony Eastwood rang to say that Samuel was driving him to Bishops Stortford Station. He would be on the London bound platform before my train arrived, and could I come to the door of the second carriage to make sure we didn't miss each other. I smiled and thought about the dichotomy of someone so flamboyant, also so particular about the detail. I presumed he inherited that trait from his father, who used that skill to his advantage and became a successful businessman. Whilst I waited for the train to start its journey, I read the poster on the train inviting people to visit East Anglia. This one was about Bishops Stortford and explained that it was a market town and the birthplace of Cecil Rhodes, founder of Rhodesia. I wondered whether Cecil Rhodes was now turning in his grave at the thought of his beloved Rhodesia now being strife-torn Zimbabwe.

The train pulled out on time. I guessed it was fuller than usual, with the commuters who had diverted from Ipswich, together with business men returning from short trips to the continent and other parts of the British Isles. Everyone looked pretty tired and washed-out, particularly the air travellers; because to make a day-trip viable it usually required an early start, and even an eight o'clock morning flight required you to be at the airport by six, which probably meant the day would start at half past four. The accountants trying to squeeze costs don't realise the fallacy of day trips, and that quite often a plane the previous day, plus an overnight stay meant the business is likely to be far more productive. I was pleased that part of my life was behind me and thought about my impending visit to Singapore.

The train pulled into Bishops Stortford Station and I went to the door of the train as it opened. I looked out along the station platform and there was no Tony Eastwood, in fact there was no-one at all. After Bishops Stortford the Stansted Express would only stop at Tottenham Hale in north London, before terminating at London Liverpool Street Station.

"Come on Eastwood, what are you playing at?" I thought to myself.

I glanced at my watch and saw that the train had arrived on time, and in a few seconds it would be departing. I looked through the opposite window to view the ticket office and see if any one was making a mad dash for the train, but the ticket office had no one waiting for a ticket. At that moment a beeping sound started to signal that the door was closing. I had to make an instant decision and hopped onto the platform; luckily I had not taken my ski jacket off.

The train departed and the platforms were deserted. Even the station staff had retreated inside the station buildings, probably to the warmth of a hot cup of tea or cocoa. I walked up the London bound platform northwards towards the way the train had arrived. Halfway along the platform there were stairs which led towards the exit, via a foot-bridge, over the Cambridge bound platform. When I could see there was no-one standing at this end of the platform, I turned around and walked south towards the other end of the platform, cursing Tony Eastwood under my breath. I decided to call his mobile. As it started ringing there was an echo, I could hear another phone ringing in the near vicinity. His voicemail cut in at the same time as the phone nearby stopped ringing. I redialled his number, and then started walking towards the ringing phone. It was coming from inside the waiting room on the platform. I could see inside the waiting room but there was no-one standing or sitting there. I reached the door and opened it to be confronted by Tony Eastwood lying on the floor. The windows of the waiting room started at seat level so Tony had been hidden from view.

I bent down towards him and said "Tony, are you OK?"

That was a pathetically stupid question with him lying on the floor with his small wheelie bag next to him. I could smell alcohol, and guessed he had either passed out, or knocked himself unconscious. As I got closer to him, I realised that his head was turned at an unnatural angle, and he was not breathing.

"Shit, he's dead!" I blurted out loud.

My mind was racing; I saw his phone near his left hand and my eye caught sight of something metallic in his right hand. His fist clenched the object hard, and I had to use all my strength to prise his fingers open one-by-one, to release the object from his grasp. I guessed what he was holding before I had it in my hand. When I had done so I was satisfied that I was not mistaken and that what he had been holding were indeed my keys, that had been lost, or stolen the previous Friday. Whilst my instincts were screaming at me to ring the police, I stopped myself, and thought about the questions they would be asking because: Tony and I rowed publicly last week; he was now the partner of my estranged wife; we had arranged a clandestine meeting at a train station late at night; he was lying on the floor of the waiting room with his neck broken.

The adrenaline had kicked in and the 'fight or flight' emotions were very strong. I decided I must get away so I could work out what had happened. My mind was racing with possible scenarios. Had Tony been assaulted and his assailant run off, or was it premeditated; whichever I was suspect number one!

At that instant I heard police sirens and could see flashing blue lights pulling into the front of the station.

"Bugger!" I swore to myself.

The only way off the platform was the footbridge because the back exit to the station was closed outside of the heavy commuter hours. I was trapped and worse I felt that it was no coincidence that the police were arriving just at the right time to find me standing over Tony's dead body.

# Wednesday Night
# River Stort

My blood was pounding in my ears. I calculated that I had less that a minute before the Police arrived and I would be questioned about the murder of Tony Eastwood.

"Come on Marc, get a grip." I said to myself.

Bishops Stortford Station was situated in a cutting, with very steep embankments to the left of the tracks. I looked south towards London, on the other side was the station itself; North was not an option for me because that would require that I go past the footbridge. South was my only way out. I didn't have a clue where I was going and the moment I stood up I would be visible above the low wall of the waiting room. Just at that moment Tony's phone started to ring, I pounced on it and pressed the 'busy' button, so the call should be directed to Tony's voicemail. I turned off his phone and decided to take it with me. Whilst the police would probably request details of Tony's mobile phone usage from his network, past experience had taught me that it would take them at least a couple of days, and by taking Tony's phone with the log of his recent calls between us may slow them up a little. Before I turned off his phone I had noticed that the last call was from a '01279' number, which I knew covered the Bishops Stortford and Harlow areas. At that moment I felt my own phone vibrate, the caller's number was the same as that which had just called Tony, which meant that someone else knew I was meeting Tony.

Who knew I was meeting Tony? I soon pushed that thought to the back of my mind, as four policemen come onto the Cambridge bound platform, adjacent to the station buildings. Two of the policemen were searching that platform, and the other two were heading towards the footbridge. If I was going to run it would have to be now.

The wind from the earlier bad weather had moderated, but was still gusting hard so the noise of my footsteps would hopefully be masked. There was nothing I could do about the open ground. From the light of the station car park I could just about discern what looked like an industrial building of sorts some fifty or sixty metres away. I was just about to make a dash for it when the first bit of good luck occurred; a train from London rolled into the other platform, and for a few seconds the view from the station would be obscured. I pulled the hood of my black ski-jacket over my head, and ran out of the waiting room down the slope at the end of the platform, onto the ground careful not to trip over the rails or sleepers. I was behind the train in the station and hoped that there would not be another on that line for at least a couple of minutes. Luckily the eastern rail network used overhead power lines, rather than 'third live rail' system.

It was only fifty metres to the corner of the industrial buildings, but there was a link metal fence between the railway, and the buildings. I was stranded in no man's land. I couldn't go back so I continued south following the railway tracks. Eventually I dared to look back and saw I was now out of direct sight of Bishop's Stortford Station. I stopped to catch my breath. I crouched down against the fencing and took stock of my options. I was on the run and shortly I felt sure to be branded a fugitive.

I studied the metal fence more carefully and realised it was designed to keep people out of the railway - not the other way around! I made my way towards the next corner post, picking my spot in the fence where I could use the stanchion of the corner post to hoist myself up about six feet where the barbed wire was angled away from the railway. Some cardboard had been dumped close by, which I used to straddle the barbed wire, I dropped to the ground and then made a mad dash for the industrial buildings.

Once I reached the wall of the buildings I made my way to the corner crouching as much as I could. I was breathing hard when I turned the corner and sat down to recover. After a few seconds I peaked round the corner of the industrial buildings back towards Bishops Stortford Station

"Shit!" I swore to myself, I left the piece of cardboard on the fence; that would telegraph my escape route. It was still quiet, but in the light of the platform, I espied the two police officers searching the London bound platform open the door of the waiting room. I was right. The activity increased the moment they found Tony's body. It would only be a short while until they started searching the environs, and I wanted to put as much distance between myself and the crime scene as quickly as possible.

Whilst I was debating which route to take my phone started vibrating; I looked at it and saw it was the same number as before, and I let it ring into my voicemail. I would not give the caller a clue to where I was at that moment. Then I realised that merely calling the mobile was sufficient to be able to track the position. I opened my phone and removed the SIM card and turned off the phone, hoping that would stop, or at least slow them being able to track me.

In the time I had spent messing around with both mobile phones, as I decided to deactivate Tony's as well, the activity at the station had spilled into the town accompanied by a continuous wail of sirens.

"Think, Marc, think!" I said to myself, trying to focus on an escape route, which would take me more than a few yards from the station.

The trains would obviously be suspended, and the police would consider how the killer entered, and exited the platform. Tony had only just arrived at the station before me, which meant the killer, was either waiting for him from an earlier train, or they passed through the ticket office. I hadn't gone through the ticket office which possibly gave me a slight advantage, although there would be eyewitnesses to describe me getting off the train from Stansted. I was hoping it would take the police a while to track down the passengers and interview them.

With the trains halted, I guessed that the police would also throw a cordon around the roads exiting Bishops Stortford, and stealing a car presented more risks and more reasons to be thrown in jail.

It was thirty five miles or so to London, and I felt it would be easier to lose myself in a big city, rather than in the countryside. I started walking, trying to follow the train-line but at the same time keeping off the main roads. In less than ten minutes I encountered my first dilemma, the main road was the only way across the railway lines, and two police cars had passed by my hiding place in less than a minute. I was forced to the right and almost stumbled into the river. I followed the path beside the river, passing under a small bridge, making good progress when I heard voices and saw the light from a torch approaching me in the distance. I turned back the way I came, but the pool of light cast by the street lamps over the road bridge would certainly reveal my presence to whoever was walking along the river path toward me. Whilst the weather during the day had been stormy it was warm for November but the temperature of the water ruled out hiding in the waters of the river as an option. I then realised that I had passed a narrow boat moored close to where I had joined the river path. I crouched down and scuttled back to the vessel, which I hoped was being used as a pleasure craft. I crept on board and slipped under the tarpaulin that covered the cockpit. The door to the cabin was only fastened by a small padlock. I was looking for something to force the padlock when my fingers touched a metallic object poking out under the edge of the rubber matting. It was a key for the padlock. When inside the cabin I did not close the door fully as I could hear voices within a few metres.

I lay absolutely still, as I could hear the footsteps coming closer, to the boat. It had just stopped rocking as a result of my boarding.

"I am sure I saw something moving close to the ground." It was a female voice.

"I didn't see anything," replied a male voice "it was probably a fox. Anyway why do only the 'special' constables have to walk the river paths, whilst the regulars swan around in their warm patrol cars?"

"Oh shut up, will you? There's a message coming through on the radio." The older female officer listened to the static enhanced message. "We're to return to the station. Someone has been spotted on the golf course towards the M11, and they are bringing in dog-handlers to help with the search."

"Thank goodness for that. I want a cup of tea and my bed," was the response from the male officer.

"Ok, I suppose we better go then," the female officer replied, and I heard footsteps walking off into the distance.

It was only a temporary respite, as I knew the dogs would very soon pick up my trail. I needed to get under way as soon as possible, but something stopped me from returning to the river path, and continuing my flight. I was becoming accustomed to the darkness and could see something lighter than the surroundings by my feet. I reached down to touch it, and as I did so I heard the faint static of a radio. One or both of the police officers were still close by. I sat motionless on the floor of the cabin. I stayed like that hardly daring to breathe, and after about fifteen minutes I heard footsteps walk away for a second time. My place of refuge had now become my prison and I needed to escape. The object at my feet was an oar of a kayak, which gave me an idea, because the police dogs would not be able to track me on the river. I knew the River Stort led into the River Lea, and the waterways connected into the canals of East London. If I took the narrow boat it would be noticed, and I had never navigated one previously, but a kayak was another matter.

Very quietly I made my way out of the cabin into the cockpit and slowly peered through an eyelet of the tarpaulin. I couldn't see anyone, but my vision was restricted. I climbed out from under the tarpaulin, nothing happened! There was no-one standing on the path ready to arrest me, and

I could hear the police sirens some way away from where I was now. I saw the kayak lashed to the top of the narrow boat and within a few seconds I had it on the river path. I returned to the narrow boat and retrieved the oar plus a dark green waterproof. My ski jacket would keep me warm, but it wasn't water proof, and I felt sure my rusty kayak skills would result in me shipping a lot of water.

The recent rain meant the river level was quite high, so getting into the kayak was not a problem, although I was quite clumsy when I climbed in myself. There was a spray cover stuffed down the front of the kayak, which I fitted around my midriff, before attaching it to the kayak. It was very dark on the water, with the clouds keeping any light from the moon well hidden, so the diffused street lighting was my only guide. I started paddling slowly because I wanted to keep close to the river bank, to avoid going in circles.

I was surprised how quickly and easily I was moving down river, the effort required to keep the kayak at a reasonable pace was minimal, as I was being aided by the river itself. The rains that accompanied the earlier storm had swollen the river which was flowing swiftly.

My confidence took a battering in less than ten minutes, when my route on the river was halted by a dead end. It was spooky on the river. It was quiet and very dark so I could not see what was preventing my passage. I could hear water passing me by and I wondered if I had paddled into a dyke of some sorts. I had to try and see where I was, so I turned on Tony's mobile phone, using the light cast by the screen to faintly illuminate my whereabouts. Even with the merest light I could see what was blocking my passage. I had come to a lock across the river. I turned the kayak around and came to steps close by the lock, probably for narrow boat users, so that they could climb up to the river bank to operate the lock. I released the spray cover and grabbed the steps, hauling myself out of the kayak, careful to put the oar inside as I exited the kayak.

Once on the river bank I pulled the kayak out of the water, I then walked around the lock carrying the kayak with me. Before I left the lock I quickly studied the map nearby, again I used the faint light of Tony's mobile, and it showed the navigation of the river as it led into the canals of London. I was at the South Mill Lock, and I counted that there were another fourteen locks to negotiate before I reached the River Lea, near Rye House in Hoddesdon.

Back on the water, it was under fifteen minutes when I reached the second lock at Twyford, and went through the same procedure as at the first lock. I found it tiring climbing in and out of the kayak, and I wondered if walking would be a better option. The tiredness was probably exacerbated by the fact I had not eaten for many hours. The adrenalin rush had well and truly subsided, and my teeth even started to chatter, which was not surprising as it was a November night.

After the lock at Twyford, the street lights of Bishop's Stortford were well behind me, and I was making better progress with the clouds breaking apart allowing the moon to shine through. The river was becoming more visible by the moonlight. The noise of the town and traffic was also gone. If it were not for the cold and damp permeating my body, I might have actually enjoyed myself.

I was thinking ahead as to what I should do next, and where I should go to avoid being arrested by the police. Establishing who killed Tony would help immeasurably. The '01279' number was my only lead. I lay the oar across the kayak and let the river drift me downstream. I put the SIM card back in Tony's mobile phone and turned it on. As I was waiting for the network connection to be activated I noticed that the time was approaching half past eleven. Nearly two hours had elapsed since I discovered Tony's body in the waiting room of Bishop's Stortford Station. I dialled the '01279' number. It rang without answer. I had the same number on my phone, so I felt safe to dump Tony's mobile, I turned it off and dropped it into the river.

I resumed my paddling, and just after midnight, I had to negotiate another lock at Spellbrook. Back on the water the temperature was falling further as the skies became clearer. I could not be seen on the river, but I would have to stop my journey as soon as I next reached a built up area - or dawn – whichever arrived first. From my recollection of the map at South Mill, I believed the river passed very close to Sawbridgeworth Station, after which Harlow Mill was the next memorable point on the river. Sawbridgeworth Station was on the outskirts of the small town and not in an urban area. My target was to be past Sawbridgeworth, and off the river, before Harlow Mill and before dawn.

With that goal in mind, I picked up the rate at which I was paddling, to reach Harlow Mill before the cold took its toll.

# Dawn Thursday
# Harlow Mill

The high spirits I had felt after Twyford seemed a lifetime away and had become low. The stretch of river from Spellbrook Lock to Tednambury Lock seemed to take ages, as it was essentially a meander in the river.

At Sawbridgeworth Lock disaster struck. I dropped the kayak as I was pulling it out of the water, and it drifted away from the riverbank. Cursing many expletives, I was at a loss to know what to do. The kayak had been taken across the other side of the lock to the sluices, which provided a by-pass for the river around the lock. I swore again to myself and thought about walking. As I made my way past the lock I noticed a lifebelt and rope, which gave me an idea. I took the lifebelt off its brackets and carried it over to the riverbank on the north side of the lock. It was surprisingly heavy. I would have no chance of throwing the lifebelt to where the kayak was drifting. I decided to try and clamber across the lock itself. I couldn't walk across, but if I lay on the top and used a technique similar to that used for crawling along a taut rope, I could keep my balance. Two problems, firstly the lifebelt was too heavy, so I dropped it into the water, after first belaying the rope around my waist thus freeing my hands and feet. The second problem was that my ski jacket was too bulky. I had to take it off even though the temperature had fallen close to freezing.

At first I made steady progress, reaching the other side of the lock in reasonable time, and climbed onto the riverbank as close to the sluices as possible. The kayak was being kept in place by the tide pushing it against the edge of the lock by the sluices. I pulled the lifebelt out of the water, which needed a lot of effort, and I threw it towards the kayak, but it fell short. It wasn't until my fourth attempt that the lifebelt fell over the other side of the kayak cockpit. I had to stop to recover my breath. My hands were numb from the cold water of the river on the lifebelt rope. I was trying to sit down before I collapsed, but failed and fell onto the riverbank. The cold was pervasive and I could feel my eyes closing. I lay there for what seemed a long time but probably was only two minutes. Eventually I recovered enough to start pulling the lifebelt rope taut, and slowly the kayak straightened and then came towards me. I was hoping that the weight of the lifebelt would be able to counteract the strength of the tide, and that the kayak remained at the same angle, otherwise it would turn and be pushed back to the sluices. I continued to pull on the rope and eventually the kayak was at the bottom of the steps beneath me.

I held it steady and gently climbed in. I paddled back over to the other riverbank where my ski jacket and gloves were lying, towing the lifebelt with me. I tied the lifebelt to the bottom of the steps and then pulled the kayak out of the water before returning for the lifebelt.

I was back on the water on the other side of Sawbridgeworth Lock, reunited with my ski jacket and gloves, but I was now very weak and the cold was affecting my mind as well as my hands and feet. It had taken me over an hour to recover the kayak and it was now after three o'clock in the morning. I was unsure how much more distance I could manage before I completely seized up.

I reached Sheering Mill Lock in what seemed no time at all, and took extra care when lifting the kayak out of the water. One more lock to negotiate and then I must find a place to stop. I cleared Feakes Lock about four o'clock. Exhaustion was again taking its toll, because when I lifted the kayak out of the water, I stumbled and the oar fell out of the cockpit. Luckily it floated beside the steps of the lock, but it still meant another journey up and down the steps of the lock. It was one mile to the next lock at Harlow, which was past Harlow Mill; I definitely needed to find a place to stop before then.

My journey on the river had started just before eleven o'clock and it had taken me over five hours to travel nearly six miles. Walking would have been quicker, but I felt confident that the police would not have discovered my unusual escape route in that time. The cold and exhaustion were letting self-doubt creep into my mind, the tracker dogs would have already led their handlers to the narrow boat, and the hunters would know their quarry was on the water. They wouldn't be able to follow me on the river because of all the locks. I breathed an audible sigh of relief, but I realised that the police would merely wait for me at the next convenient point, where the road crossed the river.

"Where was that?" I muttered to myself.

"Come on Marc, think back to the map at Twyford Lock!" I was talking to myself to try and maintain concentration.

I couldn't focus, and stopped paddling as I was convinced I was taking myself towards an ambush at Harlow, where I knew the river went under a number of roads. The river after Feakes Lock had meandered to the right and after a bend to the left it straightened again. I wasn't paddling yet I was being swept towards Harlow, and in my befuddled state of mind I was sure I could hear voices in the distance. The voices must be police, who were organising a barrage across the river.

If I had become confused because of the cold and tiredness, this had been banished by the adrenalin, and I was now very awake and alert. In the distance I could see a bridge crossing the river, and the streetlights were like a lamp, with me the moth being lured toward their luminescence.

Should I turn around, and start paddling against the current, back from where I had come? I was so tired and knew I just needed to get off the river. Despite the dangers of overhanging trees and tree roots I decided to get out of the centre of the river, navigating to the left hand side of the river, where the current was at its slowest. I was hardly moving, and the trees on the river bank also blocked out the moon. I stopped my progress by holding onto a thicker branch. I held my breath, straining to listen for any voices, but all I heard was the blood pumping in my ears.

After a couple of minutes of staying still, I used the oar to punt my way in the shallows. The bridge was only a hundred metres away, and it seemed very quiet, but beneath the bridge was just darkness. I had no idea what lay in wait for me.

I was thinking about going ashore and walking in to Harlow, when I found myself beside a small slipway, which in the summer would be hidden from view by the foliage on the trees. As I peered between the trees I saw an old wooden boathouse, or large shed at the top of the slipway, which itself was in a pretty poor state of disrepair. I edged the kayak closer to the waters' bank, being careful not to ground the kayak on the concrete, so not making any sound that might easily carry across the river to the bridge.

As quietly as possible I pulled off the spray-cover and gently eased myself out of the cockpit. My arm muscles were sore due to the paddling, as well as having to lift and lower the kayak out of the water, at each of the locks. I was definitely seizing up, and hoped this boathouse would give me brief shelter and respite. I lifted the kayak up to the top of the slipway. The large double doors leading from the building to the slipway were firmly bolted from the inside. I crept to the left keeping the building between myself and the bridge. The dead brambles were pulling at my trousers, and I could imagine that in the summer this would be a veritable jungle and inaccessible. There were windows but the darkness and grime made them completely opaque. I reached the other end of the building and saw that there was a path through the woods leading to a door. I slowly turned the handle and it was unlocked, but the door wouldn't move more than an inch. Either something was blocking it from the inside or the door was jammed. I leant against the door, increasing the pressure until it yielded, and opened with a loud creak.

"Shit!" I swore at myself, but there was no immediate shout of 'there he is'.

I went into the building which smelt musty, and was pitch black when I shut the door. I turned on my phone to give me some faint light and saw that the building was indeed a boat shed, with a small cabin cruiser on a wooden frame. There was a step-ladder at the back of the boat, enabling someone to be able to work inside the cabin cruiser, whilst it was out of the water. Engine parts were at the foot of the step-ladder, and the peeling paint indicated that keeping this vessel on the river required a lot of maintenance, and tender loving care. From the top of the step-ladder I could see inside the cabin, and saw there was a bunk which would give me somewhere to rest for a couple of hours.

I opened the door of the shed as quietly as possible, and returned to the slipway. I picked up the kayak and brought it to the front of the shed, and carried it inside. I climbed up the step-ladder into the cabin cruiser and found an old sleeping bag on the bunk. Within less than a minute I was in the sleeping bag and fast asleep.

# Thursday Afternoon
# Harlow

*I was back on the river and it was early morning with the sun shining brightly, low in the sky and mist lay on the river like a carpet giving the impression I was floating through clouds. It was very quiet; the only sound was the faint 'ssshhing' of water passing over a weir. My progress through the mist quickened and the noise of the water had grown to a shooshing. All my senses were alive to the situation which had moved swiftly from idyllic to concern. The speed was increasing every second. There was no paddle to try and change direction, I couldn't see the river bank through the mist, which was now thicker like a fog obliterating the sun. The noise was a crescendo and the kayak fell over the weir, I screamed but nothing came out of my mouth. I kept falling, falling, falling – where was the water.*

I woke up with a start, totally disorientated, the smell of diesel all pervading. Slowly I sat up. The cabin cruiser was more recognisable by the daylight, which had been able to permeate the November skies, and the grime of the windows. I looked at my watch, which showed me the time was nearly half past eleven. I had been asleep for over six and a half hours.

I was confused. Why had I not been found and arrested? The tracker dogs were bound to have picked up my scent, leading the police to the narrow boat, and they were sure to quickly establish that I had taken the kayak.

"Come on Marc!" I said out loud.

It was no good thinking what might have happened. They haven't caught me, so I should get underway as soon as possible. As I climbed out of the sleeping bag, my arm muscles screamed at me, and I realised that I would not be able to continue with the kayak all the way to London. What's more the speed was painfully slow and I could only travel by night. I couldn't afford to start walking, as I would be easily spotted once outside any built-up area; perhaps I would have to risk public transport?

Hunger pains now assaulted my stomach, and I realised that I had not eaten since Felixstowe. I went into the galley of the cruiser and found a tin of cola, together with two tins of tuna, and a tin of frankfurter sausages. A tin opener was conveniently near the tins, and I feasted on my meal of protein and sweet carbonated water, it was delicious.

I climbed down the step-ladder, and looked around my place of refuge in more detail. The smell of diesel was due to the engine being in a number of parts in a tray. There were windows on both sides of the shed and using a dirty rag, I wiped the window facing the bridge, and peered out. It was sunny, and after a moment or two, I could see there was traffic crossing the bridge. I could not see a police car sitting on the top of the bridge. I was continuing my search of the shed when I literally walked into my next piece of good fortune; two bicycles were hanging down from the ceiling of the shed.

This discovery set my mind racing. I was approximately thirty miles from London, and I could comfortably be in London in four hours. I moved the step-ladder to beneath one of the bicycles and was able to lift it off its mounting hook. The bicycle was relatively new but of an old fashioned design popular in Holland. This brought images of Gerda flooding into my mind. I stopped to think for a few minutes. OK – so I take the bicycle, and go to London, but then what do I do? It would be an absolute certainty that my flat would be watched, and I would be either arrested, or questioned about Tony Eastwood's death. Also the police would probably be keeping watch on K-P. I wouldn't want to do anything to upset Jane, as her retribution could be worse than prison.

It was also unlikely that the police would know much about Gerda, and hopefully nothing of her visit this weekend, or her mode of transport. Gerda would be arriving late Friday afternoon, which gave me about twenty-eight hours to keep out of trouble in London. What about if I intercepted her at Harwich? No, that would mean using public transport which was far too dangerous, and I couldn't cycle there in time.

I thought about staying in the shed for another night, but felt the chances of discovery were too great, plus the tinned food had only taken the edge off the hunger pains that would return shortly. I had to keep on the move, and I would feel safer on home ground in London, than in the countryside or suburbia. Deciding that I should get underway as soon as possible, I quickly pumped up the tyres, and put on the helmet that was hanging on the back of the door for safety and disguise.

It was then I thought about who owned the shed and how I was going to get onto the road. I took the helmet off and quietly opened the door, which protested less that the small hours of the night. The path through the woods led to a garden, with about twenty metres of well-kept lawn, at the back of a large modern house. French windows covered half of the rear of the house; there were kitchen windows, and what looked like the back of the garage on the other side of the building. There were no signs of life, but with the bright sunshine, the occupants were unlikely to turn on any lights during the day. Whilst there did not appear to be anyone in the house, there was no obvious exit to the road. The house and garage covered the full width of the plot, and interwoven wooden fences were flush to the outside walls of the house and garage.

"Ok, that's why the door to the boatshed was unlocked." I breathed to myself.

I was about to make a dash across the lawn to test the garage door when I noticed the alarm on the back of the building. I retreated back into the woods and made my way to the fence that was closest to the bridge over the river.

After a couple of metres from where the fence went into the woods, the neat wooden fence gave way to chicken wire, and just five metres before the river bank this was replaced by two strands of barbed wire. I returned to the boatshed, put on the cycle helmet, together with a grubby luminous tabard I found screwed up in the corner. I carried the bicycle to the chicken wired fence and dropped it over the top, then I walked to the river bank straddled the fence post, in order to be able to collect the bicycle from the other side of the fence.

Within a couple of minutes I was on the road heading for Harlow Town Centre. The time was nearly quarter to two. After fifteen minutes I was through Harlow and heading out towards Roydon, which I remembered was on the river. I was peddling too quickly and I would be exhausted if I didn't slow down. I was in Roydon within half an hour and was held up at the level crossing because of a train heading towards London. I thought about dumping the bicycle and jumping on the next train, but considered that the rail network was too big a risk, especially with the prevalence of close circuit television. Whilst cycling I was trying to formulate a plan of what would I do when I got to London; where would I go! I needed the time on the bicycle to think – I slowed my peddling and started to enjoy my journey on a gorgeously sunny November afternoon.

I wanted to keep off the main roads as far as possible, and shortly after crossing the railway line at Roydon I was able to turn into a private road that took me past sewerage works and Rye House Station, bringing me into a large housing estate in Hoddesdon. From Hoddesdon I was able to keep to suburban routes through Broxbourne, Wormley, Turnford, and Cheshunt. So after a couple of hours from setting out, I was in the Waltham Forest area, on the outskirts of London.

It was dark at half past five when I was riding through Leyton with only a few miles before I reached Hackney. The darkness acted like a protective veil, and I felt much safer, even with the luminous tabard I didn't attract a second glance from anyone. During the afternoon I had decided on a plan, the first part of which required that I visit my flat, to see whether the police were looking for me specifically, or just looking for a person – identity unknown – who had killed Tony Eastwood at Bishops Stortford Station.

I reached my road in Hackney just after six o'clock, and rode past my flat looking neither right nor left, I turned around about fifty metres past my flat and rode back again. I cycled into Victoria Park and sat there for twenty minutes before repeating the exercise, and then returned to Victoria Park, where I reflected that during the four passes of my flat everything seemed normal. The rush hour traffic was at stand-still, and Shariz's shop was full, both of which were typical for this time in the evening. There was no sign of vehicles parked outside of the shop, nor did I see any policemen waiting for my return. I felt confident enough to put the next part of my plan into operation.

# Thursday Evening
# Hackney

It was after half past six when I walked into Shariz's shop, still wearing the cycle helmet and tabard. I picked up a newspaper and walked over to the counter.

Shariz recognised me immediately and kept his eyes down, whilst speaking in a whisper, "Oh, Mr Marc, you are in very, very big trouble."

My blood ran cold in my veins and the urge to fight or flight surged through my body.

"What have you heard?" I said, keeping my eyes lowered as well.

"The police are looking for you, to question you about the death of someone. They're in the flat across the street, plus two more in my brother's workshop waiting for my signal, should you come into my shop."

"Shariz, believe me, I didn't do it – I am being set up. I need help, please!!"

Even though I was whispering, the urgency in my voice was clearly present.

"I know Mr Marc. Leave now and meet me at ten o'clock in the road behind the Hackney Empire. Go now."

"Thank you." I replied and picked up my newspaper, walking as nonchalantly as possible out of the shop, collecting my bicycle from its position on a railing outside the shop. It took an incredible effort to appear normal and not to sprint away.

I returned to Victoria Park, to look at the newspaper. The headlines were dominated by the recession, with economic forecasters predicting doom and gloom for the forthcoming Christmas season. There was no 'HACKNEY MAN WANTED FOR MURDER' headline, but Tony's death was reported on page 3, saying that Essex police were continuing their enquiries and were confident that they would be interviewing a number of people shortly in connection with his death. What was interesting was there was no mention of the word 'murder' giving the impression that Tony's death might have been an accident. I felt sure this was only a tactic to avoid panic within the public, if they knew a murderer was on the loose. Shariz's news about the stake-out of my flat reinforced my view that I was their main - or only - suspect.

I swore to myself. Despite my precautions I had nearly bumbled my way into an ambush. My plan was blown, and now I had to rely on Shariz; I was in need of food and warmth before I met Shariz, in three and a half hours. I cycled to the Mile End Road and headed toward Stepney Green. Between Stepney Green Underground Station and the London Hospital there are a number of Asian restaurants, and I chose a quiet establishment offering food from Bangladesh. I didn't realise how hungry I was and ordered a starter, main course, two side dishes and naan bread. I devoured the food very quickly, which left me with still two and a half hours before my rendezvous with Shariz. I walked to the Genesis Cinema nearby, I didn't care what film was showing, and I just wanted warmth and a place to think.

It was warm inside the cinema, but thinking was out of the question, as I was asleep shortly after the opening credits had rolled. I awoke to the closing credits and the lights being turned on. I had only thirty minutes to get to the meeting place with Shariz.

I arrived at the Hackney Empire with time to spare, and was becoming more impressed with how quick and efficient the bicycle was as a form of transport. With very few hills the old fashioned design was perfect for London, and the upright position meant my back wasn't complaining, although I was suffering from some saddle soreness not helped by five hours in a kayak. Much as it pained me I might have to re-evaluate my abhorrence of bicycles.

It was another five minutes before Shariz arrived with his brother.

"Oh, Mr Marc, you are in very big trouble." Shariz repeated what he said to me earlier in the afternoon.

I again pleaded my innocence and asked Shariz what he had been told.

"Mr Marc, I suspected all was not well since the weekend when you were hit about the head and your flat was broken into. My brother feels sure that someone had tried to force the new lock yesterday, but I didn't see anyone going upstairs – so yes I think you may have been 'set-up' as you say Mr Marc."

"The Police, Shariz, what have they said?" I asked.

"Oh yes Mr Marc, sorry, how bad of me. They came to my shop about lunchtime yesterday, asking whether I had seen you."

I interrupted Shariz "Was it a uniformed or plain clothes policeman?"

"First it was a plain clothes young man showing me his warrant card," Shariz continued "and then I saw this policeman with uniformed officers go into the building across the road. A few minutes' later two uniformed policemen asked if they could wait in my brother's workshop, should you return. I was to make a signal to the building across the street if you returned, or telephoned."

I digested what Shariz had told me before saying anything. The police had invested quite a few resources into my capture.

"Shariz, can you help me please? I realise this could cause you problems with the authorities, but I just need a little time to find out what has happened, and why me?"

Shariz spoke to his brother in a language that was a mixture of English and their mother tongue. The conversation was quite animated with Shariz seeming to advocate my case, and winning the argument.

Shariz smiled to me and said "We can help you. What is it you want?"

"Thank you Shariz." I sounded relieved as I spoke "I need shelter for tonight, and do you or your brother have connections to obtain a passport for me, in a different name?"

"We can help with the shelter, but no, we have no connections regarding passports Mr Marc, and anyway they are very expensive. How would you pay?"

Shariz shrugged his shoulders with his hands upturned in his usual manner when asking a question.

I held up my flat keys "You could rent or use my flat. Either I prove my innocence and go to Singapore for three years as planned, or I don't and I go to prison – any which way I won't need my flat."

"Sorry Mr Marc, I have no suggestions for you at the moment," he continued "anyway where is it you wish to go?"

"Holland!" I replied.

"Holland?" He questioned.

"Yes, Holland." I confirmed.

"Follow me please, Mr Marc."

Shariz turned on his heel and within twenty-five metres we entered a three-storey purpose-built apartment block.

"You need to carry your bicycle Mr Marc, otherwise it will not be here tomorrow – locked or not!"

We reached the top floor and opened the door of the first flat nearest to the stairs.

"Leave your bicycle in the hall, please, Mr Marc." Shariz instructed me.

"This is the home of our Uncle who is very ill. My brother stays here most nights. Our Uncle has had a massive stroke, and is partially paralysed, and unable to speak."

For a home of an elderly person it was warm, but did not have the accompanying mustiness. Perhaps it was the spicy food that had been prepared in the flat, or the incense, the odours of which were prevalent without being pervasive.

"Mr Marc I am sorry but we can only offer you the sofa with a duvet and pillows." Shariz said apologetically.

"Not at all Shariz, this is fantastic and I am sorry to ask this favour of you."

Shariz looked me straight in the eyes and told me under no circumstances should I leave the flat until he returned in the morning.

"I have an idea Mr Marc – and don't shave please".

Just as he was leaving I made another request.

"Can I borrow a mobile phone to send a text please?"

Shariz spoke to his brother who passed me his phone.

"I will come early before I open the shop Mr Marc. Sleep well." And with that Shariz left the flat.

I took the SIM card out of my phone and replaced it with the one from Shariz's brother's phone.

I sent a text to Gerda from the phone's memory: *"Sorry, my phone's not working. This is a friend's. Can't wait to see you tomorrow afternoon. Will call at 12. Love you xx"*

I returned the phone with the SIM card back in its place, and lay out on the sofa. Despite my sleep in the cinema earlier, I was asleep before Shariz's brother had turned off the lights.

# Friday Morning
# Hackney

Someone was gently rocking my shoulder. I opened my eyes to see Shariz smiling at me in the half-light that was being cast from the kitchen.

"Good morning, Mr Marc. I am trusting that you slept well?"

"Yes, thank you." I stifled a yawn. "What time is it?"

"Nearly six o'clock Mr Marc; I must go shortly, or I will be late." Shariz continued "I think I may have a solution for your passport problem, Mr Marc."

I sat up, consciousness quickly returning "Please tell me."

"How long do you need a passport?"

"Only a week or two, at the outside. Why?" I replied.

"I have an idea" he said triumphantly "you can use my uncle's British Passport. He is confined to his bed, and hopefully he will remain with us for the next two weeks, I pray."

I looked at Shariz very sceptically "Shariz, have you not overlooked something? I am white!"

Shariz was enjoying himself "Not at all Mr Marc," producing a bottle from his pocket "please use this to stain your skin. My cousin's wife has a bad birthmark, and she uses it to disguise the white discolouration."

I took the bottle, opened the lid and sniffed the liquid. "What's in it" I asked.

"I do not know Mr Marc, but please take care, it stains everything. Please stand on newspapers in the bathroom, and try to avoid splashing the bath, sink and toilet. After you have applied it – all over your body – wait half an hour and apply again. Then wait one hour before putting on clothes, or washing any part of your body, other than the palms of your hands or the soles of your feet, they must remain white. Do not forget the back and inside of your ears. After you have applied for a second time, my brother will cut your hair, and then you need to use this hair colour."

He produced another bottle, this was a recognised brand, but the colour was grey.

"Mr Marc, your hair and beard must be grey. Look at the picture and shave your top lip as my uncle has done for his passport."

I looked at the dog-eared passport and smiled at Shariz.

"Thank you very much Shariz, I think this might work."

I was the same height as his uncle and luckily possessed brown eyes.

"I am going to open up the shop now Mr Marc, but I will return about eleven o'clock, when my brother will look after the shop."

As he was leaving he looked over his shoulder and said "I shall be bringing clothes, and other things to help with your disguise."

I took the two bottles with the passport to the bathroom and turned on the light to get a better look at the photograph. Shariz's uncle was also called Shariz which was not unusual.

The shape of his head and face were not dissimilar to my own. I tried a small amount of the skin dye on the back of my hand and it seemed to be exactly the same colour as Shariz's skin. I found some old newspapers in the sitting room and returned to the bathroom to start staining my skin, having first carefully shaved my top lip and neck, with the disposable razor Shariz had thoughtfully left with me. It took me the best part of an hour to methodically stain every part of my skin. I even managed to be able to stain the middle of my back between the shoulder blades. I waited the recommended thirty minutes, and then started the process again. In particular I took time around the face, eyes, ears and hairline as these were the areas that would be visible for most of the time. I was much quicker the second time, but even so it was half past eight before I could start clearing up the newspapers.

I returned to the sitting room and saw that (young) Shariz's brother was busying himself in the kitchen, with aromatic smells wafting around him. He saw me and started to laugh.

"Very good," he chortled "now beard, and then haircut."

I showed him my hands and that I couldn't remove the stain from my palms.

He quickly made a call on his mobile phone, after which he said "Shariz says no problem."

Hardly the conversationalist he went back to his cooking, and I returned to the bathroom, to dye my hair and beard grey. This required two applications before I was satisfied. I had used all of the hair colour, but still had about a quarter of the skin dye left, which I decided to keep for any maintenance required. I guessed the stain should last long enough for me to make the trip to Holland and back. I smiled at what Gerda would say when she saw me, especially as I would be proposing that she takes me back to Holland with her.

Shariz's brother had prepared a large bowl of breakfast kedgeree for his uncle, and he gave me a plateful with some naan bread. I was thankful that I liked Indian and Bangladeshi cuisine.

After breakfast, Shariz's brother produced a set of hair clippers and closely cropped my hair, the result was startling. My reflection from the bathroom mirror, with stained skin and short grey hair and beard, could easily be taken as the man in the passport photograph.

True to his word Shariz returned to the flat at eleven, just a short while after his brother had left the flat, to relieve him at the shop. He was carrying a black plastic bag, from within which he produced a pair of my old black shoes, and a new pair of black socks in my size.

"I found the shoes in the clothes you left in the workshop." He seemed a bit embarrassed "I hope you do not mind Mr Marc?"

"Not at all Shariz – your friendship and assistance has been fantastic" I reassured him.

"Mr Marc, I am still worried you are looking too young, so can you please try on these spectacles."

I put the spectacles on and everything was out of focus. I needed to squint and peer through the lenses to be able to recognise anything. "Shariz, I can't see anything through the glasses!" I protested.

"Excellent," Shariz exclaimed "by straining through the spectacles, wrinkles appear around your eyes. Now try to bow your head at the same time please Mr Marc."

I did as instructed and Shariz seemed to approve. He went into his uncle's bedroom and returned with two new pairs of old fashioned white boxer shorts – still in their packaging – together with a white cotton pyjama suit and an old well worn grey jacket.

"Please Mr Marc, would you be so kind as to change into these clothes."

I went to the bathroom and did as requested. The boxer shorts, pyjama suit fitted fine, as did my black shoes. The jacket arms were slightly short.

I returned to the living room and Shariz was very pleased with the result. He pulled through the sleeves of the pyjama suit, so they could be folded back over the sleeves of the jacket. He then produced a black hat typically worn by older generations of his community.

"Mr Marc, remember that when walking, take smaller steps and stoop."

He passed me an old walking stick "I am afraid my uncle will have little use for this now. But my uncle would be happy to know that his clothes are being put to good use, by helping a friend of the family."

I merely smiled and said "Thank you."

"Now we must get rid of these clothes of yours Mr Marc."

"What are you going to do with them?" I asked.

"Put them in the nearest charity collection point." Shariz replied.

"Not my beautiful ski jacket," I implored "can't you put it with my other clothes in your brother's workshop?"

"I am most very sorry Mr Marc that is not possible. I must insist."

I shrugged my shoulders realising that Shariz and his brother had already taken great risks to help me. Any evidence to implicate them must be hidden or destroyed.

"What about the bicycle?" I asked.

"It is my cousin's son's birthday in a couple of days and he will be very grateful for such a gift."

I looked quizzical.

"By tomorrow it will be a completely different colour."

"A bit like me?" I laughed.

Shariz smiled politely.

"Can I ask one more favour please Shariz? A big one."

"What is it Mr Marc?" Shariz replied warily.

I held up my keys "Can you go into my flat and find my spare phone? It's in the cabinet drawer beside my bed."

Shariz didn't reply instantly, but after a moment or two he agreed that he would try.

We shook hands and then he left. It was quarter to twelve and my mind was turning towards Gerda's arrival later that day. I practised walking up and down the sitting room, trying to make my smaller gait more natural. I also thought about going into the bedroom of (old) Shariz to thank him personally, but thought better of it, in case the sight of his doppelganger walking towards him would give him another – potentially fatal – stroke.

It was twelve thirty when Shariz's brother returned from the shop.

"Very good, very good." He said when he saw me in his uncle's clothes. He also passed to me my spare mobile phone, which in fact was Paul van der Kohl's old phone.

I turned it on and immediately sent Gerda a text '*Hello my darling, hope journey OK. Using Paul's old phone. Call me when you land at Harwich. Love you xx*'.

# Friday Lunchtime
# Bethnal Green

The final item Shariz's brother pressed into my hands as I left the flat was his uncle's old gabardine raincoat, and the moment I walked outside I was very grateful for this afterthought. The weather for November might be mild, but in the linen suit I felt the cold immediately, and wished I was wearing my skiing undergarments.

I had been walking for about twenty minutes when Paul's mobile rang. I checked there was no-one in ear-shot and answered Gerda's call.

"Hello, my darling."

"Hello, Marc" came Gerda's soft reply "I can't wait to see you. I have just come through customs at Harwich, and if the traffic is good I might be at your flat before three o'clock."

"That's great my darling, you should beat the rush-hour."

"Why should I want to hit anything?" Gerda giggled. Her English, like Paul's and most of the Dutch nation, was very good, but sometimes the colloquial phrases might wrong foot her for an instant or two.

"Very funny," I replied "Gerda I have a surprise for you, we are going to stay in a hotel tonight rather than the flat. Is that OK?"

"Yes, that's fine. You are being very mysterious. I think I will like it, no?" There was the slightest doubt creeping into her voice.

"Can we meet at the entrance to Victoria Park? Do you remember how to get there?"

"I think so, but can you remind me please?"

"Certainly." And I gave her directions.

We were over the first hurdle, that we would not be staying at the flat, so I pushed on with the minutiae.

When I had finished giving directions, Gerda laughed. "That should be OK, I think, I just have to convert miles to kilometres."

I only hoped she would be in the same good humour when she saw me.

"Will we be seeing K-P, Jane and the children on Sunday?"

"Possibly not – it depends on the surprise." I answered truthfully, and then I thought how I might get in touch with K-P without giving away my whereabouts, and getting him dragged into this unholy mess.

My mind was wandering and Gerda picked up on it.

"Hello Marc, are you still there?"

"Yes my darling. I will be waiting at Victoria Park by quarter to three. Please drive carefully; I love you." I blew a kiss down the phone.

"Me too – chuss!" Gerda rang off.

I would have over an hour and a half before my rendezvous with Gerda. I was feeling nervous so I started walking towards Bethnel Green, trying to perfect my gait, and avoid walking into other pedestrians with the blurred vision caused by wearing the spectacles. I considered taking them off, but decided to persevere regardless. Another issue I needed to consider was how I should speak if anyone addressed me. I knew no other language beyond English and wondered if I should try an Asian accent. Speaking could lead me into difficulties, and perhaps the safest course of action would be to talk in a faux upper class clipped English accent, which would have been the vogue of Shariz's uncle's teachers some fifty plus years ago. With that sorted in my mind I was determined to try and contact K-P, as well as finding some warm underclothes.

After walking for another thirty minutes, I was in the heart of the street market on Bethnal Green Road, and so far my looks hadn't attracted a second glance from anyone. I came upon a stall selling cheap clothes, and found some thermal vests plus long-johns that my grandfather might have worn, and I purchased them. A couple of stalls beyond the clothing stall was a vendor of bags; I bought a cheap nylon bag for when I checked into the hotel, as they would expect to see some luggage, which at the moment only contained the underwear. The total outlay was under five pounds, but I had to be careful as I was running out of money, and withdrawing money from an ATM was not an option because it would be an easy way to alert the police to my whereabouts.

I found a café that also boasted cheap overseas telephone calls. It seemed to be populated by elderly people, who were unlikely to be the owners of mobile phones; therefore I did not look out of place. I ordered two vegetable bhajis and some naan bread with a cup of tea. The tea was milky, weak and already heavily sweetened, the way it was drunk in Northern India. The food and drink had a remarkable calming affect upon my stomach, as well as warming me up. I then purchased a two pound phone card and retreated to one of the booths at the back of the café. First I tried K-P's mobile number, but my call instantly transferred to his voice mail, I hung up without leaving a message. Next I tried his direct work number, and when it switched to his voice mail I pressed '0' before his recording finished, and was directed to the main switchboard.

"Can I help you?" The telephonist asked me.

"Hello, I have been trying to contact Mr Sethia, but I keep being transferred to his voice mail. Is he in today?" I asked innocently.

"I am sorry, but he is out of the office today."

"Will he be back on Monday?" I pressed.

"We do not know. Who is speaking please? One of his colleagues may be able to assist you?"

"Not to worry, it is only a rugby matter and it can wait until next week. Thank you." I hung up.

The next call was going to be much more difficult. I took a deep breath and dialled K-P's home number.

Jane picked it up on the second ring "Hello."

"Hello Jane." I spoke softly into the mouthpiece.

"I am sorry, you have the wrong number."

She hung up without saying another word.

"Shit!" I mumbled under my breath.

I guessed K-P was being watched, because usually Jane would have had no compunction to shout and bawl me out. I surmised that some one else was in the room and despite K-P's situation Jane had decided for whatever reason not to give me away.

"Shit and bugger." I swore to myself again, and I reached into the raincoat and pulled out my mobile phone. I turned it on but enabled the flight safe mode so it would not search for any networks. I looked at the call log and dialled the '01279' number that called me on at least two occasions the night Tony Eastwood died. The dial tone continued unanswered for thirty seconds, and just before I was about to hang up it was answered.

"Hello!" It was the voice of a young boy.

"Hello, could you help me? This phone number rang me and I do not know who called. Where are you?"

"Mister, why are you calling if you don't know who you are ringing?" The boy seemed very pleased with his logic.

"Because I am trying to find out who called me two days ago. Can you help me please?"

"It could'a been anyone."

"Why?" I asked.

" 'Cos, this is a public telephone!"

"Where are you now?" I tried a different tack.

"In Stortford o'course," he snorted "near Sainsbury's!" With that, he hung up.

My mind was spinning with the information I had gathered from my three phone calls. I went to the toilet in the café, and once there went into a cubicle, to put the thermal underwear beneath my other clothes.

I was back on Bethnal Green Road again convinced that K-P was being pestered by the police. Perhaps they were at his home, and that is why he wasn't at work. I trusted no-one else to talk to. Who else would want to kill Tony? The telephone call from the public call box to both mine and Tony's mobile reinforced my view that it wasn't a random killing. I didn't know Bishops Stortford particularly well, but I seemed to recall that the Sainsbury's store was quite close to the station, so it is quite possible that the killer made the telephone call. But why kill Tony? Whilst he was a stuck-up arrogant twit, that shouldn't be enough to get him killed. I also felt that the hastily arranged meeting with me was also connected with his death. Why? He had been insistent that we meet before his business trip to the USA, and he wanted to give me something. With Mércédès in Goa and Sir Hugh in London, Samuel would have known he was meeting me and he would have access to both mine and Tony's mobile telephone numbers.

"Samuel?" I said to myself and shook my head. Samuel and his family had been in the employ of Sir Hugh's family for many years, and Samuel was a big man but very gentle. I had never even heard him raise his voice and he certainly would not be a rival for Mércédès' affection. No it would not have been Samuel I reasoned. I wish I had kept Tony's mobile phone, to check the call log, to see whether he had spoken to anyone else about our meeting. Perhaps I should speak to Samuel to ask him?

"Don't be a fool." I said to myself.

The family would be grieving, and the loss of his future son-in-law would be weighing heavily on Sir Hugh, and our friendship and new job would be totally screwed unless I could prove it wasn't me who killed Tony.

Singapore was also now a very distant dream. The roller-coaster ride during the last week, made me feel giddy just thinking about what had happened to me. Then a horrible thought popped into my head. What if it was me they were meant to kill and Tony was just in the wrong place at the wrong time!

"Shit!" I said to myself again and I picked up my pace. I needed to get out of London. I had a plan how to do it, as long as Gerda agreed to be an accomplice to a suspected fugitive.

# Friday Afternoon
# Victoria Park

True to my word, I was at the entrance to Victoria Park by quarter to three, and there was no sign of Gerda. Victoria Park was bisected by Grove Road and I went into the western part of the park that contained flower beds, a lake with a fountain, and a café by the waterside. In the eastern part of the park were playing fields and tennis courts. I sat on a bench from where I could see the entrance to the park. The weak November sun was starting to fade and it would be dusk in an hour.

It was about quarter past three when I saw Gerda's silver coloured VW Golf pull up across the road from the entrance.

I dialled her number and was greeted with "So did I 'beat' you?"

"No, I have been here for a little while." I replied.

"Where are you?" She asked, and I could see her looking around for me.

Now it was going to be interesting "I am just walking towards you out of the park entrance."

"I cannot see you Marc. Are you making fun of me?"

"I am across the road from you."

"There is only an old man talking on the phone!" Gerda was starting to lose her sense of humour.

"That's me. I am in disguise." I said as I smiled at her.

I hung up and walked across the road, remaining in character.

Gerda wound down the window "No doubt you have a very good reason for this charade."

"Yes my darling." I put my hand through the open window and gently stroked her cheek in the way I knew she liked. She nuzzled against my hand and almost purred.

"Get in the car my darling."

Gerda unlocked the doors, and I had to go into the road to open the passenger door, as it was a left hand drive car.

"Where are we going?" Gerda asked after I planted a quick peck on her lips as I sat beside her.

She smelled gorgeous and I wanted to get to a hotel immediately, so we could say hello properly. First I needed to explain the reason I was in disguise, before we went anywhere, as there was a risk Gerda might turn the car around and go straight back to Holland.

"Pull over to that parking space for a few minutes, please." I pointed to a gap in the parked cars about twenty metres away.

Gerda pulled a face, but did as I requested.

When she had turned off the engine I held her hands in mine and started my tale of woe.

"Firstly Gerda I want to tell you that I love you so much, and want to marry you as soon as my divorce comes through."

Tears were starting to well up in Gerda's eyes "Yes Marc, I would love that too, but what about Singapore and Paul?"

"Singapore is the least of my problems. I am in trouble, very big trouble. That's why I am in disguise."

My hands were shaking now and it was Gerda's turn to reassure me, by squeezing my hands.

"What is it my darling?" She asked.

"I am wanted for questioning by the police in connection with the death of Tony Eastwood. I can promise you on my honour that I did not kill him."

Tears were now rolling down Gerda's cheeks.

"Why do they suspect you? When did he die?" Her questions were barely audible.

I reached forward finding tissues in the glove box. I offered one to Gerda, so she could wipe her eyes and blow her nose.

"It was Wednesday evening and I found him just after he had been killed."

I then told Gerda the whole story about my visit to Felixstowe; how Tony had practically demanded that I meet him before his business trip to the States, and I explained how I found him, as well as the two calls from a public phone in Bishops Stortford. I described in detail my escape from Bishops Stortford station, the kayak trip down the river, followed by the bicycle ride into London. Gerda eventually managed a smile when she heard I had used a bicycle, as she knew how much I detested cyclists.

I held my hand up and said "OK I might have second thoughts about bicycles in London."

I then told Gerda how Shariz warned me that the police were waiting for me in Hackney, and that Shariz had given me shelter last night.

"It was Shariz who suggested this disguise when I asked him if he could get me a passport."

"So that's why you couldn't use your telephone, in case the police could trace your call?" Gerda had caught on quickly and I nodded my head.

"Shariz's uncle is very unwell, and Shariz has leant me his uncle's passport for a couple of weeks, also these are his clothes. Gerda, can you help me? I would quite understand if you decide you can't, because aiding a fugitive could land you in a lot of trouble."

"I love you Marc, and if you say you did not kill Tony, I believe you." She gave me half a smile. "Why don't you explain everything to the police and let them investigate properly."

"I will do so in time," I promised "but I need some time to think things through. Also I want to speak with K-P but I can't get in touch with him. He wasn't at work today, and Jane hung up on me as soon as she recognised my voice on the phone, I think the police may have been at K-P's when I called."

"What can I do to help?" Gerda asked.

"Thank you. Firstly we need to go to a hotel. We will need two bedrooms; otherwise it will look very strange, as we are going to say that I am your father-in-law."

Gerda's smile widened as I explained my plan.

"We need to stay two nights in London and then I want to either go to my parents' house in Norfolk, or better still, go back with you to Holland."

Gerda sat quietly for a few moments before replying "Yes, coming with me to Holland would be better, because from what you have said I'd feel sure that the police will be watching your parents' house."

"Thank you my darling."

I then took another deep breath, and I outlined my theory that perhaps Tony was not supposed to be the victim, and perhaps I was supposed to be the target.

"What!" Gerda was obviously upset. "Marc, you are crazy. Who would want to kill you?" Gerda started the engine and said "It is good I am now here, because being alone has made you become paranoid. OK, where is this hotel?"

I directed Gerda towards the London Docklands only a couple of miles from Victoria Park. By four o'clock we were in the car park of the hotel.

"Can I put your jacket in my bag please? Otherwise I don't have any luggage which might look out of place."

Gerda nodded "Of course. And do not help me with my bags, old man!"

We walked into the hotel with Gerda holding the door for me, looking every inch the dutiful daughter-in-law. She went to the receptionist and asked whether they had two single rooms for two nights for herself and her father-in-law. The receptionist hardly looked at me, and studied his computer. After a few moments he answered that they had only one single room for Friday and Saturday.

We were just about to leave when he said "However we do have a suite with two bedrooms if you don't mind sharing with your father-in-law?"

"How much would it cost?" Gerda asked.

"It is unlikely to be wanted as a suite at this late stage, so I could let you have it for the cost of two single rooms."

"Father, is that alright for you?" Gerda asked me with a completely straight face.

I merely nodded for fear of laughing if I spoke. Absolutely perfect I thought to myself.

Within moments of being in the suite we were in each other's arms kissing deeply.

"Will this dye come off?" Gerda asked.

"Let's find out." I started to take my clothes off.

Our lovemaking was beautiful and a total distraction from the events of the past few days. Afterwards we lay on the top of my bed, with a large towel under me, in case the dye marked the sheets, falling asleep in each other's arms.

It was eight o'clock before we awoke and I was starving.

"Darling are you hungry?" I asked Gerda.

"Yes." She replied.

"What do you want to eat?"

"Well, I have just had an Indian so something different." Flouncing into the bathroom with a giggle before I could catch her. "You will have to be quicker than that Old Man!"

"We'll see" I replied.

When she came out of the bathroom I explained that I had very little cash, and I could not use an ATM, because the police might be watching my bank account.

"That's OK but we might just have to be frugal." Was her pragmatic reply.

We headed towards Limehouse and went to a gastro-pub owned by a well know TV personality chef. The food was beautifully prepared, but prices were more akin to restaurant prices than a typical pub menu, so we ate lightly. We were both very tired and so we returned to the hotel, and we were sound asleep by eleven o'clock.

# Saturday Morning Docklands

I slept right through the night until eight o'clock. Gerda was still snuggled against me, her cheek against my dyed chest. Although I couldn't feel my fingers, I did not want to move my arm for fear of waking her.

I looked down at Gerda; I didn't think I could go to Singapore without her, although that opportunity probably died with Tony. Unless I found out who killed Tony, Gerda and I would be apart for a much longer period, possibly in prison.

The first proper night's sleep since Tuesday had left me with cobwebs in my brain, and it was as though I was walking through treacle, in trying to think of my next steps. Gerda sighed and nuzzled even closer to me, and her slight change of position allowed me to free my arm, my fingers tingling with the sensation of the blood returning to my extremities. Gerda was very tired from her journey and was still fast asleep. She had given me a good tip when staying in hotels, always shut the door to the bathroom as most noise is transmitted through other guests running taps or flushing toilets.

I lay in the half-light and tried to make sense of the last seven days. A week ago I woke up in a police station, and I felt sure that the subsequent events were somehow connected to my beating, but I couldn't connect the dots. I wished I had stopped drinking when K-P left the Lamb last Friday.

"K-P! Where are you! I need to talk to you." I whispered quietly to myself, so as not to disturb Gerda.

I picked up the remote control that was lying on the cabinet beside the bed. I turned on the television and tuned into the satellite news channel, with the volume barely audible. I was waiting for the news at nine o'clock to see whether the hunt for me was gathering pace. The sports news item gave me an idea of how I might be able to get in touch and meet with K-P!

The sports news item was the first of the 2009 Autumn Rugby Internationals. It had now become a regular spot in the autumn when the Southern Hemisphere teams would embark upon a short tour to the Northern Hemisphere. Today's matches included an encounter between England against Australia at Twickenham. The news headlines came and went with no mention of a manhunt for Marcus Edge; I almost felt disappointed.

I was becoming restless to put my plan into action but as I went to leave the bed, Gerda pulled me towards her.

"Where do you think you are going my lover?"

It was gone ten o'clock before I made my second attempt to get out of bed. I picked up Paul's mobile and dialled K-P's home number, prefixed by '141', so the mobile number wouldn't show up straight away. I hoped that it was K-P, and not Jane, who answered. My fears were allayed when I heard K-P's voice at the other end of the phone.

"Hello."

"Hello K-P, its Bruce!" I shouted down the phone in the most appalling Australian accent.

When we were much younger and on rugby tours, we would spend the whole time speaking in awful Australian accents and we were all called 'Bruce' in homage to the famous Monty Python sketch.

"Hello Bruce" I was sure K-P knew it was me "how are you?"

"Gud mate. Don't s'pose you know of any tickets goin' spare for the game today?"

"No. Sorry Bruce."

"Shame. Are you goin' to watch it at the Albany as usual?"

The Albany was a pub just off Victoria Park, where K-P and I would often retreat to drink Guinness, and watch sport.

"That's the plan." K-P had received my message and would be able to meet me.

"If I don't lay my hands on a ticket I will see you there. Will Marc be there?"

I was probing for more information to get the lie of the land.

"No," K-P retorted immediately "Marc has a bit of a problem and wont' be there."

In those few words K-P confirmed that the police were still looking for me. The way he continued with the charade, the police were either in close proximity, or possibly listening in electronically.

Gerda had been slowly surfacing from her slumber whilst I was on the phone to K-P, and had heard only snippets of the conversation. I explained to her my plan. She was not convinced it was safe and she was nervous that I would be discovered, before I could clear my name.

"Gerda, my darling, when waking this morning I realised how precious you are to me," I held out my arms and drew her close to me "and I want us to spend the rest of our lives together; however, I need K-P's insight and input."

"Why K-P? You think the police are watching him. Isn't there anyone else?" Even for Gerda, who was usually so calm, this verged on a plea.

"Number one, I would trust him with my life. Number two, he's very intelligent and his naval training in analytics is invaluable. Number three, he knows the people involved."

I held Gerda for a few moments longer and she nodded her head. "Ok, I am going shopping whilst you go to the pub."

"It will just be orange juice for me, so I don't blow my disguise."

After a late breakfast, we spent the rest of the morning wandering around Canary Wharf buying a couscous salad for lunch. I had bought a heavyweight newspaper to see whether there was any more information about Tony's murder, but again there was nothing reported. Gerda left for the West End to embark upon her Christmas shopping, whilst I continued to browse through the newspaper. The sports pages occupied most of my time, particularly the rugby where Australia were clear favourites, because England were halfway through their rebuilding process in time for the next world cup in 2011.

I flicked through the financial pages, and almost at once, three articles seemed to jump out of the page at me. The first was a story about a potential hijacking of a vessel off the Somali coast by pirates. What made the story interesting was the fact that they were unsuccessful, because the vessels were guarded by highly trained security officers employed by Masterson Shipping, for all their vessels operating in the region. The journalist reporting the story highlighted the fact that the Suez Canal authorities would not allow armed security guards on the vessel whilst in the canal.

There had been a vicious catfight and a number of the Somali pirates had been killed. In the next column was an associated article about Masterson Shipping expanding into the African and Asian regions. Also how important the security of their vessels would be to succeed with these plans. The third item was that Lloyd's of London was setting up a taskforce, to investigate the mysterious disappearances of a number of vessels in the past twelve months, and that this investigation was the result of reinsurers threatening to withdraw cover. I felt sure I saw the hand of Neptune Re, and Eric Jones in this move, but then a pang of disappointment as I realised he had probably heard of my predicament and given up on me.

I went into the bathroom to reapply my disguise. I was now becoming familiar with the dark face looking back at me. I donned the spectacles, raincoat, picked up the walking stick and left to meet with K-P with a very queasy feeling in my stomach.

# Saturday Afternoon
# The Albany

I arrived at the Albany about an hour before the game was due to start. It was already busy with a local rugby team who played in Victoria Park. They had arranged an early kick-off, so they could watch the first international of the season. It suited me that there was a big crowd, as I could buy my orange and lemonade, and retreat quietly to the corner without being noticed. From where I was seated, I had a reasonable view of the television and a very good view of the entrance, with the toilets close to where I was sitting.

The pub was rapidly filling up and the noise level was increasing by the minute. This was enhanced when a group of itinerant Australians entered the pub. The bragging started about who would be the eventual winners, with ubiquitous wagers, most of which involved buying rounds of drinks. The atmosphere was fantastic, and I was dying to be on my feet drinking beer, and joining in with the banter. It was about ten minutes before kick-off when K-P came into the Albany.

He flashed a smile at the landlady and within a few seconds he had a pint of Guinness in his massive paw. The pub had obviously pre-poured a number of them, to allow the dark ale to settle properly, before topping it up for the next customer. He almost immediately started a conversation with a group near the bar. Not once had his eyes scanned the room to look for me, which instantly put me on notice that all was not as it seemed. I looked around the room but nothing, or nobody, looked out of place. There certainly wasn't anyone wearing a windcheater to cover their police uniform.

I looked around the room again, much more carefully this time, and searched for people watching K-P rather than the television screens. The teams were now on the pitch, and the national anthems were about to be played. The pub noise reached a cacophony when the supporters of England and Australia each sang their own anthems. Although outnumbered by two to one, the Australians pretty much matched the English, which I hoped was not a sign for the rugby contest which was to follow.

As best I could with Shariz's uncle's spectacles, I guessed that there were at least twelve possible candidates for police watchers in the crowd, because they either didn't join in the singing or they weren't drinking beer. I decided at some point I needed to make contact with K-P. I waited until about fifteen minutes into the first half; England had gone into an early lead through a penalty and drop goal, but it was still early days with both teams probing, to ascertain any potential weaknesses in the other side.

I got to my feet using my walking stick and tottered over to the bar. I bought my second orange and lemonade, and when I started my return journey, I walked into K-P.

He looked at me and I said "I am most terribly sorry."

"Not a problem." K-P responded but he didn't recognise me.

"I am sorry for asking but could you help me back to my seat."

"Certainly, and let me take your drink for you."

I walked back to my seat and to the onlookers it must have seemed only natural for a younger Asian to be helping an elderly Asian gentleman.

"Thank you." I said.

When we reached my table I then feigned a stumble at which point K-P had to bend down to help me. When his face was close to mine I quickly whispered "Half time in the toilets."

K-P was a terrific actor; he didn't flinch, or even give me a second glance. I pretended to resume watching the match, which was impossible through the spectacles. I looked over the lenses, or out of the side of my eye, and established that none of the twelve possible watchers were paying particular attention to me or K-P. The first half was inconclusive with the young England still narrowly ahead, adding another penalty, after Australia had scored a converted try. As soon as the whistle went I headed for the toilets, and occupied one of the toilet cubicles. I went in but held the door slightly ajar, so I could see when K-P headed for the toilet. He was the next person and I swung open the door and grabbed him.

With the door locked I felt we had at least two minutes before K-P would be missed.

"Marc, it is a brilliant disguise" K-P started "and you will need it, because you are in very deep shit."

"I didn't kill him K-P."

"No you may not have done but the evidence against you is pretty overwhelming."

"What do they know?" I asked.

"Well they know that Tony was going on a business trip to the States, and suddenly he became agitated whilst he was at The Hall, and hastily arranged to meet someone at Bishop's Stortford Station. Samuel, Sir Hugh's chauffeur, wasn't certain but believed it was you."

"Anything else?" I asked.

"They are watching your flat...."

"I know" I interjected "Shariz told me. He and his brother helped me with the disguise – also I have Shariz's uncle's passport."

"The police questioned me on Friday, asking if I had seen you since Wednesday, which I answered truthfully no. They have been keeping our flat and telephone under surveillance, in case you try to contact me."

"Do they know about Gerda?" I asked.

"No, I don't think so. Why?" K-P was curious.

"She's going to take me to Holland, or my parents' house."

"Avoid Norfolk. Joshua, your brother, has tipped the police off that your parents are away."

"Damn." Then I added "I think you might have been followed."

"Yes, I think so too." K-P confirmed.

"I need to talk to you properly tomorrow. Gerda and I are staying as father-in-law and daughter-in-law at a hotel in Docklands."

K-P raised his eyes but said nothing.

"Can you take your bicycle and go for your normal Sunday morning exercise via Docklands?"

"I suppose so." K-P replied.

"OK if you could be in the car park by eight-thirty that would be fantastic. I think we will need at least an hour.

Now you better get back to the bar in case your minders suspect something is amiss."

"See you tomorrow Marc."

He gave me a man-hug.

"K-P, be careful what you say in the flat," K-P cocked an eye, "the police might be bugging it."

I didn't care K-P thinking I was paranoid – I was on the run.

He left the toilet and I locked it immediately and then used the facilities before returning to my seat. K-P was in the process of finishing a pint of Guinness; probably to support the reason he needed the toilet for so long.

The game had restarted on a high note, and within a few moments, there was an almighty melee between the two scrums, with fists being thrown in every direction. During this distraction, my attention was drawn to a scrawny scruffy looking student-type and his companion – a woman who was dressed smarter then him. Their gazes were fixed on K-P, and they had not joined in any of the cheering or jeering, which followed the award of a penalty against England. I hadn't considered this couple earlier because they both had beer in their glasses, but now I could see that neither of them had drunk more than a sip. At that moment the woman stood up and went outside the pub. Her companion picked up his drink, tipped the glass to his lips, but drank nothing. 'Bingo' I thought to myself and then felt a shiver come over me, as I considered what the police might be planning to do.

Originally I thought that I would stay to the end of the game, and then slip out with everyone else, but now I decided I should get out of the Albany as soon as possible.

With one of the sets of eyes missing, now would be as good a time as ever. I picked up my raincoat, folded it as small as possible, before standing up and returning to the toilets. Beside the ladies toilet was a door marked 'Private'. I tried it and thankfully it was open. I guessed it led to the kitchen, and I was not mistaken. No food was being served during the match, so the kitchen was deserted, and in three steps I was outside the back door. As I came round to the front of the pub I stopped in my tracks, as I saw the woman talking to two men in a large family saloon. I felt sure the decision to leave now was a good one, and walked away from the Albany as slowly as possible, resisting the urge to run!

# Saturday Evening/
# Sunday Morning Docklands

I was back in our hotel room in just over half an hour, in time to watch the post match interviews on television. Australia had won, through another try and two penalties in the second half, which the English management felt was a stepping-stone on the way to successfully rebuilding the team for the next World Cup. Gerda hadn't returned from her shopping jaunt to the West End, and I decided to test the strength of the dye by having a hot bath. I felt shivery, and I would not be surprised if I had caught a chill, given the night on the river on Wednesday plus the flimsiness of the clothes I was now wearing.

I finished my bath and the dye had remained. Still Gerda had not returned so I climbed into bed and, despite having the television on, I was sound asleep in minutes.

I was aware of someone gently stroking my hair and I opened my eyes to see Gerda propped on one arm lying on the bed beside me. I pulled her towards me and kissed her deeply, ready to take matters further but Gerda pulled away,

"We have time for that later. First let me show you the fruits of my shopping trip."

I barely stifled a yawn with "Lovely darling."

Gerda gave me an old fashioned look and continued by putting at least ten bags of different shapes and sizes on the bed.

"How did you manage to bring those back all by yourself?" I asked.

"By taxi, and a very nice man he was too."

It was my turn to give an old fashioned look.

A lot of the bags contained either foodstuffs that Gerda couldn't buy in Holland, or presents from Hamley's for children of friends. Neither Paul nor Gerda had children, or siblings, and their parents had died some years previously. Gerda had treated herself to clothes, which she said were much cheaper than in Holland.

"For Paul, I have bought him lots of talking books on CD."

Gerda was convinced that Paul would recover and the doctors, who monitored his life signs, confirmed that there was brain activity but could not rule out that there might be brain damage.

There still remained three large bags.

"What are in these ones?" I asked Gerda.

"They contain your presents and I think they will probably be of better use to you now than at Christmas."

Gerda was smiling as she was speaking, and was obviously very pleased with herself. The first bag contained long armed and long legged underwear made of silk.

"They will keep you warm in the winter and cool in the summer," Gerda was very pragmatic "especially if you have to wear your disguise for some time yet."

The next bag held similar clothes to those I had borrowed from Shariz's uncle but they were darker in colour and heavier in weight, much more suited to autumn and winter.

The last bag Gerda passed to me saying "I know how much you like your overcoat, and you will miss your ski-jacket, but you need to keep warm."

The bag contained a thigh length quilted coat, that in normal circumstances I would not have considered wearing but in the present situation would be ideal.

"Thank you so much my darling," as I held Gerda in my arms "I love you so much."

"Food!" Gerda said.

"Food!" I replied and we ordered Indian take-away from one of the numerous restaurants that were advertising in the foyer of the hotel.

The food arrived and we feasted until we were replete. We ordered a film through the 'box-office' but were both asleep before it had finished.

I was awake early on Sunday morning. During her shopping trip Gerda had bought me a beard trimmer, but what remained was not as dark as my hair which had been dyed, and I made a note that we needed to obtain more hair dye. What I did notice, because of my darker coloured skin, was that some of my un-dyed beard was turning grey. I should not be surprised, given the stress of the past eighteen months, and the last week in particular.

Dressed in my new clothes by half past seven, I wanted to show off to Gerda, but she was still asleep. I sat down at the desk, and used the hotel's stationary to write some notes, before meeting with K-P. Hopefully this would help organise my thoughts. I jotted down various salient points that had occurred to me over the past eight days:

1. *Eric Jones Neptune Re*
2. *Beaten up*
3. *Flat burgled (nothing taken as passport found)*
4. *Job offer in Singapore*
5. *Captain Hennessey*
6. *Meeting with Tony – why?*
7. *Public telephone*
8. *Masterson ship repels pirates?*

I was not sure why I had written the last item, but somehow I felt it significant. I sat at the desk staring at the list. I closed my eyes and tried to re-create the events of Friday the previous week in my mind. There was still something just beyond my consciousness. I could sense it rather than visualise it in my mind's eye. The more I tried to concentrate, the more it felt out of reach; it was as though it was dancing beyond my senses, like two magnets destined never to touch.

Gerda was stirring and I went and sat on the edge of the bed and lightly brushed her lips with mine.

"Good morning my sweetheart." I whispered to Gerda.

"Hmm-m-m! Come back to bed." She purred, lifting the covers revealing her lithe naked body.

"I really want to, but K-P should be here in fifteen minutes and I want to meet him downstairs, before bringing him up here."

Gerda feigned a sulk and pulled the sheet up around her neck.

"Off you go in your new clothes then," she smiled "as I need to have a shower and be dressed before he arrives."

I retrieved the spectacles and walking stick from the other bedroom and descended to the ground floor, where I walked slowly towards reception. A young Asian girl was at the desk.

"Good morning Miss." I said in a clipped English accent.

"Good morning sir." She replied.

"My son-in-law is visiting me in a few minutes and we wish to have tea and coffee in our suite. Is that possible?"

"Yes sir. I will call room service and have it sent to your suite in ten minutes. How many teas and coffees, sir?"

"Two coffees and one pot of tea please."

"Any pastries or croissants?"

"No thank you, we have a large family meal later today." I lied fluently, giving background as to why we were staying in the hotel for the weekend.

It was a sunny but crisp cold morning. There had been an overnight frost, and the windscreens in the car park were in need of de-icing before the vehicles could be driven safely. I glanced at my wrist where my yacht-master watch used to sit, to be confronted by my cheap sports watch, and I checked my mobile phone. It was just before half past eight, when K-P arrived.

He was dressed in a dark blue track suit, and he had obviously been pushing himself quite hard, as he was sweating heavily.

"M-morning!" He gasped.

"Thanks for coming K-P."

I grasped his hand tightly, maintaining the father-in-law and son-in-law charade.

"I am sure I was being followed at the beginning."

"Have you lost them?" My eyes were darting around the environs.

"I am pretty sure I did," K-P had recovered his breath and had a huge smile back on his face "I went through Victoria Park and exited over the Hertford Union Canal at the south east corner. I then doubled back through the quiet roads behind Roman Road, before coming down the cycle path on the Regents Canal to Limehouse Basin, and then to here."

"Bravo."

K-P's smile flattened slightly for an instant "I think the police were lying in wait for you at the Albany yesterday."

"They were;" I confirmed "there were at least two inside the pub, taking more of an interest in you than the game, with a car load of plain clothes heavies outside. I slipped out through the kitchen, before the second half was over, and went out round the back.

"Pretty cool.." K-P was impressed.

"How long can you spare?" I asked.

"About an hour." He replied.

"Did you bring a mobile?" I enquired.

"Yes."

"Turn it off" K-P cocked his eyebrow "because they may try and call it, and even if you do not answer it, they can potentially track the signal of the phone."

K-P did as bid. We walked over to the entrance of the car park, where he was able to padlock his trusty titanium steed.

Within a couple of minutes, K-P was in the middle of a big bear hug from Gerda. I could think of no-one who didn't like K-P, and wondered how far he could progress in life, if he had a mind to do so. Then again, that was part of his innate charm, the fact that he was not pushy and he was besotted by his family.

"K-P, can you help Marc?" Gerda asked K-P.

"I will try Gerda but he is in big trouble." K-P said with a solemn face to emphasise the gravity of the situation.

There was a knock at the door. We all turned at the same time, but I allayed their fears by saying I had ordered tea and coffee. Gerda answered the door, and the refreshments were brought in by a spotty youth needing a shave.

Settled into an armchair, with a cup of tea, K-P asked "So what happened on Wednesday in Bishop's Stortford?"

"I don't know K-P. I was over in Felixstowe during the day on an errand for Eric Jones of Neptune Re. The trains were buggered up, so I took a bus to Stansted Airport. Tony called to say he needed to talk to me and give me something to my advantage. He seemed OK, not agitated, and we agreed to meet at Bishops Stortford Station where he would join the train to London with me."

I took a gulp of coffee and continued "When the train stopped he wasn't to be seen, despite me talking to him only a few minutes earlier. I got off the train to look for him, and found him in the waiting room, dead!"

I explained to K-P how both my and Tony's phones were called by the same Bishop's Stortford number, just as the police arrived, which I subsequently discovered was from a public phone not far from the station.

"Hmm," was K-P's response followed by "how was he killed?"

"I don't know. There wasn't any blood, and his head wasn't caved in. K-P I think that possibly the killer was after me, and Tony was just in the wrong place, at the wrong time."

"Possibly," said K-P "but doubtful. I think you were the target, and Tony was the bait."

"To kill me."

"Or to discredit you, and get you out of the way," K-P refilled his cup "and perhaps things just went wrong with Tony. We need to know how he was killed."

"What have the police said to you about Tony's death? Why have they not released more details to the press?"

"They're playing their cards very close to their chest. All they are saying is that they want to talk to you about Tony's death, and the fact that you ran away from the scene has made you their number one suspect. By the way, how did you get away?"

"By kayak and bicycle" I answered and K-P laughed, spluttering tea.

"A bicycle!"

"Yes, a bicycle!"

I filled in the details of my escape bringing him up to yesterday when we met at the Albany. He sat quietly for a few moments.

"K-P, I think everything that has happened since the Lamb eight days ago, is somehow connected."

I then proceeded to go through what had happened each day meticulously. K-P closed his eyes and far from tuning out I knew he was listening intently to each word, analysing and storing the facts, so he could recall them later.

I finished with "So can you fathom out anything from what I have told you?"

"Let me think for a couple of days. So what are you going to do next?" K-P asked me.

"I am going to write a letter to the police explaining everything, and then later this afternoon I will accompany

Gerda back to Holland, on the evening ferry." I said smiling at Gerda.

"Be careful," K-P was addressing Gerda "don't let him drag you into his mess."

Gerda replied "His mess is my mess."

Gerda planted a kiss on my cheek.

"K-P" I handed him a slip of paper "this is my mobile number."

"It's not a UK number."

"Correct, its Paul's old mobile," I continued "please do not phone it from yours or Jane's mobiles. Nor from your home or office number, the police might be keeping tabs on you, but please call me if you have any ideas or clues."

K-P was nodding his head "Aye, aye, Captain."

"Also can you see if there is any more information about the Masterson ship that was attacked by Somalian pirates?"

K-Ps eyebrows were working overtime.

"What I would like to know is what the ship was carrying as cargo, and where it was bound, including any intermediate stops?"

"Is that all?" K-P asked.

"For the time being, yes thank you."

"OK" K-P stood up "I had better be going before the police get too annoyed."

Gerda had a bag for K-P "These are Christmas presents for the children; I thought we were having lunch with you and Jane today. What shall I do with them?"

"Leave them with Reception saying I will pick them up this evening when I have my car."

K-P then gave Gerda a big hug and she kissed him on his cheek.

"Look after her Marc," as he hugged me "or you will have me to answer to, and good luck - you'll need it."

# Sunday Afternoon
# Harwich

After K-P left, I spent over an hour composing not one but two letters, on blank stationary. The first was a simple note to John Eastwood saying I did not kill Tony, and I would do my best to discover what did happen for the sake of both Tony and myself.

The second letter was much longer. It was a written account of what I had told K-P, almost word for word, addressed to Sergeant Smithson at Bishopsgate Police Station. I left out the current disguise and how Shariz and Gerda were helping me. I ended the letter by saying I was going to try and solve Tony's killing myself, but could the police look at the timings of:

*When Tony bought his ticket?*
*What time did the train from Stansted Airport arrive at Bishops Stortford?*
*What time were the Bishops Stortford police called to say something was amiss?*
*Who else went through the ticket office?*
*Who could have been on the platform?*

Gerda and I checked out of the hotel by eleven, leaving the bag of presents with the receptionist, together with a ten pound note for their trouble. We drove into the City, posted the first letter through the door of JPG, and handed the second one in at Bishopsgate Police Station. By noon, we were heading out of London, on the A12 towards East Anglia.

I knew Gerda was nervous about the ferry crossing, because she would alternate between long quiet periods, or incessant chatting about her friends and colleagues. I tried to ease the tension by asking her to give me a verbal sketch of each person she mentioned. We stopped at a restaurant north of Chelmsford for lunch, during which I cast my mind back to the previous Sunday, and my trip to Felixstowe with Sir Hugh.

What I was appreciating over the past few days was how invisible I was to other people. Wherever we encountered people, they would engage with Gerda. At first I thought it was just because she was young and good looking; but when Gerda said she wanted a table for herself and her father-in-law, the waitress looked straight through me. Perhaps it was because I was looking old, Asian, or a combination of the two.

We ate quickly and were heading towards Harwich again, and we arrived at the ferry port an hour before the ferry departed at five o'clock. We walked into the terminal and Gerda, with my passport in hand, requested an additional one way ticket, for her father-in-law. The Customer Services adviser issued the ticket, and didn't even seem to check the passport photograph likeness to me. So far so good. We returned to the car, proceeded to check-in which was accomplished in five minutes, and we rolled past the UK customs booth. There seemed to be little interest in people leaving the country, nearly all the efforts were centred on people coming into the United Kingdom. The Dutch customs booth was only fifty metres beyond the disinterested UK official. The Dutch official took the two passports, before asking Gerda something in their – seemingly - unintelligible tongue. Gerda replied quickly and confidently. Passports returned, we were waved through, and drove towards the holding area prior to boarding the ferry.

"What was the problem?" I asked.

"No problem" she replied "they just wanted to know why it had been such a short trip."

"And?"

"I told them truthfully that it was for Christmas shopping."

"Nothing about me?" I persisted.

"No nothing." Gerda smiled.


My theory about the invisibility of older Asian men was receiving further credibility. Whilst dusk started to descend we sat in the car chatting. We were on view to the world at large, and needed to maintain the father-in-law and daughter-in-law charade; although the conversation was far from innocent. This was brought to an abrupt end when Gerda's mobile phone rang.

"Ja?" Gerda said answering the call. The same word was repeated several times before she ended the call.

After the call had ended her eyes were moist, and I thought she was about to burst into tears.

"Gerda, what's the matter?" I asked.

"It's Paul," she gave a very small smile "his nursing home has my number with instructions to call me if there is any change in his condition."

Before I said anything she continued.

"His blood pressure and respiration have been unsteady today."

"Oh, shit!" I swore under my breath.

"The problem is that this has happened before, but this is the third time in the last two weeks."

Tears were now rolling down her cheeks. I wanted to take her in my arms and hug her tight. She sniffed, and I pulled a tissue from the glove box.

"It could be potentially good news as well as bad," she whispered while wiping her eyes "the doctors say that it might be associated with an increase in his brain activity. I have already made arrangements to see Paul tomorrow afternoon. Will you come with me please Marc?"

"Of course I will my darling." I replied squeezing her hand.

It was dark outside and we listened to the radio. I wanted to hear the post mortem following the rugby the previous day. Unusually the British sports press were being kind to the England team, saying it had been a spirited display, and a number of positive aspects pointed to the re-building of the team being on track. The expectation for the following week was much higher, when the visitors were the Argentine Pumas, before the final showdown of the season against the New Zealanders. I hoped that I would still be at liberty to watch both games.

The cars in front of us began to show signs of moving just before half past four, and we were seated on the ferry by a quarter to five. The majority of vehicles were lorry drivers, and the public areas of the ferry were less than half empty. We found two comfortable armchairs and within thirty minutes of the ferry leaving Harwich we were both asleep.

The North Sea was behaving itself, with the result that the crossing was smooth, and uneventful. We docked just after two o'clock in the morning, and were away from the Hook of Holland by half past two, heading towards Amsterdam.

# Monday Late Afternoon
# St Bartholomew's

We slept until midday on Monday, and for the first time since Friday, we were able to relax in the privacy of Gerda's flat. It was purpose built on the outskirts of Old Amsterdam, a warm functional building, where the occupants were able to maintain their privacy yet share a community spirit. We typically wore very few clothes in the flat, and now was no different, despite my dyed body. Upon waking we made love intermittently for two hours, only punctuated by food, drink and bathing.

We dressed and drove to St Bartholomew's Nursing Home, which was only ten minutes from Gerda's flat, near one of the main canals of Amsterdam. The appointment with the consultant was a weekly ritual. Paul was under constant supervision from the nursing staff, and the consultant would visit Paul at least twice a week, unless there was a change in his condition. Before leaving Gerda's flat we had debated whether I should continue to dress as an old man, and we decided that might require more explanation, so I borrowed some of Paul's old clothes. I was simply introduced as a friend from England, without any embellishment, and none was sought.

The consultant was polite and following my introduction continued the conversation in fluent English, with only a trace of an accent.

"You speak excellent English, doctor." I remarked.

"Yes, for a while I studied at Queen Mary's College, in London." He replied.

I was on the verge of saying that was close to where I lived, but hung back, not wanting to volunteer too much information. He turned to Gerda and explained that he had been contacted twice by the nursing staff over the weekend, and he had visited Paul on Sunday to assess the situation for himself.

"His blood pressure and respiration has now returned to normal, but both had been clearly disrupted over the weekend, and" he paused for a second "Paul had been moving his legs."

"Oh my God!" Gerda said with her hands clenched to my arm.

"Now, we have been here before, Ms van der Kohl," the doctor was clearly trying to manage Gerda's emotions "and we should not get our hopes up."

The doctor was probably no more that two, or three years, older than myself. He had a kindly manner, which was matched by his grey eyes, which held Gerda's gaze when talking to her. A moment passed, before the doctor continued.

"If nothing else changes I will visit Paul as normal on Wednesday, but have asked the nurse to contact me, even if there is the slightest change in his condition."

He smiled at Gerda, shook my hand, and departed on his rounds.

Paul was in a private room. Whilst Gerda had tried to personalise the room, with mementos from her and Paul's past, the smell of the building was unmistakably that of a medical facility. From a young age I had always had an aversion to such places, and I tried to dismiss that memory, supplanting it with the thought that medical advances were being made all the time. Against one of the walls opposite the bed was a table, which had a CD-Midi hi-fi system, which Gerda would use to play the talking books to Paul. On the wall were various framed photographs of Paul and Gerda as children, some with their parents, and one of their parent's wedding. What surprised me was that there was a large photograph of Paul, Gerda and myself taken after a particularly strenuous tennis match when Gerda and I had beaten Paul and his girlfriend. Paul's girlfriend had taken the photograph and I was hugging Gerda, whilst looking at the camera lens, but Gerda was looking at me. The tennis match was only a few weeks before the JPG garden party at The Hall, when I met Mércédès. Gerda had only just recently left university. Now with hindsight, I could see in the photograph that Gerda's feelings for me were much stronger than as a tennis partner.

I walked across to Gerda, pulled her towards me, whilst planting a light kiss on her lips saying "I love you!"

I looked at Paul and was shocked at how pale and thin he looked. It had been nearly five months since the last time I had seen him, and he had spent over eighteen months in bed. His tan, that he was so proud of, had gone. His skin seemed almost translucent. Also, the lack of good food, fine wines and buckets of beer had meant he had lost weight. His appearance was accentuated by the neon light. As with every bed in the home, a large cross with Jesus Christ was on the wall above his head.

"His eyes reacted to the light!" I exclaimed when the neon lights were switched on.

Gerda smiled "Yes, this has started in the last few weeks, and coincided with changes in his blood pressure and breathing patterns."

Gerda walked over to the CD player and selected a Dire Straits CD and started playing it. Dire Straits were one of Paul's favourite bands, and Gerda played it endlessly, when she visited Paul.

"This is what I have been mentioning to you Marc."

Gerda was busying herself tidying-up and re-arranging the few personal items in Paul's room.

"You know it could be a negative sign?" I tried to say as lightly as possible.

She nodded with a muffled "Yes."

"So what do you do when you come to visit Paul?" I said trying to change the subject.

"I come at least twice a week," I knew Gerda's routine but wanted her to keep talking "usually I come after work, and I bring my supper with me. I perch on the bed and talk to him about what has happened in the days since my last visit, my friends at work but mostly I talk about you and me."

I slipped my arm through Gerda's and sat beside her on the bed.

"Last week it was all about us, and whether I should go with you to Singapore. I told him that I would be seeing K-P, Jane and the children."

"Sorry I have messed all that up." I said apologetically.

"It's not your fault my darling," she continued "and after my supper I tend to put on one of the talking books, or tune into BBC Radio 4. Sometimes we listen to the sport on BBC Radio 5."

A quiet calm descended on the room until the next Dire Straits track started.

"Gerda I need to do some serious thinking over the next few days. What if I come and do it here, while you are at work?" I suggested.

Immediately Gerda's face brightened up "That would be lovely. Paul would really appreciate it. I know what he did to implicate you in his mess was wrong, but you're his best friend Marc."

"I know, Gerda," and I looked at the body in the bed which was a faint shadow of the *bonne vivant* that was Paul van der Kohl "I know."

# Tuesday Morning & Afternoon
## St Bartholomew's

We returned home after the visit to Paul, via a takeaway restaurant serving a variety of Asian food, and I was desperate for spicy food. Spicy food releases endorphins, so it can be more than habitual and cravings develop; if that was the case then I was hooked! Mércédès, because of her mother's Goanese background, could eat spicy food but chose not to. Gerda on the other hand had difficulty with spicy food but loved it. And I loved her for it, as well as all the other differences from Mércédès.

Gerda had an early start on Tuesday so we retired early to bed after our meal, but it took time before sleep enveloped us, and then we did so entwined with each other following our amour. Before Gerda left in the morning she gave me a spare set of keys to the flat, as well as the lock for her bicycle; my liking for the two-wheeled vehicles was certainly improving. I was mobile, and once out and about it was a delight to cycle in a city that separated bicycles from motorised vehicles, and more importantly pedestrians! Perhaps my dislike towards bicycles in London should be better directed against the City planners, Police and Local Authorities, rather than the cyclists who were merely competing for their own space.

Paul's room at St Bartholomew's faced the east, and when I arrived it was bathed in winter sunshine, and I wasn't alone. There were two men bent over Paul, and I recognised one of them to be the doctor, whom Gerda and I met the previous day. They turned in unison as I entered the room, and I asked them whether there was a problem.

The doctor answered very quickly "No, no" adding "this is Peter, the night nurse who called me to say that Paul had a restless night again. I asked them to let me know whenever there is a change in his condition."

I nodded and was aware of Peter the night nurse staring at me intently. I felt uncomfortable and turned to talk to him, which I hoped would break his gaze.

"Does his restlessness happen at any particular time?" I thought to be a sensible question.

Peter smiled which lessened the intensity of his stare.

"No, he can become restless night or day, but we are monitoring it to see whether there is any pattern." His voice was heavily accented which I guessed to be Afrikaans.

The consultant added "But there is no pattern yet."

I turned to the consultant and asked him the question that I had refrained from asking Gerda.

"Are these changes good signs or bad signs?"

"I really don't know," admitted the consultant "the brain is a very complicated organ. Well, your presence here has saved me a call to Ms van der Kohl, if you could let her know. I must be going now."

The consultant left the room leaving Peter with Paul and myself.

Peter was straightening Paul's bed-linen when I asked him "Peter, do you play rugby?"

"Yes, why do you ask?" He replied.

"I thought we may have played against each other?"

He looked at me strangely "I haven't played since I have been in Europe, and not many coloureds play rugby in South Africa."

'Shit' I thought to myself, I am supposed to be of Asian extraction, and being in Holland I have let my guard down on the first day.

Peter left the room and on his way out, he said "I am going off duty in thirty minutes, and I will look in again before I finish."

"Thanks." I said.

I familiarised myself with the room and went to Paul's CD collection, selecting a David Bowie compilation album, and as it played I sat on his bed wondering what life Paul could expect if he regained consciousness. Would they imprison him after eighteen months in a coma? Would he care? Would he remember anything?

I decided I needed a cup of coffee. I looked around the room, but Paul had no need of a kettle, so I went in search of a coffee machine. As I walked down the carpeted corridor towards the nurses' station I could hear Peter was on the phone. At the mention of Paul's name I slowed my pace trying to listen to what was being said. The conversation was quite animated, and could have been either Dutch, or Afrikaans. I had no way of telling the difference. I knew that Afrikaans developed from Dutch, in the same way as Canadian French had developed from French.

I didn't want Peter to know I had overheard the conversation, so I retreated back to Paul's room, opened the door then closed it again quite loudly and returned to the corridor. Peter had heard the door and looked up from behind the nurses' station, terminating his telephone call.

"Hi," I asked jauntily "can I get a coffee?"

"Ja," Peter answered "there's a machine near the toilets." He pointed down another corridor.

"Thanks."

"It costs nothing." He added.

"Great." I said as I passed the desk.

A few minutes later I was back in Paul's room, and thought I was being overly sensitive, deciding that Peter's telephone call was probably just a report on the various patients' conditions. I turned off the CD player and started to talk to Paul.

"Well, my friend, I am really up shit creek now. The police in England believe I killed Tony Eastwood."

"Why is that? I hear you asking."

I continued my monologue giving Paul a blow by blow account of what had happened over the previous ten days. As I did so I asked myself aloud various questions, and as I did so I found the piece of paper where I had written the same questions, at the hotel in London.

It was nearly twelve o'clock by the time I had finished my monologue, I had been interrupted twice, and first it was Peter checking Paul's blood pressure and respiration. The second break was my further need for caffeine, during which I met Peter's replacement, a large middle aged lady wearing spectacles with thick lenses, and her grey coloured hair in a neat bob. She came into the room only a few minutes after I had finished my story to Paul, and I took the opportunity to go in search of some lunch. The weather had deteriorated, the wind blowing hard, and sleet was falling. I was pleased that I had worn my new quilted coat, although it would not resist the rain if it persisted.

I left the bicycle at the nursing home, and walked in search of a café, or sandwich shop. I had to walk for ten minutes, before I found anything, and during my search for lunch I had the distinct sensation that I was being followed. I stopped at a jewellers shop pretending to view the window display, whilst in fact I was trying to use the window as a mirror; I couldn't see anything untoward. I found a small shopping mall, and went in the front of a clothes shop, and exited through the back. In the middle of the mall was a fast food restaurant, where I bought myself chicken and chips, and sat at a table in the middle of the mall. When I had finished, I made my way to the toilet, and remained in a cubicle for twenty minutes. No-one came into the toilet in that time, and when I returned to the mall, most of the faces I had memorised before visiting the toilet, had changed. I relaxed and tried calling K-P at work, to be told that he was out of the office, still in Lloyd's of London. I glanced at my watch and realised that whilst it was lunchtime in Holland, the UK was an hour behind, and the middle of core underwriting hours.

The weather had deteriorated further during my lunch in the mall, the icy rain and sleet was making the conditions underfoot slippery. The number of pedestrians had reduced, and my sense of being followed lifted, as I convinced myself that it was only my paranoia.

Paul's room was warm with a Dire Straits song coming from the CD player. The nurse must have moved my papers, whilst checking upon Paul and putting on the music, as they were neatly piled on the table. I waited until the end of the track before turning off the CD player.

"So, Mr van der Kohl," I asked Paul "who do you think killed Tony Eastwood?" and then I started to add comments to my piece of paper written on Saturday evening:

1.  *Eric Jones Neptune Re - Why did Eric Jones of Neptune Re pick me?*
2.  *Beaten up - Why pick on me? There is something in the recesses of my mind that kept dragging at me – a familiarity.*
3.  *Flat burgled (nothing taken as passport found) - All not what it seemed? What if it was to frighten me (which it did)? What if something(s) was taken but later returned? I was sure my passport had gone initially.*
4.  *Job offer in Singapore – Now a distant opportunity. What about Gerda – we wanted to marry.*
5.  *Captain Hennessey - He was the key to Eric's problem and I blundered that completely.*
6.  *Meeting with Tony – why? - He sounded genuine but was he just setting me up?*
7.  *Public telephone – Would there be any CCTV in the area?*
8.  *Masterson ship repels pirates? – Why shouldn't ship owners protect their assets with as much force as they deem to be necessary?*

I had been so absorbed in the writing that I had not been aware of a change in Paul's respiration. Also his legs were twitching. I stood up from the chair I had been using, and walked across the room so that I was standing beside Paul, and his breathing was becoming shallower. I put my hand on his shoulder and spoke softly.

"Sshh calm yourself, my friend."

As I did so I heard a slight moan. I thought I was imagining things, or that it was merely his breathing, combined with the way he was laying on the bed. I squeezed his shoulder again.

"Paul, can you hear me?" I asked.

The hairs went up on the back of my neck, as I discerned a definite low but faint growl, like someone trying to clear their throat as they awoke.

This was not my imagination and I went in search of the nurse. She was not at the nurses' station, and then she hove into view from the small kitchen, with a mug of something and a large cream cake.

"Hello, I am sorry to trouble you but I think there has been a change in Mr van der Kohl's condition."

The nurse did not say anything, just cocked her head to one side in a questioning manner.

"Would you come and have a look at him please?" I asked.

The nurse nodded her head and I returned to Paul's room.

Paul's breathing was still shorter than usual. I stood beside him, and held his hand, whilst trying to make contact with him again.

"Paul, its Marc."

I nearly jumped out of my skin when I felt his hand trying to squeeze my own.

The nurse was beside me and witnessed what I had felt.

"Did you see that?"

"Ja."

She gently moved me to one side, whilst she checked his pulse, and blood pressure.

I walked out of the room, so I could let the nurse get on with what she needed to do, and more importantly for me to phone Gerda. I went outside to call her and rang her mobile with no answer, at which point the unintelligible voice mail greeting started, and asked her to call me as soon as possible. I was walking back towards the nursing home when I felt the phone vibrate before it rang.

"Marc, are you OK?" Gerda asked sounding worried.

"Never better." I replied.

"Then, why did you call? I was in a meeting!" She was trying not to sound cross.

"It's Paul."

"What's happened?" She interrupted before I could finish.

"He responded to my voice – twice. Also his breathing is shallower and his legs are twitching."

I explained that I had spoken to him, and that I had heard something in his throat and that he squeezed my hand.

I continued "The grey haired female nurse saw what happened and is checking him over. Gerda, Gerda…. are you alright?"

I could hear her sobbing softly at the end of the phone. Then I realised what a bloody silly question it was. Eighteen months of worry and tension potentially was coming to an end. Gerda had warned me that if Paul did come out of his coma, that the prognosis might not be good; he might suffer from brain damage and amnesia.

"Marc, I am very worried." Gerda sniffed through her tears.

"I am sure he will be alright." I said trying to console her.

"He may not fully recover; he could be a vegetable," she blew her nose and continued "whilst he is in a coma at least I can hope he might return to normal."

"I know."

"Has the nurse spoken to the doctor yet?"

"I don't know. Not before I called you."

"OK, I will phone him now and ask him to come to the home. I will be there within the hour. I love you Marc!"

Gerda hung up and I walked back into the building, hearing the nurse talking on the telephone at the nurses' station. I looked into Paul's room and he seemed calmer now. There was an empty syringe in a surgical dish on the cabinet beside his bed. I looked to see what the nurse had administered but there was no packaging in sight. Paul's breathing had returned to normal. I tried talking to him but there was no reaction and, when I held his hand, it was limp.

I went in search of the nurse. She was no longer at the nurses' station, and I waited there for fifteen minutes, but there was no sign of her. I went behind the desk, and looked at the monitor that relayed images from the various CCTV cameras, scattered across the home. The nurses' station was in the middle of the purpose built home, and Paul's room was between the main entrance and the nurses' station, so I had not a clue what was down either of the corridors that ran left or right of the nurses' station. I looked in the kitchenette that was beside the toilets by the nurses' station; the kettle was warm but not hot. I went into the men's toilet but refrained from the ladies. I continued down the right hand corridor and all the doors to the patients' rooms were closed. When I reached the end of the corridor, I turned around and returned back past the nurses' station, working my way along the left corridor. This corridor was much longer, with double the number of rooms down each of its sides, and at the end was a large community day room. The day room had tables, chairs and easy chairs in front of a large television. The television was turned off but there were three people in the day room, two elderly men were playing chess and the third was a frail looking woman, asleep in one of the comfortable armchairs. There were French windows that overlooked a pretty rose garden, but they were firmly locked and secured against the miserable weather on the other side of the double glazed panes. It was now snowing, and there were no footmarks on the path outside the French windows, so I surmised the nurse hadn't gone outside from here.

I returned to Paul's room, passing by the still deserted nurses' station, and noticed instantly that the syringe and kidney shaped surgical dish was gone. Now I was becoming cross, as I knew I wasn't imagining what I saw and touched. The nurse could have been in the ladies toilet and waited for me to enter the day room. Then I reasoned that I was being paranoid, and the nurse might have just attended another patient, and returned to Paul's room afterwards to tidy up!

I went in search of the nurse again and immediately saw signs of activity at the nurses' station. As I walked towards the desk, I could tell that it was not the grey haired middle aged lady. The shock of long blonde hair was accompanied by very blue eyes and a figure that one would associate with the front of a calendar rather than a nurse's uniform. As I approached the nurse, she looked up and said something in Dutch that was completely lost on me.

"Sorry I am English and don't speak Dutch" I said as I arrived at the nurses' station.

The nurse said something else in Dutch, at which point I realised that I had met one of the few people in Holland who didn't speak English. The opportunity to ask about the syringe and the whereabouts of the grey haired nurse would have to wait until Gerda arrived. I tried to explain that I was a friend of Paul van der Kohl.

Whilst clearly uncertain, the nurse just said "OK."

I retreated back to Paul's room, and whilst waiting for Gerda I couldn't help thinking that something was amiss. I started examining Paul's arms for puncture marks that might have been caused by a syringe needle. I couldn't find anything on either forearm. I rolled down the bed covers, careful not to disturb the two catheters that were in place, one to deliver vital fluids and nourishment to Paul's body, and the other to extract the waste from Paul's body. Again, no sign of any puncture marks. As I pulled the covers over Paul, I decided to look more carefully at his hands. Bingo! Between the fingers of each hand there were puncture marks, indicating recent injections. I went to the bottom of the bed, un-tucked the sheet and blanket to examine between Paul's toes. Again, the tell-tale pin pricks were clear to the naked eye, when you looked for them. Immediately this told me two things: firstly that Paul had been given medication quite regularly, and secondly the person injecting him had done so surreptitiously. I decided to keep the information to myself for the time being.

I had been sitting in the chair for less than ten minutes, when it opened and Gerda came into the room.

She turned to me and I said "And I love you too!!"

"Sorry Marc," Gerda came over to where I was sitting and gave me a peck on the lips "it's just that there is so much to take in with Paul's situation, you on the run from the police plus work is very busy after my long weekend."

Just as I was about to tell her about my interaction with Paul earlier, someone knocked on the door, it opened with purpose and the doctor strode purposefully into the room. He briefly exchanged pleasantries with Gerda and me, before starting to examine Paul. He consulted the medical chart and then checked Paul's pulse, breathing, blood pressure and temperature.

"Well he seems calm and relaxed now." The doctor said, as he entered his own findings on the medical chart, beside Paul's bed.

Gerda had blushed up, and was anxious to explain to the doctor that there had been a significant change.

"Well that is obvious now, but what Marc saw, and felt can't be ignored?"

"W-well…."

I felt the doctor was about to try and justify my experience with rational medical reasoning.

I stopped him in his tracks "Doctor, I am sure you think you can explain what happened here today, and that it still fits within your current diagnoses."

The Doctor was nodding his agreement before I had finished.

I changed tack "Have you witnessed at first hand any of these episodes of increased activity?"

"No" he replied honestly "just the aftermath, when the bodily faculties are slightly higher than normal."

"Thank you Doctor," I continued "but I have not seen Paul for some months, so I too had only been told of these changes by Gerda."

Gerda looked at me quizzically, and I spread my hands in a comforting gesture, whilst giving her a broad smile of reassurance.

"Doctor, I can tell you unequivocally that there was a subconscious communication today, between Paul and me. It was verging on the conscious, with him squeezing my hand, when responding to a question I asked him. The older grey haired nurse witnessed part of what happened. Has she reported any of this to you today?"

"No, not yet" the Doctor's eyes held steady – either he was a very good liar or because he knew nothing untoward "which is not unusual, because the nurses submit their reports at the end of their shifts."

Gerda chipped in "Doctor, could this be good news?"

It was his turn to try and reassure Gerda "Possibly, so I will come and see Paul twice a day for the next week, and to closely monitor his condition. At the next sign of any increased activity, I will ask for a brain scan."

He was packing his stethoscope away in the ubiquitous black bag carried by doctors the world over.

"Thank you Doctor." Gerda was relieved that he was taking us seriously.

"Yes, thank you and Doctor, have you prescribed any sedatives to be given to Paul to calm him?"

"No, I haven't!" It was his turn to sharpen his voice in indignation.

He bid us goodnight, turned on his heel and left the bedroom.

"Why did you ask that?" Gerda looked questioningly at me.

I decided to show her the evidence between Paul's fingers and toes.

"Are they needle punctures?"

I nodded.

She looked at me aghast "If I catch the person…."

Before she finished I held up my hand and urged her not to speak.

I walked over to her and whispered in her ear "I think it is the grey haired nurse, also the room may be bugged. Let's talk about it when we get back to your flat."

We remained with Paul only another couple of minutes. Before leaving by way of the nurses' station, Gerda spoke for a few moments in Dutch with the blonde nurse.

The weather outside had changed again. The air was freezing. The sleet and snow that had fallen earlier in the day had now turned to icy treacherous conditions underfoot. We walked, careful not to fall, to Gerda's car and I left the bicycle at the nursing home overnight. It took us only a few short minutes to return to Gerda's flat. Gerda was in no mood for work. We went to bed, talking and loving for hours, until we decided we needed food. We ordered take away pizza, which we ate with a bottle of red wine, remaining warm and snuggled in bed.

The combination of mental strain, physical bonding, food and alcohol meant we soon fell into a deep sleep.

# Dawn Wednesday
# Gerda's flat

I woke early and I disentangled myself from Gerda's embrace, sliding gently from under the bedclothes, so as not to disturb her. It was still very dark, and the digital clock beside the bed was the only source of light in the room, illuminating Gerda's delicate facial features whilst showing the time as a quarter past six.

I crept slowly out of the bedroom *en route* to the toilet, only pausing to peer out of the curtains in the lounge, to see that it had been a very clear cold night. There had been no further snowfall, but the sparkles on the ground from passing car headlights meant that there had been a heavy frost. Returning from the toilet I slid as gently as possible back under the duvet. I thought I would not fall asleep again, and tried to make sense as to why the grey haired nurse might have drugged Paul, if the Doctor had not prescribed any such medication. I needed to talk to the nurse. I then returned to my own predicament, and wanted to also make contact with K-P sometime during the day, to gauge the temperature in London regarding my whereabouts.

Again the shadows of the Friday night beating returned; it was as though my sub-conscious was trying to tell me something. I closed my eyes, trying self-hypnosis to remember the bar near Spitalfields and Carla plus the others from JPG. I concentrated hard without breaking my trancelike state, I focussed on my senses and it wasn't anything I touched felt, heard or smelt. It was something I saw! What was it? Dark, very dark, it was black. That was all I could see in my mind's eye. The effort was like a release and I dozed on and off until the alarm clock woke us from our slumber at half past seven.

# Wednesday Morning
# St Bartholomew's

Gerda and I left her flat at the same time, and she dropped me close by St Bartholomew's, so that I could walk the rest of the journey.

"I need to put in a long day my darling." Gerda said as she gave me a peck on the lips.

"Not a problem, I will have dinner prepared for when you return, and I will try not to disturb you at work." I replied as I closed the door of the car.

The conditions underfoot were still awful, but on our short journey we had seen the municipal workers starting to salt and sand the main thoroughfares. It took me another thirty minutes to reach St Bartholomew's due to a combination of the ice on the ground, stopping to buy a cup of real coffee, rather than relying on the machine-made fare at the nursing home. I attempted to phone K-P at work from a public phone, and luckily the instructions on the public phone were in English as well as Dutch, but I did not have the correct coins. I had to return to the coffee shop to ask for change. I phoned his direct line at a little after nine which even allowing for the time difference, would usually have found him at his desk. He wasn't answering. I left a message on the voice mail to say overseas rugby tour is currently booked for Holland, although we were considering moving it to East Africa; however, we were concerned about the pirate situation off the coast of Somalia and wondered if you (K-P) had any further information. I added that I would try and call again before the day was out.

As I entered the home, I saw Peter just coming out of Paul's room. I was supposed to report to the nurses' station upon arrival, but I chose to ignore the protocol, as the lock on the front door was not engaged. Paul was seemingly calm, and I looked at his medical chart. There had been two further entries on the chart, since the Doctor entered his findings the previous afternoon. The late night entry was very similar to those of the late afternoon, but the stats were higher when taken in the morning, about an hour previous to my arrival. I wondered if this may be the result of Paul's subconscious being able to recognise night and day, with his body-clock kicking into action. I laid the writing pad on the table and went to report at the nurses' station.

I approached the desk and I could see a head with very little hair upon it; as I drew closer the owner of the nearly bald head looked up.

"Gutten morgen."

"Good morning." I replied in English, which I hoped would establish that I spoke no Dutch.

This did not faze the male nurse, who merely cocked his head to one side of his plump, thirty something year body, as if to say 'so what?'

I dutifully complied with his unspoken request "I am a friend of Paul van der Kohl and will be in his room for most of today."

"OK."

The chubby nurse was disinterested, and did not ask for my name or any form of identification.

"Excuse me," I continued as the nurse buried his nose in the papers on the desk "but is the elderly grey-haired nurse working today?"

This jolted him into a more fervent response "No she isn't! She called in sick, so I have had to come in on my day's leave!"

"Oh, I am sorry."

I left the reason for my question unsaid.

I returned to Paul's room selecting an easy listening CD, and started to write a more detailed account of what transpired the previous Wednesday, for what reason I wasn't quite sure. It helped pass the time, and it was past eleven o'clock by the time I had finished, so I went in search of a coffee from the machine near the toilets. There was no-one at the nurses' station, but I could hear a male voice coming from the kitchenette. Returning with my coffee, I could see Peter at the other end of the corridor, and waved to him 'hello'. I was about to walk towards him, when he waved back but then entered a patients room, near the communal day room.

Sipping my coffee, I took a closer look at the CDs and picked out a nineteen eighties compilation album. I inserted the second disc and pressed 'play' but no music came from the speakers. I pressed 'eject' and examined the disc. It was a blank disc with nothing to indicate what – if anything – was stored on it. I opened the CD's case to see if there were any clues to be found there, but there were only the two original discs stored in the space reserved for the first disc. I was curious as to what might be stored on the disc and wondered whether it might contain data from a computer. I slipped the disc into my pocket, first wrapping it in a paper napkin.

I inserted the correct disc into the mini system, and was greeted with some cheesy pop song. Paul's choice in music was fairly eclectic. The music was fairly lively and I walked over to Paul's bed, sat on the edge and held his hand. There was a reflexive muscle reaction as I squeezed his hand.

"Can you hear me Paul?" I asked him.

There was no response, if anything his hand became limper. I persisted in talking to him, recalling our previous escapades, most of which occurred before I met Mércédès. I was remembering a particular occasion when Paul came over to London, for a six nations rugby match against Italy. Italy had not long been admitted to the annual competition, and we met a pair of Italian sisters, who had come over from Italy for the match. They were supposed to be staying with their uncle in London, but the four of us ended up spending the weekend together. We had a great time and kept in touch for some weeks afterwards, until Paul queered our pitch, by going to Rome and asking the wrong sister out for dinner. Their weekend in London had been a heady adventure of adrenalin and alcohol, during which we had mixed up the sisters' names, so Paul's weekend in Rome was confined to restaurants and sight-seeing.

By the time I had finished my story, it was twelve thirty and I decided to go and get some lunch. I could see no-one at the nurses' station when I walked out of the home. I was about thirty metres away from the entrance, when I remembered I wanted to look over the account of last Wednesday, but I had left my notepad in Paul's room. I turned back to retrieve it.

I walked into Paul's room, and saw Peter leaning over Paul. He turned sharply as I entered the room, surprised to see me.

"Hello, Peter, you've been busy this morning."

I hesitated as I saw a kidney shaped dish, and syringe, on the bedside cabinet.

He saw my eyes look at the bedside cabinet.

"What's that in the syringe?" I asked.

"Oh, it's just a muscle relaxant; it is pretty routine for patients like Paul."

"How long has it been prescribed for him?" I tried to make it sound an innocent question but I could hear an edge in my own voice.

Peter shrugged his shoulders "I'm not sure?"

"Was it before you and the grey haired nurse worked here?" I tried a different tack.

Peter's eyes started to bore into me.

I pushed my luck further "The injections between the fingers and toes are not seen by the doctor, during his routine examination, are they?"

It was a statement rather than a question, and Peter's mood was deteriorating visibly.

"I think I need to make a phone call." I said as I went to open the door.

Peter sprang like a cat, covering the distance between us in one bound as he crashed into me, which also slammed the door shut. We grappled and rolled around, both too close to each other to be able to land a clear blow on the other. He tried kneeing me in the groin but luckily it did not land square. We rolled some more, then Peter's head hit the post of Paul's bed. His grip loosened for a second, and I was able to head-butt him above his nose, whilst punching him hard in the solar-plexus. He was winded for an instant. I jumped to my feet, opened the door to escape, only to be confronted by an automatic pistol in the hands of the grey haired nurse.

"Get back in the room Edge!" Her voice meant business.

The fact she knew my name could only mean that I was in deep trouble.

"Sit on the floor with your hands on your head."

I was ushered to the furthest point of the bedroom.

Peter was still groggy climbing to his feet. There was a nice clean wound on the bridge of his nose, with blood flowing freely down his face. He staggered over to me and slapped my face with the back of his hand.

"That's only the beginning Edge!" He blurted out in anger.

"Leave him," the grey haired nurse called out to Peter "and go wash your face, and make sure that fat lump at the nurses' station didn't hear anything."

Peter cleaned himself up as best he could, before straightening his clothes, and leaving the bedroom.

"I didn't think you were feeling very well today." I said sarcastically.

"Shut up Mr Edge!" Her cold calculating voice sent shivers up my spine. "Yes, we know who you are, and shortly so will the police. You made your first mistake when you talked about rugby to Peter, no Indians play rugby."

I would have liked to debate that point with her as I thought about K-P.

"The dyed skin disguise was good, but when you chased around the home after I carelessly left the syringe in the room, we guessed who you were."

"I suppose the Doctor also mentioned that I asked about the sedative medication." I wanted to engage her in a dialogue.

"Ja, that is why I could not come to work today; he wanted my report."

The door opened and Peter came into the room, sporting a plaster between his eyebrows, and a clean jacket.

Peter addressed the grey haired nurse, in either Afrikaans or Dutch, and she replied in the same tongue.

"I will be back to deal with you shortly!" His voice was pure venom as he spat the words at me.

As Peter left the room, I spotted that during our scuffle he had knocked the syringe onto the floor, and it was lying within reach of my right foot. When the grey haired nurse turned to watch Peter leave, I stretched out my foot and was able to slide the syringe under my foot, towards me. She was further distracted whilst pulling the chair in front of me, by which time the syringe was in my hand, and I kept it out of sight behind my back.

"English is your first language isn't it?" I asked but got no response. "So you're not Dutch, South Africa perhaps? I bet you both are Zimbabwean."

"No we are Rhodesian!" Her reply was fired back at me.

I kept quiet for a few moments whilst I disseminated the information.

"I don't suppose it is a coincidence that you and Peter work here, is it?"

The nurse was smiling.

"Does Sir Hugh pay well?" I was guessing and tried a shot in the dark.

"He doesn't pay us anything; he doesn't have to."

"Why not?" I asked instantly trying to keep the conversation going.

"You will not leave Amsterdam alive, Mr Edge, so I guess it does no harm to tell you that I am Peter's mother, and Sir Hugh is his father."

I was stunned and my jaw actually dropped.

The grey haired nurse started to laugh at me.

I shook my head in disbelief.

"Yes, Mr Edge, Peter is actually related to you until your divorce is finalised."

"Does Mércédès know about Peter?"

I was still floundering around blindly, trying to overcome my astonishment at this news.

"No! And she never will," she snarled "not from your lips anyway!"

"How?"

"How do you think, you stupid man?" Her vehemence was increasing.

"I was pretty once, and I nursed Sir Hugh's grandfather, during which time Sir Hugh and I became very close, but I was already married to the son of a neighbouring farmer."

"So why are you sedating Paul?" I nodded towards Paul.

As she turned involuntarily to look at Paul, I threw the syringe like a dart at the nurse. I couldn't have aimed better because it hit her in the neck. She screamed and dropped the gun on the floor. I jumped to my feet, and as I knocked her off the chair, she fell to the floor. She fell onto the syringe, and the angle of the fall injected the contents into her neck.

"Bastard!!!" She screamed at me and fell to her knees.

The bedrooms would be reasonably sound-proofed, but there was a good chance Peter might have heard the commotion, and I needed to get out fast. I ignored the gun, and left the bedroom before Peter's mother could recover.

As I was leaving the home I heard Peter's voice behind me shouting "Moeder, Moeder!"

I started to run as fast as I could.

I dismissed any thoughts about using the bicycle, because the icy conditions were such that it was nearly impossible to run, let alone cycle. I turned the first corner, stumbling as I did so to see that Peter had given chase on foot, and seemed to be carrying something in his hand.

"Shit, he's got the gun."

I ran as fast as I could, trying to ignore the conditions underfoot.

The idea of a shoot-out in the middle of Amsterdam was not very appealing, and with one possible murder hanging over me in the United Kingdom, if I was caught I would be dead meat. I turned right down a small side street, towards a cluster of industrial buildings and warehouses, next to one of the canals. I managed a quick glance over my shoulder to see if Peter had followed me. There was no sign of Peter, but at that moment a small silver car with an over-revving engine, came skidding around the corner. It screeched to a stop just a few metres behind me, the door opened, and Peter jumped out.

"Shit!!"

I started running for all my worth towards the warehouses.

I could hear Peter's footsteps behind, but the roar of the car was now filling my ears, which meant it was underway again and would be behind me in an instant. The warehouse was closed, in fact it looked vacant, and I scrambled along its perimeter with the car gaining ground. I came to a fenced gate and tried to open it, but it was restrained by an old chain and padlock. The car was nearly upon me. I scrambled over the fence with seconds to spare, into a concrete loading area, just as the car hit the fence.

With no salt or sand, the ground was unbelievably slippery. Initially I could hardly walk let alone run, but then found my balance. I turned towards the fence; Peter had caught up with the car and he was climbing over the fence. I couldn't go back, the warehouse was secured. The only way was towards the canal. As I stumbled across the open ground, the car had backed up about twenty metres and then the roaring of the car reached a crescendo, followed by a mighty crash. The silver car smashed through the gates of the fence. The car was skidding and sliding wildly in my direction; it flew past Peter and was accelerating directly towards me. Peter's mother was hunched over the wheel, her head seemed to fall forwards, and she recovered only for her head to loll backwards.

"The sedative!!" I said to myself.

Her head fell forward again, she was no longer in control, but the car kept accelerating. I had to dive sideways, to avoid being hit. The car continued forwards until it was five metres from the canal, when it started to slew to the right, and for a second I thought it would stop. But it hit the low kerb of the canal broadside and the force of the impact tipped the car onto its side. Then as if in slow motion, accompanied by a stomach churning scraping, it slid toward the canal. Right on the edge of the canal the car teetered for a moment, before it tipped over falling out of sight, with the engine noise still filling the air.

I stood rooted to the spot in total disbelief. Peter ran past me, screaming for his mother, and I followed in his wake. I reached the edge of the canal just as Peter jumped. I could see why. The canal had frozen; and although the ice had cracked, the small car was still on the surface. The canals of Holland were famous for holding long-distance speed skating races on their frozen surfaces, but it was November, and this was the first heavy overnight frost. The ice wasn't thick, plus the force of the car hitting the ice had created a fissure the breadth of the canal. Peter was on the ice crawling towards the car. Whether it was his additional weight, or just the inevitability of the ice cracking, but the car disappeared to the bottom of the canal and with it Peter was sucked under as well.

As soon as the car was below the water, the ice recovered its shape and the hole disappeared, trapping Peter beneath the surface. I looked around for help, but the area was deserted, and it looked like no-one had seen the accident. The wail of sirens could be heard in the distance, and they were getting closer with each passing second. I did not want to be answering difficult questions by the Dutch Police, holding a false passport and on the run from the English Police.

I walked, half ran back towards the warehouse, and tried the doors again. They were firmly locked, and there were no windows. I went to the nearest point between the warehouse and the gate, pushing myself into a shallow alcove, in the wall of the warehouse. I didn't have to wait long before a fire tender and ambulance came screaming through the gate, and even before they had halted I made a dash for the gate.

There was no other vehicle following them and I walked to the end of the street. I rejoined the main road and made my way towards the nearest tram, as quickly as I could away from the scene of the accident, without drawing attention to myself. Sitting on the tram, two more fire tenders and a police car streaked past in the opposite direction, with their lights flashing and sirens wailing. It was not until we reached the central station that the blood stopped pounding in my ears. I made my way to a drab café, ordering a black coffee and a large brandy. The waiter didn't give me a second glance, but if he could have seen my hands he may have been more interested, because they were shaking uncontrollably.

By the time the coffee and brandy arrived, I was able to hold the glass and cup without spilling the contents. I drank the liquids nonchalantly, as normally as possible, and left enough money to cover the cost plus a small tip. I walked about fifty metres until I found another unassuming café and repeated the order, but I had to force myself to drink the caffeine and alcohol, because I was feeling sick inside.

Could I have stopped Peter? I killed his mother by injecting her with the sedative. I needed to speak with Gerda, and quickly.

It was just after half past one, when most people would be at lunch, or just returning. I dialled Gerda's number from Paul's old mobile and she answered on the second ring.

"Hi my darling, are you ok?" she asked.

"Gerda, we have a problem……."

# Wednesday Afternoon
# Gerda's flat

It was half past two when I walked through the door of Gerda's flat. There was a large glass of wine in front of her, and it looked like the glass had been refilled once already. When she saw me she stood up, ran over to me, threw her arms around me, and then burst into tears. This was very unlike Gerda, normally a very cool person when under pressure; and it was as if she was reading my mind.

She blurted out "Marc, will this craziness stop? I can't lose you. I love you so much. I need you!"

I held her tight in my arms until her sobs subsided. I had only given her the briefest details over the phone. Gerda had told her colleagues that she had a meeting out of the office, and would be back in an hour. I then explained to her in detail what had happened.

"So, did anyone see Peter's mother try to run you down?"

I shrugged my shoulders "I don't think so, but I can't be sure, plus the emergency services were very quickly on the scene. I don't know who raised the alarm."

Gerda walked over to the television and tuned into the local news. Instantly the screen was filled with pictures from the canal. The ticker-tape underneath the pictures was in Dutch, and I looked to Gerda for enlightenment.

She translated "Early this afternoon, a driver of a small silver car lost control, and the car crashed into a canal in the centre of Amsterdam. A passer by was seen to jump in after the car. No casualties have been located by the emergency services; their progress is being hampered by the ice on the canal."

Gerda continued "There is no mention of you."

I smiled and replied "That's good, but it will only be a matter of time before they recover the car, as well as both Peter and his mother's bodies." I paused for a moment "We probably have one day, possibly two before the police will want to question the staff of St Bartholomew's, and the person I asked about Peter's mother will remember me very clearly."

"So what should we do?" Gerda asked.

"My darling, I think you need to go back to work to give yourself an alibi, and I need to get back to London double quick."

Gerda was about to disagree with me, and I held her shoulders with my hands.

"You would not be able to help Paul, or me, if you were detained by the Police?"

"I suppose not." Was Gerda's hesitant reply.

"We must make it appear that my return to England was planned for today, so can you drop that into conversation with your work colleagues? Also, stay as late as possible at work, to support your story."

Gerda nodded.

"You can collect your bike tomorrow." I gave Gerda the keys to the bike lock.

Again Gerda nodded.

"If Peter and his mother knew my real identity, we cannot risk that others know I am in Holland, and we both will be safer if I am back in England. Also the Police are probably watching for me to leave the country rather than enter it!"

"So how are you going to return?" I had been waiting for Gerda's question.

"Train," I replied "I checked the times whilst I was calming down at the central station. It takes between four and a quarter and four and a half hours. If I catch the five o'clock train I could be in London by half past nine, London time allowing for the time difference, including a change in Brussels."

"Where will you stay, Marc?"

I was not exactly sure and replied "Somewhere safe."

Before Gerda could reply I made three further requests.

"Gerda, my darling, have you any cash for the train travel? Also I found this disc in Paul's room, and I think it might contain data rather than music. Could you check it for me please? And finally can you buy me some more credit for my mobile phone?"

"How can I refuse?" Gerda replied in mock seriousness.

I put my arms around her and gave her a big hug "That's my girl."

"I have three hundred Euros in the house, and I can buy the top-up for the phone on–line."

"Thank you my darling, I must pack, and change back into my disguise again."

Whilst I had been in Amsterdam I had worn jeans and sweatshirts over tee shirts, dispensing with the spectacles and walking stick.

"I will give you a lift to the station," Gerda offered "but you must be quick!"

"I'll be fifteen minutes, tops" I shouted over my shoulder, as I left the lounge.

I went to the bathroom and re-dyed my beard and hair, because the growth over the last few days was a different colour, and would be noticed. I was changing into my new long-johns when Gerda came into the room and picked up my phone.

"There you are I have added fifty Euros credit."

"Thanks my darling."

We both went back to the bedroom, where I drew her close to me kissing her long, and deeply.

"Marc, what are you going to do in England?" Gerda asked in a whisper.

"I am going to send a further letter to the Police Station in Bishopsgate, and then I am going to confront Sir Hugh."

"What are you going to say?" Gerda looked worried.

"I am going to tell him that I know that his former lover and illegitimate son were nursing Paul. Also that I know they had been sedating Paul."

"I am worried Marc," Gerda was again on the verge of tears "what if you were correct and Tony's murder was a mistake, and you were the real target."

A chill went though my body despite the warmth of the flat and the silk underwear. I poo-poo'd her fears, hoping not to show I was shit scared, I really was.

"I will be in disguise, plus the advantage of knowledge, and surprise."

"I want to come with you;" Gerda was shaking when she spoke "why don't you wait until Friday when I can take more holidays, and we will return to England together?"

"No, my darling, I need you on the outside helping me."

There was a firmer tone in my voice than I would have liked.

"I need to be focussed and it will be safer if I am not worried about your safety as well. Also, I think that it is possible that Paul's condition may change, if no sedatives are being pumped into him."

Gerda's smile was the one which I had come to know and love, it conveyed both understanding and agreement.

I finished dressing, quickly packing my battered holdall, and I put on Shariz's uncle's spectacles. I just remembered to retrieve the walking stick from the corner of the bedroom. Gerda was at her computer when I returned to the lounge diner.

"Marc, come look at this?"

I walked over to the dining table to where she was sitting.

"You were right; the disc you found has spreadsheets, documents and other files."

"What's in them?" I asked.

"I can't open them. They are all password protected."

"What are the files called?" I couldn't make any sense of the file names because they were written in Dutch.

"They are all names of places in Holland;" she hesitated "they are all holiday destinations, where our parents took us to when we were children."

"Hmm?" Was my unhelpful response.

"Sorry Marc, but I have no clue as to what Paul would have assigned as a password."

Gerda turned off the computer and we were ready to leave.

# Wednesday Afternoon
# Train to Brussels

Neither Gerda nor I said anything in the car during our journey to the Central Station. Both of us knew saying goodbye would be too painful, plus the uncertainty of what might happen to me when I was back in London weighed heavily upon the atmosphere in the car.

Luckily we found a parking space close to the Central Station; Gerda could remain there for only fifteen minutes, but only by feeding the parking meter an extortionate amount of Euros.

"I can take it from here to save you feeding the meter." I said.

"No!" Gerda replied firmly "You must now act in character, as an elderly man, and it would be normal for a younger person to carry your bag."

I merely smiled and nodded in acquiescence.

As Gerda fed the parking meter, I slowly got out of the car, and Gerda collected my bag from the back seat. I was instantly grateful for the long padded jacket that Gerda had purchased for me in London. It was very cold, but the shiver going through my body was at the thought of Peter and his mother's frozen graves. I hoped their demise was swift.

I shuffled behind Gerda to the ticket office where she requested a single ticket to London King's Cross – the new London terminus for the Eurostar trains.

The ticket vendor asked Gerda a question and she turned to me, "He would like to see your passport."

I fished it out of the inside pocket of my padded jacket. The ticket vendor passed it back to Gerda, after entering the details in his computer, which gave me an idea about the disc that I had found in Paul's bedroom. Gerda gave me my ticket and Shariz's uncle's passport.

"Gerda, do you think you can remember the year, and possibly the month your parents took you to the various places mentioned on the disc?"

She thought about it for a moment or two. "You think that might be the passwords."

I nodded.

"I will try later tonight," she replied.

I could sense rather than see that Gerda was looking me in the eyes, because Shariz's uncle's spectacles put everything slightly out of focus.

"Phone me lots, and look after yourself, I love you so much." She gave me a peck on the check as would befit the departure of an elderly relative, or friend, and she walked off towards her car.

I had mixed feelings seeing her leave, but I had a sense of purpose, although if all failed I could end up in jail - for a long time. As ridiculous as the last twelve days had been, I felt more alive than I had been for a very long time. The sadness was the uncertainty as to when I would next see Gerda, because the last twelve days had reaffirmed that we were meant for each other, and I wanted to spend the rest of my life with her.

It was a little after half past three thirty, and my train wasn't due to depart for another eighty minutes, also the train for Brussels had yet to arrive. I went to the public telephone booths, repeating the morning's exercise, but with much more success.

"Hello?" K-P's soft deep gravelly voice was at the other end of the telephone.

"Hi K-P," I replied "how's tricks?"

"OK at the moment," and he added "the compliance department have left us alone yesterday and today."

I presumed he was referring to the police.

"Good, because I am on my way back to London and with any luck I should be there by nine tonight. Could you possibly see the nephew of my sponsor, and ask him whether I could stay another night, with his uncle?"

"I will try but it will not be until late."

I could sense hesitation in K-P's voice.

"OK! What is it?" I enquired.

"I met your friend Eric Jones of Neptune Re, by chance, at lunchtime."

There was obviously more to tell otherwise K-P would not have teased me.

"So?" I played his game.

"He asked me how you were, and whether the police had you in cuffs yet?"

"What!" I shouted down the phone.

"I thought the police had kept their search for me a secret?"

"As did I." K-P replied.

"What did you tell him?"

I could hear anxiety in my own strained voice.

"I played it cool, and said that I had no idea what he was talking about."

I could imagine K-P's poker face, the one he would reserve for when an underwriter had made a mistake with the premium they wanted, or the fact that they had underwritten a difficult risk at all!

"I was non-committal and then Eric smiled, which was not a pretty sight, and suggested we meet to discuss - hypothetically - what may have happened to Tony Eastwood."

Before he had finished, my question was out of my mouth "Did you accept?"

"Of course I did," K-P answered "but not straightaway. I kept up the pretence that I did not know what he was inferring, when he said it might be to your advantage. I relented by saying that the least I could do for you was to listen to what he had to say."

"Good boy K-P."

I was encouraged by his approach and coolness.

"When and where are you meeting him?"

"Half past four at a quiet bar off Cornhill."

"That's interesting," I remarked "not a normal insurance watering hole. It's more for bankers."

"I thought the same." K-P agreed. He continued "So it is unlikely I will get to Shariz until after six o'clock."

"Ok, please can you phone me on Paul's old mobile number, after you speak to Shariz."

"Will do, and can you give me the number again? I will phone from a public telephone."

"OK, and when you see Eric can you ask him about Masterson's recent fracas off the coast of Somalia, and whether they or another of their sister company's vessels have been involved in a similar incident?"

"If it is opportune to do so, I will."

I could hear in the background K-P was shuffling papers and closing his slip case.

"I have to go and see some underwriters."

Eric Jones was no fool and I was unnerved by his remarks to K-P about Tony Eastwood. The only connection between K-P and Tony Eastwood was me! So the underlying message to K-P was really meant for me. The police had kept Tony's death out of the media; presumably this had been deliberate, to try and ensnare me if I made a mistake. Eric was obviously well informed, and was his knowledge the product of intuitive guesswork or a well educated grapevine. More ominously, was there the possibility that he was being fed information by the police or another organisation? I looked across to the large station clock, and even through the blurred vision caused by Shariz's uncle's glasses, I could make out that twenty minutes had elapsed since Gerda had departed from the station. I looked over the top of the spectacles, trying to read the train indicator, and I could just see the platform number. I looked over to the platform and saw that the gate was yet to be opened to the eager travellers. I decided to make a couple more telephone calls. The first was to Masterson Shipping, the phone was answered on the second ring, and I asked to speak to Ms. Syrani. Her clipped New York twang filled the receiver.

"Hello, Ms. Syrani speaking. How may I help you?" I lowered my voice to a whispery rasp.

"Yes, its Marcus Edge, I thought you might like to know why I had not been in touch."

If she was surprised to hear from me, she recovered instantly, because there was no trace of hesitation in her voice.

"Well, yes, Mr Edge, we had been wondering why we had not seen you in the office. We have left several messages on your mobile telephone."

"I am sorry but I have been very ill in bed with the H1N1 flu virus. I was staying with a friend and the credit on my phone is exhausted. I didn't want to blot my copybook with my new employers, and infect you all with my germs."

There was no riposte about catching my death of cold on the River Stort, but a genuine concern about my health.

"I quite understand Mr Edge, that was very thoughtful, and when might we see you back in the office?"

"Monday, I hope. Is Sir Hugh in the UK at the moment?"

I had to try and make my question sound as innocent as possible, and unusually Ms. Syrani was open with her reply.

"Yes, he is around until the middle of next week and we hope you are well enough to see you on Monday."

My next call was to my brother, and thankfully his voicemail cut in immediately. I repeated the lie that I had told to Ms. Syrani. Hopefully one of them would mention this to someone, who might tell the police, and it might mean they look in the wrong direction after I returned to East London. The train was ready for boarding and I thought about calling Bishopsgate Police Station to establish whether Sergeant Smithson was on duty. I was stopped by my own good sense taking hold of my irrational impulse. I did not know the telephone number of the Police Station, and to find the number would mean that I would need to replace Paul's SIM card with my own, thus running the risk of being traced. I would wait until K-P called me later, and I would ask him to find out if Sergeant Smithson was on duty.

It was time to board the train for Brussels. I picked up my battered holdall, made sure the walking stick was in the correct hand, and shuffled like an old man towards the platform. I had gone only a few feet when a young girl in a uniform walked up to me, and spoke the unintelligible tongue of the Netherlands.

"I'm so sorry but I do not speak Dutch." I smiled as I replied in a clipped English accent.

The girl offered "Can I help you to your train? You are going to London, no?"

"Yes, I am catching the express train to Brussels, and then the Eurostar to London."

"It is wonderful how quick it is now," she proudly announced "and it is much more civilised than flying."

"Yes, it is my first time I have travelled by train to London."

I tried making myself more helpless by feigning a small stumble.

The girl looked at me, pulled out a mobile phone, and called a speed dial number. This was all in one smooth action, without breaking step, or hesitation. She spoke crisply for less than a minute, ending the call as we reached the train.

She turned to me and asked "Are you travelling First or Second Class?"

"I cannot afford First Class," I said apologetically "may I have a seat close to the WC please?"

The girl looked slightly bewildered and then said "Oh, the toilet, no problem."

As I boarded the train, her mobile rang.

"Ja, ja, danke." She turned to me as I took my seat "Is this good, yes?"

"Very nice. Thank you." I nodded my head as I replied.

"I have made arrangements for you to be met in Brussels for assistance to the Eurostar."

I started to protest but she insisted.

"We are very proud of our efficient railways and of our service."

I shrugged my shoulders and smiled.

The train departed on time, and five minutes later my – Paul's old – mobile rang. The name on the mobile screen showed *Gerda 2*, which I recognised as her work's telephone number.

"Hi." I whispered softly into the phone.

"Did your train leave on time?"

"Yes and a very attractive female employee of Dutch Railways aided this elderly gentleman onto the train."

Gerda giggled.

I continued "Plus she made arrangements to have me escorted to the Eurostar at Brussels."

"Be careful, Marc, that you do not attract too much attention."

I would do well to heed Gerda's warning, because I was liable to get carried away, and believe in my own bullshit.

"Marc!" Her voice was quite earnest.

"Yes my darling" was my *sotto voce* response.

"I have been able to open some of the files on the disc. The password is the month and the last two numbers of the year we went to the various destinations for our holidays."

"That's fantastic Gerda!" I said in a slightly raised voice.

"Hmmm" her reply was intended to manage my expectations.

"What is it?" I asked.

"Everything is in code."

"Damn it." I swore softly.

"But it definitely has amounts of money." She tried to sound hopeful.

"Gerda, it is a great start, and I am sure with a bit of time we will be able to work it out. Any news from St Bartholomew's?"

"No," she paused "I am just checking the news, and the car still has not been recovered yet. The weather for tonight is predicted to be freezing so they are going to try again in the morning."

I felt sick and could see Peter's mother's eyes blazing as she drove like a maniac trying to kill me. She obviously loved Sir Hugh enormously, and would do anything to protect him, and her son. I shook myself from my reverie and asked what time would she be visiting Paul.

"About half past six," she added "and then I will come back to work for a couple of hours, to catch up.

"Good, that will tie up with when I arrive in London, and I will call you then my darling. I love you so much."

"Me too!" And she blew a kiss down the phone.

As the train picked up speed, various emotions were tugging at me. The news that the car would remain under the ice for the night meant that I probably had a twelve hour start before the police started making connections between St Bartholomew's and Paul van der Kohl's recent visitor. It was also possible that Paul's regaining consciousness might not be too far away, and whilst that might aid me in clearing my name with Lloyd's of London, it would not make a ha'pence of difference as far as the murder of Tony Eastwood was concerned.

The memory of Tony's death galvanised me into writing a more detailed version of the events from the previous Wednesday. In fact I started with the briefing by Eric

Jones, followed by a brief account of the visit to Felixstowe. My recall of the moments as the train drew into Bishops Stortford station, through to the point I made my escape, were so vivid. I tried to record every aspect of what I saw, and what I had deduced subsequently; in particular the calls to my mobile from the public telephone in the town centre of Bishops Stortford. The details of my escape by river to Old Harlow, cycle ride to East London, plus the disguise and journey were all kept out of the account. I finished this as the express train was pulling into Brussels station.

I felt more certain than ever that the answers to so many of my questions would be found at The Hall, possibly during an interview with Sir Hugh Masterson, if I could engineer such. Was the Scorpion playing a very dangerous game, and why the heck could I possibly be a threat to him? I didn't have any dirt on him and, until my disgrace with Lloyd's of London, we had the perfect father and son-in-law relationship. Even after my ban we communicated, so I realised I was doing him a disservice by believing he wanted me out of the way. Was I making a mistake about his involvement? Perhaps he was just being philanthropic and very generous to give me a chance to start again? Could I really confront him without going to pieces? When his piercing blue eyes stared into my own I would feel as though he was looking straight into my soul.

# Wednesday Evening
# Train from Brussels to London

As the train stopped in Brussels Station, the doors slid open, and a very large negroid man climbed on the train. His clothes looked like they were at least one, or possibility two, sizes too small for him.

"Bonsoir monsieur. Je vous aide." He pronounced in very broken French, with a heavy accent.

Although it did not seem possible, he was even darker than Sir Hugh's manservant Samuel, and I assumed he must have hailed from deepest Africa.

"Merci." I replied.

Without any fuss he picked up my holdall, giving me his hand, it felt as though he could have carried me to the electric cart on the platform. As he towered above me, I suddenly and involuntarily recoiled, snatching my hand away. My head was swirling, and I was reliving the beating I received in London, twelve days previously. The porter's eyes were wide open with shock at my reaction to his touch. He was embarrassed and concerned, and the last thing I wanted, was to be examined by a doctor.

"Pardon, Monsieur je suis un petit soufre, ce n'est pas de problème."

The porter nodded at my poor explanation that I had just caught my breath. The electric cart was like a magic carpet that whisked me to the entrance of the Eurostar platform. I had to show my ticket, passport and then be security screened, as if we were at the airport. Passing through security, I then had to be cleared by UK immigration, where I held my breath as my passport was scanned. The immigration officer fixed me with a stare and then handed the passport back to me.

"Enjoy your journey sir."

I waited for a few seconds before I dare breathe out.

The large African porter was waiting for me, and again I was on the electric magic carpet, speeding me along the platform. We reached the appropriate carriage, and I was safely installed on the train, before most of the passengers had embarked. The time was twenty to seven and the train was due to leave at a minute before seven. With the one hour difference, the journey time of just over two hours would mean I should be in Kings Cross by a quarter past eight.

K-P would have been with Eric Jones for less than an hour, so I shouldn't expect a call from him for another hour or so. Similarly, Gerda was going to visit Paul in ten minutes, so I should not expect a call from that direction either. I settled into my seat as my fellow passengers joined the train. There was about fifteen minutes before departure, I was studying the questions I had written at the end of my latest account, and my eyes felt very heavy.

*I was in a bar. It was noisy with people talking loudly over the music, which was intended to create an atmosphere, but meant that people were on the verge of shouting. Then I did hear someone shout and swear, before crashing to the ground. A girl was helping the person on the floor to his feet. I recognised the girl, it was Carla, and the person on the floor was me!*

*"Tony, you've pushed me too far this time," I was slurring "I'm going to bloody thrash you."*

*"Marc, shut up!!" Carla was shouting at me to be quiet as two 'bouncers' were starting to make their way towards me.*

*"Tony's not even here you piss-head. Go outside and calm down before we all get thrown out and banned from our favourite bar!"*

*Carla and one of the other employees of JPG helped me stand up. She leaned me up against the wall and asked me "Can you get yourself outside on your own?"*

*I nodded because I felt I was about to throw up.*

*I just stood there leaning and muttering curses and oaths against Tony Eastwood.*

*"Are you feeling sorry for yourself Edge?" The voice came from the dark, and was familiar from the past, but I could not recognise it.*

*"Well you will after this!"*

*A gloved fist came out of the shadows and pole-axed me.*

I woke up with a shudder, and I was surprised that there were people around me, and they were on their feet. I was disorientated. Had we arrived at our destination? I looked more carefully at my surroundings and saw that there were new passengers embarking on the train. Through the window, I could see that it was snowing. I peered hard through the spectacles, my blurred vision just making out the sign of Lille, in Eastern France.

I settled back in my seat, determined to fall asleep again, and hoped to be able to pick up my dream from where it ended. I was able to doze off quite quickly, but deep sleep associated with the dream, eluded me. Four aspects from the dream stuck with me, and the more I tried to sleep, these kept popping into my mind like a revolving door. The first was that whoever attacked me knew me by name; it was not a random beating, by a bunch of local thugs. Secondly the person knew where I was, so they had been tipped off by someone, or they were following me for part of that day. Thirdly, whilst I could not recognise or place the voice, I had definitely heard it before. The last was the gloves.

I added another question to my list:

*'9. Who in the last twelve days have I met wearing gloves?'*

I added this to my account for Sergeant Smithson, saying it was not a random beating, and the reasons behind my statement.

I checked my mobile, there were no calls, so I settled back again and sleep without dreams came swiftly. I woke again with my ears popping. The train's speed was still quick, due to the tunnels and cuttings through the undulating Kent countryside, and we were heading towards the North Downs and London Kings Cross. I checked my mobile, still no calls from either K-P, or Gerda. I opened my wallet, counting the Euro notes Gerda had given to me. The exchange rate was very firmly in favour of the Euro, and I was hoping to be able to net nearly one pound sterling for every Euro.

As the train climbed another inclination, my mobile vibrated with a message that I had received two voicemails. Either the speed of the train, or the fact that whoever called me had done so whilst I was under the English Channel, meant they had been diverted to voicemail. At the third attempt I connected with my voicemail. There were two messages waiting to be opened. The first was from K-P, saying Eric Jones had delayed the meeting for a couple of hours, which apparently would be to your (*my*) advantage so K-P agreed, but it meant he might not be able to see Shariz before my arrival.

I swore quietly under my breath.

I cleared the message, and then listened to the second message, which was from Gerda. She had visited St Bartholomew's. Nothing was mentioned about Peter and his mother, but Paul had been restless, so she would stay with him until the doctor visited.

The Eurostar sped towards London passing over the River Medway, and then stopped at Ebbsfleet. Ebbsfleet station was created for Eurostar, and for one of Europe's largest shopping centres, Bluewater. No one from my carriage disembarked at Ebbsfleet, and I wondered whether the station would become a white elephant, similar to Ashford International, when the prosperity promised for Ashford failed to materialise.

Within minutes the train was on the north side of the Thames, and running speedily through East London, past the large Ford works at Dagenham, before turning northwards, towards Stratford and Kings Cross. The new station at Stratford, built for the Olympics, was not yet operational. During the Olympics, the trains are scheduled to stop every six minutes, but after the games were finished the number of Eurostar trains stopping at Stratford would be few and far between. I thought perhaps the new station at Stratford should have been designed as a temporary structure, like a number of the other venues for the Olympics.

The train was running perceptibly slower, we were starting the final part of the journey, as we approached the terminus at Kings Cross.

# Wednesday Night
# East London

The arrival at Kings Cross Station was smooth and slick, with the area reserved for the Eurostar more akin to an airport than a train station. I wasn't sure why I was surprised, because the girl from Dutch Railways had admitted their aim was to attract passengers away from flying.

I shuffled my way down to the underground station. I was gratified to see that I could purchase a travelcard with Euros, which would allow me full access to the buses, Underground and DLR. I bought one for the evening, and another, for the following day.

I made my way to the platform where I would be able to take an underground train to Liverpool Street Station. I didn't have to wait long, and the train was half empty, although that would change dramatically when the theatres and cinemas emptied.

When I had made my way out of Liverpool Street Station, the snow I had seen in Lille was in London, but it was not cold enough to stay on the ground, and formed a wet slush on the pavements. The weather conditions made it difficult to shuffle along, and I changed the walking stick into my other hand, to give me greater stability. Shuffling fifty metres along Bishopsgate brought me to the entrance of the Police Station, just after quarter to nine. I had to be reasonably quick, so I could get to Shariz, before he closed the shop under my flat. I searched for a letter box where I could deposit my latest account of events for Sergeant Smithson. There was no sign of anywhere that letters could be posted, which I supposed was a security measure, along with the fact there were now very few rubbish bins on streets of Central London. There was no alternative; I had to hand the letter in myself.

I walked in and rang the bell on the counter. My blood ran cold when the person who came to the desk was the career-minded WPC who interviewed me the Saturday morning after I had been attacked. I had to fight the urge to turn and run.

"Yes, how can I help you?" She barely looked at me, probably annoyed that she was on duty in the station, rather than out in the public arresting people.

"I would like to hand this letter in to Sergeant Smithson, please?"

I spoke softly, as would befit an elderly gentleman, and in my best English accent.

Still she did not look up when she answered me "Sergeant Smithson is not on duty until early tomorrow morning."

"Would you be so good as to pass it on to him please?" I asked.

She looked up "What is it?"

"I do not know." I explained as I lay it on the table.

She crinkled up her nose "Then why are you here?"

I had been waiting for this question "A very nice young man asked me to hand this letter into this Police Station, and he gave me a five pound note, if I delivered it for him."

I smiled my sweetest grin.

"Wait here!" It was more a command than a request.

She walked off with the letter.

I could walk out and the deed would be done, but that might blow my disguise, so I decided to do as I was bid.

She returned shortly "Can you describe this man?"

"I will try. He was about my height. A well-spoken young Englishman in his mid-thirties, wearing a ski-jacket," I added "which I thought was just as well in this weather. I do not like this weather, the damp goes right….."

"Yes, yes," the WPC was becoming impatient "what is your name and address, in case we need to contract you?"

I gave her Shariz's uncle's name but a fake address and hoped they would not check it until I was in the clear.

"Do you have a phone?"

"No sorry. I cannot afford one," I pulled my coat around me to feign a shiver "can I go now?"

Just at that moment a policeman was bringing in an angry young man, which distracted the WPC.

"Yes!" She dismissed me.

I returned to Bishopsgate, very pleased with my performance. I switched the walking stick, back to the other hand, and made my way across the road to catch the bus towards Hackney. I shuffled on the bus, a young girl stood up from the disabled seat to offer me the one near the exit. I sat down, checking my mobile, but still no calls from either K-P or Gerda.

The bus dropped me about hundred metres from my flat above Shariz's shop. I shuffled along the pavement, and stopped opposite to the shop, glad that the snow had relented whilst I was in the Police Station. As I looked into the shop, I could see Shariz talking to his brother, and there didn't appear to be anyone else with them. I shuffled on for another twenty metres, to where there was a crossing. I crossed the street, looking across to where the police had been watching my flat, the previous week. There were no suspicious vehicles outside, or curtains twitching at the house they had commandeered.

I opened the door, but kept my head bowed, so that Shariz did not recognise me immediately. I kept my back to him as I selected some milk from the chilled cabinet. I walked up to the counter, and then Shariz turned away from his brother, to focus on his new customer. His jaw dropped perceptibly when he saw it was me.

"Shssssh." I hissed quickly to stop him saying anything "Hello, Shariz, how are you? Is your uncle well?"

"Hello," he replied "I am sorry to say that he is quite poorly at the moment, and that is why his sister and his niece are living with him now."

"Oh!"

I could hear the disappointment in my own voice.

Shariz came around the counter to help an elderly relative, and he took me by the elbow, carrying my holdall into the room behind the shop. He spoke quickly to his brother, who came and took up station by the till.

As soon as we were alone in the back room he put on the radio, and turned up the volume.

"Mr Marc, you gave me such a shock," he said shaking his head from side-to-side "I did not recognise you at first."

"Thank you, Shariz," and I shook him warmly by the hand "I presume I can't stay at your uncle's?"

"Sadly no," his face was long "unfortunately his health has deteriorated, and I fear you might not be able to use his passport for very much longer."

"I'm sorry," I fished the document out of my pocket "here it is."

Whilst he did not say anything, I could tell he was pleased that I had handed it back to him.

"Mr Marc, I think if you are careful, you could stay in your own flat."

I lifted my head and looked at him enquiringly.

He continued "The Police left the house across the road on Tuesday morning."

I was about to question him how he knew.

"They are not very clever, because the same two people kept coming into the shop, for snacks and cigarettes."

Nothing much got past Shariz.

"Also the police came back and searched your own flat again today. They were there for over an hour, and when they left I could see wires were hanging out of a bag, so I think they have taken away some surveillance equipment."

I was surprised by how much information Shariz had been able to gather, but also I thought how much time and effort had been invested by the police. Then a thought crossed my mind.

"Shariz," I started my question "are you sure they were policemen?"

"Yes, of course!"

"How did you know?" I probed further "Did they show you a warrant card?"

"Yes they showed me their identification," then the fallacy of his assumption "who else could it be, this is England!"

Shariz was proud of England and the thought that dark forces would operate here was beyond his ken.

"Yes," I murmured "who else indeed."

We decided not to take any chances, and Shariz left the radio blaring out strains of sitar music, whilst we climbed the stairs to my flat. At the top of the stairs, Shariz turned off the light, so nothing would shine through the window when we opened the door. The reflection from the street lights cast shadows across the living room. I could instantly tell that the flat had been well and truly searched. I nodded to Shariz, as he gave me my key, and shook his hand.

"This will all be over in a couple of days." I whispered to him.

He cocked his head to one side.

I added "One way or another!"

"Good luck, Mr Marc, please be careful!"

These were wise words and I was going to completely ignore them. A plan was forming in my mind, which required that I act decisively; but not quite yet, I needed more information. I took off my shoes, so as not to make too much sound, whilst turning my mobile phone to vibrate. My eyes were slowly acclimatising to the dark. I went into my bedroom. There were not many places to store things in the bedroom, especially as I had already had a clear out, in anticipation of a four year stint in Singapore. I took off my padded jacket, and Shariz's uncle's suit, but kept on the silk underwear as I slid beneath the sheets and duvet of my bed.

I wasn't ready for sleep, but being back in familiar surroundings meant I was able to relax. As I lay there looking out of the window - I daren't draw the curtains together - my mobile vibrated. It was Gerda.

I pulled the duvet over my head as I whispered into the phone "Hello my darling."

"Hello, Marc?" I could tell she was concerned "Your voice sounds strange. Are you in trouble? Are you hurt?"

"No, I'm fine."

I explained that I was in my flat and just being careful in case anyone else was watching or listening.

"Marc, I have great news; Paul was more responsive again this evening," I could tell she was excited "and the doctor saw it happening."

"Fantastic!" I was genuinely pleased for Gerda because of the number of previous false dawns.

"The doctor is going to recommend another series of tests, plus a nurse will be permanently stationed by Paul's side."

"Won't that cost a small fortune?" I asked.

"No, nothing," she laughed "he wants to use Paul – how do you say – as a guinea pig."

"I think he may be suspicious about Peter and his mother," I was more sceptical than Gerda "and he is trying to cover his own back."

"Possibly, but I am so happy Marc;" she sniffed "I love you so much my darling. If it was not for you, those bastards would still be feeding him drugs."

The vehemence in her voice shook me "I love you too!" I said in reply.

"Marc, why would they want to sedate Paul?" Her voice had recovered to its normal tone.

"I have an inkling of a possible reason. I think with some more information, I might be able to clear up this situation, and reverse the Lloyd's of London ban."

"How?" Gerda sounded worried "You won't do anything stupid, will you?"

"Of course not!" I lied very poorly.

"Hmmm."

She was unconvinced, and rightly so, because I intended to march straight into The Hall and confront Sir Hugh Masterson.

"My darling, I am going to use tomorrow and Friday to get my facts straight." As I was speaking, an idea popped into my mind, "Gerda can you check tomorrow if any names of ships are contained in the data on the disc please?"

"Ok, my darling Marc." I could hear tiredness in her voice.

"Thank you Gerda. You sound exhausted. Try and get some sleep, we can talk in the morning." I blew her a kiss with "I love you."

"I love you too." Gerda replied as she rang off.

It was less than a minute before my mobile vibrated again, but no number showed on the little screen.

"Hello." I whispered from under the bed clothes.

"Marc, are you OK?" K-P sounded as concerned as Gerda was a few minutes earlier.

I repeated to him, what I had said to Gerda about being in the flat, and being careful.

"I don't think it is the police who have been watching the flat" K-P answered.

"Why do you say that?" my voice rising more that I would have wished.

"I can't tell you now, because I am in deep do-dos with Jane, being out so late without warning. I will meet you for lunch tomorrow in Brick Lane; wear that disguise of yours, it will be perfect."

K-P ended the call, and the familiar surroundings of my bedroom allowed me to assimilate the information both Gerda and K-P had imparted. Weariness enveloped me, and the sounds of the traffic seemed a comfort, rather than an annoyance. I fell into a deep and surprisingly untroubled sleep.

# Dawn Thursday
# Hackney

I woke with a shock, blinking and rubbing my eyes, to dispel the feeling of disorientation. Dawn had broken. I checked my watch, remembering not to illuminate the room, relying on the watery November sunlight. I jumped out of bed and was instantly grateful for the long silk underwear. It was cold.

I went to the toilet, and on my return I looked out of the living room window; I could see that it had snowed during the night. There was a light covering of snow on the window ledge, and elsewhere, but none had settled on the roads or pavements. As I looked down the road I saw a police car approaching, with its blue light flashing, but no siren. About thirty metres away, the blue light was turned off, and the police car drew up alongside the shop beneath my flat. The markings on the side of the car indicated it was from the City of London Police.

"Strange, they're operating outside their area?" I said to myself as Hackney was serviced by the Metropolitan Police.

The two policemen were getting out of the car, and the hairs on the back of my neck were bristling, and I felt that I might be the likely focus of their enquiries. If I was right, I was trapped in my own flat, because the only exit was down the stairs and past the entrance to Shariz's shop. I had to get out of the flat another way - and quickly.

I pulled up the covers of my bed, quickly dressing in my clothes from the previous day, whilst not forgetting the warm quilted jacket. I went into the bathroom, climbed onto the bath and opened the Velux window. Immediately I was showered with wet snow, which had lain on the top of the window, and fell on me when the window passed through ninety degrees. I used the handle of the Velux window to help me leverage my way out through the window opening, onto the flat roof above. Once on the roof, I kept as low as possible, creeping over to the parapet at the front of the building. The police car was still there, and it had not been joined by any other vehicles. Perhaps it was just a routine enquiry. I decided that I could not afford to take that risk. I erected a television aerial myself, shortly after I bought the flat, and therefore knew the layout of the roof.

Still crouching, and keeping low to the roof, I made my way across to the back of the building. I peered over the parapet to see whether the alley, which ran along the rear of the terrace, was clear. It was. I climbed over the parapet, holding onto a downpipe, praying it was firmly fixed to the wall and that it would take my weight. The pipe was cold and wet. My shoes were leather and slipped. I started to slide down the pipe far too fast. The back of Shariz's shop was three metres below me, where there was a ground floor extension, and it was careering towards me. If I landed heavily on the store-room, not only would I hurt myself, but the noise would undoubtedly alert anyone in the shop of my escape route. In an effort to try and slow my wild descent, I put the soles of my shoes flat against the wall, and pulled the pipe, trying to wrench it off the wall. It slowed me sufficiently that my impact with the roof of the store-room was a dull thud, rather than a crash. My torso would be bruised again, but there were no cries or shouts, so the policemen did not hear me.

I dropped off the store-room, onto the ground where I made fresh footmarks in the snow. I made my way to the end of the store-room, where there were double doors opened onto hard standing, and then on to a locked gate which gave access to the alley beyond. The key was in the padlock of the gate, and one of the store-room doors was slightly ajar, plus there was no snow on the hard standing. I guessed that Shariz's brother was probably working in the store-room when the police arrived. I walked over to the gate leading to the alley, unlocked the padlock, and slipped into the alley. I made sure that there was a clear imprint of my footsteps in the snow, before stepping into the middle of the alley, where there were already tracks of other pedestrians. I then walked backwards, careful to ensure that my feet traced my original footsteps, until I returned to the hard standing. I then turned around, walked towards the open door, and quietly slipped inside the store-room.

Immediately I was inside Shariz's storeroom, which doubled as his brother's workshop, I could hear the policemen trying to force their way into my flat. A large crack signalled that my door gave way. The wet snow on the floor of the bathroom, would give them sufficient evidence to show that I had stayed in the flat, and then they would soon be on my trail. I retreated to the rear of the storeroom, where a pile of timber was covered by a tarpaulin. I squeezed behind the stack of wood and crouched down.

I would be unlucky if the policemen themselves found me, but if they called for dogs, I would be discovered immediately. I was hoping the police would fall for my ruse that I left via the alley.

As I huddled down, I listened to the noises coming from my flat, and my hands started to burn with the wet and the cold. I shivered involuntarily, hoping that I didn't sneeze. My knuckles were raw from the grazes on the brickwork, and blood was dripping onto the floor. At that moment I heard footsteps clattering down the stairs, the owner of the footsteps came through the storeroom, going outside and then returning to the entrance. The static of his radio crackled into life.

"He has got away through the alley!" He announced to his colleague.

There was a muffled expletive from the radio.

The policeman in the store-room replied "Yes, I am sure!" The tone of his voice was rising. "Twat!" he said under his breath.

A metallic voice came across the airwaves "Pardon?"

"That's that, I said," the policeman lied fluidly "should we look for him?"

The radio crackled in response.

The policeman in the storeroom walked outside, and I heard the rasp of a flint lighter. He was having a crafty cigarette, whilst waiting for further instructions. I could hear the door of the shop opening and closing, as Shariz's trade commenced, and London started to wake up to a cold and murky November morning. I recalled a recent national newspaper advertising campaign, which boasted they were the only paper who could guarantee delivery to Londoners, because Londoners woke up forty minutes before the average for the rest of the United Kingdom.

There was a crackle of the policeman's radio, followed by the sound of metal on concrete, as the policeman ground out the cigarette with the reinforced heel of his boot. I heard my flat door closing, which meant the other policeman would soon be joining his colleague. He had come downstairs and was speaking to Shariz. His partner sauntered in from the cold, and I was sure I could smell his nicotine laden breath, from my hiding place. He continued through the storeroom and was reunited with the younger policeman at the door of the shop.

The smoker asked his colleague "What's the score?"

A softer voice replied "We are to remain here until Sergeant Smithson has spoken with the DI."

"For Pete's sake!" The smoker was obviously a man who disliked hanging around "He's probably half way to Paddington by now!"

"I saw the walking stick upstairs."

I held my breath for a moment. My disguise is blown.

The smoker retorted "An old Asian-looking man running will stick out like a sore thumb. I think we should cruise the roads between here and the City."

At that moment the air filled with radio static.

"Yes, Sarge?" The smoker replied first.

I could hear a voice, but I could not make out the words.

"OK. The resignation in the policeman's voice was obvious. "Do you want a cup of tea?" He asked his colleague.

"But we are to remain here?" asked the younger policeman.

Whilst I could not see them, I had imagined that the older policeman was much more cynical than his colleague.

"I'm going outside for a few minutes," the older policeman announced, and I could hear his heavy feet walk into the shop, followed by the sound of the storeroom door closing a few seconds later. The younger policeman shuffled from one foot to the other. He was moving closer to me. Had I left a trail when I came into the store-room? He was moving things along the shelves. Was he just curious, or was he looking for something? The faint sounds on the radio were definitely clearer, I felt he was less than two metres away, and I was trapped if I was discovered. I thought about pushing the stack of timber in his direction and making a dash for freedom. Despite the rush of adrenaline, sense prevailed, and I sat tight.

My prayers were answered by a crescendo of static filling the air.

A voice sprang from the policeman's radio "Suspect spotted running towards Cambridge Heath Road Station. Please pursue and apprehend?"

This was immediately followed by the rasping voice of the smoking policeman, acknowledging, and confirming their pursuit.

The door of the shop opened violently, followed by a shout of "C'mon tenderfoot, he won't fool us in his disguise, the chase is on!!"

The older policeman was about to get his daily fix of 'blues-and-twos'.

The door of the shop closed. I waited a couple of minutes after the noise of the police car's sirens had melted into the background of East London's morning traffic rush-hour. Shariz and his brother were talking animatedly as I eased my way out of my hiding place. I gently crept towards the shop, Shariz's brother saw me first, and his eyebrows shot up his forehead.

Shariz swung round "Oh gosh Mr Marc, you are still here!"

"Yes." I replied.

"They thought you ran into the alley and towards the station."

"Yes, I heard it on the radio."

"They know about your disguise!" Shariz made a very solemn face "They accused me of helping you!"

"What did you say?" I asked.

"I said that I hadn't seen you since Wednesday morning, a week ago."

"Good!" I said.

"They knew it was you because of the CCTV outside Bishopsgate Police Station. They compared it to when you had been there previously," Shariz continued "even in your disguise, they could tell it was you by the way you walked – it was your gait."

I had been careless on Bishopsgate, because of the snow on the ground, and did not use the walking stick properly. More foolishly I changed hands when I walked with the stick.

"Apparently it is nearly impossible to change your gait," Shariz was proud to impart this piece of trivia "and the police identify more people through their gait, than their faces on CCTV."

"Hmmm! Where are my old clothes I asked you to store for me?" I asked.

Shariz spoke to his brother, who smiled as he led me back into the store-room, and I took the bag and headed towards my flat.

"You can't go up there Mr Marc." Shariz said to me.

I ignored him, and was halfway up the stairs, until I saw the reason for Shariz's warning. The door was closed and the younger policeman had spent his time placing 'Scene of Crime' tape across the entrance. To enter the flat, would only drop Shariz and his brother in the brown stuff.

"Can I change in the store-room?" I asked at the bottom of the stairs.

"Of course Mr Marc; perhaps you should give me my uncle's spectacles, and other clothes?"

I nodded.

Shariz continued "And your quilted coat is very distinctive."

This I was not keen to give up in a hurry. First my ski-jacket, then my British Warm crombie, and now the coat that Gerda had only bought for me at the weekend.

"Please keep it safe for me Shariz."

"Of course Mr Marc!" Shariz replied, nodding his head vigorously.

In the store-room, I shed the coat, the light cotton suit and the black shoes. I kept the silk underwear, as I would need it more than ever with no coat. I pulled out an old pair of trainers, worn jeans, a grey training top, a ski base layer, a black sweatshirt, a lightweight nylon shower proof jacket, and a Yankees baseball cap. The last item I had brought back from the USA and never worn.

With the baseball cap covered by the hood of the training top, and the nylon jacket over the top of the hoody, I hoped I would look like any number of young Asian men that could be found in East London. I went to the toilet behind Shariz's shop, and looked in the mirror and I was astounded by the transformation. My shoulders hunched, I could hardly recognise myself.

# Thursday Morning
# Whitechapel Road

I left Shariz and his brother just before nine o'clock, when the peak of the morning trade was at its zenith. I decided to avoid the Cambridge Heath area, and headed south towards Victoria Park, my preferred route anyway even if plagued by bicycles.

I checked my phone. No calls. I was surprised that I hadn't received a call or text from Gerda. I tried calling her but it just went to her voicemail.

"Good morning, my darling. Just checking how you are and to tell you - I love you".

I hoped my message conveyed the warmth of feeling I felt for Gerda. I slipped the mobile into my jeans pocket, but not before I switched the phone to vibrate, so I wouldn't miss her call through the noise of the traffic.

It was a nothing sort of day, the evidence of snow from the previous day could only be seen in a very few places, and the watery sunlight was quickly defrosting the overnight frost. There was no wind, and grey skies; a depressing day, if it were not for the tasks I had designated to accomplish before sunset.

I was reaching the southern exit of Victoria Park when my phone vibrated once; I had received a text message. I fished out the mobile and saw that it was from Gerda.

'Sorry, can't talk, I am in a client meeting until four o'clock, and then going to see Paul at the hospital. I will call you from there."

I replied *'No problem. Love you. X'*

Four o'clock in Holland would be three o'clock in London, by which time I should have finished lunch with K-P. With that thought in mind I brought up his contact details and selected his office number. He answered on the second ring.

"Hi!" I said.

"Good morning," was his reply "still at large then?"

"Only just."

Before he asked what happened, I enquired whether we were still meeting for lunch.

"Yes, but no alcohol for me today. Jane was furious when she smelt my breath after my meeting with Eric Jones."

"No problems for me either," I said eagerly "there's a lot to catch up on, and I need my wits about me."

"Why's that?" He sounded worried.

"I will tell you over a curry and a sweet lassi."

"Alright, the Shalimar at twenty past one." He instructed me.

"Perfect. See you then." I hung up.


I walked by Regents Canal, past Queen Mary University, and when I reached the Mile End Road I climbed the stairs to street level and turned towards the City. As I walked towards Stepney Green the results of the recession were clearly visible, with a number of premises closed, and there was very little sign of fresh tenants looking to occupy these retail units. The thinning out of the weak in tough times was always thus, whether a physical or a financial battle. The influx of immigrants that were attracted to the United Kingdom in the boom time were starting to return to Eastern Europe and elsewhere in their droves. The fact that the United Kingdom boom was built on credit, and so closely associated with the USA, meant the economies of Europe were recovering quicker than the United Kingdom. The Celtic Tiger economy was broken and very nearly bust, so the Irish were running for European cover and agreed to ratify the Lisbon Treaty. The United Kingdom was dithering, more concerned about the impending election, and troops dying in Afghanistan.

All was not depressing news; the banks were quickly re-building their balance sheets, and increasing their solvency margins. The investment banks' employees, who had caused so much damage in the first place, were in grave danger of earning large bonuses again as the phoenix started to rise from the ashes. The weakness of the dollar and pound against other world currencies, particularly the Euro, meant the United Kingdom was becoming an obvious and financially attractive destination for tourists. It would be wonderful if the exchange rate and low inflation could remain until after the Olympics in London. The cost of the Olympics was a fear for every Londoner, but the lack of competition for materials and labour during the worldwide construction slowdown, was resulting in the construction being ahead of schedule. This was starting to dispel the natural English sceptical view, being that we would be unable to deliver the Olympics on time, within the 'real' budget. The London Mayor, Boris Johnson's comments that the London Olympics will be achieved in a quintessential English way, rather than the lavishness of the Chinese games, had gone a long way to manage the world's expectations.

I passed Stepney Green underground station. The London Hospital was now visible, as was the street Market on the opposite side of the road. Predominantly the stall holders were Bangladeshi, and for a moment you could actually believe you were in a city on the Indian sub-continent or the Far East. Suddenly the idea of going to Singapore was still very appealing, but if what I was planning happened, that would be as likely as me becoming the next Prime Minister.

My destination for the next few hours, before my rendezvous with K-P at lunch-time, was the Idea Store – modern name for the Public Library - on Whitechapel Road. I paid the minimal fee required to use the Internet and settled into my research. I felt the future plans of Masterson Shipping were a key to the events of the past two weeks. I know that Sir Hugh's family farm was in the dry wind-swept south-western region of Zimbabwe known as Matabeleland. Ever since Robert Mugabe's accession to Presidency he has slowly and cruelly seized the farms of the white farmers. Whilst a legacy of the former colonialisms that pervaded Zimbabwe and other African countries, Mugabe's systematic seizure was hailed as a triumph by the African National Congress, even though the farms were passed to his supporters and army cronies, rather than going to the impoverished black population. Successive harvest failures led to amelioration of sorts in 2007, when leases were granted to a number of white farmers. The power-sharing with Morgan Tzvangerai's Movement for Democratic Change was a severe 'slap-in-the-face' for Mugabe. So, in an effort to show he was still 'all powerful', at his 85th birthday in February, he avowed that the last white farmers would be asked to leave Zimbabwe.

Displaced white Zimbabwean farmers had tried elsewhere, with only limited success in Mozambique, Nigeria and Zambia, probably due in part to Mugabe's strong arming of his fellow African National Congress leaders. Only a few hundred white farmers now remained. A number of Zimbabwean farmers joined South Africans and signed an agreement with the Republic of Congo to lease two hundred thousand hectares of land. The Congo needed the expertise to be able to farm 'in-country' and reduce its dependence upon imports.

If my hunch was correct, the announcement by Mugabe at his birthday may have galvanised Sir Hugh into taking action, before it was too late. Since independence, Zimbabwe's primary goal has been to try and redress the socio-economic imbalances that existed during the era of colonialism. They wished to do this without alienating its white population, whose skills were of vital importance to its economy; but this became a false objective as far as the white farmers were concerned. At the point of independence, Zimbabwe was fortunate in having a relatively diversified economy. It had a good infrastructure, strong manufacturing and agricultural sectors, plus a vigorous financial services sector and extensive mining. One of its misfortunes is the fact that Zimbabwe is landlocked, with the closest seaport being Beira in Mozambique, five hundred and sixty kilometres away.

I had a break from my research, and bought a coke from the newsagent, next door to the Idea Store. I would have loved a coffee, but it would have been totally incongruent, given I was trying to portray myself as a young Asian man.

Returning to the Internet, I noted that a new company planned to set up an inland port to serve as a regional cargo hub, handling both inbound and outbound cargo via the railroad and air networks. It would also handle container traffic, *en route* to and from Beira.

A number of different events may have set in motion a plan but what was the plan? I searched the columns of various newspapers, reporting the news from Zimbabwe. The most reliable news service – the BBC - was banned from Zimbabwe, so I scanned the Internet sites of newspapers pro- and anti- Mugabe.

I was starting to lose heart when I found a report regarding the Conservative Allianz of Zimbabwe. The Conservative Alliance of Zimbabwe was styled as the final incarnation of a party formerly called the 'Republican Front', and prior to that the 'Rhodesian Front'. In the immediate post-independence period, the 'RF' sought to promote the position of whites in Zimbabwe. Another party was spawned from the Conservative Alliance of Zimbabwe, known as the Forum Party, attracting support mainly from the whites and urban middle class blacks. The Forum Party appeal was too narrow and failed to make an impact on the mass electorate. However, the concept of the broad based, non-ethnic opposition movement was born. Other parties were forming in the democratic vacuum including the Zimbabwe National Congress, which hoped for defections from the Movement for Democratic Change and the Zanu-PF parties.

I sat back in the uncomfortable plastic chair, playing a number of scenarios through my mind, but all incredibly improbable. I decided to turn my attention back to the

movements of Masterson Shipping vessels. The obvious
place to start looking was the web-site of *Lloyd's List*. Their
web-site included a section called 'Lloyd's Loading List',
which listed all the countries of the world and for each
country their principle ports. Within the port you can select
a particular date, and there was a list of the comings-and-
goings of vessels, together with the name of their Master.
I checked my watch, it was just approaching ten thirty,
still three hours before I was to meet with K-P. Plenty of
time, but time I knew I would need, as it would take ages
to find the needle in the haystack I was seeking. I selected
Mozambique as the country, Beira as the port and started
searching from the beginning of March two thousand and
nine – the day after Mugabe's birthday when he called for
the remaining white farmers to clear out of Zimbabwe.

As there was no leap year, there were the records for two
hundred and fifty four days to research. I started the long
arduous task, and it took ten minutes or so before I found the
shortcuts, to be able to search the web-site more efficiently.
After an hour I had reached June, with only sporadic hits on
Masterson Shipping vessels, there was no pattern emerging.
As I paused a horrible thought occurred to me: What if
my theory was right, but Sir Hugh was using vessels from
other companies in the Masterson Shipping Group, or even
leasing vessels from completely separate companies?

I swore to myself for not thinking of this before.

I accessed the Masterson Shipping web-site, and made
a note of all the companies mentioned, whether they were
wholly or partially owned by Masterson Shipping Group.
Then another thought occurred to me, Sir Hugh would
only trust his most senior of Masters, so I again searched
the Masterson Shipping web-site which helpfully listed the

Captains of his vessels. What did investigators do before the Internet?

With my lists of companies and captains, I resumed my search. I decided to continue where I had left off, because I couldn't recall any of the company names leaping out at me when I had searched from March to the end of May. What was also noticeable was that the number of vessels was decreasing, which probably reflected the world recession biting into the number of voyages, and the pirates attacking ships off the east coast of Africa.

I had reached the end of August, and was feeling downhearted that my theory was just that, a ridiculous theory. But as soon as September started I hit the mother lode, with four hits in September, one each week and never the same company twice. October proved to be equally fruitful, as was the first week of November; since then nothing, which coincided with the last two weeks!

## Thursday Lunchtime
## Brick Lane

I left the Idea Store at one o'clock, and the weather had deteriorated into a drizzle of freezing rain. The stallholders of the street market were huddled under the canopies of their stalls. There were only a few hardy shoppers; most pedestrians were bound for London Hospital or the underground station at Whitechapel. I pulled my training top tight over my baseball cap, grateful for the nylon waterproof, and bowed my head as I walked quickly westwards towards Brick Lane.

The City of London's eastern border is Aldgate, and Brick Lane was very close to Aldgate East underground station, famed for its Asian restaurants. Recently the northern end of Brick Lane had become a hip cosmopolitan tourist attraction.

I turned into the southern end of Brick Lane at quarter past one as the freezing rain started to increase in intensity. The Shalimar was in the middle of Brick Lane, where the restaurants were at their most dense. Usually there would be employees outside each of the restaurants, persuading passers-by that theirs was the best value in the area. Today the street was nearly empty, the weather dissuading diners from venturing out of the City for lunch.

The Shalimar offered a good value buffet on Thursday lunchtimes, making it a favourite of K-P's, and other *Lammers*.

"Yes, can I help you?"

I was surprised at the tone, and then I caught a glimpse of myself, in the mirror behind the bar.

"I am having lunch here today with my uncle," the waiter eyed me suspiciously "he will be here shortly."

The waiter pointed to a table in the corner, away from the only other table occupied by diners. I pulled the hood of my training top off my head, removed my baseball cap and then took off the nylon waterproof. I only had to wait a couple of minutes before the door of the restaurant was filled by K-P's profile. I waved at him, he looked around the restaurant, and then he waddled towards me.

"Another disguise?"

"It's even better when I put on the baseball cap and hood over my head."

"I am surprised you haven't been arrested, for being a juvenile delinquent, looking like that?" He smiled as the waiter came over with two poppadums and menus. "Two buffets and two sweet lassis" K-P ordered.

The waiter retreated without a word.

"So how was Eric Jones?" I couldn't contain my curiosity any longer.

"In a moment," K-P had a very solemn face "tell me what happened in Holland, and what you have been up to since you have been back in London? Jane received another visit from the police mid-morning, asking whether you had been in touch."

He paused as the waiter served our non-alcoholic yoghurt drinks.

"Jane warned me and I took precautions by ducking through a department store in Fenchuch Street with a back door to Leadenhall Market, and caught a cab from Gracechurch Street."

"I wondered why you were not wet."

I took a sip of my drink, before continuing "Whilst I stayed with Gerda, I spent some time visiting Paul in hospital. When I was talking to him he very nearly became conscious, but the next day, he was completely unconscious again. I asked the doctor whether he was sedating Paul, which he denied, yet I had seen an empty syringe by Paul's bed. Paul's nurses included a young man with an Afrikaans accent as well as an older female nurse."

K-P was listening intently as I took another sip of my drink.

"The following day I walked into Paul's room unannounced, and saw the Afrikaans accented man with a syringe in his hand, so I confronted him. He knew exactly who I was, and the elderly female nurse walked in to Paul's room brandishing a gun. She was his mother, but the kicker is that Sir Hugh was his father!"

"Was?" K-P interjected.

"A scuffle broke out; I escaped from the room, and ran out of the nursing home. The weather conditions were appalling, through a combination of snow, and ice. Sir Hugh's illegitimate son gave chase, on foot, and we headed towards the Prinsengracht. His mother then tried to run me down using her car, and she skidded, hit the kerb and flipped into the canal. Peter tried to save her, he jumped on the ice, but the ice cracked and they both disappeared beneath the surface."

"Bloody heck!!" Was K-P's response and he was genuinely shocked by my account.

"The Dutch Police hadn't recovered the bodies when I phoned Gerda last night, but I am expecting them to do so today, and it won't be long before the police come to the nursing home."

Again I paused to finish my drink "Then they will want to interview people with Gerda being asked the whereabouts of her Asian guest."

"I suppose at some stage you are going to confront Sir Hugh, with the fact his illegitimate son was drugging Paul?" K-P knew me only too well.

"That, plus some other interesting tit-bits." I replied.

"Well before you do so," K-P started his expected warning "he will probably know what has happened, from what Eric Jones told me last evening." He rubbed his stomach, "Let's get some food, I'm starving, and it will help my hangover."

We piled our starter plates high, returning to the table, and we ordered two more sweet lassis.

"When you were with Eric I went to Bishopsgate Police Station, and left another more detailed account of what happened on the night of Tony's death."

K-P looked at me askance, knowing there was more to come.

"I then went back to my flat and stayed the night, only to be woken by the arrival of the City Police."

K-P actually stopped his fork in mid-air, whilst he waited for the next instalment.

"I hadn't been very careful when I went to the police station."

"So why are you not now languishing at Her Majesty's pleasure?" K-P said as he finished his starters.

"I escaped through the Velux window in the bathroom, slid down the drainpipe, and laid a false trail in the snow."

"But you hid in the store-room."

"Exactly," I replied "and hence a different disguise."

I resumed eating as K-P said "I suppose you're feeling pretty pleased with yourself?"

I merely gave him a very supercilious grin.

"But seriously Marc," his tone became deeper "you are an amateur, and I think you are going into the lions den with well organised professionals. Someone is going to get hurt; I should say, more people are going to get hurt, people you care about."

I knew he was right, but I could see no alternative but to continue down the path I had chosen to take.

"K-P, I know. But what else can I do? Run away like a fugitive?"

He shrugged his shoulders "No, I don't suppose you can."


We helped ourselves to the main course, although what K-P had said had taken an edge off my appetite. We ate in silence for a few minutes, and then I repeated my earlier question, about his meeting with Eric Jones. K-P ate a couple more mouthfuls before he started his story.

"Mr Jones is a very complicated and well informed character." He started.

"How so?" I asked.

"We met at half past six at the bar off Cornhill, and he said 'So you and Edge are really that close'. I asked why would he say that, and Eric replied that your brother didn't want anything to do with you, and that he and I were your last chance."

K-P took a long sip from his drink, followed by another two large mouthfuls of food before he recounted the meeting of the previous evening.

"Eric was at pains to point out that he was only a claims manager for Neptune Re, but he used to be in the armed forces, and he kept in touch with 'friends' of his from the Admiralty. When Eric first had his suspicions about these unusual marine claims some two years ago, he and his 'friends' would meet to chat-things-over. In particular, the pirates of Somalia were gaining more confidence, and it was only a matter of time before they would start targeting larger commercial vessels. His 'friends' had informed him that there was an attempted attack on a vessel, owned by a sister company of Masterson Shipping."

"Yes, I know about that," I interrupted "I want to know whether Eric Jones knew anything more than what had been reported."

"You mean the attempted hi-jack this month?" K-P enquired.

"Yes!" I said firmly.

K-P smiled "Don't get cross. No, the one that Eric's 'friends' advised him of happened nearly eighteen months ago, and apparently the pirates were literally blown out of the water, with no survivors."

"Why wasn't this reported?" I asked.

"Because the crew were paid a lot of money to forget about what they saw, and were warned that it would be bad for their health if they talked about it."

K-P went to re-charge his plate from the buffet whilst I digested the information he had just provided.

As he started on his second plate, I asked him "Was the vessel *en route* to Beira, Mozambique, by any chance?"

"Yes." He replied through a mouthful of food.

"And was our missing captain the Master?"

341

"Bravo. Go to the top of the class Mr Edge."

"So how did the news get out?" I asked.

"*Vino veritas.*" He answered.

"Sorry?"

"One of the crew got drunk in Rotterdam, and told a bar full of sailors, how they blew the pirates boat to pieces and then machine gunned any bodies they could find."

"My goodness." I said.

"And guess who was in the bar, that fateful night?" K-P was teasing me, but his eyes were deadly serious.

"Not a clue." I replied.

"Really?"

"Yes, really!" I said in a firmer tone.

"Paul van der Kohl." K-P said before returning to his food.

"Well I never would have guessed."

My voice trailed off until the last word was barely a whisper.

It was just under eighteen months ago when Paul was accused of fraud and I suffered my own subsequent fall from grace.

"What are you thinking?" K-P asked.

"That Paul, with his gabby mouth couldn't keep quiet, and that he mentioned this to someone he shouldn't have." I hesitated for an instant "Possibly Mércédès, or even, Sir Hugh himself?"

"Hmm, that's interesting."

"Why?" I asked.

"Because Eric Jones thinks exactly the same as you, and he thinks it was Mércédès, especially as she has never had a particular liking for Paul."

I was astonished that Eric would know such a thing and told K-P so in a very old fashioned manner.

"Oh, come on Marc!" K-P placated me "It was obvious, when they were together the body language between them was awful."

I said nothing.

K-P continued "Eric thinks that it may have been Sir Hugh who tipped off Paul's employers about this siphoning off the commission. Sir Hugh, as Chairman of JPG, was bound to have access to the information of commission payments."

"Shit!" I murmured.

"And there's more." K-P's voice had deepened and I looked up into his face.

"Far from being your supporter on the Committee of Lloyd's, he was privately the most vociferous, and played the martyr by saying 'even if it affects my own family, we must drive corruption out of Lloyd's'."

"The bastard!"

Again my voice only above a whisper, as the shock of K-Ps revelations started to sink in.

"K-P," I was starting to feel angry "Sir Hugh probably poisoned Mércédès against me."

"Probably so." K-P agreed.

"Do you think Eric Jones knew all of this when he asked me to investigate the disappearance of Captain Hennessey?"

"Almost certainly," K-P continued "and it would not surprise me if he made sure that Sir Hugh was made aware of his actions."

"Whatever for?" I asked.

"Can't you guess?" K-P was smiling.

I shook my head.

"You were Eric's blunt instrument; he wanted you to go blundering in, to start a chain reaction." K-P explained.

"But why" I was at a loss to see the end-game "all the fuss about this vessel and the Captain?"

"I don't know" K-P answered "truthfully I don't, but after the softening up through your beating, the Singapore offer was probably to try to get you out of the way."

We ordered coffees and asked for the bill. It was dawning on me that both Eric and Sir Hugh were treating me as a pawn in their own games. I felt sure it was linked to vessels delivering cargo to Zimbabwe, via Beira in Mozambique. K-P paid the bill and started to make for a return to work. As we walked towards Lloyd's, I briefly outlined my research into the political situation in Zimbabwe, and also what I had found out through the Lloyd's List web-site.

"All supposition," K-P said as we passed through Spitalfields near the bar where I received my beating almost two weeks previously "and guesswork that you have chosen to fit around your own fanciful theories."

"Many thanks for your support, and" I turned to him "whose side are you on?"

"Marc, it is not a question of sides, and I hardly need to remind you that you are being hunted for one possible murder in the UK, and before long another two suspicious deaths in Holland."

He stopped talking until we were through Artillery Lane, which was near the London headquarters of Inter-Continental, my previous employer.

"And you need to have hard facts before you are caught, because as it stands, the next time you see your god-children, they will be at university."

He let this sink in as we exited Devonshire Square.

"What will you do now?"

"Have more coffee and a think." I replied.

"Well be careful, and give me a call at work about half past five, before I go home."

"Will do, and thanks for lunch".

As I was about to turn away, K-P warned me not to return to my flat.

"Why not?" I asked.

"Eric Jones dropped a hint that not only were the police watching it, but also his 'friends' from the Admiralty were interested in your movements, and they spotted another couple of heavies hanging around."

"It's a wonder I got away at all!" I said gleefully.

K-P brought me down to earth with "Only because they wanted you to run amok. And your disguise may be wearing a bit thin, as the tint on your skin is becoming lighter."

"Thanks!"

"It's nothing." K-P smiled and waddled off to Lloyd's of London.

# Thursday Afternoon
# Liverpool Street

It was nearly a quarter to three when I left K-P on Bishopsgate, almost outside the police station. The urge to go into the police station, to explain all to Sergeant Smithson was strong, but I suppressed the idea and carried on to get a coffee. The rain had stopped during lunch, but the sky was dark and leaden; it was like my mood - very depressing. I was expecting a call from Gerda shortly, so I headed for shelter afforded by Liverpool Street Station. Within two minutes I was seated at the same table at the coffee shop I shared with Carla the previous week.

I had finished my coffee by the time Gerda called, just after quarter past three.

"Hello my darling." I greeted her.

"Hi Marc," Gerda sounded up-beat "sorry about this morning, but I had completely forgotten about my client meeting today."

"Not a problem," I reassured her "how did it go?"

"Fine, no, very good in fact" her cheerfulness was evident and I only hoped it continued.

"Are you at the nursing home?"

"Yes," Gerda replied "and the new nurse has said that Paul has continued to float in and out of consciousness."

"That's brilliant news." I then asked "Any news about Peter and his mother?"

"Apparently they recovered the car from the canal late this morning," Gerda replied quietly.

"Hmm, the police will soon be at the nursing home."

"I know," was Gerda's matter-of-fact reply "but it is their problem to track you down. I will merely say you returned to London as scheduled yesterday afternoon."

"The doctor may give us some breathing space, as he has probably worked out that they were up to no good."

"Possibly" Gerda sounded unconvinced "I don't think he is a very confident man."

She then asked the question I had been dreading "Are you OK? What have you been doing?"

I tried to play down the morning's escapade "I nearly had a close encounter with the police at my flat."

"What!" Gerda was obviously upset.

"It's not a problem" I lied badly "I slipped out the back door of the storeroom of the shop."

"Why did they come to the flat?" Gerda asked.

"I am not sure," then I changed the subject "anyway I had lunch with K-P, and his meeting with Eric Jones was very productive."

"How so?" Gerda enquired.

"Eric Jones thinks Sir Hugh may be behind the tip-off about Paul's taking of commission."

Gerda said nothing.

After a moment or two I spoke again "Are you there?"

"Ja."

"And I think all the events are somehow connected to Zimbabwe.

"Why?"

The brevity of her reply indicated that Gerda was struggling with strong emotions.

I explained about my research at the Idea Store, and the fact that Eric Jones may have wound me up like a toy solder, to flush out Sir Hugh.

"Normally I would tell you to do the exact opposite, but I know there is no other way than to confront Sir Hugh with this information."

The pragmatism of Gerda was sometimes amazing, and this was one of those occasions. Before I could agree with her she pointed out that I needed to do it quickly; before he became aware of Peter's and his mother's death, because he would then know that I knew about his involvement in Paul's sedation.

"Why do you think Sir Hugh wanted to keep Paul from gaining consciousness?" Gerda asked.

"I believe it is because he heard about a massacre of Somali pirates by a heavily armed Masterson ship." Before Gerda said anything further I added "This was before the current wave of hi-jacks, and it may have had something to do with the cargo that was being carried."

"When and how are you going to confront Sir Hugh?"

A hint of nervousness had crept into her voice.

"Tomorrow, at The Hall," I hadn't really formulated my plans properly but I knew I had to act quickly "Sir Hugh often works from home on a Friday."

"Marc, I love you so much. I have to go now because the doctor is coming towards me, and he does not look happy."

"Ok my darling. Can you call me again when you are at home later tonight?"

"Sure. Chuss and love you." Gerda hung up.

I bought another coffee, and sat in the corner planning my next move. I checked my wallet, and I still had most of the three hundred Euros Gerda had given to me, the previous day.

I finished my coffee, and then walked to a currency exchange desk on the concourse of Liverpool Street Station, where I exchanged the Euros into Pounds Sterling. If the teller was curious as to how a scruffy young Asian had so much cash, he kept his thoughts to himself, and I had over two hundred and fifty pounds a few minutes later. With cash in hand, I then walked over to Boots the chemists and made various purchases. When I exited the shop I had a bag filled with two large bottles of make-up remover, two bottles of hair dye, shower sponge that had a rough side, a razor, toothbrush and two packets of cotton wool pads. I also picked up a couple of sandwiches and a coke.

Taking the escalator out of the station, I returned to street level and to my right – near to the site of where the Old Broad Street Station used to stand – were a number of men's clothes shops. The recession meant there were permanent sales, and 'massive discounts' were advertised in each shop. I chose a well known shop, at the cheapest end of the range, which would be able to provide me with a suit, shirt, tie and shoes. The shop assistants were mainly Asian, and I picked the youngest, explaining quietly that I was starting a job on Monday and needed everything for under a hundred and fifty pounds. He managed it with two pounds to spare. The suit was slightly damaged, so it was at a knock down price and thankfully fitted well with no alterations required. The shirt and tie were fairly plain, but the shoes were an awful modern design, and I thought it was no wonder that they were in the sale.

I made my way back towards Brick Lane; it was approaching half past four and dusk had already settled over London. As I walked I felt a sense of purpose and, whatever the outcome of the next day or two, I would never again stay in my flat feeling sorry for myself. I reached Brick Lane in ten minutes, and then took a road off Brick Lane, at the end of which was a run-down hotel. The elderly receptionist looked at me as I walked in, greeting me in a foreign language.

"Sorry, I only speak English." I replied.

"What do you want?" was the accusatory question.

"A cheap room for one night please?" I tried to look bewildered "This is my first time in London, and I have a job interview tomorrow."

This seemed to appease the old man "Cash up-front sixty five pounds!"

I counted out the requisite amount and used Shariz's uncle's name but a false address in Leicester.

This seemed to be in order, he handed me a key saying the room was on the top floor, and he pointed to a lift with battered doors.

The room was on the fourth floor, at the end of the corridor; it had a single bed and threadbare carpet. I was not worried about the state of the room, as I started filling the bath and hand basin with plenty of warm water. I stripped off my old clothes and looked at myself in the mirror. The dye was still dark over most of my body, but in places it was starting to become pale, as the skin cells flaked off. I opened one of the make-up removal bottles, blotted one of the cotton wool pads, rubbing the pad and lotion on my forearm. If I rubbed hard the dye came off my skin, but it was not going to be easy; so I concentrated on my hands, wrists, neck and face. I put the make-up remover to one side and turned off the wash basin taps. I then applied the first application of hair dye. As the hair dye started to do its work, I climbed into the bath with the sponge and a bar of soap supplied by the hotel. After thirty minutes I stopped scrubbing, rinsed my hair under the shower, and then attacked my face and hands with the make-up remover again.

Just before half past five I phoned K-P.

"Are you OK?" he asked.

"Yes," I replied "I am trying to change my appearance, again!"

"Any success?"

"Limited so far." Was my honest appraisal.

"I have had a call from the police asking whether you had been in contact."

"That's not surprising" I replied.

"No, but watch your step." A short pause and then he enquired "So what is your next step?"

"I am holing up tonight, and then a full frontal attack on The Hall tomorrow, because Sir Hugh normally works from home on a Friday."

"Does Gerda know what you plan to do?"

"Yes," I replied "it's Hobson's choice really."

"I know," he agreed with me "but don't expect me to like it. Try and call me when you can. Good luck, Marc."

"Thanks K-P."

I re-applied the hair dye, and scrubbed myself again, in fresh hot bath water. I watched the television that only received terrestrial channels, through an aerial, precariously balanced on the top of the television. The weather for the following day was due to improve, with heavy rain over the weekend following a winter storm blowing in from the Atlantic.

"Bloody English weather." I cursed to myself.

I was eating the first of my sandwiches when Paul's mobile rang. It was Gerda.

"Marc, lots of news," she said before I could speak "Paul woke up and he recognised me and smiled."

Gerda was crying, with her sobs and tears clearly audible across the airwaves.

"That's fantastic news" I said after I heard Gerda blow her nose "I wish I could be there with you my darling."

"Not at the moment you wouldn't!"

"Why not?" I asked.

"The police came to the nursing home asking questions about you."

"Did you stick to the story we planned?"

"No" she said "they knew it was you Marc. They also know about your disguise."

"I am changing it again."

"Good, but they also know that you are back in the UK. They have spoken to the police in London, who said they missed you by a whisker today."

"They exaggerated" I lied.

"Hmm," she sounded unconvinced "but more good news, apparently a crane driver on the opposite side of the Prinsengracht saw the whole accident. It was he who called the ambulance and police."

"Thank God." I said.

"The police still want to interview you. They want to know what led up to the accident, and how you were able to get in and out of Holland."

"I am sure they do."

Gerda spoke again "I think they know I was involved, but they were there when Paul woke up, and have gone away for the moment."

"I am both pleased, and sorry for you, my darling. What are you going to do?"

"I have spoken to my boss, and told her about Paul; she has agreed that I can work remotely tomorrow from the Nursing Home, in case Paul wakes up again."

"That's great my darling."

"What about you?"

Before I could answer the question, she said that the Dutch police made a connection with Sir Hugh. "They will close in on you."

"That's the least of my worries," I countered "I am more concerned about Sir Hugh finding out about the deaths of his son and former lover before I confront him at The Hall first thing in the morning."

"Please be careful Marc. I love you so much, and with Paul coming back to me, I want us all to be together at Christmas."

I laughed "I will do my best. I love you too, and will text you in the morning. Try and sleep my darling."

"You too." Then she was gone.

I ate the rest of my sandwich, and then went back to the bathroom to survey the results of my scrubbing, and hair dye. The hair was certainly fairer although there was a slight orange tinge. I opened the second packet of hair dye, which was for women and much stronger than the first; it smelt instantly of peroxide. Whilst the bleach on my head was working away I tried a little on my skin with immediate results. I re-read the instructions on the back of the hair dye bottle, which explicitly warned about contact with the skin. I filled the wash basin with warm water and rubbed my face quickly with the diluted hair dye, rinsing it off almost immediately. I was extra careful around the eyes. The result on my skin was such that I now looked like I had a winter tan. After eating my other sandwich I showered, careful to clean the bath and wash basin. I towelled my hair and opened the shirt and tie from their packaging. I tried them on, together with the suit, and the awful shoes. The effect was passable, not exactly a City gent, especially with the dyed hair, but hopefully enough of a chance to not stand out too much. I hung my purchases in the rickety wardrobe, turned the television so I could watch it from the bed, and fell asleep in minutes.

I woke up bathed in sweat, I was burning up, the television and lights were still on. I switched off the television and checked my watch, it was midnight. I got out of bed to visit the toilet and get a glass of water. As soon as I switched on the bathroom light, I could see why I felt so hot. I was pink from head to toe and my face was blotchy. I laughed at my own stupidity, and just hoped my skin would recover to be less of a red hue by the morning.

I lay on top of the bed, hoping the Hotel's central heating would soon finish for the day. As I lay in the darkness, I realised that the following day was probably the most important day of my life, and the outcome would determine my future for years to come.

# Friday Morning
# The Hall

I slept fitfully during the night, waking at least three times again after midnight; but each time I resisted the temptation to go to the bathroom, and see if my skin was any less pink. I climbed out of bed at half past six and went through to the bathroom. I was still a bit pink but a vast improvement from the first time I woke up. I strip-washed and dampened my hair before dressing. During one of the times I was awake, I was concerned how I would get past the hotel reception with my changed appearance. I decided that I would wear my training top, plus nylon jacket over my suit, and then put on the baseball cap with the hood over the top of the cap. I would walk out of the hotel without looking backwards.

With the rest of my belongings in the suit carrier, I walked down the stairs, hovering out of sight from reception, until someone came out of the lift and went across to the check out. Whilst they engaged the receptionist, I walked quickly towards the exit, and I was out of the door in seconds.

It was a crisp dark morning, with dawn still yet to fully break. I walked briskly towards Liverpool Street Station, arriving at half past seven, with the next train to Bishop's

Stortford leaving within five minutes. I was hungry. Whilst I had left the hotel full of bravado, I realised that other then the possibility of Sir Hugh working from home on a Friday, I didn't really have a plan. I went to one of the fast-food restaurants on the station concourse, and brought myself a cheap breakfast burger. I retreated again to the coffee shop that had been my regular haunt over the last two weeks, ordering a coffee that was complimentary, as I had filled their loyalty card.

As I counted my remaining coins and notes, I was worried how I would be able to get to The Hall, which was some miles from Bishop's Stortford. I had enough money for the train from either London to Bishop's Stortford, or a taxi from Bishop's Stortford station to The Hall, but not both or the return fare. I could not risk being caught on the train without a ticket, albeit the return ticket may be redundant if I was able to meet and confront Sir Hugh. A depressing thought occurred to me; for all my tenuous theories, I may have it completely wrong and my visit to The Hall could be nothing more than a wild goose chase. I finished my coffee, and sat thinking about what I should do, when I got to The Hall.

I looked around the coffee shop at my fellow customers, and idly wondered what the day had in store for each of them. Despite the recession, Christmas decorations were adorning most shops and as this was the last Friday in November, the advertising was in full swing. A couple approximately my own age came into the coffee shop holding hands tightly, looking deeply into the others' eyes. I wondered if the alcohol had flowed freely for them on 'Thirsty Thursday', and their inhibitions had been lowered, with this morning being the aftermath of a night of passion. The man took his coat off, laying it on the spare chair, as they held each others hands across the table. I turned my eyes away because I felt as though I was prying into the couple's private moment. My own thoughts then turned to Gerda, who undoubtedly would be at the nursing home, and then I quickly sent her a text telling her '*Love you deeply and all is well xx*'.

It was ten past eight when I made my way over to the ticket machine on the station concourse. I selected Bishops Stortford as my destination and pressed for a return ticket, which unfortunately was more that I could afford. I cancelled the transaction and walked across to the ticket office. I waited in line, with the other infrequent travellers, who didn't have a season ticket. When my turn came, I asked what the cheapest fare to and from Bishops Stortford was. I could afford a cheap one day return, but I would not be able to travel until after nine o'clock. I thanked the ticket vendor, but didn't purchase a ticket. The discounted cost of a cheap return ticket was about half the price of the full fare, but it would leave me with no money. Should I risk trying to withdraw money from my own account, or would my account have been frozen by the police? I didn't know what to do, so I returned to the coffee shop buying yet another coffee, from my meagre funds.

I sat down in my familiar seat, and saw that the couple had gone, but the man's overcoat was still on the chair. I looked into the middle-distance, yet all I could see was an abyss, which was the lack of a plan to get myself out of this god almighty mess. 'Vanity, vanity, all is vanity' I could hear my paternal grandmother's voice ringing in my ears. She always said that 'being too big for his breeches' would get me in trouble, and would probably be the death of me. How right she was? Whilst the last two weeks may have brought me to life again, my vain belief that I was a self-styled *uber* sleuth was proving to be a big joke. My previous appointments were in truth nothing more than crumbs from the tables of my friends. And now when I really needed to be professional, to save my own skin, I had merely crashed around hoping that something might happen. I was going to do exactly the same with Sir Hugh today. The thought of running away appealed, but I knew that was not really an option, and anyway where would I run to on less than fifteen pounds!

I was committed to action, foolhardy or otherwise. I decided to act now, before I changed my mind. I wandered over to the chair with the overcoat and picked it up, checking the pockets to see if it had any clues as to its owner, who had not returned to claim it yet. The only item in the pocket was a travel season ticket between London and Harlow. Harlow was only two stops from Bishops Stortford, and if I paid the small excess fare I now had the wherewithal to travel to Bishops Stortford; plus I would have enough money left for a taxi to The Hall.

I should have felt bad about using the season ticket, but I felt nothing other than good fortune, as I slipped the overcoat over my clothes. I caught a glimpse of myself in the window of the coffee shop the overcoat was a vast improvement, helping me to melt into the background of the commuting masses. Anyway I was only going to borrow the coat and season ticket; I swore to myself that I would hand them into Lost Property, upon my return to London.

I walked nonchalantly through the automatic gate that was activated by the season ticket, and within a few seconds, I was sitting on the eight thirty-five train for the journey northwards. The trains arriving into Liverpool Street Station were packed to the gills, but those departing back to commuter-land were only a quarter full. The destination of this train was Cambridge, and my fellow passengers consisted of business people having meetings in the City of Cambridge, as well as a number of tourists off to visit the universities. I had read that the universities at Cambridge had recently celebrated eight hundred years of being one of the two premier seats of learning in England, when a group of drunken professors were thrown out of Oxford and established a rival to the 'dreaming spires' in the flat-lands of East Anglia.

We departed on time, and as the train slowly drew out of the station I could see that dawn had fully broken, but it was a grey day that did nothing to lift my sense of foreboding. We passed close to my flat in Hackney, and the morning rush-hour was in full swing. Being the eve of the last weekend in November, most people's thoughts were probably focussed on Christmas, hoping that the New Year would bring some improvement to the economic climate. I picked up a newspaper left by a previous commuter. It was a broadsheet that was determined to be rid of the labour government at the earliest opportunity. Signs, albeit faint, were apparent that the UK economy was starting to climb out of the recession, albeit the UK was way behind the other major economies of the world. The UK's massive debt had disguised some structural flaws in the economy, which were now painfully exposed. The row being played out on the front page of the newspapers was centred on bankers' bonuses. The government needed a scapegoat for the debt fuelled recession, and smart city boys in sharp suits and fast cars were an easy target. UK plc does not manufacture much anymore, and the invisible earnings of finance plus insurance are pivotal to the UK's terms of trade; therefore, if clever bankers are not rewarded properly, there will be a 'brain drain' and the UK will be poorer because of it! I smiled, as I once was thought of as one of the bright stars of the insurance industry, doing my bit for the UK invisible terms of trade, before I had fallen from grace. I would like to see the bankers taken down a peg or two – but not to the detriment of the UK economy. A change of government was almost certain in the New Year, and I hoped the circus of current government would soon be at an end.

Thinking of the New Year, I pulled out my mobile phone from my suit pocket, and saw that Gerda had sent me a message '*I love you*' followed by '*BE CAREFUL*'. I sent a text back saying that I loved her too, and that I would be in touch after meeting with Sir Hugh. I considered calling The Hall to check Sir Hugh was there, but I was concerned that might act as a warning of my impending arrival, and he may try to avoid me. I looked out of the window just as we were pulling into Harlow Town station. The weather was much worse than in London, with the rain pouring from the heavens, and the passengers were huddling under the lee of the staircase on the 'down' platform towards London.

We pulled out of Harlow Town Station and the ticket collector came through the carriage almost immediately, and I paid him the additional fare, leaving me just over ten pounds cash. The train stopped briefly at Sawbridgeworth, and my mind cast back to nine days previously, when I was kayaking past the station in the early hours of the morning. Only a few minutes later the train pulled into Bishop's Stortford Station at just after twenty past nine. I drew the collar of the borrowed overcoat around my neck against the elements, as I walked down the platform. I was very pleased my face was covered, because as I turned into the ticket office I caught a glimpse of Samuel, pulling away from the drop-off zone in front of the station. I looked around to see why he was at the station. I was worried Sir Hugh was taking the train, which he did on rare occasions, but I was relieved to see Ms Syrani walking directly towards me. I pulled the coat collar even higher around my neck, bowing my head, so she did not recognise me. I thought this was a good sign that Sir Hugh was probably working from The Hall.

The bad weather meant that taxis were in short supply. Two middle aged ladies were in front of me waiting for taxis. They were travelling together so hopefully they would also be sharing a taxi. After a few minutes a taxi did arrive. It was a people carrier and one of the ladies turned to me to ask where I was heading. I replied the village close to The Hall.

"That's just a little bit further on from where we are going" the other lady replied "do you want to share the cost of the taxi young man?"

"That's very kind." Perhaps that might mean I would have enough money for a return journey by the bus. I hoped good fortune continued to smile upon me, because I would need a lot of luck to be able to walk out of The Hall with my objective completed.

The taxi driver dropped the ladies at their destination. They paid the fare up to that point, and I then gave the driver directions to The Hall. The weather was still foul, with the result that large puddles were forming at the edge of the country roads, slowing our progress. It was five minutes past ten when the taxi drew up at the front door of The Hall.

I thought about asking the taxi to wait until someone answered the door, because Sir Hugh might refuse to see me and send me away. However, with no obvious transport, I was hoping he would agree to talk with me. The additional fare was only four pounds, and I gave the taxi driver five pounds. Whilst the taxi was preparing to leave, I looked around for signs of the Range Rover, which Samuel had used to drop Ms. Syrani at Bishops Stortford Station. Samuel and Ms. Syrani did not get on with each other, so I guessed little conversation would have passed between them, during the journey. Each saw themselves as Sir Hugh's private confidante, and my betting would be on Samuel having the edge, due to the number of years Samuel's family had worked for the Masterson family. No car was in sight, but Samuel could have already put the Range Rover in the old stables, where Sir Hugh's other three vehicles were kept. I took a deep breath and rang the bell.

There was no response, and after half a minute had passed, I rang again. My heart was sinking, until I heard noises coming from inside The Hall. As the footsteps became more audible I grew increasingly nervous. Then the door swung open and Sir Hugh was standing in the doorway, wearing the same clothes as he wore when he invited me to The Hall nearly two weeks previously.

"Marc," he was obviously taken aback by the sight of me door-stepping him "what are you doing here?"

His tone was one of surprise rather than anger.

I decided to try and put him on the back foot immediately "I wish to have a serious chat about a few things."

Sir Hugh recovered very quickly "You will have to be quick, I am due to leave for a business trip this evening, and I have a lot to do before then."

My tactics seemed to have no effect on Sir Hugh; he was very casual "Come on in out of the rain."

I walked into the entrance hall and hung up the overcoat on the stand by the front door.

"Coffee Marc, I was just making some for myself?"

Sir Hugh asked as he walked through into the kitchen.

"Yes please," I replied following him "no Samuel?"

"He has gone into town to do some shopping for me."

He looked up at me as he filled the kettle "Why do you ask?"

"I thought I saw him at the station," I paused before continuing with "dropping off Ms. Syrani."

Sir Hugh didn't say anything immediately, as he busied himself with the cafetière and the mugs for coffee.

"Milk or sugar?"

"Neither, thank you." I said as my self confidence was ebbing away.

The kettle boiled, and Sir Hugh added water to the coffee grains in the cafetière. Whilst waiting for the coffee to brew, he fixed me with his steely blue eyes.

"Ms. Syrani informed me that you phoned, to say that you have been unwell, what was wrong with you?"

"I lied" I answered abruptly, trying to unsettle Sir Hugh.

"Why?"

"Because I have been on the run from the police, following the death of Tony Eastwood; but you know that anyway, don't you?"

"Perhaps I should call the police now and tell them I have caught the fugitive."

Sir Hugh's eyes were dead like a fish's, as he stared at me.

"Perhaps you should, or perhaps you should wait until we have had our chat."

"And why should I do that?" he asked.

"Because in the last week I have been to Amsterdam, and to the nursing home where Paul van der Kohl is being treated."

Sir Hugh remained impassive.

"I met with two nurses, a mother and son; perhaps you might know them, they came from Zimbabwe?"

Sir Hugh's eyes bore into me, and I noticed that a slight tic was noticeable in his left eye.

He pushed the plunger of the cafetière, and poured the coffee into the two mugs on the tray.

As he picked up the tray "We will be more comfortable in my study."

I naturally assumed we would be going to the study on the ground floor, but instead he started to climb the stairs to his private sanctuary next to his bedroom. The room was just how I had remembered it; from the first and only time he showed it to me previously, with so much pride. A tension now existed between us, as Sir Hugh was trying to regain control of the situation, by bringing me into the lair of the Scorpion. He sat behind his desk, which further increased his psychological advantage of the situation.

"What do you have on your mind laddie?"

The tone in his voice was much frostier than in the kitchen.

"*Sea Cargo III* and Captain John Hennessey," I asked "where are they?"

Sir Hugh just cocked an eye at me.

"Do you not understand my question?" I tried to push him.

"I am not playing your games Marc."

The tables had turned, and he wasn't going to let me dominate the proceedings again.

"I think that you are smuggling arms into Zimbabwe, storing them at an inland port."

"And why on earth would I undertake such a foolish venture?"

He was almost smiling, almost but not quite.

"I think you may be a patron of the Conservative Alliance of Zimbabwe party, hoping to hasten the departure of President Mugabe as he nears his forty year rule of Zimbabwe."

Sir Hugh said nothing and his face once again was staring impassively at me.

I continued "About eighteen months ago, one of Masterson Shipping's vessels was attacked in one of the first of the pirate raids, off the coast of East Africa. But the commando style raid was unsuccessful, because the raiders ran into real commandos on the Masterson ship and there was a massacre. The result was that all the raiders were killed, and sent to the bottom of the sea, together with their speed boats. The Captain and all the crew were sworn to secrecy, probably involving a fat bonus payment. The ship continued to Beira, where the cargo was unloaded before its transit by road to the inland port."

Sir Hugh picked up his coffee, which he sipped noiselessly, thus maintaining the tension.

"The Master was Captain John Hennessey" I was hoping this might unsettle him "the details were easy to find, as are all the voyages of Masterson Group vessels to Beira, over the last eighteen months. The pressure in Zimbabwe has been increasing, and the power-sharing with the Movement for Democratic Change has seen the first chinks in Mugabe's dictatorship. So it was important that you and the Conservative Alliance of Zimbabwe party were prepared for a sudden change in government."

I paused and sipped my own coffee, during which Sir Hugh never took his eyes off me.

"But there was a security breach. One of the crew got very drunk in a bar near Europort in Rotterdam, and he mentioned the massacre, but Paul van der Kohl was in the bar that night. I am guessing that he approached you at some point, asking you whether it was true, and if so how much would you pay him to keep quite. Paul was already on the fiddle, taking the commission payments on the insurance he arranged through JPG, and sending it to a different bank account. You knew this because, as Chairman of JPG, you would have access to payments made by JPG. You decided to blow the whistle on his nefarious activities to his employers. What you didn't know was that Paul had inadvertently implicated me in his fraud. You couldn't risk me siding with Paul, and whilst he was in a coma you engineered my removal from Inter-Continental, Lloyd's of London and my marriage to your daughter. To make sure that Paul didn't recover from his coma too quickly, you somehow were able to get your former lover and your son employed at the nursing home as nurses. They drugged him constantly, to ensure that he didn't regain consciousness."

At the mention of his son the nervous tic returned to Sir Hugh's left eye; but still he didn't move or say anything.

"All was going to plan until the loss of *Sea Cargo III*. Perhaps you were getting greedy, and you needed an injection of funds, I don't know why. Was it the recession, which meant that your assets couldn't be converted to cash for guns quickly enough? So you persuaded Captain Hennessey, I guess with a large number of the crew who were on the vessel when the massacre occurred, to lose the vessel. It wasn't lost of course, it just changed name and went to Beira. But Eric Jones, and some of his shady government 'friends' had you, and Masterson Shipping, under suspicion. News of the massacre had reached their ears from other sources."

Sir Hugh finished his coffee. He was lounging arrogantly in his leather desk chair, waiting for me to continue, which I did after finishing my own coffee.

"Eric Jones had picked me, not because of any investigating ability, but because he hoped it would provoke a reaction from you; which it did! When you knew that Eric Jones was going to try and hire me to investigate the loss of *Sea Cargo III*, you had me beaten up. Things couldn't have gone better for you, because to whom do I turn in my hour of need, but yourself. You played the part of the benefactor very well, and whilst you had me drive you to Felixstowe on the Sunday, you had someone search my flat. It was probably the same person who battered me on the Friday night, because they had kept my keys. I presume they were looking to see if I had been given any evidence regarding the loss of the vessel, and they stole my passport, to prevent me from travelling abroad. Then you had a brainwave, rather than try to get rid of me through force, you tried – and succeeded – through guile and my vanity by offering me a post in Singapore. Also it would get me out of the picture with Mércédès, whom you had turned against me, as well as pulling strings in Neptune Re to make it very difficult for Eric Jones to use me as an investigator. All was going to plan, until Tony Eastwood phoned to arrange to meet me, before he left for his business trip. I don't know why you had him killed, or maybe it was an accident, and the killer was supposed to kill me. Perhaps it was because I had been to Felixstowe and spoken with Captain Hennessey's brother. His brother was very upset, probably because his brother had gone missing, but he reported my meeting with him to you, and you knew that despite your best efforts I was still investigating for Eric Jones. That's when things started getting out of your control because I slipped through the police's fingers. What I couldn't understand, until yesterday, was why the police didn't publish pictures of me in the media."

Sir Hugh shrugged his shoulders as I paused.

"It was because they knew I wasn't the guilty party. Poor Tony, he was a total prat, but he didn't deserve to die. I escaped from the UK to Holland, where I met your former lover and son. Did you know they are both dead?"

I was hoping this was the catalyst that would open him up, but there was still no reaction from Sir Hugh; he just sat immobile in his chair.

"It was a nasty death for them both. They froze in the Prinsengracht. Your lover tried to run me down, but she skidded, and the car careered into the frozen canal. Her - your - son jumped in, without a thought for his own safety, to try and rescue his mother. The ice cracked, they fell through the surface and drowned."

Sir Hugh's blood must run as cold as the icy waters of the canal, because there was only the merest reaction in his left eye during my monologue.

"Also you should know that Paul woke up yesterday, and Gerda - his sister - has already found some data he had been keeping about his affairs, which will clear me from any wrong doing." I was now about to lie my head off. "I have been able to obtain a first hand account of the massacre, and details of the ships cargo, which I handed in as part of a written account of what I have just told you to Bishopsgate Police Station."

Sir Hugh continued to stare at me in silence for a full two minutes, and then he lifted his head slightly so he could look over my shoulder.

"Samuel, Mr Edge is leaving now, and will not be returning – EVER!!"

I turned to look at the door of the study, and saw Samuel standing there, his bulky frame filling the entrance. I turned back to Sir Hugh, but he had now turned his attention to papers on his desk, and then reached for the phone. The audience was over, and I had lost. I stood up and walked over to the door. Sir Hugh didn't even bother to look up from his desk. As I closed in on Samuel he brought his hands from behind his back, and what I saw stopped me in my tracks; his massive hands were covered with black leather gloves. Then the beating in London came flooding back to me, it was Samuel who had thrashed me so badly, also he was in The Hall when Tony Eastwood called me.

"You!!" I yelled at the top of my voice "It was you, you bastard, who beat me up!!"

Something snapped within me and I ran headlong towards Samuel, my head hit him square in the chest, which knocked him backwards across to the wall the other side of the corridor. He was only kept upright by the wall behind him, so I charged at him again, but he was ready for me this time. He hit me hard, very hard in the stomach, and then again on the chin.

# Friday Afternoon
# The Hall

It was pitch black, it was cold, and I couldn't move my feet or my hands. My face was grazed by the concrete of the floor. My head was throbbing insistently, and I could taste the sickliness of blood on my tongue. I wriggled my arms, until I realised my hands were tied behind my back, which were attached to the bonds holding my feet together. The dark musty smell suggested that I was in the cellar, beneath the kitchen in The Hall. I had no idea what the time was, nor how I could stop shivering. I wriggled a bit more, and could just see the faint outline of a door above me, which was at the top of the cellar stairs. I remembered that there was a metallic wine rack in the wine cellar, and it should be behind where I was laying.

It took me ages to wriggle backwards until my hands could feel the wine rack. Each time I tried to manoeuvre myself, I would scrape my face on the concrete floor. My hands fumbled around aimlessly for the edge of the wine rack, but every movement exhausted me. I rested for a while, then tried again with more vigour but only succeeded in bruising myself on the tops of the bottles at the bottom of the wine rack. I stopped again realising it would take more energy than I had to cut my bonds on the metal. My head sank at the futility of my situation. Then my muscles flexed again, and I touched a wine bottle, which gave me another idea. I reached out to the wine rack, pulling a bottle out of its home, and then dropped it on the floor. There was a loud bang, followed by the sound of the bottle rolling away from me, across the floor of the cellar. Before it rolled too far, I jerked my legs backwards, which wrenched my back but I managed to kick the bottle against the wine rack. The sound of the breaking glass was deafening, and I felt sure it would bring my activities to the attention of Samuel or Sir Hugh.

Once again I wriggled and shuffled across the floor, my hands reaching for the broken glass. I could feel the contents of the wine bottle seeping through the trousers of my new suit. My hand touched the first piece of glass, and it sliced through my thumb. I tried again, but with more care, searching for the neck of the bottle. After three or four more attempts, each resulting in further lacerations on my hands and fingers, I felt the neck of the bottle. I manipulated the neck of the bottle to saw through the rope tying my hands to my legs. After only a short while the rope was cut, releasing my feet; but my hands were still tied, although I was able to first kneel and then stand-up. Once up, I found a sharp metal edge to the banisters of the cellar steps, and by pushing my weight down on my bonds I was free in a matter of seconds.

Blood was now flowing freely from the wounds on my fingers and hands. I walked up the cellar steps, expecting to find the cellar door locked, but it wasn't. I opened it slowly, and could hear raised voices coming from upstairs. I crossed to the sink and picked up a tea towel to try and stem the bleeding. The kitchen light was not illuminated, and I was working from the dull grey light outside, concluding that the time was somewhere between three and four in the afternoon. The audience with Sir Hugh probably lasted about forty-five minutes; therefore I must have been unconscious for at least four hours. I instinctively rubbed my chin, it was very sore. The only consolation was that Samuel's fist must hurt equally as much as my chin.

The bleeding had stopped, and I made a futile effort of wiping my blood from the porcelain sink with the tea towel. There were huge splotches on the red sandstone floor tiles, and I mopped these as well.

I could still hear the voices from upstairs, and whilst not actually shouts, a tirade of sharp words was being exchanged between Sir Hugh and Samuel. I knew I should escape from The Hall with all possible haste, but the fact that Samuel had bound me and thrown me in the cellar, was not the action of someone just acting out of self-defence. I was just about to open the back door of The Hall that led from the kitchen, when the tone of the raised voices grew to a full blown argument between Sir Hugh and Samuel. The lure was too much for me, and I turned from the back door, into the kitchen.

I crept up the back stairs, which led to the landing opposite the door of the guest bedroom, where I had stayed only two weeks ago. I made my way on tip-toes along the landing towards the open doorway of Sir Hugh's inner sanctum. I was pressed flat against the wall of the landing, so as not to cast any shadows into Sir Hugh's study, until I was just a foot away from the doorway itself.

I caught Samuel speaking my name.

"I will kill Edge and dump his body near his flat in Hackney."

"Don't be a fool Samuel!" Sir Hugh replied curtly "Your blood lust, and incredible stupidity by killing Tony Eastwood, has caused us to change our plans. You have potentially put the whole project in danger."

"Eastwood knew something, he saw me with Edge's Yachtmaster, and I think he had worked out that I had given Edge his beating." Samuel tried answering in his defence.

Sir Hugh yelled at him "Admit it, you lost your cool, because Tony was going to be a permanent fixture in Mércédès life?" Sir Hugh paused. "For years I have seen the way you drool after her, and finally your jealousy was too much to bear."

"Shut up!" Samuel screamed.

But Sir Hugh did not stop.

"Even if she were free, she would never look at you. You repulse her!"

The cruel sneer in Sir Hugh's voice was clear to hear, even from outside of the room.

"I was good enough for her as a playmate in Africa, when we were children. She said she loved me."

Samuel's voice had broken and he was crying, the sobs clearly audible.

"She played with you, like any servant's child, and she played you well."

"Perhaps she will pay me more attention, when the Movement for Democratic Change recognise my part in our plans."

"Really Samuel, I think you are now having delusions of grandeur. Your 'friends' of the MDC will have no time for you, as I have no time for them. They have been neutered by Mugabe, and that's why we have had to fund and arm our own party." Sir Hugh paused for a second before continuing "In fact Samuel, you have become a liability. I've had enough of you, and have decided to dispense with your services."

373

"So you can have the bitch Syrani here all the time!" Samuel spat the name of Sir Hugh's private secretary.

"Samuel," Sir Hugh's voice was ice cold "your father and grandfather would be so disappointed that you have developed into such an envious, uncouth, loutish ruffian. To think you might even contemplate lusting after my daughter is enough for me to know I can no longer trust you, and it is time for you to return to Africa."

For a moment I thought that Samuel had completely gone to pieces, as he registered Sir Hugh's decision to cut the link with his family, which had existed for three generations. The muffled sobs from a grown man were just the beginning, as Samuel's distress increased and the anger poured into his heart, at which point he let rip an ear-splitting roar of a wild animal. I nearly jumped out of my skin, as the wall behind me vibrated, and I could hear the noise of metal scraping on metal. There was a faint whooshing noise, followed by the sound of a soft thud, and a small grunt. Then silence, total silence descended on The Hall.

It was eerie; I could hear my own breathing, and little else other than Sir Hugh's long-case clock ticking in the entrance hall downstairs. What had happened? I was desperate to peak through the doorway. I was thinking that Sir Hugh had shot Samuel, with a silenced pistol, hidden in his inner sanctum. But the sound of scraping metal and whooshing, what could that have been? I was frozen to the spot when I heard the sound of crying again.

I realised it was Samuel who was alive, and if Sir Hugh was dead, Samuel would want to blame Sir Hugh's death on someone else. And what luck we have Marcus Edge unconscious in the cellar, who had a grudge against Sir

Hugh turning up uninvited and unannounced to confront him.

I started back-tracking down the landing, as fast as I could, before Samuel came looking for me. I was on the top step of the back stairs when my phone vibrated, and in a second or two it would start to ring, I desperately pulled it from my jacket. I rejected the call on the first note of the ring. I glanced down at the screen, it was K-P, and this was the tenth missed call I had from him today. The others must have been whilst I was out cold in the cellar. I couldn't take the risk that Samuel had not heard my phone, and I threw caution to the wind, flying down the stairs into the kitchen. I was across the kitchen and out of the back door in a couple of seconds.

Once outside I had a problem, because it was nearly half-a-mile to the end of the drive, from The Hall itself. I would be a sitting duck until I managed to reach the village, which was another half-a-mile away. I ran in the opposite direction, into the kitchen garden, towards the potting shed that leaned against the brick wall at the other end of the garden. Being autumn, the cover was very bare, but I made it to the low-slung building in the gathering gloom that was the end of a short November dusk.

I lay under the table at the end of the potting shed; hoping the plastic table cloth that hung over the sides of the table, would keep me hidden. I strained to hear any sounds, beyond the rustle of the last remaining leaves on the trees in the small orchard, which adjoined the kitchen garden. I heard the sound of a diesel engine coughing into life, followed by some severe over-revving. I could swear it was Sir Hugh's old Land Rover, being driven down the drive, to head me off. I relaxed, and I could feel my heart pounding, the sound of blood pumping through my ears.

I lifted the plastic table cloth, but could see nothing but dark shapes in the early evening penumbra. I stood up and made my way out of the potting shed. I then darted out of the kitchen garden into the old stables. The stables were Sir Hugh's garage, and immediately I noticed that the Land Rover was missing, with one of the stable doors still wide open. I was taking a risk, but I needed to get to the village as soon as possible, and decided to use one of the remaining vehicles. The keys to the Range Rover never left Samuel's pocket, so that was out of the question, and with the Land Rover gone it only left the Peugeot. Samuel intensely disliked this car, perhaps because it reminded him too much of Africa, and the keys were hanging on the hook just inside the open door of the stables.

I grabbed the keys and started the engine. I daren't put on any lights, so I gently edged the long car I had driven to Felixstowe out of the stables. I couldn't use the main driveway, for fear of running into Samuel, so I turned towards the kitchen garden and the orchard beyond. At the other end of the orchard was the entrance to a paddock, behind which there was a bridleway, which led to another village two miles away. I was through the gate into the paddock, when the bright lights of the Land Rover loomed in my rear view mirror. Samuel must have careered to the end of the drive, and now driven back again, without the aid of headlights. With nothing to lose I switched my lights on and floored the accelerator. I tried to smash through the five-bar gate between me and the bridleway.

The impact was bone-shattering but I managed to crash through the barrier, and I travelled about twenty metres before I came to a grinding halt. The wheels were spinning, and the more I revved in the wet mud, the more noise I made – but little forwards progress. I opened the car door, jumped on to the bridleway, and started running for my life. The horses used this route often, and their deep footprints in the mud made my progress in the dark tortuously slow. The Land Rover just drove alongside me in the field beside the bridleway. When Samuel was opposite me I heard the blast of a shotgun, and then felt a searing pain in my left arm, side and leg. I just crumbled to the ground, the mud almost enveloping me.

I couldn't remember much of the journey back to The Hall. Samuel threw me into the back of the Land Rover, and then manhandled me up the stairs of the Hall, into Sir Hugh's inner sanctum. I was close to fainting, from the pain of the gun-shot wounds, and again blood was seeping into my clothes. Even with all I had been through over the previous two weeks, I was totally ill-prepared for the sight that greeted me. Sir Hugh was still seated in his chair, behind his desk, glasses in his hands but it would take more than one man to get him out of his chair. Straight through the centre of his chest and his heart was an ornamental African spear, the force of which had pierced all the way through Sir Hugh's torso and through the back of the chair. So that's what accounted for the whooshing sound.

Samuel had brought the shot gun with him, placing it in Sir Hugh's hands, before discharging the second barrel into the floor. He then dropped me on the carpet that was now shredded by shotgun pellets.

"You'll be dead when they find you," Samuel announced "because I won't phone them until your life-blood has flowed out of you."

He then put his gloves on my hands; the gloves that I could see in my dreams, but could not connect with Samuel, until too late. I coughed, tasting blood in my spittle; I realised that one or more of the pellets had punctured my lung. Samuel was right I was going to die here today.

"Hurry up and die Edge!" he tried to coax me to my final destination.

"Sod off you maniac!!" I yelled back at him, but it was only a faint wheeze, which just made him laugh.

He was laughing so much; he didn't hear or see, what was moving in the shadows behind him. The fist that chopped him on the back of his neck would have probably killed most people, especially when delivered with the ferocity and strength of K-P.

Samuel fell to the ground, and immediately K-P jumped on him before he had time to recover. K-P pinned Samuel to the floor, and then Samuel went limp, before K-P released his grip for an instant. In that split second Samuel managed to roll away, and in one movement, he sprang disoriented to his feet. K-P just ran at him as though he had the rugby ball, and was only five metres from the try line. He hit Samuel in the mid-rift, which lifted Samuel out of his socks, and he continued until he rammed Samuel against the wall.

The impact should have just winded Samuel, but he would never take another breath. The ornamental spears hung on the wall in pairs, behind a shield, and the scraping sound I had heard was Samuel taking one spear from its position. The other had remained on the wall, but pointed slightly away from the wall, and Samuel was now skewered onto the other spear. Blackness enveloped me and I passed out.

# A few days later
# Princess Alexandra
# Hospital, Harlow

Lots of flashing lights, people staring at me wearing green outfits with no faces, someone kneeling on my chest. This seemed to be a recurring nightmare, which was so vivid that I would wake up regularly in a hot sweat, unable to breathe properly before falling back into the dark mire again.

Later I was told that I regained consciousness five times over a period of three days, and the doctors had to monitor me carefully, as I recovered from major surgery to stop me drowning in my own blood. The shotgun pellets had indeed punctured my lung, which collapsed, and I was choking to death. My heart stopped briefly on the way to the hospital. The paramedics in the ambulance, who arrived only moments after K-P's final encounter with Samuel, were able to revive me immediately. K-P had heard the shotgun, at which point he called '999', before following Samuel and me into The Hall. The people in green outfits were the staff of the operating theatre in the Princess Alexandra Hospital in Harlow, and luckily the surgeon who operated on me was very experienced in the treatment of gunshot wounds.

I regained consciousness properly the following Monday afternoon. The nursing staff told me it would take a day or two for the anaesthetic to wear off, and that Monday afternoon was approximately thirty-six hours after the last dose of anaesthetic. I opened my eyes and could see a large machine with a face mask, which had been used after the surgery to aid my breathing, and the face mask had only been removed earlier that day.

A drip providing saline was still attached to my arm. It still felt as though someone was kneeling on the side of my chest.

"Hello." A familiar soft voice came from nearby my bed.

I tried to reply, but my mouth was so dry, I could only wheeze loudly.

"Don't talk my darling." Gerda's head came into view.

I could feel soft warm tears rolling out of my eyes, and onto the pillow. My vision became blurry and I fell into a deep untroubled sleep for another few hours.

It was dark when I woke up again, and I could hear voices in the room.

"He's awake again."

I recognised the voice immediately, but was very surprised that he was at my bedside.

"The nurse said he could sip a little water to clear his throat."

K-P's booming voice was as deep and reassuring as ever, and I guessed that he had brought my other guest with him to the hospital.

Gerda's head came into view again, and she kissed me lightly on my lips. My dry lips tried to form a smile. She brought the plastic cup to my mouth and a few drops trickled down my throat. The feeling was wonderful, pure nectar, and I thought that I would never again be dismissive of water. I had about three sips before K-P told Gerda not to give me too much. Gerda then brought a tissue to my face, wiping away the water, which had dribbled down my chin and neck.

K-P loomed over Gerda's shoulder and smiled at me.

"Thanks." I croaked.

It just came out as a grunt, but K-P understood and nodded in acknowledgment.

The third person in the room came into my peripheral vision. Joshua looked uncomfortable, not wanting to look me in the eye.

"Sorry Marc," Joshua studied his hands which he was wringing constantly "I don't know the full story, but I think I have been unfair on you."

Joshua never liked to admit he was wrong, so this statement was tough for him, and I made no comment.

"I have spoken with Mum and Dad," he continued "they have cut short their trip, and will be back by the weekend. They suggested that you stay with them until you are fully recovered. We are going to spend Christmas with them in Norfolk, and they would like Gerda and Paul to come as well."

I smiled, as I thought of Paul and me recovering by the sea, with Paul embarrassing my mother with his schmoozing.

I just smiled and nodded.

"I better be on my way back home to catch up on my e-mails from today. I will be in touch soon."

Joshua shook hands with K-P, kissed Gerda on the cheek, and left for home in Epping not many miles from Harlow.

K-P's glance followed Joshua out of the door, and within only a few seconds broke out into a huge guffawing laugh, that Joshua couldn't have failed to have heard in the corridor.

As his laughing subsided, he said "You probably have a multitude of questions, but the doctor is insistent that we must not exhaust you."

Gerda added "I am staying with K-P and Jane for a few days, before returning to Holland on Friday, when Paul will be released from St Bartholomew's. I will be in touch with your parents next week to make arrangements for Christmas."

"We will not return until tomorrow afternoon, because you will be exhausted." K-P had a solemn look on this face.

"Why will I be exhausted?"

It was an improvement on the earlier grunt, but still pretty incoherent.

"Until this morning we have been accompanied by a policeman," K-P explained "and when you woke up today, he said he would be back tomorrow with Sergeant Smithson from Bishopsgate Police Station."

I nodded my understanding.

"Right, I am gong to find a coffee machine, and leave you two love birds together."

K-P flashed a smile with his amazingly white teeth and left the room.

Gerda perched on the bed and stroked my face gently.

"Hi."

"Hi" I replied.

"What are we going to do next?" She asked.

"Get married as soon as we are able".

Gerda's eyes welled up and tears rolled down her cheeks, but she was smiling and nodding. I closed my eyes and very soon I was asleep again.

I woke in the middle of the night, my mouth was parched. When trying to reach for the water, I managed to knock the cup and its contents onto the floor. The night nurse heard the noise, and came in to clear up the mess, whilst helping me with some water. She asked whether I needed a bed pan, which I declined. As I lay in the bed trying to sleep, I recalled the events of the past two weeks, but each time a whooshing filled my ears, followed by the image of Sir Hugh impaled by the ornamental spear. I felt sick. Eventually I dozed off, but it was a fitful sleep, and I didn't feel rested when my visitors arrived at nine o'clock.

A young policeman, from Harlow, escorted Sergeant Smithson, Chris Worcester – my solicitor, Eric Jones and John Eastwood into my room. Seeing how cramped it was, John Eastwood made his excuses, saying he would speak to me privately later. He and the young policeman left the room.

"Hello Marc." It was Eric Jones who opened proceedings.

"I have explained to Sergeant Smithson the terms on which I appointed you, and that together with your written account you left for him has pretty much filled in the gaps up to Thursday, but we need to know what happened at The Hall."

Sergeant Smithson interjected, "We have spoken with the Dutch police, who have agreed that we can take a statement from you, and they will decide whether they wish to interview you themselves."

Before Sergeant Smithson could complete his sentence, Chris Worcester interrupted him "Don't worry Marc, no charges will be brought against you. The crane driver who called the emergency services has given a full account of the incident, where Peter's mother tried to run you down, with her car."

Sergeant Smithson shot Chris a look of disapproval, adding "However, both the British and Dutch Customs would like to know how you managed to travel to and from Holland, undetected."

"That's easy," I replied "I used someone's passport, then returned it to them when I was back in the UK, before they noticed it was gone."

Sergeant Smithson cocked a disbelieving eyebrow in my direction "Hmmm, so Shariz didn't know you had his uncle's passport?"

I felt as though I was flushing up, so I merely nodded.

Sergeant Smithson looked very unconvinced.

"That's not really why we are here today." Eric Jones regained direction of the meeting. "Did K-P brief you after my conversation with him last Wednesday?"

Again I nodded.

"I thought so." He made a note in an exercise book on his lap before continuing. "We need to close down Sir Hugh Masterson's nefarious affairs in Zimbabwe. It will do more damage, in the long run, to the chances of lasting peace in Zimbabwe.

He didn't need to explain, but he did so anyway; whether for the benefit of the other two people in the room, or just to marshal his own thoughts. As he set the scene, recounting the background of Sir Hugh's life and his rise to prominence in the shipping industry, I realised that his own background must have included a stint with the Security Services at some stage.

"…so we know that Sir Hugh was smuggling armaments into Zimbabwe, and we guess he was stockpiling them at the new inland port. We also have intelligence that he was the main source of funding of the Conservative Alliance of Zimbabwe. We also assume that he had been planning some type of 'show of force', before or at the fortieth birthday celebrations of the birth of Zimbabwe, next year."

"That's what I believe as well."

I confirmed Eric Jones assumptions, and again he made a note in his book.

"So what happened from Wednesday night, when you dropped this into the police station?"

Sergeant Smithson held up the document I had prepared in Holland.

Eric held up his hand before I could start and he looked at Chris Worcester.

"Please do not make a record of this conversation. I will make notes and then send them to you for your approval."

Chris put his pen away in his jacket pocket, and his note pad back into his briefcase.

"Sorry Marc, take your time, and no detail is too small."

Eric leaned back in his chair which was the signal for me to begin.

"I returned to my flat secretly, trying not to implicate Shariz. In the morning I was woken by Sergeant Smithson's colleagues, and made my escape out of the bathroom window."

Sergeant Smithson's face showed no emotion whatsoever about this episode.

"I spent the morning at the library in Stepney Green, where I was able to establish the shipping movements of

Masterson vessels in and out of Beira. This also confirmed that Captain Hennessey was the most frequent Master of the vessels taking this route, and that he was the Master of the vessel involved in the massacre."

Eric nodded, but to Sergeant Smithson and Chris Worcester the information of the massacre was obviously new. Both in unison sat more upright in their chairs.

"I met K-P at lunchtime, when he briefed me fully after your meeting with him," I was looking directly at Eric who continued to nonchalantly make notes in his exercise book "and I decided that I would confront Sir Hugh with all I knew the following day."

I paused and took a long swig of water, my voice was getting stronger, but I was feeling tired and dehydrated.

After a moment or two, I recommenced my recollection of the remainder of Thursday, of how I bought a suit and then tried to scrub myself clean of the skin dye at the hotel in the East End, which seemed to amuse them.

"Where did you get the skin dye from?"

Sergeant Smithson asked the question in a very innocent manner, to try and put me off my guard; but I knew what he was driving at, so I lied my head off by saying I had found it in the storeroom behind Shariz's shop. He knew I was lying, I knew he knew I was lying, so I punctuated my answer with as innocent a smile as I could muster.

"Anything else happen on Thursday night?" Eric was ensuring that he maintained the momentum of the questioning.

"No."

"Which leads us to Friday and The Hall?" Eric asked "So how did you know Sir Hugh would be there?"

"I didn't, not for certain, but when I phoned earlier in the week Ms. Syrani told me he was planning a business trip.

He often worked from The Hall on Fridays, particularly in advance of a trip," I paused for a second, "I suppose I just got lucky."

Again I took another sip of water before continuing "I made my way to The Hall by train and taxi."

"Did you steal the overcoat and season ticket from the coffee shop in Liverpool Street?" The question was from Sergeant Smithson.

"No," I replied honestly "it was left on a seat and I only borrowed it. I was going to hand it into lost property when I returned to Liverpool Street Station."

Sergeant Smithson's unconvinced look returned, and I swear if we had been alone, he would have stroked his chin in the universal motion of disbelieving someone.

I turned my face back towards Eric and resumed my story. "Sir Hugh was alone when I arrived at The Hall; Samuel had dropped Ms. Syrani at Bishops Stortford Station – I saw them when I was waiting for a taxi – and he was as charming as ever. He made me a coffee and then took me into his private office, which was unusual in itself."

"Did he seem agitated, or perturbed, in any way?" Eric asked.

"Not at all," I replied "and I then told him all I knew, plus I tried bluffing him as well."

"What did he say?" Again Eric was leading the proceedings.

"Nothing, he just told Samuel that I would be leaving, and would not be returning," I could see Eric was about to clarify something, so I explained that Samuel had obviously returned, and was listening at the doorway "which was behind me so I couldn't see him."

More water, then I asked Chris to call for a nurse, and a bedpan.

It was the first time I had voluntarily urinated since Friday morning, so what should have taken only a minute or two lasted nearly half-an-hour, as the effects of the anaesthetic inhibited my bodily functions. My visitors had adjourned to have a coffee, and it was after ten o'clock before I was comfortable to start talking again.

"When I saw Samuel in the doorway, my eyes caught sight of his gloves. He never used to wear gloves, but he wore them on the Saturday morning when he collected me from your cells." I was looking at Sergeant Smithson. "Over the last two weeks, I have been having vague memories of my beating, and each memory was becoming clearer than the previous. I remembered seeing black gloves hitting me." I turned back to Eric "Something inside me snapped, and I launched myself at Samuel. I caught him off-guard for an instant, but he recovered and kicked and punched me senseless."

"Then what happened?" Eric asked, eager to get to the nub of the enquiry.

I explained about waking up, bound, in the cellar. Of how I freed myself; and that as I was about to escape, the raised voices of Sir Hugh and Samuel arguing lured me upstairs.

"What were they arguing about?" Sergeant Smithson asked.

"Tony Eastwood."

"Why?" Eric asked.

"Sir Hugh accused Samuel of killing Tony, because he was jealous of Tony's affections for Mércédès."

"Don't tell me that Mércédès and Samuel were lovers?" Eric asked.

"Not exactly."

I told them of how Mércédès had led Samuel along, when they were children, and Samuel thought that one day they could be together.

"I should know that Mércédès is capable of creating such an illusion."

"So Samuel confessed to killing Tony?" Sergeant Smithson asked.

"Yes," I replied "his excuse was that he was worried Tony knew that he had beaten me up, and he was going to tell me; hence why he drove Tony to Bishops Stortford Station, and he was the one who phoned from the telephone box." I was making an educated guess on the last point. "Sir Hugh was taunting Samuel about never being with Mércédès; how his friends in the Movement for Democratic Change would ignore him, and anyway they were useless hence why he had to fund the Conservative Alliance of Zimbabwe."

I paused again for water as the image of Sir Hugh's dead body filled my head. I closed my eyes, opened them again, and continued my tale.

"I was outside the door to Sir Hugh's study and although I did not really know what was happening I heard Samuel take the spear off the wall. I heard the whooshing sound, as the spear flew through the air, plus the soft plop as it hit Sir Hugh. At first I thought Sir Hugh had shot Samuel with a silencer gun."

"So you didn't actually see Samuel kill Sir Hugh?" It was Sergeant Smithson asking the question.

"No, but there was no one else there, except me."

Eric stepped in "We have already ruled Marc out of any implication in Sir Hugh's murder."

"Just checking."

Sergeant Smithson didn't seem offended by Eric's comment, and I supposed he was just doing his job properly.

"I was sneaking away when K-P called my mobile. I cut him off, and ran out of the house, as quickly as possible."

"Why didn't you use the drive to escape?" Sergeant Smithson asked.

"I was going to, but I heard Samuel in the Land Rover, so I decided to try and go in the other direction. The Range Rover's keys weren't available, so I had to take the Peugeot, and I made it so far until I got stuck. It was nearly impossible to walk or run down the bridle-path, and the Land Rover drew alongside me, when Samuel shot me."

I paused again before completing my account of Samuel's demise.

"I can't remember much after that, except being back in the study with Samuel threatening to kill me. Also he was trying to make it look as though I killed Sir Hugh."

"Is that when K-P arrived?" Eric asked.

I nodded, then closed my eyes, trying to erase the picture of Sir Hugh pinned to his chair.

Eric thanked me, saying that what I had told them was how he imagined events played out, and he was sure that I would not be troubled again by the British Authorities on this matter. He looked at Sergeant Smithson, who initially shrugged his shoulders, before nodding his head in agreement.

"Good."

It was Chris Worcester who stood up first.

They shook my hand in turn, and Eric said that John Eastwood would like a word with me, if I wasn't too tired.

"For John, I would do anything."

Eric smiled and left the room.

John came in almost immediately, and sat down in the chair nearest the bed.

"How you doing Marc?" he asked, ever the gentleman.

"Tired, to be honest John." I replied, and he nodded in empathy.

"Me too, Marc." He closed his eyes briefly, and then he opened them again. "Eric has given me a brief outline of Sir Hugh's activities at Masterson Shipping. As far as JPG was concerned we were never involved, and for me he was the perfect Chairman and owner."

"I could see that was the case" I agreed.

"Yes it was, wasn't it?" John seemed happier that I thought as he did.

"Somehow I knew you didn't kill Tony. I gave him too much too soon; I always hoped he would turn out like you Marc."

There was nothing I could say, without sounding pompous, so I said nothing.

"Mércédès was good for him; I am sorry to say that you and Mércédès were doomed from the beginning Marc. She was too selfish, and you were too nice for her."

"You didn't say anything to me when Mércédès and I were married."

"How could I?" He looked hurt. "Sir Hugh thought you were great for Mércédès, and it would only look like I was jealous that Tony had lost out to you."

I nodded "Yes, I probably would have assumed that was the case."

"I have tried to speak with Mércédès, but she, her mother and grandfather are out of touch. I want to tell her of my decision to retire in one year's time."

"Why? JPG will need you more than ever, after everything that has happened." My voice sounded really concerned.

"No they won't, because they will be in safe hands, yours!" He smiled benignly, like a kindly uncle "It will take you a year to get back into the swing of things, and for me to hand over to you properly."

Tears were in both our eyes.

"You will be the successor I would have liked Tony to be."

# The day before Christmas Eve, Near Brancaster, Norfolk

Three weeks have passed since my parents picked me up from the Princess Alexandra Hospital in Harlow. K-P had visited my flat and packed essentials into a large holdall, and I was whisked away in the back of a people carrier taxi, which my parents had booked from Heathrow Airport.

My mother turned white, nearly fainting when she saw the extent of my injuries, dressings and how thin I looked.

My father much more stoical said "He's young and will recover."

Upon arriving at my parent's home a fire was lit in the grate, and it had not been allowed to die since my arrival. My parents preferred the heat from the fire, rather than central heating, to draw the moisture out of the walls. Three months had passed since they left for the Southern Hemisphere, so the moist sea air had permeated the whole house. The range in the kitchen meant that room was always warm, thus living room and kitchen were magnets, with other rooms used sparingly for sleeping and bathing. In fact the first three nights I slept in the living room, gazing fitfully into the flames, and reliving recent events.

By the weekend, after my release from hospital, a routine had developed. It started with a hearty home cooked breakfast followed by a daily constitutional down to the beach, with an elderly neighbour's dog. Initially my father joined me, and slowly, I gave him a very detailed account of what had transpired. He would then tell my mother most of what I told him, because in the afternoons whilst my father napped, she would ask pointed questions about what I had told my father. Neither of them offered an opinion, critical or otherwise. They just listened, and understood, which was very comforting.

My father's words that I would recover were justified, when two weeks after leaving the hospital we all drove to Kings Lynn, where my dressings were changed and medication reduced dramatically.

"The New Year will see dramatic improvement, just keep walking and eating your mother's home cooking" the surgeon advised, whilst my mother blushed.

The visit to Kings Lynn coincided with the start of the preparations for Christmas. The festive season was going to be a large family affair, with Joshua and his family being joined by Gerda and Paul, for a whole week. I was missing Gerda desperately, and our daily phone calls were both joy and pain. It was such a pleasure to talk with her, but each time we spoke was a reminder of how much I loved her, and that I hated being apart from her.

Since the visit to Kings Lynn, I had increased my walks to two perambulations a day, and the glee of the dog was obvious by the frantic tail wagging and incessant barking. John Eastwood sent me a contract of employment which I signed. He smoothed over the termination of my services at Masterson Shipping on the basis I was more important to JPG, than being a manager of Masterson Shipping in Singapore. My father allowed me use of his computer for only an hour a day, whilst he took a break from his part time consultancy which supplemented his pensions. John Eastwood sent me bite-sized e-mails, so I could get a feel for the current state of the insurance market, and the financial position of JPG. I had also been in contact with Chris Worcester, to try and commence divorce proceedings with Mércédès; however, with the death of her boyfriend and father, I expected matters to take some time. Chris had offered me some hope, by saying that Mércédès' solicitors had let slip that she, and her mother and grandfather would be coming to England before Christmas. I presumed that was to start to sort out Sir Hugh's estate. I did not envy that task of Mércédès, and what she might discover about her father, so I told Chris to tread carefully.

It was the day before Christmas Eve. I had returned from my morning's walk, and I was watching the clock, counting down the hours until Gerda and Paul arrived. They had landed at Stansted at nine o'clock, and were currently on the coach to Kings Lynn, from where my father and I would collect them. So I was surprised when I heard the noise of a car on the drive, shortly followed by the sound of the car doors closing. I opened the front door to see Chris Worcester paying a taxi, flanked by John Eastwood and K-P.

"Hello," I greeted them "this is an unexpected surprise. Why didn't you telephone to warn me you were coming? I might have been out!!"

"We knew you would be here," K-P spoke for the trio "I spoke with your father yesterday afternoon."

"So why did he not tell me you were coming?" I was becoming cross at being left in the dark.

Chris responded "When we told him why we were coming, he suggested that we should tell you, face to face."

"You had better come in out of the cold." I opened the door for them to be able to file past me.

My mother and father were already waiting for the audience in the living room. I noticed that a tray had been prepared with six cups, a plate of biscuits, plus freshly brewed coffee and tea. When I looked at them they merely shrugged their shoulders.

"Marc, can I suggest we all sit down, we have some bad news." It was John Eastwood who was leading the proceedings.

I sat on a chair, which I had brought from the dining table, feeling as though I had been summoned to the Headmaster's study.

"There is no easy way to break the news. Mércédès is dead."

"What!" I exclaimed.

"She, her mother, and grandfather - Phillippe de Souza - were travelling to the airport, and were involved in a bad accident. They were all killed instantly."

"H-h-how?" I asked in barely a whisper.

K-P answered "Apparently they were late for a flight to London, and their driver was overtaking on a blind bend, where they were hit head-on by a fully laden lorry."

No-one said anything for a whole minute.

It was Chris who broke the silence "Marc, I am not sure you realise the implications of what we have just told you."

"In what way?" I asked.

I felt sorrow at the news of the accident but not much more. I had moved on from the hurt, which I had felt when Mércédès had left me.

John Eastwood replied "Sir Hugh was an only child, brought up by his grandparents, when his mother died. Both of them are now dead. Mércédès mother was also an only child, as was Mércédès. You and Mércédès were separated, but divorce proceedings have not yet commenced."

I was seeing where this was leading, but I could have had no sense of the magnitude of what Chris was about to tell me.

"Marc, Peter and his mother could have had a tenuous claim; but as they are both dead, you are the sole heir to the estate of Mércédès. She in turn was the sole heir to her mother's, grandfather's and Sir Hugh's estates."

Chris took a large draught of coffee before continuing "Some of the assets are tied up in trusts, but what with the properties and land in Goa, Zimbabwe, London and Essex, together with Sir Hugh's financial stake in Masterson Shipping, JPG, and other companies, the value of Mércédès estate is somewhere in excess of two hundred and fifty million pounds."

One could literally have heard a pin drop, and the only noise audible was the wood burning on the fire. I stood up, picked my jacket off the peg, and walked down to the beach. I must have stood there looking out to sea for fifteen minutes, before I was aware that K-P was by my side.

"You OK?" He asked.

I nodded my head "No matter what Sir Hugh was involved in, the price he and his family have paid is too high."

"I agree." It was K-P's turn to nod.

I turned and looked at him "K-P, you're my best friend, and you saved my life. I want you to share in my fortune."

"Now don't be silly." K-P was shaking his head.

"I want you, Jane and the children to live at The Hall."

He laughed "I couldn't even afford a gardener, let alone the maintenance."

"I agree," I replied "which is why I am going to continue to own it, and be responsible for any costs associated with the upkeep and heating. I would like you and your family to live there for as long as you want to – for free!"

"I suppose it would be a great place for the *Lammers* to have their annual dinner."

We both laughed, and hugged each other, on the sand.

# The Players

| | |
|---|---|
| **Marcus ('Marc') Edge** | Former Lloyd's insurance broker |
| **Mércédès Edge** | Marcus' estranged wife and daughter of Sir Hugh Masterson |
| **Sgt Brian Smithson** | Policeman at Bishopsgate police station |
| **Sir Hugh Masterson** | Shipping magnate/owner of a Lloyd's insurance broker |
| **Knapp-Pahl Sethia** ('K-P') | Friend and Lloyd's insurance broker |
| **Jane Sethia** | K-P's wife |
| **Samuel** | Sir Hugh Masterson's chauffeur |
| **Eric Jones** | Claims manager at Neptune Re |
| **Jimmy Black** | Lloyd's insurance broker at Judge Palmer & Gown |
| **Tony Eastwood** | Lloyd's insurance broker at Inter-Continental |
| **John Eastwood** | Managing Director of Judge Palmer & Gown |
| **Christopher Richardson** | Recruitment consultant |
| **Max Huntley** | Chairman of Inter-Continental's marine company |
| **Paul van der Kohl** | Friend and former client of Marc Edge |
| **George White** | Legal and Compliance Officer of Inter-Continental |
| **Carla Nottage** | former colleague and former girlfriend at JPG |
| **Gerda van der Kohl** | Girlfriend and sister of Paul van der Kohl |
| **Chris Worcester** | Marc Edge's solicitor |
| **Shariz** | Owner of the shop beneath Marc Edge's flat |
| **Phillipe de Silva** | Mércédès grandfather |
| **Jacqui Syrani** | Sir Hugh Masterson's private secretary |

| | |
|---|---|
| **Omar Aziz** | *Masterson Shipping's Middle East Regional Manager* |
| **Stuart Myhill** | *Bank employee* |
| **Joshua Edge** | *Marc Edge's brother* |
| **Stacey** | *Receptionist at Tomline House* |
| **Caption Mark Hennessey** | *Master of a Masterson Shipping vessel* |
| **Peter** | *Night Nurse at St Bartholomew's nursing home* |

Lightning Source UK Ltd.
Milton Keynes UK
26 March 2011
169923UK00001B/2/P